Howie walked to th... ...nced Ruger. He eased the end of the silencer against the sleeping man's head.

"Amigo, it is time to come awake one last time," Howie said in colloquial Spanish. The drug dealer mumbled and tried to roll over. The force of the silencer against his head brought him awake. His eyes snapped open, and he saw his situation even in the faint light.

"Hey, hey. What's this? You playing games? I am Cuchi. What the hell are you doing?"

Howie snarled, "You were Cuchi, amigo. El Padre doesn't like the way you're moving in on other men's territories, especially his. El Padre wanted me to tell you that before you die. So long, sucker."

Cuchi's eyes went wide for a millisecond, then his muscles tensed.

The Ruger spat twice, and his muscles relaxed forever.

Titles by Keith Douglass

THE SEAL TEAM SERIES:

SEAL TEAM SEVEN
SPECTER
NUCFLASH
DIRECT ACTION
FIRESTORM
BATTLEGROUND
DEATHRACE
PACIFIC SIEGE
WAR CRY
FRONTAL ASSAULT
FLASHPOINT
TROPICAL TERROR
BLOODSTORM
DEATHBLOW

THE CARRIER SERIES:

CARRIER
VIPER STRIKE
ARMAGEDDON MODE
FLAME-OUT
MAELSTROM
COUNTDOWN
AFTERBURN
ALPHA STRIKE
ARCTIC FIRE
ARSENAL
NUKE ZONE
CHAIN OF COMMAND
BRINK OF WAR
TYPHOON

SEAL TEAM SEVEN
DEATHBLOW

KEITH DOUGLASS

BERKLEY BOOKS, NEW YORK

Special thanks to Chet Cunningham for his contribution to this book.

This is a work of fiction. Names, characters, places, and incidents are either the product of the author's imagination or are used fictitiously, and any resemblance to actual persons, living or dead, business establishments, events, or locales is entirely coincidental.

SEAL TEAM SEVEN: DEATHBLOW

A Berkley Book / published by arrangement with
the author

PRINTING HISTORY
Berkley edition / July 2001

The Penguin Putnam Inc. World Wide Web site address is
www.penguinputnam.com

ISBN: 0-425-18074-3

BERKLEY®
Berkley Books are published by The Berkley Publishing Group,
a division of Penguin Putnam Inc.,
375 Hudson Street,
New York, New York 10014.
BERKLEY and the "B" design
are trademarks belonging to Penguin Putnam Inc.

PRINTED IN THE UNITED STATES OF AMERICA

10 9 8 7 6 5 4 3 2 1

This novel of
military fiction is
gratefully dedicated to
all those veterans of all the wars
that we have fought over the past sixty years.
May those of us who are living always remember those
who did not return home after the war
and remember the parents,
spouses, and children
of those veterans
who also
served.

FOREWORD

Hello, and thanks for picking up this copy of Seal Team Seven. Every writer wonders who is reading his small gems and what they really think of them. Were they entertaining? Did they hold together? Did you like or hate the people?

Input from readers is one of the ways that any writer can learn just how his books are being received by the public. So take time out and drop me a quick line. Let me know what you think of the series, the characters. If you have any plot ideas you're just dying to tell me, slip them in. Who knows, I might use one of them.

So send me a card or a letter. Praise the book or shoot it down, I want to know what you think. I'll be glad to hear from you and will write you back. Send your comments to:

> Keith Douglass
> SEAL TEAM SEVEN
> 8431 Beaver Lake Dr.
> San Diego, CA 92119

Thanks and I hope to hear from you.

—Keith Douglass

SEAL TEAM SEVEN

THIRD PLATOON*
CORONADO, CALIFORNIA

Rear Admiral (L) Richard Kenner. Commander of all SEALs.

Commander Dean Masciarelli. 47, 5'11", 220 pounds. Annapolis graduate. Commanding officer of SEAL Team Seven and its 230 men.

Master Chief Petty Officer Gordon MacKenzie. 47, 5'10", 180 pounds. Administrator and head enlisted man of all of SEAL Team Seven.

Lieutenant Commander Blake Murdock. 32, 6'2", 210 pounds. Annapolis graduate. Six years in SEALs. Father important congressman from Virginia. Murdock recently promoted. Apartment in Coronado. Has a car and a motorcycle, loves to fish. Weapon: Alliant Bull Pup duo 5.56mm & 20mm explosive round. Alternate: H & K MP-5SD submachine gun.

ALPHA SQUAD

Willard "Will" Dobler. Boatswain's Mate. Senior chief. Top EM in platoon. Third in command. 37, 6'1", 180 pounds. Nineteen years service. Wife, Nancy; children, Helen, 15; Charles, 11. Sports nut. Knows dozens of major-league baseball records. Competition pistol marksman. Weapon: Alliant Bull Pup duo 5.56mm & 20mm explosive round. Good with the men.

David "Jaybird" Sterling. Machinist's Mate Second Class. Lead petty officer. 24, 5'10", 170 pounds. Quick mind, fine tactician. Single. Drinks too much sometimes. Crack shot with all arms. Grew up in Oregon. Helps plan attack operations. Weapon: H & K MP-5SD submachine gun.

*Third Platoon assigned exclusively to the Central Intelligence Agency to perform any needed tasks on a covert basis anywhere in the world. All are top secret assignments. Goes around Navy chain of command. Direct orders from the CIA.

Ron Holt. Radioman First Class. 22, 6'1", 170 pounds. Plays guitar, had a small band. Likes redheaded girls. Rabid baseball fan. Loves deep-sea fishing, is good at it. Platoon radio operator. Weapon: Alliant Bull Pup duo 5.56mm & 20mm explosive round.

Bill Bradford. Quartermaster's Mate First Class. 24, 6'2", 215 pounds. An artist in spare time. Paints oils. He sells his marine paintings. Single. Quiet. Reads a lot. Has two years of college. Squad sniper. Weapon: H & K PSG1 7.62 NATO sniper rifle or McMillan M-87R .50-caliber sniper rifle.

Joe "Ricochet" Lampedusa. Operations Specialist Third Class. 21, 5'11", 175 pounds. Good tracker, quick thinker. Had a year of college. Loves motorcycles. Wants a Hog. Pot smoker on the sly. Picks up plain girls. Platoon scout. Weapon: Colt M-4A1 rifle with grenade launcher; alternate, Alliant Bull Pup duo 5.56mm & 20mm explosive round.

Kenneth Ching. Quartermaster's Mate First Class. 25, 6' even, 180 pounds. Full-blooded Chinese. Platoon translator. Speaks Mandarin Chinese, Japanese, Russian, and Spanish. Bicycling nut. Paid $1,200 for off-road bike. Is trying for Officer Candidate School. Weapon: Colt M-4A1 rifle with grenade launcher.

Vincent "Vinnie" Van Dyke. Electrician's Mate Second Class. 24, 6'2", 220 pounds. Enlisted out of high school. Played varsity basketball. Wants to be a commercial fisherman after his current hitch. Good with his hands. Squad machine gunner. Weapon: H & K 21-E 7.62 NATO round machine gun.

BRAVO SQUAD

Lieutenant (j.g.) Ed DeWitt. Leader Bravo Squad. Second in command of the platoon. 30, 6'1", 175 pounds. From Seattle. Wiry. Has serious live-in woman, Milly. Annapolis graduate. A career man. Plays a good game of chess on traveling board. Weapon: Alliant Bull Pup duo 5.56mm & 20mm explosive round. Alternate: H & K G-11 submachine gun.

George Canzoneri. Torpedoman's Mate First Class. 27, 5'11", 190 pounds. Married to Navy wife, Phyllis. No kids. Nine years in Navy. Expert on explosives. Nicknamed "Petard" for almost hoisting himself one time. Top pick in platoon for explosive work. Weapon: Alliant Bull Pup duo 5.56mm & 20mm explosive round.

Miguel Fernandez. Gunner's Mate First Class. 26, 6'1", 180 pounds. Wife, Maria; daughter, Linda, 7, in Coronado. Spends his off time with them. Highly family-oriented. He has relatives in San Diego. Speaks Spanish and Portuguese. Squad sniper. Weapon: H & K PSG1 7.62 NATO sniper rifle.

Colt "Guns" Franklin. Yeoman Second Class. 24, 5'10", 175 pounds. A former gymnast. Powerful arms and shoulders. Expert mountain climber. Has a motorcycle and does hang gliding. Speaks Farsi and Arabic. Weapon: Colt M-4A1 rifle with grenade launcher.

Tran "Train" Khai. Torpedoman Second Class. 23, 6'1", 180 pounds. U.S.-born Vietnamese. A whiz at languages and computers. Speaks Vietnamese, French, German, Spanish, and Arabic. Specialist in electronics. Understands the new 20mm Bull Pup weapon. Can repair the electronics in it. Plans on becoming an electronics engineer. Joined the Navy for $40,000 college funding. Entranced by SEALs. First hitch up in four months. Weapon: H & K G-11 with caseless rounds, 4.7mm submachine gun with fifty-round magazine.

Jack Mahanani. Hospital Corpsman First Class. 25, 6'4", 240 pounds. Platoon medic. Tahitian/Hawaiian. Expert swimmer. Bench-presses 400 pounds. Once married, divorced. Top surfer. Wants the .50 sniper rifle. Weapon: Alliant Bull Pup duo 5.56 & 20mm explosive round. Alternate: Colt M-4A1 rifle with grenade launcher.

Anthony "Tony" Ostercamp. Machinist's Mate First Class. 24, 6'1", 210 pounds. Races stock cars in nearby El Cajon on weekends. Top auto mechanic. Platoon driver. Weapon: H & K 21-E 7.62 NATO round machine gun. Second radio operator.

Paul "Jeff" Jefferson. Engineman Second Class. 23, 6'1", 200 pounds. Black man. Expert in small arms. Can tear apart most weapons and reassemble, repair, and innovate them. A chess player to match Ed DeWitt. Weapon: Alliant Bull Pup duo 5.56mm & 20mm explosive round.

1

Tijuana, Mexico

Howard ("Howie") Anderson faded silently into the shadows against the wall of a closed shop that sold cheap pottery. He pulled down the stained slouch hat that had part of the brim torn off and hunched over so anyone seeing him couldn't tell how tall he was. He wore two sweaters, both moth chewn and filthy but warm. His double layer of too-large pants had been patched several times. He walked quietly on dirty, rundown sneakers. In his left hand, he carried a half-filled wine bottle partly hidden in a paper sack. He had bought the clothes three weeks ago at a thrift store on the other side of Tijuana. It had taken him twenty minutes to finish his disguise by layering dirt and grease paint on his face and hands.

The clothes were untraceable. He carried no wallet or identification, only two thousand pesos for an emergency. Hidden under the sweaters, a .22-caliber automatic pistol rested in a belt holster. He tensed as a Tijuana Police car made a sweep along the cross street half a block down. The TJ cops were getting better at their job. He didn't want them to see him.

Howie checked both ways on the litter-strewn side street. No cars, no people. He worked his way painfully into the street, dragging his right foot, which turned outward so far he couldn't step on it solidly. A car flashed by in the narrow street, missing him by three feet and bringing a screech of Spanish vulgarisms from strident young voices. Howie didn't even look up. He was bilingual in Spanish. What they said was crude and challenging, but he wasn't concerned about the newly rich TJ teens. He had bigger prey.

The building he had been watching for the past four hours now showed lights on the second story. There had been none there for the past three hours of darkness. Howie jammed himself between a garbage can and a large wooden packing box in front of a tattoo parlor. It would be impossible to see him in the heavy shadows from ten feet away. From there had a good view of all six windows on the second floor of 4343 Blanco Street. Reymundo "Cuchi" Hernandez must be home. "The Knife" wouldn't have much use for a blade, not after tonight.

For the past three Sundays, Howie had tracked Cuchi, carefully recording every detail of his lifestyle. The afternoons he spent at the bullfights, then a big dinner and lots of drinks with his current *mujer* at an expensive restaurant. After that a long night with her in his bedroom. There had been few signs of the protection that Cuchi's position had earned for him. His bodyguards must leave him after making sure he was inside his apartment. The eight-room bachelor pad hovered over a fancy ice cream parlor. Tonight looked to be the same for Cuchi. He usually came and went from a rear entry.

Howie went over his plan again. It never hurt to question every detail on an operation, especially since there was no one to double-check with and no backup. The shed on the rear of the store was an easy climb to the first-floor roof. From there he would work the second-floor window in the rear of Cuchi's apartment and be inside before the drug supplier knew it. Cuchi was pushing too hard for more territory, taking over three or four smaller suppliers without permission. The powers who supplied the third level of the huge operation with the product, didn't like it. A spokesman four layers removed from the man at the top, El Padre, had talked to Howie one night a month ago in the El Gallo Colorado. The bistro/cantina was owned by one of Howie's long-time friends. Most weekends Howie was at the café, down from San Diego, eating too well, drinking just enough, and sampling the always available bevy of eager *muchachas.* Sometimes the best things in life all depended on who you knew.

Howie didn't move for two hours where he hid beside the packing box. His muscles began to scream at him, but he'd stayed in one position for three times that long on many missions. He relaxed and waited for the lights to go out in the apartment. Three hours later the lights snapped off one at a time.

Shortly after 0200, a sudden light from a downstairs entranceway slashed into the dark street. A woman came out quickly. The door closed. The light snapped off.

Howie grinned. Everything was perfect. He'd never seen the woman of the night sent home this early before. Everything was in place. Tonight was the night.

He was ready. His special Ruger Standard .22 long rifle pistol felt good in his hand. It was his favorite handgun. It was a classic 1982 upgraded model of the 1949 weapon that launched Ruger's empire. It had a hold-open latch, a new magazine catch, new safety catch, and a modified trigger system. The basic weapon had a 120mm barrel, weighed 1020 grams, and had six grooves of rifling in the barrel.

He had been extremely careful handling the pistol to avoid fingerprints. He had worn surgical gloves for loading the nine rounds in the main magazine and nine in the spare. There would be no fingerprints on the shell casings. He kept the thin plastic gloves on when he cleaned and oiled the Ruger last night after the team came off a night exercise. He did that work at home in his Coronado apartment. It had cost him six hundred dollars to get a custom-made silencer put on the weapon three months ago. That extended the barrel by four inches but it had been invaluable twice already.

Howie smiled in the darkness, cracking the layered-on dirt and grease. He lifted up, stretched as he had seen street people do, and worked across the narrow passageway dragging his right foot as before until he made it into the shadows. Then he hurried down the darkness to the alley and up it to the third store, the ice cream parlor. It even had a marked rear entrance.

Howie slid the Ruger into the belt holster and stood on a barrel next to the shed's rear wall. He climbed up the back of the one-story building, finding foot- and handholds as the skilled hard rock mountain climber he was.

After he swung up on the roof, he froze and listened. There was no cry, no window banging open, and no voice in the night. No ominous shape of a guard hiding in the shadows. He moved on soft-soled sneakers to the windows of the second story where he found the same one unlocked that had been left wide open last Sunday night. Cuchi was getting sloppy. Too sloppy to live.

With infinite care and quietness, Howie edged the double-hung window up, letting the sash weight settle into its chamber gently and without a sound. He paused and listened again, inside and outside the open window.

Nothing.

Howie stepped through the open window into what he knew was a storage room. He drew the pistol and screwed on the four-inch silencer. The room was filled with boxes, cartons, and cones for the store below. He edged through and around them noiselessly, and turned the door knob. It was unlocked as he had hoped. He eased the panel inward an inch and peered through the slot. A small night light glowed at the far end of the hall giving a strange half light to the area.

Howie slid through the door, then stopped, a prickle of alarm darting down his spine. Twenty feet down the hall, a man sat in a chair that leaned back against the wall. Howie could hear the guard's slow even breathing. He growled in his sleep and moved just enough so the chair slammed down with the front legs hitting the floor. It woke up the guard. He swore softly in Spanish, turned the chair so it faced Howie. The man shook his head and blinked.

"What the fuck? Who'n hell are you?"

Howie had the Ruger up, he refined his head shot just a moment and squeezed the trigger. Just like on the close combat range. The guard clawed for his weapon in a shoulder rig. Before he could get it out of leather, the .22 caliber messenger sent an urgent message to his brain. The lead slug shattered as it tore through the skull and splattered into a dozen vital brain centers killing the guard in a half second. He slumped in his chair.

The whisper sound of the shot couldn't be heard ten feet away. Howie scowled. Something always had to go wrong. He'd never seen a guard inside. But then he'd never had a good look inside before. He moved up quickly, checked the man, dead. Howie took the revolver from the man's holster and stepped soundlessly to the door just beyond. It had to be the bedroom. That's where the last light of the night always showed.

He listened at the door, his hand tightening on the pistol. Someone snored inside. Howie snorted softly and shook his head. Why did he have to make it so easy? Howie turned the knob. Locked. He saw the old-style door lock that had a key hole. He selected from a pocketful of keys an old time skeleton key and gently inserted it. A small metal clink sounded.

The snoring stopped for a moment, then charged on as if to make up for lost sound.

Howie turned the key in the lock and heard a soft click. He rotated the knob and the door eased inward. Now Howie wished he had his night-vision goggles. Some light came in the window. A double bed sat against the far wall. One figure on it sprawled over most of the bed. He wore only pajama bottoms, and used no covers.

Howie walked to the edge of the bed and lifted the Ruger. He eased the end of the silencer against the side of the man's head.

"Amigo, it is time to come awake one last time," Howie said in colloquial Spanish. The *cucillo* mumbled and tried to roll over. The force of the silencer against his head brought him awake. His eyes snapped open, and he saw his situation even in the faint light.

"Hey, hey. What's this? You playing games? I am Cuchi. What the hell you doing?"

"You were Cuchi, amigo. El Padre doesn't like the way

you're moving in on other men's territories, especially his.
El Padre wanted me to tell you before you die. Good-bye,
asshole."

Cuchi's eyes went wide for a millisecond, then his muscles tensed, but before he could move the Ruger spat twice.
The muzzle blast even through the silencer left two deeply
burned powder circles on the side of Cuchi's head. He died
before his muscles could react. Two rounds to the head. It
would look like a Mafia hit.

The two *fsssssssst,* sounds could not be heard outside the
room. Howie nodded, turned and retraced his path down
the hall, past the dead guard, and through the storeroom.
He stepped out the window to the roof, then gently closed
the double-hung window. He didn't think about the dead
men. He didn't know either of them. They were criminals
who sold dope that killed hundreds of men, women, and
kids every day. They deserved no sympathy. Howie
shrugged. Hell, it was just a job, an assignment, a mission.

He crouched by the window, and looked quickly at every
potential trouble spot. No noises, not even a dog. No late-
night drunk getting home. He crept to the edge of the shed
and crawled down the same way he had gone up. There
was no evidence that anyone had climbed up this side of
the wall.

Howie walked down the alley at his foot-dragging rate.
If anyone saw him they would look right through him.
Street bums were of no consequence, especially in Tijuana.
It took him twenty minutes to go down the two blocks to
where he had left his car. Actually it wasn't his. He had
"borrowed" it in Coronado, and changed the rear license
plate to one he had taken off a wrecked car in a junk yard
a month before. It always paid to be prepared. He'd drive
the '92 Chevy back to Chula Vista, just over the border on
the U.S. side where he had left his Ford Mustang the night
before.

Leave nothing to chance. Plan, plan, plan, and then work
your plan. He had the system down. It worked. He stopped
two miles from the kill house and cleaned up his face and
hands with baby wipes, changed into a sport shirt and

perched a Padres baseball cap on his head covering up his military crew cut. He had no trouble crossing the border.

An hour later he came out of the shower in his Coronado apartment. It was nothing fancy. He could afford much better, but it wouldn't fit in with his public middle-class lifestyle.

He checked a small book that looked as if it held times and distances of his daily workouts and runs. The book showed a date last week and 112.6. He would call the bank tomorrow night and have the computer voice read off his balance. Then he would write down the new time for a run. It should be 122.6. Yes, ten thousand dollars in two e-deposits would be added to his bank account tomorrow morning. This was in a bank he didn't use regularly and where he didn't put down his real name. The name and numbers were hidden in the book of running times dating back five years.

Howie had stashed the Ruger and its silencer in a secret compartment he had built into the floorboards of his 1998 Mustang. The hiding place was barely three inches deep and eight inches wide. The top was designed to look like an access panel under the floor mats.

Now he toweled off, checked the news on the all-night TV station and looked at his hand-held computer calendar.

Today was Monday, nearly 0330. The platoon would have muster this morning at 0700. He wouldn't be late. Had never missed a roll call since the day he signed on with SEAL Team Seven four years ago.

2

Dushan, People's Republic of China

United States Senator Gregory B. Highlander stared at the paper a Chinese soldier had just given him at the door of the small house they had been provided in this remote village 20 miles northeast along the coast from Zhanjiang in south China. They were a 150 miles southwest of Macao in one of the poor peasant backlands of China. Senator Highlander knew the message had to be bad news.

The Republican senior U.S. senator from Idaho couldn't believe it. He had his wife read the formal document for him a second time. It was written in Mandarin and she was half Chinese. They had come to this small, poor village a week ago to track down his wife's last known relatives. Several had been killed in the great Mao purge, others sent into the countryside. Some simply disappeared.

"The orders are clear, Greg. It says we are considered enemies of the Chinese people, and we are required to stay within our house until further notice. We are not to contact any Chinese in the area and may leave only with an escort to obtain food. It doesn't say how long this house arrest will last."

"Surely our embassy—" The senator stopped. The State Department and the embassy in Bejing had argued against this trip by the chairman of the U.S. Senate Armed Services Committee. They told him he was the most important man in the Senate for getting military expenditure bills through Congress and that a person with his knowledge of the U.S. military establishment and weaponry simply shouldn't go on a tourist jaunt into the People's Republic of China, which had remained belligerent.

Now he sat heavily in one of the three wooden chairs in the sparsely furnished living room of the modest house that his wife's distant cousin had arranged for them to use for their stay. It was owned by another distant cousin, and there had been a lot of bowing and chattering as the cousins met for the first time in their lives just a week ago.

Senator Highlander had believed that he, his wife, and their daughter would be in no danger on this visit. He was an important person in the U.S. government. The Chinese would not dare think of curtailing his travel or do anything that might make him uncomfortable, let alone that he might complain about to the embassy. Yeah, he had been dead wrong on that one. He winced at the word *dead*. No he couldn't think that way. Now he realized that he had been wrong to agree to come. His wife thought that things had loosened up enough in China for a trip she had been planning for over fifteen years.

He was an idiot. Now what he had to do was think of some way that he could get out of this burning house situation. Contacting the embassy was out. The house didn't even have a telephone. He wouldn't play his ace card unless he had to. As a powerful U.S. senator he had grown accustomed to getting his own way, of winning fights in the Senate about military spending, and even having his own way at home with his wife and daughter. He had earned the right, damn it. He had come up the hard way, from a farmer father who was blown out of the Nebraska dustbowl in 1937. Then the long trip to Oregon, where the family had done a little better; but still they ate a lot of grapefruit and oatmeal that first year of 1937–1938, mainly because it was cheap and good for them. He had made it through high school, played in the band, and graduated somewhere in the middle of his small-town high school class of ninety-eight seniors.

The Model A Ford Roadster he had bought in his senior year cost him $225. It had yellow spoke wheels, a top that came down, and a rumble seat, a 1931 Model A. When he

bought the car, his grades went down but he stayed on the
tennis team and graduated. Not until the second half of his
senior year did he think about going on to school. His parents couldn't afford to pay college tuition or buy books.

A small private college in his home town suggested he
might want to play on its tennis team. They had no schol-
arships, but they could help him get a job on campus to
pay the tuition: $225 for the first semester. He sold the
Model A to get the money.

The senator looked outside the small Chinese house and
saw something new. A military guard with a submachine
gun slung over his shoulder, stood just beyond the small
gate in front of the house. He guessed there would be one
at the back door as well.

*Damn fine mess I've got us in this time. Not so bad for
me, but Lydia and Darla. God damn it to hell!*

Lydia Highlander watched her husband. She had inher-
ited her English father's fine coloring, a peaches and cream
complexion that was flawless at fifty-two years. The Chinese heritage showed in her almond eyes that slanted de-
lightfully, and in the flat bridge of her nose. Her sleek
absolutely black hair hadn't been cut for two years. It
flowed around her shoulders and down her back. She
touched her husband's arm.

"Greg, it will be all right. They wouldn't dare hurt you.
We must figure out how to get you back home."

"How to get all of us back. I won't go and leave you
two here." He paused, then shrugged. "There's only one
way now. You know about the heart stimulator machine I
brought with us?"

"Yes. I knew it wasn't that. What is it?"

"I'll show you." He took one of their unpacked suitcases
and opened it. The maze of wires, dials and readouts built
into a metal box looked medically complicated and professional. He moved the unit to a small table and unscrewed
a plate on the back. From the metal case he pulled out a
long rectangular, metal object.

"It's called the SATCOM for satellite radio communications." He took a small dish antenna from inside the box

and spread open the dish part into a circle. He set it on a small tripod by the window and moved it around a little.

"Should work there." He hooked it to the radio. "With the proper frequency I can call up any phone number in the world, access the president or the chiefs of staff, my own office, the CIA, anyone." He looked in a small notebook that had been in the fake metal box and pointed at a frequency.

"Yes, I think we'll talk to the CIA. This is really their jurisdiction. First I have to make sure the antenna is tuned toward one of the satellites overhead that will relay the signal. There are supposed to be such satellites all around the world. They told me it would work."

He moved the knobs then adjusted the dish antenna twice and waited each time. A moment later a beep came from the speaker on the radio. The radio itself was about five inches square and sixteen inches tall. It had a built-in round flexible antenna and a handset. The whole thing including batteries weighed only ten pounds.

"We have the satellite tuned in, now here's hoping I did everything right." The senator picked up the handset and pushed the send button.

"CIA, this is Senator Highlander calling from a small town in China. Looking for some help. Do you receive me?"

He turned the set to receive and listened but the speaker remained ominously silent. He tried the same words again, and then a third time. Then a voice came through faintly.

"Senator Highlander. Your signal is weak. Increase your power to eighteen watts. What do you need?"

"CIA, moving to eighteen watts. We've been put under house arrest here in China. Armed guards at the front and back doors. We need to get out of here. We're at Dushan, a small village about twenty miles north of Zhanjiang which is on the south coast of China. We're about three miles from the South China Sea. Can you help us? I have a lot of information about this country. She's on a wartime footing."

"Senator, understand your problem. Will take it up im-

mediately. Keep your SATCOM on burst sending so China
can't pick up your signal. It's all encrypted in the set. Will
contact you in two hours and every two hours after that.
Have the set turned on."

"Thank God. We'll be waiting."

Darla, his sixteen-year-old daughter, had been in the next
room, but came in when she heard the radio speaker. She
stood wide eyed watching the exchange.

"Is it dangerous here, Daddy?"

"It could be. I'm trying to get us out of China."

Darla's eyes went wider. Their slant was less than that
of her mother's but apparent and her nose was more
rounded. Her skin was not as perfect as her mothers. She
wore shorts and a T-shirt, her soft dark hair kept cut short
for easy care. "Not much ice skating here, huh, Daddy?"

"Not that we've seen. Now, how is our food supply? We
could be here for several more days. Do I need to go out
and get something from that small market and store we saw
when we came in?"

The senator looked at his wife. He was maintaining a
steady calm on the outside. Even as he asked about food
he was thinking about a story he had read on Chinese pris-
ons, and detention camps. He shivered as he remembered
the pictures of what China did to some of its own people.
Now those visions kept slamming into his mind.

NAVSPECWARGRUP-ONE
Coronado, California

The clock in the equipment room of Third Platoon, SEAL
Team Seven, showed 0730. The sixteen SEALs had been
called out early to get the news.

"We've got work to do," Lieutenant Commander Blake
Murdock told his men. "We move out from North Island
Naval Air Station at twelve hundred. We go fully loaded
with weapons, double ammo, and anything else you can
think of that we might need on a hot firefight. I'm not sure
which direction we're traveling, but Commander Masciareli
asked me if Kenneth Ching was fit for duty."

"China? We're heading for China?" Jaybird Sterling, machinist mate second class, asked.

"Speculation," Senior Chief Boatswain's Mate Will Dobler snapped. "You heard what the man said. Let's get cracking. We've got an hour to get our gear ready to travel. Double loads of ammo in your drag bag. Uniform of the day will be desert cammies. Take one change of clothes. We'll work out weapons assignments now." He looked at Murdock. "Commander, what mix do you want?"

"We don't have the slightest idea what we're going to be getting into. Let's take two of the EARs, five of the Bull Pups, and the rest standard. We'll leave the fifty here this time. The Bull Pups can do the same job. Check for ammo supply on the Pups."

"Aye, aye, sir," Dobler said. "Move it you swabbies. We've got an airplane to catch."

Murdock put his gear in order, then inspected the men at 0830. Speculation about where they would be going was running wild.

"Not a clue," Murdock told them again. "Orders came through channels from our beloved commander, that's all I know."

"Seems kind of lonely without Don Stroh giving us a call on the SATCOM," Bill Bradford, quartermaster's mate first class, said. "He still gonna be sticking his big nose in here from time to time?"

"I'm sure he will," Murdock said. "The through-channels flap will be hot for a while, then calm down. He says he's free to talk to us after we get an assignment."

They had special chow at 1000, then another inspection and lined up to board two six-by trucks for transport to North Island, only two miles away. They were early. Their bird was being turn-around serviced. It was a Gulfstream II (VC11). The troops grinned. It was a fancy business jet the military used for VIPs or for fast moves of small groups of men.

The plane had a low wing with a twenty-five-degree leading-edge sweep, three degrees of dihedral from the roots, and low wing fences at midspan. The trailing edge had one-piece single-slotted, Fowler-type flaps inboard of insert ailerons.

The T-tail had a broad, slightly swept vertical fin with a small dorsal fillet and full-height rudder. At the top of the tail were swept, horizontal stabilizers with full-span elevators. Two Rolls-Royce turbofan engines with Rohr thrust reversers were mounted on short stubs that were located high on the rear fuselage; the inlets overlapped the trailing edges of the wings. Fuel was carried in wing tanks.

The Gulfstream Aerospace plane had a crew of three, and normally carried nineteen passengers. Its wingspan was sixty-eight feet ten inches and it was seventy-nine feet eleven inches long. Maximum cruise speed at 25,000 feet was 581 mph. It had a ceiling of 42,000 feet and a range, with maximum fuel, of 4,275 miles.

The SEALs lounged on their drag bags and packs on the tarmac fifty yards from where final fueling of their jet took place.

"Damn, this time I hope we draw one of them tasty little Air Force women stewards," said Jack Mahanani, hospital corpsman first class.

"Hell of a lot better ride than a C-130," said Paul Jefferson, engineman second class.

They loaded at 1130; stowed their vests, weapons, harnesses, and drag bags; and settled into civilian-type, lean-back, first-class seats.

"Now this is living," Colt Franklin, yeoman second class shrilled. "This is really living."

A tall black woman in an Air Force uniform with three stripes on her sleeves came out of the plane's flight cabin. "Gentlemen," she said, and everyone shut up and looked up. "My name is Andrea, and I'm crew chief on this bird. Anybody barfs gets to clean it up himself. You be nice to my baby, or I'll razz you all the way to our first fuel stop. Y'all hear me?"

"Yes ma'am," the sixteen SEALs said almost in unison.

"Good. Just so we understand each other. I hear you haven't eaten since ten o'clock. Poor babies. I'll have some high-quality Air Force box lunches for you an hour after takeoff. Now settle back and enjoy. Usually I get admirals and senators and generals for passengers." She frowned, lifted her brows, and shook her head. "From admirals to this. Please, Lord, have mercy, I got saddled with a whole passel of froggy guys."

She grinned, and the SEALs hooted as she went out the main door.

T'aipei, Taiwan

Thirteen hours and two stops later, the sleek business jet rolled to a stop at T'aipei airport and the SEALs transferred quickly to a U.S. Navy bus that took them to the port where they were bunked down in a Navy building. It had a small mess hall and twenty bunk beds.

That was where Don Stroh contacted them through a base telephone.

"Enjoy your tourist flight?" Stroh asked Murdock.

"Terrific, especially the in-flight movie. Now who in hell is going to tell us where we're going and what we're supposed to be doing?"

"That would be me. Uncle Sugar has a small problem, three of them actually. This blunderbuss senator, who also is chairman of the Senate Armed Services Committee, is stuck in China. They have him under house arrest at a little village in south China down below Macao somewhere. He says China is at a fever pitch, that the whole damn place is almost on a wartime footing. He expects something big and wild to pop at any time. He wants out."

"I can understand his thoughts."

"His wife and teenage daughter are with him. Three packages, all must come out untouched and totally unharmed."

"Our job is to go in and bring them out?" Murdock asked.

"You're quick, Murdock. Except when those calico ocean bass are biting. You have to wait for the second nibble, then strike with a good upward snap with the rod. That's the reason I can outfish you any day in the week."

"Not on a clear day, Stroh. Now, how do we get from

here to down there? How far is it? Do we have Navy power in the area?"

"Questions, questions. You are to meet with Admiral Barney Chalmers. His place in half an hour. Bring along your team."

"You're here in T'aipei?"

"Bingo, I told them you were quick. Been waiting for you. I've been here all of four hours. But I had an eight-hour head start. See you soon. A man is on his way to bring your people."

Twenty minutes later Murdock, Lieutenant jg Ed DeWitt, Chief Dobler, Jaybird Sterling, and Joe Lampedusa (operations specialist third class) walked into Admiral Chalmers's office two buildings down and came to attention.

"Admiral, sir. Lieutenant Commander Murdock and team reporting as ordered."

"Yes, Murdock, men, sit down. This may take some time. Don Stroh has been telling me that if anyone can bring out our gallivanting senator, you and your men can."

Murdock nodded in response. He saw Stroh sitting across the table from them and waved at him.

"This little Chinese village is three miles inland, and about seven hundred miles by air from us here," the admiral continued. "We have some assets in the area, namely two destroyers and a light cruiser. The destroyers are about a hundred miles off Macao and steaming south as we speak to get in position as close to the village as possible while staying twenty miles at sea."

"Yes sir," Murdock said. "We can work off a destroyer if it's cleared to land a CH-forty-six."

The admiral looked at one of his aides.

"In that area is the Guided Missile Destroyer *Gonzalez*," a three-striper said. "I know that she can service and rearm the SH-60 chopper."

"That fits," Jaybird said. "The sixty has a rotor diameter of just over fifty-three feet. The forty-six has a rotor diameter of fifty-one feet so it should work."

The admiral looked at Murdock. "Sir, I rely on my men

to assist in all phases of an operation. If Jaybird says the CH-46 will fit on the deck, sir, it will."

The admiral frowned, then shrugged. "Fine. Now how to we get a forty-six to the *Gonzalez*?"

"Sir, we have the Amphibious Assault Ship *Bataan* about two hundred miles north and west of the *Gonzalez*," a captain near the Admiral said. "She has six or eight of the CH forty-sixes. The *Bataan* is about four hundred miles south of Kaohsiung on the tip of Taiwan. We have three of the forty-sixes there."

"So she's within range of the destroyer." The admiral looked up. "I can order the chopper to fly to the destroyer whenever you say, Commander. I've had word through channels directly from the CNO that you are to get whatever you want."

"Thank you, sir. We'll need two hours to plan out the operation. Do we have any kind of visual on the area, on the house, or the beach along there?"

The admiral looked at his staff. Each man shook his head.

"Not a thing. You'll be going in blind. I do have one directive. We are not to commit any more aircraft than absolutely necessary to the operation. One chopper in and out would be the preference of the CNO. He said that way there will be less flack when China accuses us of violating her airspace and committing aggression on Chinese soil."

"And we accuse her of kidnapping three U.S. citizens," Murdock said.

"Two of whom have dual Chinese citizenship," Ed DeWitt said.

"Really?" Admiral Chalmers asked.

"Yes, as I understand Chinese law," DeWitt said.

There was a pause. Everyone looked at the admiral. He reached for his pipe. He picked it off its decorative stand on his desk, carefully cleaned the bowl while the others waited. Then he put the stem in his mouth and nodded.

"All right, let's see what you men come up with in two hours. My planning people will also be working on an extraction plan. Let's see who can make the better one."

Ten minutes later, back in their assigned building, the
SEALs gathered around a fold-out table and began to put
ideas down on paper. Ed DeWitt held the pencil and pad.
Don Stroh came in and walked up to the table.

"Well, well, the honorable Donald P. Stroh of the elite
CIA," Murdock said. "Have you asked for detailed satellite
shots of that village? When can we have them and any other
intelligence details you CIA guys have on that area?"

"Just as soon as they fax it to me. I requested it five
hours ago, so it should be coming soon, if we have anything. Murdock, do you know how many little villages there
are in the world? You can't expect us to have details about
every one."

"Just this one would be fine," Murdock said. "We'll take
what you give us. Now who has some ideas?"

"To start, we fly off the destroyer the twenty miles to
shore and three miles inland," Joe Lampedusa said. Then
he laughed. "Not a chance. We'd have a jillion Chinese
rifles pointing at us before we got ready to fly out."

"So we go in by a launch of some kind and the last five
miles by rubber duck," Jaybird Sterling said. "We go in
quiet. We get inland as far as we can without a sound. Use
suppressed shots if we need to."

"Quiet approach," Murdock said. "Put that down. What
else?"

"We use the EAR whenever practical," DeWitt said.
"That way the China News Agency won't have any bodies
to show the world on TV for a month after we leave."

"Yeah, I like this. But how do we find the guy?" Dobler
asked. "They said he has a SATCOM. Can we contact him
at a specific time and have him give us directions from the
beach?"

"Good point," Murdock said. "Stroh, can you get what
frequency he's using so we can contact him from here or
from the ship? We want to have him describe everything
to us before we take off."

"I'm on my horse to the radio. If we don't get anything
visual, he can fill us in about the area. I'm outa here."

"So it has to be a night operation," Lampedusa said. "We

hit the beach at 0100. Most of the locals should be asleep or drunk by then. Should leave us plenty of time to run in three miles and walk out, get to our boats and leave."

"Flotation with three extra bodies?" Dobler asked.

"The IBS can take two hundred more pounds easily," Jaybird said. "If there's any problem, we dump overboard all of our ammo, that's easy two hundred pounds per squad."

"What if we run into an army patrol?" Murdock asked. "The report said there were two soldiers with submachine guns at the house."

"The two Chinks we can convince not to hamper us," DeWitt said. "The EAR would be ideal."

"What about a patrol?" Murdock pressed.

"Everything we take with us is silenced," Dobler said. "If we stumble into a patrol, or if they spot us, we fire silenced, work our way out of it. As the last resort we take off the suppressors and cut loose."

Murdock gave him a thumbs up. "We get to the beach, load up, and motor out to our yacht and get on back to the destroyer." He looked around. "Any final words of wisdom? No choppers, all silenced. In and out attracting as little attention as possible. Let's go back and see the admiral."

A half hour later, the SEALs stood in front of the same group as before in the admiral's office. Only Don Stroh was missing.

DeWitt laid out the plan for the Admiral and his staff.

"So, Admiral Chalmers. We think a launch from the destroyer at the ten-mile limit, then the IBS boats for the last two miles will give us a silent approach and exfiltration as well. We might be able to get in and back out with the packages and not ruffle more than a few Chinese soldier's feathers."

The Admiral turned to his men at the table. They conferred for a moment. Before they could make any comment, Don Stroh came into the room with a sheaf of papers.

"Admiral, sir. I have some late developments."

"Pertinent, Stroh?"

"Absolutely. They could change our plans."

The admiral settled back, picked up his pipe again, and put it in his mouth. He nodded at Stroh who stood beside Murdock.

"We have a group of faxes from my office. Nothing that gives us much to go on. One aerial shot of the general area of Zhanjiang, but that's twenty miles from ground zero. What I do have are some printouts of transmissions from the senator within the last half hour by SATCOM.

"He says their small village is on a river that runs fifty feet in back of their house. It isn't large but he's seen thirty- and forty-foot craft moving up and down the river. They don't look to be flat-bottomed boats. They are three miles from the ocean, but the river runs almost straight from their house to the beach."

"Anything else, Mr. Stroh?"

"Yes, the senator has given me detailed directions how to come up the river and where to land. He can talk the SEALs in with his SATCOM if they have any trouble. The river looks to be our best bet."

The admiral looked at Murdock.

"Yes sir, I agree. A slight change in plans. The amphibious landing ship should have a Pegasus on board. If they can airlift it to the destroyer, we can use that for our run in and back from the river. It can throttle down for the last five miles, putting us within two miles of the mouth of that river. Then we go by IBS to shore, up the river to the house, take out the guards with our enhanced acoustic rifle, a non-lethal weapon, grab the packages, and have them in the IBS craft and back down the river before the Chinese change guard shifts."

The admiral looked at his staff. Two nodded. The captain lifted his brows. "Looks better than what we had in mind, Admiral. Let's go with the commander's plan."

"When?"

Murdock looked at the admiral. "Sir, that would be insertion from the destroyer so we could hit the river at 0100. With a good operation and no surprises, we should be back to the Pegasus not more than two hours later."

"Entirely covert, Commander?"

"If at all possible. If we can use the EAR. The soldiers hit will be unconscious for four to six hours and will wake up confused, slightly nauseous, but not having the slightest idea what happened."

"Very well. Commander, what's the present position of the ships involved?" The admiral looked at his staff.

"The *Bataan* is four hundred ten miles from the airfield at the bottom of this island. She's on a southwest course at eighteen knots. The *Gonzalez* is roughly fifty miles off the target and about two hundred and fifty from the *Bataan*."

The admiral checked his watch. "Gentlemen, it's a little after 1235 here local time. I know you've been across the International Date Line and six or eight time changes, but sun time here is just after noon. The COD doesn't land on our amphibs, so we go with a Sea Knight. Martin, check with the *Bataan* to be sure she has a Pegasus available to airlift to the destroyer. Also alert them of a mission and to have a Sea Knight flight checked and ready to go in seven hours. The usual signals to the two ships involved in the action and their part in it." The admiral turned to the SEALs.

"Men you have a little over five hours of flight time in those choppers. One from the air field in the south to the amphib, another one to the destroyer. I'll have them airlift the Pegasus from the amphib to the destroyer. This all should put you on the *Gonzalez* at about 1900. Then you can push off in time to get the Pegasus to that river mouth by 0100."

"We can be ready to take off in a half hour, sir," Murdock said. "Oh, one last request. Could you see if the *Bataan* has a pair of expendable IBS units they could have deflated and in the Pegasus or tied on board?"

"That's a roger, Commander." The admiral pointed to one of his men who stood and left the room.

"So, we'll see you at the airstrip at 1305."

South China Sea
Off China

Navy air power performed flawlessly, and the sixteen SEALs stumbled out of the CH46 onboard the gently pitching chopper pad on the *Gonzalez* twenty minutes ahead of schedule. Most of them had slept on the two legs to the amphibian ship and then to the guided missile destroyer.

A four-striper met them on the deck and hurried them into the compartment they would use for their short stay.

"We heard you were coming," the commander said. "I'm Randolph."

"Murdock here," Blake said and shook the man's hand. "Do you have a Pegasus for us with two IBS craft?"

"We do. Right now we're back up to speed and making thirty knots toward your small stream. It's called the Yibin River on my chart and shows navigation up about twenty miles. We're still eighteen miles off shore and paralleling it until we come off the Yibin. Another two hours at the most. How about some hot chow? I've alerted the mess and your men can order whatever they want from steak to lobster. It isn't often that we get a combat mission onboard the *Gonzalez*."

The sixteen SEALs ate, slept a while, and were on the fantail on the chopper pad twenty minutes early and ready to go down a rope ladder off the stern into the Pegasus, which rode gently as the destroyer made five knots forward in a slow three-mile box ten miles off shore from the Yibin River.

A coxswain came up and talked to Murdock.

"Sir, I'm your driver. We're ten miles off the river. I understand you want to move in modestly, then the last five miles at no more than ten knots. We stop two miles off and put you in the IBSs."

"Correct, Coxswain. Then you meander around out there for about two hours when we should be two miles out in the IBSs to meet you with the three packages."

"We have a SATCOM on board," the coxswain said. "We're set on channel one and will wait for a radio check with you when you get your packages in the boats in the river."

"Sounds good. We'll have light sticks for the pickup. If you hear any firing at all, come in closer, we might need more help than we figure right now. You have live ammo for your shooters?"

"Absolutely and good men with the guns."

"Great, time we get onboard."

Murdock lined up his men in their combat gear and with their weapons and then went down the rope ladder into the gently bobbing Pegasus. Ed DeWitt brought up the rear. Any nervousness Murdock had felt evaporated once he stepped on the Pegasus and moved forward. This was it. Once more into the fray, into the breach, as the poem went. He never went into a mission thinking that this could be his last. It wasn't in his nature. He went in knowing that he would come out. Knowing that he was serving his country and doing a damn good job. But this wasn't just another mission. This was the one right now, the most important one he had ever been on. The current one had to feel that way.

He turned and hurried the men into their seats in the cramped insertion craft that could do forty-five knots in a calm sea. Good, the quicker they got up that river the better.

Now that it had started, Murdock couldn't wait.

3

South China Sea

The loaded Pegasus growled along at twenty knots and Murdock went to the coxswain.

"Making too much noise, Chief. Cut her down to ten knots and we'll listen. Not supposed to be any Chinese out here, but we can't count on that." The coxswain cut the speed. The new sound of the big twin 4,500-horsepower diesels was a lower growl, but Murdock shook his head and asked to cut down the speed again. At last they crept through the soft swells at five knots and Murdock was satisfied.

"Our timetable isn't important going in," he told the driver. "I don't want to alert anybody along shore that some boat is heading toward the river."

"Hey, I don't want to get shot at either," the coxswain said.

Murdock called for a full stop when he figured they were a mile and a half offshore of a cluster of lights. Dobler inflated the first IBS and put it in the sea. The Pegasus had stopped, and the big engines idled.

Bravo Squad went in the first IBS and then Dobler inflated the second one and dropped it in the wet. Alpha Squad and Murdock moved into it, drag bags and all, and cast loose. The two boats were tied together with a forty-foot line as they turned toward shore. Both engines started on the second pull and they purred along at five knots, heading in with what Murdock decided was an incoming tide.

All of the SEALs had on their personal Motorola radios.

24

They had a transceiver clipped on the belt, an earpiece, and a mike that fastened around their neck and perched a half inch from their lips.

Murdock made a radio check, and all fifteen men signed on in the correct order. "Ten minutes to the river mouth. If there's no traffic, we go right up the middle of the stream," Murdock told the SEALs. "Doubt if we can keep the SAT-COM antenna on target for a talk with the senator, but we have detailed directions how to find him. Up the river two miles then a slight bend to the left. His house is another mile on beside two tall trees. He'll have the lights on and be on the riverbank with a flashlight if he can get there without the guard spotting him."

"How close do we motor to the house?" DeWitt asked.

"Let's beach it a hundred yards before we get to the right place," Murdock said on the Motorola. "Jefferson, it's your turn in the barrel. You'll stay with the IBSs to ensure that we'll have them safe and secure when we come back and save a five-mile swim."

"Yes, sir, Commander," Jefferson said.

"All of you make sure your weapons have suppressors on them, that your mags are full, and that there's a round in the chambers. No twenty-millimeter mags in the Bull Pups, at least not yet."

The men ducked low in the rubber ducks as they passed over a small bar and into the channel of the Yibin River. It was no more than forty yards across here. Murdock wondered how it could be navigated for twenty miles upstream.

The cluster of lights turned out to be three buildings near the left-hand side of the stream. They had a dock with night lights. One boat had tied up there, but Murdock could see no people. At less than thirty yards they motored quietly past the lights and back into the dark.

Clouds scuttered over the moon. Now a dark period. Murdock watched along the left-hand shore for the features that the senator had told Stroh about. He saw a temple to the left. Yes one sign post. A short way on a small stream came in from the left. Second indicator.

A shot jolted into the quiet night. The men in both boats

ducked lower. The sound came from the right.

"At ease," Murdock whispered into his mike. "That was a rifle shot but it was half a mile off. No concern of ours. Stay low."

A boat came chugging toward them showing one pale light forward.

"Left shore now," Murdock said to the mike. Both boats turned sharply toward the left shore and stopped against a grassy bank. The diesel engine chugged along, and the small wooden boat steamed downstream.

"Fishing boat," DeWitt said. "Getting an early start. Must be some good shoals or banks offshore."

The boats moved back to the middle of the stream. Now they could see houses and sheds crowding the bank on both sides. How could they spot the house they needed? Murdock wondered.

"Three miles up the river now," Jaybird whispered into the mike.

"Watch to the left shore," Murdock said.

They saw two houses with lights still on. It was almost 0130 hours. The third house was another hundred yards upstream. It had two lights on and beside it stood two tall trees.

"Hit the shore," Murdock said. "Lam, take a look at that house with the two tall trees. See if you can spot a guard. Let's hope he's a smoker."

Both boats grounded against the shore and one man stepped out and held them there. Lampedusa lifted out and vanished into the night without a sound.

The lights in the house ahead by the tall trees snapped off, one room, then the next.

"This might not be it," Murdock whispered into his mike.

They waited. Murdock checked his watch. Lam had been gone five minutes. Murdock's earpiece came alive.

"Cap, this is the one. I heard a guard yelling at the man inside. That was just before the lights went out. The inside guy yelled back in English with some highly uncomplimentary terms. Must be the senator. I've got an EAR. You want me to take out the rear guard while I know where he is?"

"Roger that. Your weapon is free."

They all listened for the typical *whooshing* sound of the enhanced acoustic rifle, but heard nothing.

"Bingo on the back guard," Lam said. "Want me to find the front one and send him to beddy bye?"

"That's a roger, Lam. We're moving up. Everyone on shore, quietly and move forward in squads. Alpha Squad hold while Bravo moves to the house. Bravo will try to contact the senator and enter from the rear. Move."

Another rifle shot jolted into the night, again on the other side of the river. Trigger-happy guards? Someone celebrating? Murdock guessed that the average Chinese citizen was not allowed to own a gun. He let Bravo Squad move out first, then followed with his own, waving to Jefferson who held the boats and dragged them higher on the gently sloping shoreline. Murdock took the point and moved slowly, silently through a smattering of hardwoods along the riverbank. There were no other houses this side of the target.

A moment later Murdock heard the *swoosh* of the EAR weapon. It was quickly followed by his earpiece activating.

"That's two down, Cap. Second guard was a smoker, dumb fucker. He'll have a long sleep and a headache tomorrow. I can see no other army units of any kind along the street. No cars. A few bicycles here and there, but nobody riding them. Looks all clear."

"Concur," Ed DeWitt's voice said on the radio. "Clear front."

Murdock hurried then, running as silently as possible the last thirty yards to the house. He flattened against the door pointing for his men to take cover at various spots. Then he tried the door. It was not locked.

He turned the knob and pushed the door open.

"Senator, is anyone home?" Murdock said in a loud stage whisper.

Murdock heard movement to his left and swung the MP5 submachine gun to cover, his finger on the trigger.

"God bless the U.S. Navy," a throaty voice said. The

sound was so choked with emotion, Murdock could barely make out the words.

"Senator, the Chinese guards front and back are unconscious. Are there any other soldiers around here?"

Quiet sobbing was the only answer. Then another voice came through the blackness.

"No, there are no other troops anywhere nearby that we know of. I'm Mrs. Highlander. You must be Navy SEALs. We're ready to travel. No luggage, only my purse and my daughter's purse, and Greg's briefcase. We can take those, can't we?"

"Yes, Mrs. Highlander. But we must be so quiet we can't even hear ourselves. There are fifteen men outside around this house, did you hear any of them?"

"No, only a funny *whooshing* sound."

"Good, get your daughter, and we'll leave. Senator, are you all right now? We need you to move about a hundred yards downstream with us."

"Yes, yes, I'm good now. I just couldn't stop—"

"No problem, Senator. Alpha Squad, and three civilians coming out the rear door. Bravo and Lam head for the boats. Give us perimeter along the way facing out. Alpha let's be a circle around the senator and his wife and daughter. Almost shoulder to shoulder. You know the protective routine. Do it, now."

He felt the senator touch his shoulder, then his wife came holding the daughter's hand.

"Come out the back door right behind me, Senator. Hook your hand in my webbing. Mrs. Highlander you hold your husband's belt in back, and hold your daughter's hand. Now, Let's move smartly, but try not to make any noise."

They left the rear door, then moved into the yard and the brush. Six SEALs appeared on each side and in back and in front. They all could reach out and touch the senator or his family. Nobody said a word. Murdock saw the Bravo Squad spread along the one hundred yards in a protective shield.

Murdock faded back to walk beside the civilian. "Senator, you'll be in the boat with me. These are rubber inflatable boats, sturdy, can't sink and each has a silent motor. Your wife and daughter will be in the second boat to distribute the weight. We must sit low and bend over on command if we come into any trouble. Understand?"

"Yes, sir," the senator said.

"I heard too," his wife said. "We'll do whatever you say."

It took them ten minutes to work their way slowly to the boats. Jefferson knew they were coming from the radio com. He had the boats turned around for easier boarding. The SEALs put the civilians in first, two SEALs getting their feet and legs wet in the process.

Mrs. Highlander started to apologize for letting the men get wet. Kenneth Ching shook his head. "Ma'am, us SEALs are wet most of the time. No big deal. Just so you're safe."

"Everyone onboard?" Murdock whispered in the Motorola.

"Bravo Squad boarded," DeWitt responded.

Murdock counted bodies in his boat. Nine of them. The senator wasn't as big a man as he had feared. There should be no trouble with the IBSs.

"Move out and start motors," Murdock said.

They were fifty yards down the river flowing with the current, making a good ten knots with the help of the motors, when they heard an engine, then saw lights bobbing along a road just off the river.

"Guard change," The senator whispered to Murdock. "They come every night at two A.M. I forgot to tell Mr. Stroh that."

"Things are going to get hairy in about five minutes," Murdock whispered into the mike. "Open up the motors for a little more speed. Like to get to the mouth of the river before any troops arrive."

The boats picked up speed, but the motors gave off a soft rumble. Murdock knew an alert guard could hear it. But would there be anyone on guard duty in a tiny village on a small stream like this? He doubted it.

The stutter of machine guns at the house they had just left surprised Murdock. The weapons fired six or seven ten-round bursts. Enough to wake up everyone in the area.

"Lift it up another notch on the motors," Murdock said. "Let's trade noise for speed."

The little craft churned downstream faster, Murdock figured about fifteen knots. They still had two and a half miles to go.

Lights blossomed along the right shore. They moved to the other side of the river trying not to hit any bars or trees. Now a rifle shot sounded behind them and to the right side. More lights snapped on. They heard motors starting, then gears grinding as heavier trucks moved out.

"Anderson, unwrap the SATCOM. Have somebody hold the dish until you get your beep, then try to contact the Pegasus. He needs to know we're coming out."

Howie Anderson, gunner's mate second class, was the new radioman in the platoon. He knew the radio. Jaybird held the antenna and moved it back and forth until Anderson stopped him.

"Pegasus, this is Rover, we're coming out. Your reception will be spotty. Over."

There was no answering call. Howie tried it again, kept Jaybird moving the antenna a little until he received the beep and at once he sent a signal. "Rover coming out. Rover coming out. Pegasus, this is Rover coming out."

This time there was a broken up response. "Peg——, Hear y——. Com——ut. Co——out."

Murdock tapped Anderson on the shoulder. "He got it, wrap it up, we've got to stay low."

Somewhere behind them another submachine gun fired. The sound came in angry six-round bursts. Murdock figured they were aimed at the water. What better escape route from the house. He bent lower and tried to will the IBS to move faster.

"Full throttle," Murdock said into the mike. "Let's get our eighteen knots plus another five out of the current and get out of this fucking river."

The engines gave a small growl, then steadied down to the new power surge.

More lights showed along the riverbank on the right, then

Murdock saw lights coming on at the opposite side of the river as well. Headlights poked along the road. Now and then a truck seemed to pull in to face the river and stop. Troops must be deploying along the river. Why would there be truckloads of Chinese troops in a small area like this? Maybe brought in especially to protect the prize catch of the tourist season.

Downstream a mile, the SEALs and the senator and family saw two star shells blossom over the middle of the river. Their brilliant light glowed for thirty seconds, then faded out.

"That's going to be a problem," Murdock said. "Unlimber those EAR guns. Anytime you see activity along the near shore by trucks or men ahead of us, send them a round. One EAR in each boat?"

"Roger that," someone said softly.

"Pick your targets so you don't both hit the same one. Do it."

Three hundred yards ahead a truck ground to a halt with its headlights throwing a bright path across the water.

"I've got it," Lam said. A moment later the familiar *whoosh* sound came, but there was no noticeable effect on shore.

"At least the driver is in dreamland," Lam said.

A quarter of a mile on downstream they saw floodlights snap on along the right shore and three army trucks were brightly lit. Men jumped out of the trucks. "Both EARs," Murdock said.

The guns got off two shots each and the SEALs could see the Chinese soldiers fall to the ground and not move.

"Senator and family, that's our EAR weapon. It's non lethal. It's our enhanced acoustic rifle, that sends out a powerful pulse of sound waves that knocks out the victims. They'll be unconscious for four to six hours and wake up with a headache but unharmed."

When a squad of men came into the light to check on the downed soldiers, Lam fired again putting them into a dream world as well.

Fifty yards on downstream a machine gun began chat-

tering six-round bursts. Murdock thought he could hear
them slapping into the water, but he wasn't sure.

"Move to the left bank," Murdock said to his mike. Both
boats swung that way. They were still less than forty yards
from the far side of the narrow river.

"Anyone spot the muzzle flash on that MG?" DeWitt
asked on the net.

"Got him," Jack Mahanani said. A moment later a
whoosh came and the machine gun stopped firing.

"Halfway to the sea," Murdock said. "They don't know
where we are, and that helps. They must have more tricks."

A moment later a guttural growl came from far downstream and Jaybird groaned. "Got to be a patrol boat motor,
Cap. We've heard the bastards before. We can't stop it with
the EAR."

"Can't stop it, but we can stop the men from operating
it," Mahanani said. "When they get close enough, we pop
a couple of EAR rounds at it and there will be nobody on
the throttle or the wheel, she'll go dead in the water and
wash out into the South China Sea."

They listened, then heard the motor as the patrol boat
came toward them. It was sweeping both sides of the shoreline, probably with small S loops. As they watched a
searchlight jolted into the night cutting a swath of brilliance
along the shore and the river.

"What's the range on the EAR?" somebody asked.

"Effective is six hundred yards, tops," Jaybird said.

"Hold fire," Murdock said.

Another machine gun blasted away from the right-hand
shore. More truck lights bounced along the road but no
more aimed lights into the river. Lam fired twice more and
silenced the machine gun.

"Range on the patrol boat at seven hundred," Jaybird
said. "A guess, but what have we to lose."

"Mahanani, take two shots," Murdock said.

The *whooshes* came ten seconds apart. The sound of the
patrol boat engine slowed, then nearly stopped before it
picked back up to its original sound.

"Too far," Mahanani said.

"Hold fire on the boat," Murdock said. "Let's be sure next time."

They powered toward the patrol boat at twenty knots, Murdock figured. The next time he checked the river boat, he estimated it was no more than four hundred yards. "Both EARs one round," Murdock ordered.

The blasts came almost at the same time, like both men had been sighting in on the patrol boat waiting word.

This time the engine slowed gradually and then stopped. The regular route of the boat wavered, then it turned lazily in the now moonlit river and began to drift slowly downstream.

"Oh, yeah," Lam said. "I get to paint a half a patrol boat on my locker record board."

They were close enough now so they could see the lights at the entrance to the river. Now new lights turned on, on the right hand side across from those they had seen before

The chattering of the machine guns came at the same time from opposite sides of the river, and this time Murdock could hear the rounds splashing into the river ahead of them.

"Interlocking machine guns," he said. "Too far off. When we're three hundred yards away, we hit them with two rounds on each MG nest. We knock them out, or we eat rice for one hell of a long time."

The senator touched Murdock's shoulder. "Commander, I'm sorry I got you into this mess. My fault entirely. I should have known better. My view of my importance made me think the Chinese wouldn't have the guts to bother me, let alone arrest me."

"Senator, you can worry about that only if we don't get you out of here. This is no sweat for my men. We train to do just this sort of rescue mission. Of course, we'd rather not get shot to pieces doing it, but those are the chances we take as SEALs. Sometimes people do get hurt."

"Have you had KIA's on missions like this, Commander?"

"In the past two years I've lost twelve good men."

"All that and the public doesn't have the slightest idea

of what you do, right? All of your missions are covert, like
this one is. I won't be allowed to say a word about it when
we get out. There will be no newspaper story or TV flash.
It will be buried in the records of your after-action reports
somewhere, forever hidden from civilian eyes."

"Way it has to be, Senator Highlander."

There was a long sigh. "Yes, I know. But I wish it didn't
have to be that way. I know damn well that I'll never skimp
on appropriations for the SEALs."

Murdock chuckled. "Hey, maybe this will be a good mission for the SEALs as well as the Highlander family."

A rifle cracked from the right-hand shore. Murdock heard
the round hit and a startled cry from someone in his boat.
"Lam."

The answer was a *whooshing* shot from Lam's EAR.

"Saw his muzzle flash, Cap. He must have spotted us in
the ribbon of light the moon casts across the water."

"Who got hit?" Murdock asked.

Nobody responded. Then Lam whispered to Murdock.
"It's Vinnie Van Dyke. He's unconscious. Hit bad somewhere but I can't find any blood. Not a head or neck shot."

"Try and find the wound and stop any bleeding," Murdock said. He looked at the machine guns that now fired
sporadically. They were less than two hundred yards from
the bar into the South China Sea. "Let's knock out those
machine guns," Murdock said

Lam fired three times, allowing ten seconds for the
weapon to recharge. After the second shot the MGs on the
right bank stuttered. The third shot closed it down. Mahanani did his work on the other shore and the machine gun
fell silent after two EAR rounds.

"Anderson, see if you can get the SATCOM working.
Tell him we're nearly out of the river and into the sea."

Howie Anderson tried twice but couldn't raise the Pegasus. Murdock used the radio. "DeWitt, I'm cutting power
so we can get a better shot at the satellite. Cut power both
boats now."

This time when Howie tried he got a response from the
pickup boat.

"Pegasus here. We're about two miles out from the mouth of the river. If you saw no shore batteries, we'll come straight in until we spot your light sticks."

"That's a roger, Pegasus. No shore batteries. We wiped out the machine guns. Good sailing."

"Skipper, found the hole. Looks like it went into Vinnie's right lung. Knocked him out. Not bleeding a lot but his pulse is slow and his breathing is ragged. He's alive but I don't know how long he can hold out."

"Soon as we're on the Pegasus, I'll see what I can do for him," Mahanani said. "I've got some tricks."

"Motors full speed," Murdock ordered.

Two minutes later they passed over the shallow bar and were in the South China Sea. Ken Ching bent two light sticks, mixing the chemicals and turning them into bright wands of light. He held them as high as he could facing front in the rubber duck.

Khai did the same thing in the other boat as they powered forward through a choppy sea toward the Pegasus. Every other wave broke hard on the bow of the small rubber boat, showering the riders with spray.

Senator Highlander crouched there in the IBS, tears running down his cheeks. His eyes were closed and he looked as if he were praying. When he opened his eyes, he touched Murdock.

"Commander, I don't know how to thank you for saving the lives of my wife and daughter. They are the valuable ones in this trio. I was ready to trade my life for theirs. Now I don't have to. How does a man who made a huge mistake thank the men who came and pulled his family out of the jaws of death?"

Murdock couldn't think of any way to answer. He patted the senior senator from Idaho on the shoulder and heard a shout from Ching.

"I've got running lights slightly to port, Captain. I think the Pegasus has found us."

Twenty minutes later in the dry cabin of the Pegasus, Mahanani worked quickly over the prostate form of Vinnie

Van Dyke. The bullet had penetrated his webbing and slammed into his right lung.

"The lead must have been misshapen and flattened out when it broke through a rib," Mahanani said. "Lots of damage in there. I gave him some morphine in case he gets conscious. Other than that we keep his head high and keep him warm so he doesn't go into shock. If the bullet chopped up some of the major tubes in there, he could bleed out in fifteen minutes. So far, so good. Nothing else I can do. They'll have a doctor onboard the *Gonzalez* who will have a good shot at saving him. Vinnie wouldn't live through a five-hour chopper ride back to T'aipei."

They had cut the Pegasus speed to fifteen knots to reduce the pounding. The coxswain said it would take twenty minutes to get to the destroyer. He had alerted the medical staff onboard about the wounded man, and they would be ready for him on the chopper pad on the stern of the ship.

Murdock sat beside Vinnie. He was still unconscious. That wasn't good. Damn it, he wasn't going to lose another man. He wouldn't permit it. He looked at the senator and his family huddled together not yet believing that they were safe and free. Three for one, it would be a good trade-off. But not if that one dead man was one of his SEALs.

Murdock closed his eyes. This was the toughest part of being a SEAL commander. Watching one of his own lying there with a bullet in him, and no one being sure if he would live or die. *Well, Vincent Van Dyke, you big sonofabitch, you are going to live if I have to pump my own blood and breath into your body. You hear me, you cocksucker? You're going to live!*

4

T'aipei, Taiwan

Senator Gregory B. Highlander had spent two days writing down what he remembered from his ten-day stay in China. He had talked with his wife and put down what she told him from the daily newspapers and television reports she had seen. He had it all spelled out and now he tried to tell the State Department's Far Eastern Desk supervisor what he had seen. He sent it on a secure encrypted line from the Navy's base there in T'aipei.

"I know what the feeling is at State, but I was on the ground, Phil. I saw with my own eyes, and my wife heard them talking and she listened to their TV and radio diatribes. I tell you that China is getting ready for war. She's on a wartime footing, and goading her people into believing that whatever the government does will be right and with the best interests of one and a third billion Chinese. . . .

"Yes, damn it, I told you, there has been absolutely no mention of Taiwan. I and my wife both have the impression that this is not about Taiwan; they are gearing up for something else. I've put everything I saw and heard in a dispatch that went out by secure wire an hour ago. I wanted to alert you that it's coming. . . .

"Don't be surprised at whatever the Chinese do, and they are going to do something. I believe it will be military, they will strike somewhere, and I don't have the slightest idea where. There has been nothing in their talk about the target of all of this building war hysteria. They might go anywhere along their borders, from North Korea to Mongolia to Kazakhstan or Kyrgyzstan, even India. Now there would

37

be a prize, but it would be a tough fight. India has nuclear weapons as well."

He listened for a moment.

"Yes, I know this is a surprise. Where are your China watchers? Don't you have anyone in Bejing anymore? Now, I've told you, my hands are clean. I think this is justification for the trouble I've caused by this trip. I just hope to God that somebody back there will take this warning to heart. They have to, Phil. Somebody has to believe me. What?"

"Coming home? We'll be traveling by commercial air so it will take us a few days. We've rested up two days here in Taiwan, and now we're ready to travel. How did we get out of China? That's between my family and a few good men we can't mention. Let's just say that we got out and nobody on either side was killed. Well, one of our men did get wounded, but I don't know what his situation is. We're out and coming home."

Lieutenant Commander Blake Murdock sat in the waiting room in the Ladies of Charity Hospital in T'aipei. It had been three days since Van Dyke had been shot on the Yibin River coming out of China. He had made it to the destroyer where a team of doctors dug into his chest and took out six fragments of the lead bullet that had fragmented when it hit his rib after penetrating his web harness.

Van Dyke was still alive. The doctors had done what they could on the destroyer, then when it was safe for him to travel, had sent him back to Taiwan via the amphibious ship in a helicopter. The trip had set him back but the doctors at the best hospital in Taiwan had corrected that problem and now he was what the doctors called out of danger. Still Murdock decided to stay with him. Orders had come through sending the SEALs to an aircraft carrier in the 27th Fleet just south of Japan in the East China Sea. The SEALs would stand watch there in case there were any more Americans in China who needed to be extracted. The platoon would replace a group from SEAL Team One, who had been stationed on the ship for the past two months. Mur-

dock requested that he stay with his wounded man until
Van Dyke was ready to be flown to the Naval Hospital in
San Diego.

Ed DeWitt had hustled the SEALs into a Navy COD
plane at T'aipei. The carrier onboard delivery plane was a
Greyhound C-2A, developed from the airborne early warning aircraft, and its primary job is to ferry goods, mail, and
personnel from land bases to carriers at sea. It can land
and take off from the aircraft carriers. It has a crew of three
and can carry thirty-nine troops or twenty-eight passengers,
or a payload of fifteen thousand pounds. It has a cruising
air speed of 299 mph and a range of twelve hundred miles.
In less than two hours out of Taiwan, the Third Platoon
landed on the carrier *John C. Stennis*, CVN 74 cruising in
the East China Sea two hundred miles south off the southern most island of Japan, Kyushu.

Still in Taiwan, Murdock put down the magazine and went
to the hospital room to talk with Van Dyke. He was alert
now, and the doctors said he was on the way to recovery.
They figured it would be five more days before he could
be sent home on a Navy jet fitted with a litter section. It
would be the same type of business jet they had arrived in
little more than a week before.

Tijuana, Mexico

Detective First Class Hector Villareal had been the first
officer on the scene after a hysterical woman reported the
two homicides early in the morning. Hector was thirty-two,
married, and had four children. He was only five feet six
and sensitive that he was shorter than most of the other
detectives. But he had a strong desire to do well at his job,
and had become one of the best detectives in Tijuana. The
woman who called was the housekeeper who cleaned the
rooms and fixed meals for the man who lived there with
one friend.

Hector had handled it by the book. He called his superior, Captain Carlos, who called the chief and together they

went over the murder scene carefully, examining every detail.

Captain Carlos was tall, with a pencil-thin moustache and deep-set piercing eyes. He was forty-two, and a widower. He stared at the bodies and scowled. "Yes, I agree this is not the usual type of Mexican Mafia killing. Those hired killers always go with three or four gunmen with submachine guns and spray a hundred and fifty bullets into the victims, making sure the targets are dead."

"This looks almost surgical by contrast," Detective Villareal said. "There is no sign that the apartment here on the second floor has been broken into. No smashed glass, no forced entry at the doors. Three of the windows are unlocked, but that is normal—there are no locks on them."

"Someone could have come in one of the windows off the shed," the chief said. "I will send a man to check that out." The chief was more politician than lawman. He held his post by appointment after the former chief had been gunned down on his way to work one morning. The former chief and three bodyguards were all slain. Reports showed that at least two hundred rounds had been fired from submachine guns. The chief stood tall and heavy, swearing that he was going to lose weight, but never could.

"No struggle, no broken furniture, nothing disrupted," Captain Carlos went on, summarizing the scene. "It could be that the victims knew their attacker. Knew him and even let him in the door, then the bodyguard reacted when he heard the shots, charged into the hall and was shot down himself. Small-caliber weapon, two shots to the head of this big-time drug businessman. He was the main target. The bodyguard must have been a complication. The two shots to the head are the mark of a professional killer. Someone who has to make sure of the death so he can collect his blood money."

"A *gringo*?" the chief asked.

Captain Carlos cringed. He didn't like the term. "Yes, it could be someone from north of our border, an *Americano*. But if so, how could he do this deed without being seen? Our detectives and uniformed men have canvassed the neighborhood, the street, and the alley. No one could remember seeing anyone who did not belong. No *Americano* walked up to the door, went upstairs, and shot down the two men. Someone would have seen him."

The chief looked at his captain. He rubbed his face with one hand and stopped at once. He had to get rid of that habit when he was unsure of himself.

"So, Captain Carlos. You still have friends in the *policia* in San Diego just across the border?"

"*Si*. Several in the detective bureau. Good friends."

"So, Captain, why don't you take a copy of Detective Villareal's report and have a two-day vacation in San Diego. There you can show the report to your gringo friends. They might recognize the techniques, and might know some *Americanos* who are capable of such a professional job of murder."

"Yes, Chief. I will go tomorrow early and talk with my friends across the border. Perhaps they will have some ideas that will give us some leads."

Bejing, China
In a secret room, ten floors below ground level, the four highest men in the Chinese government sat around a table. Before each man lay a folder that was marked "Operation Self-Sufficiency." The room was brightly decorated, had carpet on the floor, and soft upholstered furniture around the sides; at one end was a living room–type area with a large-screen television and a CD player with large speakers. On the other end of the forty-foot-long room was a bar and a small kitchen filled with supplies. The room had been built four years ago to specific designs that would withstand a direct hit of a forty-megaton nuclear explosion.

The four men consulted the file and nodded. They had been working over the plan for months, now it was ready and they had agreed to talk about it one last time before final approval.

General Hui Hon Yuen was the only one in uniform. It was his meeting. General Hui had come up the hard way through the vagaries of the Chinese Army. He attached himself to one top general after another, side-stepped when they were deposed or died, and rapidly climbed in the hierarchy until he had the top spot. He was taller than the other men at nearly five feet ten. He was fifty-three years old and silver was invading the sides of his black hair. He wore glasses and was clean shaven. Sometimes details of an tank battalion.

At Hui's right hand sat the head of state, president of the People's Republic of China, Chen Shung Wai. Chen was a politician of the old school; had ridden every phase of Chinese politics for the past thirty years; and weathered each one, moving upward with each purge and each switch in the agenda. He was fifty-six, father of one child and grandfather of one, hewing exactly to the party line on one offspring per marriage.

The second man in the country was called the head of government. He sat to Hui's left. The fourth man was the defense minister.

General Hui rose and stared at the three men. "We have worked hard on this plan, this operation. It will ensure our future as a powerful nation for the next two hundred years. It will allow us to grow without becoming dependent on any other nation. We will be self-sufficient, we will be able to rule this part of the world with total impunity."

The defense minister looked up. He was a general himself now out of uniform and in the cabinet of President Chen. He peaked his fingers, frowned, and motioned to the general. "Sir, I know of the powers of our Army and Air Force. I have agreed that we will have no trouble taking the first objective and even the second. Our troops can carry enough food for a week. Ammunition and shells and equipment repair will be a factor. Resupply of our troops is my main concern. Resupply is the key in any battle, any campaign. No matter how sharp and experienced and determined a fighting force may be, it will be whipped without timely resupply of ammunition, supplies, and food."

General Hui frowned. "You are aware that we have stockpiled huge amounts of food, equipment, ammunition, and other ordinance within a few miles of our border at both the first two objectives. Once we are victorious, we begin drawing support and food from the captured enemy."

General Hui stared hard at his one-time colleague in the military. "General, let me assure you once again, we have the resources and the placement of those items to do the job."

"What about our ally in this operation?" President Chen asked.

"They are fully ready and well equipped. We have furnished them with some of their military needs over the past year, paving the way for this operation. They will be ready to attack the same time we do; and together we will turn this into a three-day war."

The president smiled. "Three days now, but what about the second phase, the vital one."

The general frowned. "Yes, the vital one. True, the crux of our whole operation. By the time we are ready to light that fire, we will have almost two hundred thousand Chinese military in the guest country in a supposed buildup for a strike at a third nation. We will have specific targets and objectives, and we expect no more than a three-day engagement before we have won that phase of our operation."

President Chen had another question. "General, I've been talking with some of my experts on world opinion. Right now China is in a rather neutral position. That's better than the negative ten percent we were last year. However, this major war, particularly the opening shot, is going to have a dramatic negative effect on world opinion. My experts say that fully fifty percent of the nation's governments will condemn us for that act alone."

General Hui turned and walked to the living room end of the area, paused a moment and then walked back. By that time, the rage that had struck him had melted away and he controlled it. There was no sign of anger or displeasure when he turned to his only superior.

"Mr. President, world opinion means nothing to me compared to the tremendous benefit this operation will bring to us. It is ludicrous to even try to compare world opinion with our own self-sufficiency for the next two hundred years. Opinions come and go. For example we have strong commercial and business ties with the United States. Do you think they will break those contracts, deliveries, and imports because of our first strike or the resulting bad world opinion? Of course not. Our thrust will be quick and sure. World opinion will work back in our favor in only a few years."

General Hui looked around the table. The other two nodded. At last the president gave a little sigh and bobbed his head.

"Good. Saturday is the day, dawn is the time. General, communicate with our friends about their movements and have everything primed at dawn. That will be about five fifteen A.M." General Hui smiled at them. "Gentlemen, it will be a good war, a fast one, and we will be set for the next two hundred years."

5

Coronado, California

Nancy Dobler sat in her Coronado apartment in the robe
she had pulled on quickly that morning. She had overslept,
and fourteen-year-old Helen had to wake her. Helen was
ready for school, but eleven-year old Charles wasn't. She
hustled him and got them both off to school on time with
lunches.

"Mom, do I have to carry a brown paper sack lunch? All
the kids I know buy their lunch at the cafeteria. It's just
not cool to take a sack to school."

"Cool or not, you do it. We aren't made of money, child.
Your dad is Navy, right, and we scrimp and save where we
can."

"Yeah, like that model power boat Dad bought. Wasn't
that something like a hundred and fifty dollars?"

"Hush up, young lady. Your father gets little time enough
for his own enjoyment."

They were gone then, and Nancy had regretted some of
the things she said. But if the money just wasn't there . . .

She ran to the bathroom and lifted a full bottle of whisky
from inside the toilet tank where she had hidden it. Just a
short one. Just one to get through the day. Hell, it was going
to be another long one, and then Will wouldn't be there at
night. She missed him.

The one drink turned into four; and when Nancy checked
the clock through fuzzy eyes, she figured it was somewhere
around eleven o'clock. She knew she should get dressed.

"Dressed for fucking who?" she asked out loud. It
seemed funny coming that way and she said it again. This

time she shrilled with laughter. She turned on the TV in the living room and had another half a glass of the straight stuff and sipped at it. Before she knew it the glass was empty.

"Hell, must have spilled it," she said and giggled. For a minute she felt like she was going to throw up, but she didn't and lay on the sofa. The whisky bottle tipped and half of it ran out onto the fabric and soaked in. When she saw it she whooped.

"Oh, damn and God damn, I done it this time." She stared at the stain, stood the bottle on the floor and whooped in delight ending in a raucous laugh. "Fuck, I'll just send the thing out to get cleaned." It seemed uproariously funny and she said it again. Then she bent over and vomited on the living room carpet.

"Shit."

The doorbell rang. Nancy squinted dark eyes and tried to focus on the front door. She couldn't. When she tried to stand up, she fell down. "Oh damn."

She heard the door open.

"No, no, don't come in." she shouted, but the words were slurred and she wasn't sure that she heard what she thought she said.

"Oh, fuck, company."

Maria Fernandez had found the door unlocked and pushed it open just a little. She looked in and called.

"Hey, Nancy, anybody home? You missed our lunch. Thought you might be gone or something."

Maria headed into the living room with Milly right behind her.

Nancy tried to sit up where she had fallen on the floor, but after getting halfway up, she fell again, this time with her face in the pool of vomit soaking into the floor.

"Oh, shit," Nancy said. "Don't come in. I ain't dressed for polite company."

That's what Nancy thought she said. It came out a series of sounds and half words and other words slurred together.

"Work time," Maria said, peeling out of the light blazer she had worn. She put it on the back of the couch and lifted

Nancy up so she could lean against the couch. "Washcloth and towel and some clothes," Maria said.

Milly hurried to the bathroom and brought back a warm, wet washcloth and a towel. She vanished into the bedroom and came back with a blouse and a pair of matching pants.

It took them twenty minutes to get Nancy on the couch, washed up, and into her clothes. Milly cleaned the rug, dumped the rest of the whisky out in the sink, and trashed the bottle. She put on some strong coffee and let it perk.

As they watched, Nancy slumped over and either passed out or fell asleep on the couch. Maria covered her with a light blanket and put a pillow under her head.

"We're a day too late," Maria said. "The men have been gone only a week. It may be a long trip for them. I had an e-mail from Miguel last night. He said they were on a carrier in the East China Sea below Japan waiting to see what happens. Evidently, they are worried about China."

"I'll take the kids to my place," Milly said. "I live closer to the school than you do. That way I can still get to work. You get Nancy at your place. Do you have room?"

"Plenty. I'll just put Linda on the couch. Now, when she wakes up, how do we convince her to split up her family?"

"No idea, but we have to try. She hasn't gone off this way since that last suicide try and her stay at the hospital. Here the men have been gone only a week. It could be a long deployment for the home folks."

Maria frowned and began cleaning up the house. It wasn't that bad but did show signs of neglect.

"Milly, you get back to work. I'll handle the negotiations. Come back over here . . . no call me when you get off work. I should have Nancy convinced to come to my place by then. You missed enough work as it is."

"Sure you'll be okay?"

"Oh yes, I had a father who tried this same routine about twice a year. I know the drill."

When Nancy woke up three hours later, the house was clean, the kitchen spotless, the dishes done, and a load of wash in the dryer.

"Oh, God did I fuck up." Nancy moaned the words.

"Headache." Maria brought her three ibuprofen and a glass of water.

"Just a small drink to get me back in the water?" Nancy asked. She shook her head when Maria did. She sat up on the couch and grabbed her head. "Oh, damn, I tell myself never again." She blinked and looked at the room. "You cleaned up after me. I owe you, big time."

Nancy started to stand, then sank back on the couch. "Hear when the guys are coming home?"

"Nothing yet," Maria said. "They've only been gone a week."

"Hell, I know that," Nancy shouted, then stopped and tears burst out and she cried. Maria sat beside her, put her arm around her, and held her tightly.

"It's all right, Nancy. We all go through these spells. Just let us help you get over this one. I want you to stay at my place tonight. The kids can stay with Milly."

"No. We all stay here together. A family. We're a God-damned family, and we stay that way." The words came out angry, flat, and cruel, intending to leave no doubt.

"Nancy, I know about drinking. My father. I know you could use some help right now. I want to help. I don't want to be pushy or get in your face, but come on, don't you think you could use some support about now?"

"Hell yes, and fuck no." Nancy's eyes were steel balls inside a steel shell. "I know exactly what I am and that sometimes it takes over and I can't stop it. Hell yes, I know that. Damn right I have to fight it. But it's my fight. If I can't win it, then I don't deserve the great family I have. Have you looked at Helen lately? What a gem, what a wonderful young lady. Going to be fifteen in a month. A beauty, a real beauty and I don't know where she got it. Glistening dark hair, eyes you can drown in, and a smile that lights up the whole damn countryside. And Charlie, he's a go-getter. Already he knows twenty times as much about computers as Will or I do. He spends some time with them, but he's working on programming, not watching porno channels. Sure I know what I have here. Damn right I'm fighting to keep it."

Later, Maria came in the living room and shook her head. She had made a search in the usual hiding spots but couldn't find a single bottle of booze. It was here, she just hadn't found it.

"I've got to get back home before the kids come home, Nancy," Maria said. "Be all right if I stop by on my way home? Tell you what. You invite me to dinner tonight, and I'll have you and the kids to my place for barbecue tomorrow night, deal?"

Nancy looked at her a long time. "Mean me cook dinner for us and you?"

"Sure. You're a good cook. I've had a taste of your work before, remember?"

"Yeah." She almost threw up both hands. "Okay," the emphasis was on the last part of the word showing her absolute frustration.

"Good. I'll call you later. See you about six thirty." Maria turned but she wasn't ready to leave yet.

Maria fussed around the living room, straightening curtains and pictures, picking up things in the wrong places.

Nancy stood and put her fists on her hips. "Maria, you are a good person and trying to help, but you have no fucking idea the kind of hell I've been going through. Yes, I worry myself sick about Will. He's almost thirty-eight years old. How do they expect him to keep up with those muscle-bound twenty-two-year-olds? In the SEALs if you don't keep up, you can die. I know that damn well. Now they are out there somewhere, and people will be shooting at them, and they may get messed up in a real war, and then won't that be just ducky."

"That's why I'm here, Nancy. We all worry about our men. There are three of us, that's more than in most SEAL outfits. I worry every day Miguel is gone. I used to lose ten pounds when he was on a mission. I'm getting better, now I only lose five pounds. When I worry I don't eat so well. All I'm saying is you're not alone in this. Milly and I and Ardith are all around to help. Ardith isn't here much, but when she is, she's a good strong person."

Nancy waved her arms in the air and paced around the

room. She scowled at Maria and then did another round of the living room. When she stopped she turned to Maria. "Look, I'm sorry I get so bitchy. I know all this shit you're talking. Know it by fucking heart. I also swear a lot when I'm frustrated and angry and feeling sorry for myself. Don't pay it any attention." Nancy flopped down on the couch. "Maybe I should just lay down and take something so I never wake up."

"Sure, and leave the kids with all the problems that would cause? Do you think that Helen could suffer through that and not be traumatized for life?"

"Shit, oh damn. Never thought of that. Won't do that to my Helen, to my baby." Nancy threw one arm over her face and began to cry.

Maria stayed with Nancy until almost three, then hurried home to be there when the kids got out of school. She made it a point always to be there. The kids deserved it.

Just at 6:30, Maria rang the bell at the Fernandez apartment. Nobody came. She rang again. This time after a wait, someone came to the door and peered out through the glass. Then the door opened a crack.

Helen looked out. Maria saw the tear stains on her cheeks.

"Mom isn't feeling well, and she said we should do dinner another day."

"Your mother isn't feeling well? Helen, are you sure? Let me talk to her."

"No, no, Mom said you shouldn't come in."

"Helen, do you want some help? Did your mother find another bottle after we left?"

Helen didn't answer. Tears came again, sliding down soft perfect cheeks. The sobs came a moment later. Maria edged the door inward and Helen let go of it. A moment later Helen fell into Maria's arms.

"Helen, don't worry. Your mom will be fine again. This is a sickness, drinking too much is a disease. You know about it. You have to remember that. There are ways to cure people and we're going to try to help your mother get well again. We're going to want you to help us."

The sobbing stopped. Maria eased away from the young girl and lifted her chin. "Look, young lady. I'm going to need you to help me. Did your mother start anything cooking?"

"No."

"Good. You go to the market at the end of the block and bring back four frozen dinners. Here's some cash to cover it. And get something for desert. Ice cream maybe. Now run along, and I'll take care of your mother."

Nancy looked up and snorted when Maria came into the living room. She lay on the couch. The bottle she held was over half empty and the bowl of ice cubes had melted down to a lone survivor. A glass lay on its side on the coffee table.

"So Florence Nightingale, the Salvation Army lass has returned to save the drunken bitch from her own vomit . . . again, and again, and fucking again."

"We're having dinner, remember? Helen went to the market shopping and then we zap them in the microwave. Now before she gets back, how about a shower?"

"No shower."

"Yes, shower. It will perk you up, dry you out a little and might even make you a little hungry. Come on. No objections. They are all overruled and countermanded and shot to hell. On your feet, girl, move it."

The last two sentences had the snap of a top sergeant ordering around his Marines. Not exactly understanding why, Nancy sat up, then stood on shaky feet and caught Maria's hand as they walked toward the bedroom and the shower.

The shower helped. Maria just being there helped. By the time the shower was over and Nancy dressed, Helen was back with the frozen dinners. Nancy had her choice from the four dinners. She took the barbecued steak strips.

Helen called Charlie out of the den. He carried a sheet of white paper with a short message on it.

"Got an e-mail from Dad," Charlie said. Nancy grabbed it out of his hand and read it. She sat down and the edges of a smile touched her face, fought with the frown and won until the smile bathed her whole face.

"He's back on an aircraft carrier somewhere south of Japan and the first mission is over and only one man got wounded and he's recovering. He says they don't know how long they will be on the carrier, but it's like a mini-vacation. They'll do a little training but not room to do much, and twenty-mile hikes are definitely out. He says he loves us and misses us and hopes they will be sent home soon."

Nancy Dobler sat down at her place at the table and ate every scrap of the frozen dinner. Then she served the group desert, ice cream sundaes with three kinds of toppings, whipped cream, nuts, and a maraschino cherry.

Nancy smiled and almost glowed. "Hey kids, your dad is fine, he's well, and he thinks they might be coming home soon. Isn't that great!"

6

Howie Anderson had stripped down for his workout in the weight room on the carrier. He had been onboard for two days and this was his first time in the gym. It was adequate. He wore only a pair of shorts and sneakers.

He had warmed up for twenty minutes on the treadmill at near the maximum, now he worked his quads. He was at the bar again and felt his muscles tighten. *Four.* His muscles were on fire. He strained and moved it slowly. *Five.* He powered hard to get the last inch, then dropped his feet again and came back up, muscles screaming with fatigue. He bleated in pain and shut his eyes as he willed his legs to come up. They did, a half inch, then another half inch to the max. *Six.* He dropped his feet and started again. The burn was tremendous, but he couldn't stop. He needed one more inch. His legs felt like they were burning in a furnace. One more inch. No, he failed. He always pushed himself to total muscle failure. That way he knew he had gone to the max.

He toweled off and slumped on the bench, too tired to move. Somebody sat across from him. As the pain eased he looked up and saw a woman in a sports bra and shorts. She was nicely put together. Good boobs. Her straw-blond hair was damp from her workout. She grinned.

"You're getting pecs," she said.

"Need a lot more work," he said, cautious. In here you could never tell the officers from the enlisted women.

She stood and waved. "Got to go. Have the duty in twenty."

He waved back and returned to his workout. He used his system when he could. The first day he concentrated on his shoulders and arms. The second day was for chest and back. Then the third day was for the delts, triceps, and biceps. He liked to work his forearms hard, using the rubber ring squeezes until his muscles bellowed in agony from the buildup of acids.

Howie liked to bench press. He did pyramids, then ten reps at 350 and two at 370, then two more at 390. He loved to do seated behind-the-neck presses. He filled in with the usual curls, working up to 80 pounds on the dumbbells to build his biceps. At the end he slumped on a bench panting as his breathing and heart rate slipped back to normal.

"You always work out that hard?" the question came from a guy who had a pot belly and lots of flab. He had to be in his late forties.

"Usually, when I have time. You just getting started?"

The guy laughed. "Not hard to tell. My annual physical is coming up and if I don't hit the marks this time, I'm riding a park bench in New Jersey."

"Start slow and work up," Howie said. "Get a good coach to train with you and then stick to a routine. You should be in here at least an hour every day."

The guy with graying in his temples sat down and shook his head. "That park bench might be sounding better all the time."

"No way," Howie said. "Hey, there ain't no free lunch. You earn your way. If it's there, you grab it and be grateful. Otherwise you go out and dig in and pay your dues and then you can look for the gravy."

"Ah, yes. The philosophy of youth." He stared at Howie for a minute. "What are you twenty-two, twenty-three?"

"Twenty-five."

"Enlisted?"

"Yeah. You're an officer?"

"Of a kind. I'm a chaplain, a priest."

"Oh, boy. I better get going."

"Why," the priest asked.

"Before I say something that could bring me up on charges, like insulting an officer, disrespect, all that."

"Why would you do that?"

"Because I think all religions are shams and ripoffs. The end result of fear and superstition that's been formalized and organized and turned into a huge, monstrous business for profit. I think it sucks. I firmly believe that all ministers, reverends, and priests are fakes and phonies and can't possibly believe what they say they believe. No religion is logical or reasonable."

The priest moved to the free weights and took ten pounders and began to do curls, working on his biceps.

"You don't think I haven't heard this before, young man? I've heard and seen it all. Still I have my faith. What do you have faith in?"

"Natural laws. Gravity, the planets, the tides, weather, the rebirth of spring that has nothing to do with Easter or Christ. I believe in things that can be proved. I don't have to make a leap of faith that two and two are four. I can prove it. A leap of faith is a dive into stupidity."

"What's your job in the Navy?"

"I'm a SEAL. I'm trained to kill people."

The priest frowned. "Have you ever killed anyone?"

"Is the pope Polish? Of course, I've killed people. A lot. I don't keep track. It's my job. I kill the enemies of my nation. I believe in the United States, that's something else I believe in."

"My country right or wrong?"

"Something like that, Padre." He stood, using the towel on the sweat as he headed for the shower. "Got to go, Padre. I'll let you take your turn sweating, then you can dream of heaven. But remember, that's all it is, a dream, a figment of man's collective imagination."

"I'd like to talk to you again, SEAL."

Howie stared at the man of the cloth. He shook his head. "Afraid not, Padre. Then I really could get in trouble, especially if you had your officer's uniform on. What are you, a full commander?"

"Actually, I'm a captain, taking an every-three-years cruise as required by our head chaplain. It keeps us grounded. Looks like I have a lot of grounding to do here."

Howie waved and walked into the showers.

Western China
In a H-6D Badger Strategic Bomber

Colonel Lin Pota checked his compass bearing and adjusted the automatic pilot slightly to stay on course as the Badger flew high over western China on a most important mission. Colonel Lin was the best pilot in the People's Liberation Army Air Force. He had more flight hours, had more kills in combat and had mastered flying every aircraft that China had. He was fiercely loyal to China and had not known what this mission was until an hour before takeoff. None of the rest of the crew knew the target. Only two knew what weapon they carried below in the bomb bay. Usually this Badger carried YJ-61 ASM (C-601), the land-based missile version of the antiship missile with a range of 120 km at mach 0.8. It had a large search-and-track radar on its nose to provide target coordinates for the missiles. Today it had a far more deadly cargo. The Badger had been reconfigured to its original capability for this mission.

"Weapons check," Colonel Lin said in his communications mike. "Make sure our friend is riding comfortably and that there is no vibration loosening of the tie downs."

"Yes sir, right away."

Moments later an affirmative signal came back. Colonel Lin nodded and monitored his own controls. On course, at the right speed. From their base in Congqing, China, it was a 1,350-mile flight to target. At the top speed of the Badger at 650 mph, it would take them a little over two hours to make the trip. The Badger had a ceiling of 49,215 feet, but that kind of altitude was not needed. They were flying at 19,000 feet for good fuel economy. They would get to the target and return without refueling. The Badger's range with a warload was 4,475 miles. Lots of room to spare.

Colonel Lin expected no trouble. They were over the friendly skies of China for all but the last few miles. They would make the bombing run and return. Routine.

Colonel Lin was taller than most Chinese his age. At thirty-eight he was young for his rank, but he had earned it. He had never disobeyed an order in his life, but he had to think about his current mission. He would be doing something that only two or three men had ever done before.

Would he be cheered or condemned? He knew the world would call him a monster, a villain, a mass killer. He had come to peace with that. He was doing a job assigned to him by his superiors. It had to be done.

Lin stretched in the pilot's seat. He looked over at his co-pilot. The Major did not know what the mission was. He was not aware of any of the massive movements that the bombing run would set off.

Lin thought about it again. Yes, he would do it. Yes he would carry out his orders. He would drop the bomb on target as ordered and blast away at maximum power to escape as much of the blast and detonation problems as possible. The crew would be affected to a certain degree. They all would be examined carefully when they returned to base. Both he and the co-pilot wore special lead chest and lap protectors.

"One hour and ten minutes to target," his bombardier reported.

"Yes, understood," Lin said into the intercom. He adjusted the helmet, checked his instruments, and peered into the black sky ahead. Nothing there. There shouldn't be. There wouldn't be anything there. No enemy aircraft to contend with.

For no reason, Colonel Lin thought of his wife and one child at home. He and his wife obeyed the edict of one child per family in an attempt by the government to limit population growth. The plan had worked fairly well in the cities; but in rural China, there were still many four- and five-child families. He and his wife had been lucky, they had a son. He knew of two officers who had determined the sex of their child before birth and aborted girl babies. Male children were highly prized in China.

At once he thought of the wives and children who would

never have another day in their lives. He shivered slightly.
There could be a hundred thousand casualties. The target
was a city of 135,000 people. True, they were not Chinese,
they were the enemy. Lin had been surprised when told of
the target. How could that small country harm the greatness
of China? Certainly, it was no threat and there had been no
buildups or threats or war between the countries.

The timing had been carefully plotted out so the bomb
would fall on Biratnagar at precisely 0530. That would be
at the official time of sunrise in the city.

"Starting gradual climb to 25,000 feet," the co-pilot said.
Lin looked round. Yes, it was time. Two minutes past time.
He had been daydreaming.

"Right, climbing to 25,000 as programmed."

"Thirty minutes to target," the navigator said. "Colonel,
I have more than two dozen blips on the radar of aircraft
coming toward us from the south and east."

"Yes, transports, those are ours. No worry. They will
follow us over the target by thirty minutes. Everything is
going as planned. Good work, crew. Stand by for bomb
drop in twenty-eight minutes."

Bomb drop. Two words that would change the course of
the world for the next few years. The world would never
be the same. He was the trigger that would start it. He had
no idea where it might end or what else he might do in the
plan. After they returned to their base, he was to be flown
directly to Beijing for a ceremony and a medal. That much
he knew. After that, he had no idea how he would serve
China. If there were an air war, he hoped that he would be
in the thick of it.

Twenty minutes later the navigator came on the IC, the
intercom, again. "Seven minutes to release time. Seven
minutes. Starting prerelease check off and count down."

Colonel Lin went over the procedure again. The bomb
would be released at the proper point for forward motion
toward the target. It would drop fifty feet and a parachute
would deploy, slowing its descent. It would still fall at 120
feet per second, giving it two minutes to descend to 10,000

feet over the target where the altitude sensors would trigger the bomb.

That gave the Tupolev Badger two minutes to get out of the way of the atomic explosion and tremendous heat and air blast. Two minutes at 650 mph would be twenty-two miles. Twenty-two miles away from a blast that could only be described as pure hell on earth. A roiling, boiling mass of flames, blast, destruction, radiation, and instant immolation of buildings, vegetation, and human beings.

Colonel Lin tried not to think about it. He had an airplane to fly, a mission to complete. *He would complete his mission!*

"One minute to release," the navigator said. "On proper target course. About eleven miles from release point."

"Release checklist completed. We have a green light for release by the Colonel."

"Acknowledged," Colonel Lin said. He felt sweat seeping down inside his helmet. His right knee hurt. It always began to ache when he went into combat. He had no idea why. For a moment his visor fogged over, then cleared. All he could think about was his family at home in Beijing.

"Counting down from ten," the bombardier said. "Five, four, three . . ."

Colonel Lin felt tears streaming down his cheeks. He could think only of his family in Bejing, and the 130,000 souls below who might never see another sunrise.

". . . two, one, release."

Colonel Lin pushed the button on his console that had been especially rigged to release the twenty-megaton bomb in the underfuselage weapons bay. He felt a sudden upward surge of the aircraft as the extremely heavy bomb left the craft.

"Your airplane, Major," Colonel Lin said.

"Right, full throttle, gradual turn to the left, about two minutes to blast," the co-pilot said. "We'll be riding the tail of the air surge. At twenty-two miles it should be moderate but on our tail."

"Agreed, flip down face mask shields now," Colonel Lin

said. The crew moved down shields that let them see almost nothing.

Colonel Lin tried to count down the two minutes. The navigator did it for him.

"A minute and fifty seconds from release," he said.

Almost at once, a searing brilliant flash overrode the sparse sunlight of early morning, stabbing through the face shields, followed a few seconds later by a crashing mountain of air that spasmed out of the huge ball of fire and away from the mushroom cloud back there twenty-two miles.

Colonel Lin checked the controls through his shield. What he could see looked normal.

Then the flash of light dimmed, and he jerked up the shield and saw that all instruments were in the usual ranges.

"Good work, crew, our job is done, we're heading home," Colonel Lin said.

"I have more than forty blips on my radar of incoming planes," the navigator said. "They are still more than a hundred miles off but closing fast."

"Crew, we have just started a war. We have bombed Biratnagar, in southeastern Nepal. The cargo planes coming are filled with paratroopers, who will drop in on every large city in Nepal. Our leaders think this Nepal war will last no more than two days."

"Why are we going to war with Nepal?" the navigator asked. "What does that little mountainous country possibly have that China could want?"

"That they didn't tell me," Colonel Lin said. "Now our job is to get back home. Navigator, check our course and speed."

7

East China Sea
John C. Stennis, CVN 74
The carrier's wardroom was crowded with officers watching the large-screen TV that picked up CNN off a satellite. It was not yet noon on board and no one knew what time zone Nepal was in.

"Whatever time it is over there, they are in one shit pot full of trouble," an ensign said. "China will walk all over them in three days and there won't be anything left of that little country but a few high mountains."

Murdock and DeWitt had just finished coffee when the reports came through on CNN.

"I can't believe that China would waste a bomb on Nepal," DeWitt said. "Hell, she could walk across the border there anytime she wanted to without turning a hundred thousand people into crispy critters."

"CNN said this town they hit with the bomb used to have a population of a hundred and thirty-five thousand," Murdock said. "Most of them must be gone by now. Of course maybe China wanted to prove she had a tactical nuclear weapon. India would return tit for tat with a nuke, so Nepal would be safer."

Somebody turned up the volume on the TV.

So far that's all the information we have. We have no correspondents in Nepal. As most of you know it's a small country, only fifty-four thousand square miles, that's a little smaller than the state of Ken-

*tucky. Nepal has just over twenty-four million people
and Kentucky has only four million.*

*The military experts say that Nepal has a standing
army of only 47,000 men. China has almost three
million men under arms. Nepal is a kingdom with the
highest mountains in the world. That is where Mount
Everest climbs up to twenty-nine thousand twenty-
eight feet. The Himalayan Mountain Range bisects
the length of Nepal and has twelve more peaks that
are over 25,000 feet. By contrast, Mount McKinley
in Alaska, the tallest spot in North America, is only
20,320 feet.*

*Worldwide condemnation of China and Pakistan is
pouring into the news media. We have statements
from half the nations that are awake at this hour
naming China and Pakistan as monsters, bullies,
warmongers, outlaw nations, the devil's spawn, and
those are just a few of the nicer names that world
governments are calling China and Pakistan that
we're allowed to tell you about.*

*Which brings us to the question of why. Why would
a huge country with a billion and a quarter population, team up with a smaller nation and assault and
devastate a tiny country with only twenty-four million
residents? We've asked some outstanding experts on
China, including a U.S. Senator who was rescued
from South China less than a week ago. He has some
interesting comments. First let's go to the man who
has made his reputation predicting what China will
do, retired Army General—*

Murdock felt somebody poke him in the shoulder and
looked around to see Don Stroh in a garish blue, red, pur-
ple, and brilliant yellow Hawaiian print shirt showing tropical flowers, and matching pants. The vision slid into a chair
next to Murdock.

"It's really hit the fan, just like your favorite senator
predicted."

"Thought you had flown back stateside," DeWitt said.

"Convinced my boss that your senator wasn't as crazy as State said he was and wrangled another two weeks over here. Looks like it paid off."

"Hey, Stroh, we're not in this tussle," Murdock said. "None of our people were nuked."

"Haven't you heard of the Joint Southeast Asian Defense Alliance?" Stroh asked.

"Not a whisper," DeWitt said.

"Neither have I," Stroh said, "but there's something like that out there that damn well could *commit* us to take up the defense if one of the signatories is attacked. Could be something like that here. If we signed a treaty like that with Nepal, we're committed to defend that little ridge of mountains."

"Not another Vietnam," DeWitt said.

"Whatever you call it, I'd say there is a high and big fucking chance that you boys will be busy here quickly, often, and up to your gonads in Chinese and Pakistanis."

"But it still has to go through channels, right?" Murdock said.

Stroh gave a big sigh. "Oh, yeah. That little admiral who runs the SEALs is still in a bodacious snit. Wants another stripe on his sleeve. But if things get hot, we can go right with the CNO. The man himself told me so."

"Stroh, you putting on weight?" Murdock asked. "You look a little pudgy around the waist again and those jowls are barfing out like crazy. You been working out at all?"

"None of your damn business."

One of the mess stewards came up and stared at Stroh. The CIA man noticed and turned. "So?"

"Are you Mr. Stroh?"

"He is," Murdock said.

"Sir, the ship's captain requests your presence with Commander Murdock and Lieutenant (jg) DeWitt in his cabin at once. There is a guide outside to take you there."

"Duty calls," Murdock said.

Stroh didn't move. He hadn't touched the cup of coffee he brought with him when he sat down. "Be damned. This captain is getting touchy. He ordered me, that's as in ordered me, to put on some fancy officer khaki uniform. I told him I never made it past corporal in the big war, so I couldn't wear officer khaki; and he snorted, and said didn't matter. Guess I'll get a real ass chewing."

"Not likely, Stroh. You've still got connections, and the captain is always looking for one more wide gold stripe on his arm. Let's go see what he wants."

Ten minutes later they were shown into the outer room in the captain's cabin. It looked like a small living room with a sofa, two large upholstered chairs, a floor lamp and a small table. On one wall was a six-foot-wide map opened to large-scale views of northern India, Nepal, Bhutan, and Bangladesh.

"This is gonna be business," Stroh said.

"Relived?" DeWitt asked.

"Damn right. I've got a boss, too, you know."

They turned as a large man came into the compartment. He was nearly six feet six, with gray streaks in heavy black hair at his temples, and a face that looked like it had been assembled by committee. His nose was too large for his round face. His cheeks held a perpetual pinkness. Steel blue eyes surveyed the three men in front of him as he moved with an easy grace many tall men don't have, and pushed behind his desk. He eased into the tall leather chair.

"Seated," he said. An order.

"I'm Captain Robertson and this is my ship. I usually take orders through channels, and I'm not comfortable having the CNO of the whole damn Navy calling me on the radio." He paused. "Which doesn't mean a thing to you men. SEALs and a CIA officer. My lucky day. I don't mind you taking board and room on my ship, but the CNO said you may have some work to do. He wasn't specific, but said it had something to do with the nuke bombing this morning and the attack by China and Pakistan." The captain paused and looked at the men with a steady gaze.

"From what the CNO said, you men have been through this procedure before. I haven't. He told me that if we get a go-ahead on a mission for you, it takes total priority over anything else I might be doing or want to do, except the

safety of my ship and my men. That's an order I've never
had before. In short, anything you need or want that I can
provide, I give to you. In effect, you own me and my ship.
I'm not pleased with that procedure. Whatever you need
for your mission is yours. That could be a destroyer, a
chopper, a COD, a squadron of F-18s, anything short of a
nuclear weapon, which not even the CNO can initiate.

"The CNO told me to tell you that he's putting orders
through channels that you are temporarily assigned to my
ship, and you will stand by under a red alert for further
orders. My task force is to steam at once toward the South
China Sea and generally closer to China off the Chinese
island of Hainan. We have a twelve-hundred-mile move.
Any idea why, Mr. Stroh?"

"Sir, that would put us closer to the conflict in Nepal."

"True, but still twelve or thirteen hundred miles from the
fighting. I understand that more than twenty thousand Chinese and Pakistani troops have entered Nepal, elite units by
air drop, others from helicopters. Mounted troops are fighting their way into the small country by the few roads that
link China with Nepal."

"My guess is that in three days the war will be over,"
Stroh said. "Nothing to stop them, and China and Pakistan
will put as many ground troops in as they need. China alone
has two point nine million men under arms; and as we
remember from Korea, they don't mind taking a high body
count if it gets results."

"At thirty knots it'll be over long before we get there,"
the Captain said. He rubbed his face with his right hand
and winced, then massaged his right thumb. "Damned ar-
thritis." He looked up at Murdock. "Any requests, Commander?"

"Conditioning. We do need a place to run six to ten miles
a day."

"Try the flight deck when there's no air operations. It's
almost eleven hundred feet long. Five laps to the mile. Talk
to a white shirt down there before you run. He'll help you
work out a safe route. In fact he'll find an area for you to

run and work out even if we are having air operations. Anything else?"

"No, sir. If we get a mission, then I'll want to talk to you, your CAG, and probably somebody in ordnance."

"Will do, Commander. Now we head for the South China Sea and see what the big Chinese dragon does." He watched them a moment, then nodded. "Yes, I think this will work out. That will be all, gentlemen."

The three men stood, came to attention, then turned and left the cabin. When the door closed, Stroh let out a long breath.

"Oh, yes, I'm glad that's over. Not a word about my shirt." He grinned. "I guess the CIA has some clout after all. At least my clothes will make it easy for anyone trying to find me."

Murdock looked down the companionway and shook his head. "What can we do for Nepal? Nothing. I guess we have an embassy there, but we're twenty-five hundred to three thousand miles from that spot. Well, I guess we could have landing permission in India, if we pulled the right strings. India is to the south of Nepal if I remember right. New Delhi can't be more than two hundred and fifty miles from that nuked-out Nepal city."

"This is the biggest mistake China has ever made," Stroh said. "She has stepped in a deep vat of shit and world opinion is gonna drown them in it. Reports coming in are all negative, especially from nations in the area.

"India pulled out her embassy staff from Bejing and broke off diplomatic relations. Gonna be all kinds of ugly shit flying around this one for years."

"In the meantime China gobbles up Nepal," DeWitt said. "What's next for her? She want to take on India?"

"India has the bomb, too," Murdock said. "We're forgetting one element here. The official announcement of a state of war came from Bejing and it said the China–Pakistan forces are invading Nepal. What the hell is Pakistan doing teaming up with China?"

"I don't see what Pakistan is trying for," Stroh said as they worked their way through the big ship to the quarters assigned to the SEALs. They had one large compartment where they stashed their gear, weapons, and ammo and where they could hold meetings.

Murdock called the fourteen men around him. "The j.g. and I just came back from a chat with the Captain of this tub. He says he has orders to proceed to the South China Sea. We are assigned to stand by for possible work off this ship. That means we stay in top shape. Welcome to Fitness International. Senior Chief Dobler will take the platoon to the flight deck, check with a white shirt for a safe spot, and we will do an hour of calisthenics followed by a two-mile run. In case you wonder, this ship is almost eleven hundred feet long. Five laps to a mile. Uniform of the day, cammies. We have ten minutes before the Senior Chief leads us up to the flight deck. Any questions?"

"Yes sir," Jaybird said. "What's Pakistan have to do with this attack on Nepal?"

"Pakistan is supposedly an equal partner in the aggression; however, it was a Chinese nuke that opened the show. That's all we know so far."

"A week-long war?" Mahanani asked.

"The betting is for three days," DeWitt said. "Take that long to get the Chinese and Pakistani troops in place. There won't be much of a fight with only forty-five thousand troops with Nepal name tags."

"Let's get moving," Murdock said and the men scattered to their lockers to get in uniform.

Katmandu, Nepal

Three thousand feet over the capital city of Nepal, Sergeant Chiang Pio adjusted his gear and eyed the jump light. The door of the big transport was open and he stood by it holding his first out man by the shoulder. They were the first troops into Nepal since the big bomb hit the town well to the north. Now their mission was to go in and capture the civilian airport at the nation's capital, which then would be used for military supply by air. He had been surprised when the word came down that they would be attacking Nepal. He had always considered the tiny country a fly speck on the edge of China. A nonplayer in international politics. So why were they and Pakistan going in there with troops after dropping a nuclear bomb on one of the northern cities? It didn't make much sense to Chiang, but he was a soldier and did as he was ordered.

Then Chiang didn't have time to think about the mission or his family back in China. The light went from red to green and a horn sounded.

"Go, go, go," Chiang shouted, as he gave the man a gentle push and he jumped out the door into the new light of dawn over Katmandu. Twenty-seven men left the door, then Chiang held up his hand stopping the next man as he made sure his own cord was attached to the sliding rail, then he jumped out into the suddenly chilly air. His chute jerked him severely as the wide straps jolted into his legs and shoulders, then the sudden pain eased as he saw the chute opening above him and his rate of descent slowed to a normal jump and he eyed the ground coming up at him. He had come out at the right time. Some of his men would land just before the border of the airport. He would be about fifty yards down the runway. He pulled the cord on the right side of his chute to dump some air and aim to the side of the concrete runway into the softer grass and bushes. He held his feet up a moment as the ground rushed up at him, then he dropped them and ran as he hit the ground. He overtook his chute and fell on it to collapse it, then jerked his harness off, grabbed his submachine gun from the straps on his side and shouted to two men he saw. They were from his platoon.

"Get the men over here," he shouted. "We have the two sheds at the end of the runway to clear. Move it."

The men scurried around finding more men, sending them to the sergeant. Soon he had twenty of his thirty men and they formed up in a line of skirmishers and rushed the two sheds fifty yards away. There were only two workmen there getting ready to check the night lighting system. Neither of them had weapons.

The one man in his platoon who spoke Napali had not joined the group yet. Chiang shouted in Chinese at the men to continue their work. Then he used his hands to show the men to go on working. At last they nodded and picked up their tools.

Chiang assembled his men and marched them toward his second objective, a guard building at the south entrance to the airport used mainly for maintenance trucks. He picked up the ten missing members of his platoon. One man had a broken leg. They left him on the edge of the runway with another man as a backup and double-timed toward the guard shack.

At three hundred yards they took their first enemy fire. It was short. They fired their long-range weapons and kept running forward.

At two hundred yards, Chiang directed his troops into a small ditch at the edge of the runway. He put his Ultimax machine gun on a gentle rise and had it open fire on the guard shack. Now he saw it was made of concrete blocks or bricks and had sand bags at two windows, but none at the third.

The 5.56mm rounds from the Ultimax slammed into the window and around a facing door. That slowed firing from inside. Chiang took the opportunity to send one squad around to the rear of the small building while the rest of the platoon fired at the shack with their type 86 rifles. They were good weapons, Chiang knew, firing 7.62mm rounds and could be fully automatic or single shot. All of his men used the 30-round magazine, and each carried six loaded magazines, giving each man 210 rounds without refilling magazines.

His first squad came up behind the building and fired into it, reducing the answering fire. A moment later a pole came out of the building with a white T-shirt attached.

Chiang smiled and ordered a cease-fire. The men ran forward and charged into the small building without firing another shot.

Chiang made sure the position was secure and that he had the four Nepal soldiers captured and bound. Then he called in to his company commander on his radio.

"Sir, Red Platoon of Red Company has secured our two objectives. Where do you need us?"

"Red Platoon, hold your position for five minutes, then charge forward toward the hangar at the south end of the field. Resistance there is heavy."

"Right, hold five minutes." He turned off the radio and put it back in the holder on his combat webbing. "Reload all magazines. We go into a tough fight in five minutes."

The riflemen filled partly empty magazines. The two machine gunners put on new one hundred-round drums. Chiang checked his watch. He looked out the window at the building three hundred yards ahead. It was a hundred feet wide, he couldn't tell how long. He saw no soldiers, but he could hear firing.

"Two squads to the left and two to the right. Let's go on a sweep. Five yards apart. Move out."

Chiang kept in the center of the four squads. Nobody faltered, all stayed on line. As soon as they took fire they all went prone and returned fire. He saw two machine guns firing from bunkers at the front and back corners of the building. When did they have time to build sand-bag bunkers at a civilian airport? Chiang wondered.

With hand signals he moved the farthest right squad into a ditch that ran toward the hangar. He told them to move up and get the machine gun in a cross-fire. He was too far away for his submachine gun, but he fired a dozen rounds anyway.

More hand signals told the two right squads to concentrate on the rear machine gun. Three hundred rounds poured into the position and a moment later it went quiet. The two right-hand squads jolted upright and ran for the target. The other two squads bore down on the front machine gun and cut down its firing.

A short time later, the far right squad laid down a barrage of rifle fire from the corner of the building and wiped out the machine gun at the other corner.

"Charge!" Chiang bellowed and the other two squads blasted forward, secured the corner and the machine gun placement. Then they could look into the hangar. Two large civilian jetliners sat there, but Chiang saw no soldiers. He frowned. He sent a scout into the building and waited. The man ran from one side of the huge building to the other, then came out at the far corner and gave the all-clear sign.

Chiang waved his men forward. They were halfway across the one-hundred-foot-wide building with the thirty-foot-high front folding doors, when three machine guns opened up on his platoon from inside the hangar. He and his men had no cover on the concrete floor and taxiway.

"Take cover," Chiang shouted. He saw three of his men mowed down right in front of him before they could react to the weapons. Some of his men fired into the building, but they couldn't see the hidden machine guns.

Five- and seven-round bursts chattered from the three positions. Chiang ran back the way they had come. The wall there was his only cover. He saw three more of his men charging for the wall. Two fell almost in front of him. He hurdled the bodies and dove forward, rolling once to get to the wall. He rolled again with bullets chipping concrete all around him. He rolled again and slithered around the wall into safety. Chiang stared at the carnage on the cold concrete floor in front of him. He had come in with twenty-eight men. Two more were back on the tarmac with the broken leg.

He counted men dead and dying in front of him. Tears seeped from his eyes. He saw two men lunge up and try to run. One dragged his right leg. A burst of five rounds hit him in the chest and leg and he went down and didn't move. The other man almost made it to the wall and safety with two guns trained on him and two seven-round bursts plunged into his body jolting him into instant communication with his honorable ancestors.

Chiang wiped tears off his cheeks. He had four men with him, only four. The rest of them, twenty-four, lay on the hangar floor dead. He grabbed his radio.

"Captain Company Red, this is Red Platoon." He waited but there was no response. He tried again: "Captain of Company Red, this is Red Platoon. We have trouble."

A moment later the speaker came to life. "Yes, Red Platoon. Have you secured the south hangar?"

"No. We tried to capture the south hangar. My platoon was wiped out by hidden machine guns inside the hangar. We cleared it but missed them. I have five men left. The rest are dead. Instructions."

"Take the hangar, Red Platoon. Surprising heavy resistance at other areas of the airport. Do the best you can. Grenades maybe."

Chiang looked around the edge of the wall. He was low to the ground and practically invisible from anyone inside. He watched for five minutes. No sound came from the big building. Then he saw movement. One of the civilian airliners had a rear passenger access door open. He saw movement inside the shadows in the plane. That had to be one of the machine guns. He motioned for a rifle, set it on full auto and in one swift movement moved the rifle around the wall and drilled twenty rounds into the open airliner door. He jerked the rifle back as two machine guns fired at the wall, splintering it in a dozen places where he had been moments before.

Now he had more places to watch from. The hail of bullets stopped and he watched again. There were two more guns in there, but where? He figured he had silenced one of them. Again he watched the other areas of the big hangar. They had to have good fields of fire at almost all of the front of the building. That limited the spots they could hide. He narrowed down the possibilities, then watched them on a grid basis.

He sectioned the areas and concentrated on one of the squares at a time. The second time he came back to a square near the back of the building he saw that a doorway was opened more the second time around than the first. Yes, it would have the right field of fire. He reached for another rifle, made sure it had a full thirty-round magazine.

This time he barely nosed the muzzle around the wall, sighted in on the door and hosed it down with all thirty rounds in the weapon. The first burst of five rounds may have done the job. He drilled the rest of the magazine rounds into the door jolting it fully open. For a fraction of a second he saw the ugly muzzle of a machine gun there, then a round slammed it backward.

The third machine gun was later this time in firing, missing the tip of the rifle and the man firing it.

"Two down," he told his men. One of the soldiers had vanished for a while, now he came back.

"Sergeant, there's a back door down there near the rear. It's locked, but I can shoot off the lock and roll in some grenades. Might catch somebody by surprise."

"Do it when you hear me firing. I'll try to distract them."

Sergeant Chiang gave his man time to get to the other end of the hangar, then he pushed the weapon around the door and fired at the back of the hangar. He jerked the weapon back a second before the MG there fired again. Over the murderous sound of the weapon he heard two explosions. They were muffled and he hoped they were grenades. The machine gun stuttered, then stopped. A moment later he heard the flat barking sound of the infantryman's rife. Then all was quiet.

Four minutes later he heard another grenade go off and more rifle fire. He looked around the wall and saw his soldier running across the hangar toward him.

"Hangar clear, Sergeant," the soldier said. A door opened on the other airliner and a submachine gun stuttered. The soldier on the floor stopped in mid stride looking up in surprise at the Nepal soldier in the airplane who had killed him.

Sergeant Chiang bellowed in surprise and anger and stepped around the wall and fired fifteen rounds from his submachine gun at the man who stood in the airliner door. The Nepalese soldier shuddered as half the rounds punctured his chest. He dropped his weapon, turned halfway around and fell off the airliner to the concrete twelve feet below.

Chiang slumped to the floor and took out his radio. "Red Platoon to Red Captain. We have captured the south hangar. It's secure. I'm down to four men. No more missions possible."

8

Coronado, California

Girl talk. That's all it was supposed to be. They had agreed to meet at Maria Fernandez apartment at 6:00 P.M. that Tuesday. Milly came five minutes late.

"Some trouble at the office," she said. Milly worked at Deltron Electronics where she was a lead supervisor in computer services for some of the biggest companies in America. Their hardware and software problems were her problems and she hustled herself and her crews to find the answers before whole computer systems went down. "We fixed the huge glitch, but it took longer than we figured." She looked around. "No Nancy yet?"

"Not so far. Don't worry. I talked to her on the phone about noon and her spirits seemed to be up."

They had coffee in the kitchen around the table. Neither one mentioned the China–Pakistan war that was all over the news media. Maria talked about kids and school and anything else.

"God, it's almost six twenty," Milly said. She crinkled her forehead. "You suppose Nancy isn't coming?"

Maria let out a long sigh. "Lord, I hope she comes. That woman worries me. She just can't let go of her fear. That's what's behind it all, raw, blundering, agonizing fear for the safety of her man."

Both women were silent for a moment. Both thinking the same thing. They had the fear, too, but over the years had learned to cope with it, push it aside, and concentrate on something else.

A horn honked outside, three shorts and a long.

"That's V in Morse code," Maria said. They looked out the front window. Nancy sat on the front fender of her car. She saw them looking and waved.

"Bet you tarts didn't think I'd show up," she crowed a minute later when she ran up the stairs and into the front room.

"Wondered," Maria said.

"Hey, I knew you'd be here," Milly said. "Who can pass up the cherry pie that this girl promised us along with our fancy cups of tea?"

Inwardly, Maria groaned. Nancy's eyes were bright and her head held high. She had that cocaine swagger that Maria had seen often when she had worked in drug rehab.

"Well, we're all here. Coffee or tea, Nancy?"

"Take tea and see," Nancy said doing a little dance over to the third chair at the table and sat down. "Where's this delicious type pie I was promised?"

"Coming up."

Milly turned to Nancy but before she could say a word she saw Nancy starting to unravel. She slumped, elbows on the table, one hand holding her chin. It slipped off and she barely recovered before her chin hit the table. The cup of tea skittered to one side, tipped over and flooded half the white table cloth.

Without a word, Maria tossed a kitchen towel to Milly to start mopping up.

"Oh fuck!" Nancy said. She leaned back in the chair and began to laugh. "I sure as hell fucked up again. Damn it. Shit why can't I do it like you two bitches do? Why in hell can't I be normal for just a few God-damned more days?"

Tears spilled out of her eyes and she cried silently. She made no move to wipe the tears away.

"Yeah, Will is still gone, over there beside fucking China where the bastards are killing people. They'll try to kill my Will, I know it damn well as I'm sitting here."

Her mascara had melted and ran down each cheek in a long black line.

"Nancy, the men are all on the carrier," Milly said. "Nobody is fighting with the U.S. We're out of it. We'll probably stay out of it. The TV says China and Pakistan will overwhelm the little country of Nepal in two or three days. Washington can't even get an order through channels in three days. Our guys are going to be fine."

"Oh, hell yes. Just like when they went into China and one of our guys got wounded. Ardith Manchester called me about an hour ago. She confirmed that our guys went in and brought out that senator who escaped from China a week ago. You bitches know that? No, I didn't think so. One SEAL was wounded and fancy britches Ardith didn't know which one it was. One of us could have a shot-up man right now and we don't even fucking know it."

"Ardith called today?" Maria asked.

"Just the fuck said so," Nancy snarled. Then she lifted her eyes and brows and shook her head. "Oh, fuck, I'm doing it again. I'm sorry, Maria. I didn't mean to. . . . What the hell?"

She stared at Maria for a moment, then began to sag and tilt out of the chair. Milly caught her before she came un-seated. Slowly Milly eased her back into the chair and stood beside her, pinning her there without seeming to.

Nancy looked at Milly a moment, then across the table at Maria who was not good at hiding her emotions. Concern flooded her face, generating a small frown.

"Dear, is there—" Maria cut it off as Nancy's eyes closed and she sagged down until her face rested on the table. Milly eased her up until she was sitting almost straight again and her eyes came open.

"Oh, God, I need a nap."

"First how about some of that cherry pie you were look-ing forward to," Maria said. "Whipped cream or ice cream on top. Which one?"

Nancy shrugged, sagged toward the table again. Milly held her up. Maria set before her a small plate with a wedge of cherry pie with a lattice top crust and smothered with whipped cream.

For a moment Nancy smiled. She reached for a spoon, but before she could take a bite she threw up, the vomit that had been held in too long exploded across the table splattering the whole table and Maria as well. Nancy heaved again, then once more. Maria threw Milly a small towel and she wiped off Nancy's mouth and face, then eased her back in the chair.

"Now you'll feel better," Milly said. "How about lying down for a while?"

Nancy nodded and tried to stand. She couldn't.

It took both of them to walk her to the living room sofa and ease her down on the pillows. Maria brought a blanket and put it over Nancy and tucked it in.

Nancy blinked open her eyes and let tears wash out of them, then she whispered. "I'm so sorry, so sorry."

"Hey, that's what friends are for," Milly said. "Now, you get some sleep and you'll feel better. Somebody with the kids?"

But Nancy had turned off her lights and went to sleep in a half second.

Maria went to the phone and called the Dobler home. Helen, the fourteen-year-old answered.

"Hello, this is the Dobler residence."

"Helen, are you all right?"

There was a pause. "Mrs. Fernandez? Oh good. Is mom there? I told her she shouldn't drive. I said I could drive her over there. Did she make it?"

"She's here, but she ill. Right now she's resting on the couch."

"I'm sorry, Mrs. Fernandez. I tried to stop her. She's been sick all afternoon. Every since I came home from school she's been up and down. Pills and booze and some coke from what I saw. I'm so sorry."

"Helen, I'm concerned about you and Charlie. Do you want to come over here?"

"No," a pause. "No, we're fine here. Chas is playing with his computer. I have some homework." She paused again. "And some cleaning up in the house to do. You heard anything about Dad?"

"No. We get an e-mail now and then but they don't tell us much. The Platoon is still on the carrier *Stennis* from what we understand."

"The war over there . . ."

"I don't see how we can get involved, so don't worry. Now, are you sure you don't want me to come over there? Milly is here, you remember her. Could she come and stay until you guys go to bed?"

"Mrs. Fernandez, I'm fourteen. I don't need a baby-sitter." She stopped. "Oh, great, that sounded brattish and juvenile. I'm sorry. You're being kind. No, thank you but Chas and I will be okay. Will Mom stay there tonight?"

"I'll try to talk her into staying here. We have that spare room." Neither of them talked for a minute. "Helen, if you want anything, need any help, you just call. Have you locked all the doors and windows? Do that right now. You'll be fine. You're so grown-up I can't believe it sometimes."

"Thanks, that was cool. We'll call if we need anything. Right now I'm making some Easy Mac for dinner. Thanks so much."

They said good-bye and Maria hung up. She checked on Nancy. She lay with her head thrown back, her mouth half open and a soft snoring sound came out. Maria tucked the quilt in again and went into the kitchen. It smelled of Lysol.

Milly looked up from where she washed the last of the vomit off the refrigerator and the side of the stove. The kitchen tablecloth lay on the floor with a mound of soiled kitchen towels on it. The room was cleaner than it had been two hours ago.

"Thanks, you didn't need to."

"Yeah. Now we need to make some plans. Nancy stays here tonight, and I go over to her place?"

"I just talked to Helen. She and Charles are in good shape. Helen doesn't want a baby-sitter. She'll manage. Nancy could sleep for six or eight hours. Let's go check the e-mail."

The computer growled at them, came on, and settled down. Maria had learned to use the computer in self-defense. Miguel was so good at it she had to get on board. She called up her AOL program, hit the sign-on key, and waited. They heard the small musical electronic tones and sounds from the hardware; then the screen came on with the e-mail window, and a voice said: "Welcome, you've got mail."

There were two entries. The first one with the subject of "Uncle Henry's ill."

She looked at the second one. "Dull in China Sea."

She clicked on the second message and it came on the screen.

Hey, Maria and Linda. Love you guys. All quiet here on the big tub. Just floating along. We're on standby but don't see how we can get involved. Nobody is talking much. At least they haven't started to censor our e-mail. That will be when we know something is afoot.

Linda, you still want to take riding lessons? We'll talk about it when I get back. Might be able to give you a few to see if you really do like horses. Hey, just heard that we have another five mile run up on the flight deck. Gets monotonous doing all those laps. Five times down the flight deck for a mile. So, take care, and I'll write again as soon as I can. Love. Miguel.

As soon as she saw the message was from Miguel, Milly turned away and looked at a book on the shelf. When Maria had read both messages, she looked up.

"Milly, you want to check your e-mail. Easy, we just go back to the start and list you as a guest and . . ."

"No, we know that nothing is happening there right now. What was the date and time it was sent?"

Maria giggled. "Tomorrow about two in the afternoon."

"Yeah, they are ahead of us time-wise," Milly said. They went back to check on Nancy. She hadn't moved and still snored softly.

Milly looked at her friend and worry clouded her face. "Maria, you worked in drug rehab. What can we do for Nancy?"

Maria waved her to the kitchen where she fixed them the

tea they hadn't had time to drink. She also saw that the pie had not been hit by the vomit and set out wedges of the pie with vanilla ice cream on top.

"In rehab we made suggestions. We showed a path they could follow. It's like with an alcoholic. First the person themself has to want to quit, to dry out, or nothing that we could do would make any difference. They know what they're doing. Some of them really didn't know how to wean themselves off the drugs. When they admitted that and asked for help, then we could do some good and get some of them straight again. It didn't happen often. We had no clout, no court orders, and no big money charges so we could insist that people dried out. We were county and advisory only. A real mess and mostly a waste of money."

"So what can we do for Nancy?"

"We hold her hand, we clean up after her. We let her know that we love her and want only the best for her. We make ourselves available twenty-four hours a day for her. We baby-sit her when we can."

"What shouldn't I do?"

"Both of us shouldn't scold her or put her down. We can't indicate that we're ashamed of her. We don't let her think that we disapprove of anything she does. We tolerate it, we turn a blind eye to her tantrums and her drunks and her drug bashes. We maintain and do everything for her that we can."

Something thudded in the living room. Both women hurried in. Nancy had fallen off the couch. She sat there, leaning against the couch, hair a mess, no make up, her blouse spotted with the vomit and the contrasting pants dark stained at the crotch.

"What the hell? Where am I? Oh God, do I feel like shit. Where?" She looked around, then nodded. "Yeah, good old Maria. The drunk's favorite savior. What the fuck did I do this time, good old Maria?"

"You were sick, Nancy. You had a little nap."

"Now, I'm going home. Just get me to the car and I can drive. Nobody else to drive. Damned lousy husband is off playing war games again. Fuck him!"

She struggled to stand but couldn't. Maria and Milly hurried to her and helped her to her feet.

"Home, I want the fuck to go home."

Maria nodded. "Sure, Nancy, we'll help you get home. Might be better if we drive you. I know, I know, it's only a little over a mile and a half. But it'll be better. No trouble. That's what friends are for, Nancy. We'll help you however you want us to."

"Home," Nancy said. There was a pleading in it they hadn't heard before. Not a sober tone, but closer to it.

They helped Nancy down the steps and to her car in the parking lot. Maria pointed to the back seat of the three-year-old Chevy and they eased her in where she promptly slid down with her face on the seat cushion.

Maria pointed to Milly to follow them in her car. Nancy's keys were still in the ignition.

9

Dhangadhi, Nepal

Lieutenant Farooq Yuahya Khan stood behind a wooden frame building in this Nepalese town of twenty thousand and looked down the street two hundred yards at the police station. It was the last hold out of any organized opposition. He and his platoon of sixty Pakistan paratroopers had dropped in on the town at dawn the preceding day. They knew exactly where the town's small military garrison was.

They caught most of the men in their bunks, killed half of them, and took forty prisoners. In rapid order they had captured the telephone center, the city administration building, and the town's only hospital/medical center.

He and his men had flown in Chinese transport planes from Pakistan near the border and refueled in China. Then they flew in here two days ago, jumped, and lost only one man with a broken leg on the drop. They quickly quashed most of the opposition.

Now he gave hand signals and thirty Chinese-made rifles opened up on the police station from two sides. There was little return fire. He signaled again and his two best grenade men sprinted from cover to cover, then with increased support fire, they plunged across the wide street and slammed against the side of the police station. A red star shell broke high over the station. It was the signal to throw in grenades. Each man threw six grenades through three different windows and probably into six rooms.

Firing from inside the police station trailed off and then stopped. At once Lieutenant Khan ordered two squads to rush the station with a frontal charge using full-assault fire.

A few return rounds came from the station but not many. The soldiers kicked in the front door and threw in grenades; when the shrapnel stopped whizzing past them, soldiers jolted through the door and into the front and rear of the building.

In five minutes it was all over. The Pakistan lieutenant had no long-range radio, but a sergeant came out the front door and gave the move up signal, and an all-clear sign.

Lieutenant Khan worked down the street to the police station and hurried inside. There were more than a dozen dead Nepal police. He had them hauled out and put on the sidewalk for relatives to claim. He found two working radios. One a shortwave set was tuned to an Indian station in New Delhi, which was only two hundred miles to the southwest.

The broadcast was in English, and Khan could understand most of it. He sat quickly in a chair and he knew his face must be pale as he heard the news for the first time.

There is no estimate of the dead and mortally wounded, and critically sick in the city of Biratnagar, Nepal. The only authority CCN could contact was a corporal in the city's police who was twenty miles into the countryside at the time of the bombing. The nuclear bomb exploded over Biratnagar the day before yesterday at dawn. At the same time the Pakistani and Chinese troops launched their invasion of the tiny Himalayan nation of Nepal. The corporal said, on a personal ham radio he carried with him, that the city is in total ruin. Most of it simply disintegrated in the fire ball. The rest of the buildings were flattened by the tremendous explosive force of the bomb. It could have been a twenty-megaton bomb, or one of forty megatons.

The corporal said the total devastation reaches out more than fifteen miles each way from the city center. He said the winds swirled and changed with the explosion and may have carried deadly radiation into

*several more population centers in this essentially flat
land in the southwestern section of the nation.*

Lieutenant Khan turned off the radio. He would have it
taken to his headquarters in the old army fort at the edge
of town. The buildings had cooking facilities, quantities of
food, and places for his men not on patrol to sleep. More
men were promised, but none had parachuted in. He had
no way to contact his superiors or those of the Chinese. He
looked at his map again and frowned.

The town he now occupied was only fifty-five miles in
a direct line from the nuclear-bombed city. He wondered
which direction the winds blew. Was there a chance they
would blow to the west and slightly north? If so, his town
of Dhangadhi would be right in their path.

He had not questioned his orders to parachute into Nepal
from the Chinese planes. He did not question the Pakistani
Army leaders when the officers were told of the attack on
Nepal. There was no reason given, no justification. He wondered about the alliance with China to go into Nepal. It was
a small nation. Why did China need help to take it over?
He knew that China had almost three million men under
arms. They could take the small nation quickly by themselves. Why would they want an ally?

There were all sorts of rumors in the Pakistan Army,
especially with the officers who knew more of the plans.
The enlisted men were told nothing of the attack or the
alliance. Some thought that China had its eyes on Afghanistan. The feeling was that while China had many resources,
it was short on good oil reserves. Others said that Afghanistan was not a prize package for conquest. It had no oil
reserves at all if that was China's ploy. The nearest good
oil nation was Iran, Pakistan's neighbor to the south who
had ninety million barrels of oil reserve, nearly four times
the reserves that China itself had. Yes, Iran could be the
eventual target. But why the thrust into Nepal? Was it only
a ploy to show the world that China had the nuclear bomb
and wasn't afraid to use it? Sounded reasonable.

Lieutenant Khan sat wearily in a chair in the police station while his men organized the place and assigned men there. He thought of his family back in Pakistan. His wife would be worried into a state. His two small sons would wonder where their papa was. He had been a reserve in the Army and working daily at his job as a lawyer. Then the orders came and his unit was mobilized and sent to two weeks of special training and three jumps, then they were loaded into the Chinese transport planes and here they were. His unit had been lucky not to be shot up. He had lost two dead and three wounded. Lucky indeed.

Lieutenant Khan tried the small radio he had, but he knew it would not reach beyond the mountains. His only hope was that it would link up with some Pakistani units nearby.

He drove in a commandeered Nepalese Jeep to the telephone center. There he found most of the phone lines in operation. He called Dipalal, a larger town than his to the north about thirty miles well into the foothills of the mighty Himalayan Mountains. The lines were working.

Soon he was talking with his friend Captain Multan who led the attack on the larger town.

"Yes, almost no opposition. I lost only two dead, three wounded."

"Why are we here, Captain? You heard about the nuclear bomb attack on that Nepal town?"

"Yes. We didn't need such an outrageous blow. The Nepalese Army is small and spread out over the entire country. My friend, I don't know why we are here. Either one of us could have captured Nepal in a week. Now it could be three or four days."

Lieutenant Kahn talked to his classmate from the Military Academy for ten minutes, then they said good-bye and hung up. Kahn was trying to figure out how he could find out about the prevailing winds coming from Biratnagar. Would they bring deadly radiation with them? Or would it blow the other way into the mountains?

He had just hung up the phone when one of the Nepalese men who had been instructing the soldiers how to run the switchboards pulled a pistol from a desk drawer and shouted at Lieutenant Kahn. He bellowed a dozen words, then began firing from six feet away. He fired four shots. The first hit the lieutenant in the chest, driving him backward. The second hit his neck, bringing a spurting gush of blood. The third and fourth missed but Kahn slumped to the floor, his life's fluid spurting to the ceiling from a ruptured carotid artery in his neck. Each spurt came lower, from six feet down to five in the air, then four and at last a bubbling at his throat as the soldiers around him tried to stop the flow.

The Nepalese man with the pistol threatened the rest of the soldiers, then fled out the door. Two guards at the front of the building had heard the shots. They saw the man rush out, his eyes wild, waving the pistol.

They shot him four times and he died in a screaming storm of angry words and the last two shots in the pistol all aimed at the invaders.

New York City
United Nations Headquarters

For the third day, the UN Security Council tried to hold a special session. Fewer then half of the thirteen delegates were at the emergency meeting. No business could be conducted, but some delegates there charged China, a permanent member, and Pakistan with butchery in their unwarranted invasion of Nepal.

Chinese delegate Chou Kao-Feng reached for his microphone and stared hard at the other members. "I am shocked that delegates to this august body would lower themselves to use such undiplomatic language. The People's Republic of China has for many years claimed most of the area called Nepal. We are simply taking back what was stolen from China many, many years ago. We are a peaceful people, but when our rights and our borders are threatened, we will respond with devastating effect.

"Yes, we have used a nuclear bomb. Even as the Americans did twice in recent history. And we say as the Americans did at that time, that despite the loss of life at the target, the bomb itself has reduced the fighting and has saved thousands of lives on both sides.

"We have welcomed our ally Pakistan in this struggle. They too have territory in the area that is under dispute with India and Nepal and have cooperated with us to settle these disputes once and for all in a way that the world can understand."

The session continued with each nation presenting its view on the use of the nuclear weapon against defenseless women and children.

The delegate from China sat back and turned down the volume on his translation ear phones until he could hear only a few whispers. Then he kept his eyes open and concentrated on his small garden in his home near Nanjing where he had a fountain, several plants, a small stream, and a bridge. He concentrated so hard that his face fused into a soft smile and he was totally oblivious to everything that was happening around him. His aid would gently bring him back to the present if there was any need for him to make a comment.

South China Sea
John C. Stennis, CVN 74

Captain Irving B. Robertson II glanced at the two envelopes that had come to his desk the day before. One was marked with a heavy blue line an inch wide. The other had a heavy red line just as wide. Both were inscribed: "Sealed Orders. To be opened only by order of the Chief Naval Officer by radio contact."

Sealed orders. The last time he had seen those had been on training exercises, but outside of that he had seen sealed orders twice in the Gulf War. They usually meant action, but action of what type here, he had no idea. The only thing he could think of was a job for the SEALs onboard his ship. Yes, it could be for the SEALs.

He put the envelopes out of his mind and concentrated on the flight operations training drill they had in progress. They were launching F-18s, refueling them in air, and then recovering them. Drills were essential to keep every man

involved sharp and sure. Every phase of the operation was
important. In most of them, the smallest mistake or mis-
judgment, could lead to one or more instant deaths of his
aviators and those on the deck. He wouldn't allow any such
mistakes to be made. Drill, drill, drill.

It was the third day of the Nepal invasion. CCN had
flown a reporter in with Chinese permission and now the
world had up-to-date details on the rapid takeover of the
small nation. CCN was the only media news team allowed
in the area. Reports told that by the end of the third day,
90 percent of the population centers of Nepal were under
China–Pakistan control. Only a few mountainous areas had
not been touched, and would not be until there was some
administrative need.

The CCN feed was carried throughout the ship on TV
sets and the men of the carrier were current on the war.

Lieutenant Commander Blake Murdock and Lieutenant
(j.g.) Ed DeWitt sat in the wardroom watching some bul-
letins. The video showed a Chinese armored personnel carrier smashing into a small army garrison in some unnamed
town. The six soldiers there had been routed quickly, three
killed and three captured.

"And so it goes," the reporter said. "China and Pakistan
continue to mop up any last resistance to their invasion.
One Chinese general, who I talked to this morning, said he
would declare the fighting over sometime early in the evening."

"That's one we missed," Murdock said. He finished his
coffee and stretched. "We had all of our workouts today,
or is there one more?"

"We're wrapped for the day," DeWitt said. "Eight miles
this morning, then PT this afternoon followed by four more
miles. The troops are sharp and ready to go anytime."

"Good, I'm ready for a short nap before chow."

"Go ahead. I have a half-finished chess game with Jefferson. He won the last one and I'm mad as hell. Well,
almost. You have a good nap. I have to go play war on the
chessboard."

The call came at 2030. Murdock and DeWitt were both

in quarters, a six-man officer's bunking area. DeWitt had answered the phone.

"The Captain wants to see us right now," DeWitt said. "He told me that Don Stroh would be there, too."

"That means we've got some work to do," Murdock said. "At least I hope that's what's afoot."

Ten minutes later, the two SEALs and Don Stroh, dressed in officer's khaki without any insignia, sat in front of the captain's large desk. Two other officers Murdock didn't know were present. The captain didn't bother with introductions. Two files lay on top of it. He pointed to one.

"Orders just came through from the Chief of Naval Operations in Washington, D.C. I have been ordered to open sealed orders that have been on my desk for two days. I talked to the CNO a half hour ago. He said he has early advice that China will invade Bangladesh at dawn tomorrow, less than eight hours from now. The president has given orders that the Bangladesh Embassy will be evacuated at the first possible moment. He said he had no idea of our distances, but that he had been assured that there had been arrangements made for U.S. military planes to land in Calcutta, India, which is only a hundred and fifty miles from the embassy in Dhaka, Bangladesh."

"But, Captain, if we're still way up here by Hainan Island, we're one hell of a long way from Calcutta," Don Stroh said.

The captain smiled. "Yes, we were up there. So how would we get permission for an overflight of Vietnam, Cambodia, Thailand, and Myanmar? That's what we'd need if we were up there by Hainan so we could fly directly west to get to India."

"So what do we do?" Murdock asked.

The captain grinned. "Didn't tell you that ever since we hit the area around Hainan, the brass figured we would be of more value farther down south, so we've been sailing south along the coast of Vietnam. We're now below Ho Chi Minh and about to turn west into the Gulf of Thailand."

DeWitt looked at the map of the area. "So we're down

here near the Gulf. We're mostly south of those four countries, but not much closer to Bangladesh."

"Close enough," the captain said. "The important part is
we won't get shot down trying to fly over Vietnam. They
are still touchy about their airspace. We will have to overfly
a small piece of Myanmar that used to be called Burma.
It's only fifty miles wide right there and we'll be over it
before they know we're coming."

"We're talking about a COD?" Murdock said.

The man next to the captain spoke up. "Men, I'm Cress-
well, the CAG. Yes, we have a COD onboard that can make
the trip. It'll be empty except for your team and should be
able to do the run with no problem. Our navigator figured
if we get within fifty miles of the shore on the Gulf, we
should have an eight-hundred-mile run up to the tip of
Bangladesh, then two hundred and eighty miles more to
Calcutta. This bird will do a thousand seven hundred on
ferry and we won't be much heavier than that. So from the
hardware standpoint it's a go."

"How long will it take us to get there, Captain?" Murdock asked the CAG.

"The COD cruises at three hundred, so that means we
should have a nonstop of three and a half to four hours,
depending on any headwinds we hit."

"That's a good-size town there in Bangladesh," Don
Stroh said. "We'll need some directions how to find our
embassy."

"Yes, sir," the third man with the captain said. "We have
faxes from the State Department showing pictures of the
embassy building and the surrounding area. Also faxes of
a list of those personnel still incountry. They did a mini-
evacuation a week ago when their intelligence people said
something was going to happen with China."

"How many left there to evacuate?" Ed DeWitt asked.

The same man looked at his notes. "Another fax shows
that there are eight and a half million people in Dhaka. The
last report from the embassy said there were nineteen people to evacuate."

Murdock looked at the CAG. "Does the Navy have any

helicopters in Calcutta? We'll need two Sea Knights, the CH-forty-six, preferably both with door guns."

"That could be a problem," the CAG said. "we have no base there of any kind. Calcutta is well inland. We do have some elements in the general area. We had a four-ship group on a goodwill tour, a pair of guided-missile destroyers and two guided-missile cruisers. They were somewhere near the Bay of Bengal, which is just below Bangladesh." He turned to the third man, the one with the figures.

"Johnson, check out their position and what choppers they have on board. Ask specifically about the CH-forty-sixes."

The man nodded and left the Captain's cabin.

"Would one CH-forty-six do it?" the CAG asked.

"Specs call for it to carry twenty-five troops," Murdock said. "Assume that's combat ready. We'll have fifteen combat ready, but nineteen civilians in shirt sleeves, might squeeze in under the weight, and might not. We'd prefer to have two birds."

"The range is no problem, a top of four hundred and twenty miles."

"We'll have to take the ordnance we need from here," DeWitt said. "Who should I see, and when are we leaving?"

"The COD can leave anytime you're ready," the CAG said. "I'll get it warmed up and the preflight done."

"Should be a nighttime operation," Murdock said. "Not a chance we can make connections and get to Calcutta and into our choppers and to that town while it's still dark. No way. So, we make it tomorrow night. We're too far away to do it any other way."

"Give us more time to get some choppers flown in for you," the captain said. "They probably won't have door guns. You'll have to use your own."

"We'll check our team and let you know what ordinance we need. This will be a hot mission, live ammo all the way. Oh, do you have any of the laser-aimed twenty-millimeter air-burst rounds?"

The CAG shook his head. "Read about them. You have that new rifle?"

"Four of them," DeWitt said. "Great for shooting guys hiding behind buildings and around corners."

"We'll call you when we get the choppers tied down," the CAG said. "We'll try to fly three into Calcutta, so we can have two up and ready to go. We've got an amphib landing ship somewhere in that area. I'll get back to you."

"That will be all, gentlemen," the captain said. The SEALs and Stroh stood, turned and left the cabin.

Outside, Murdock looked at Stroh. "Did you know about this Bangladesh caper?"

"Yeah, but it was sealed and on the captain's desk. Knew it might happen, not that it would. It even came through channels. Your little admiral will be pleased about that."

DeWitt looked to be in a hurry. "Come on, let's get back to the men and find out what ammo we need. This could get hairy if we have to go up against those Chicoms."

Murdock frowned. "Chicoms? I haven't heard that term since the Korean War."

"Like you were around then. That was fifty years ago."

"I read about it. Chinese Communists, shortened into Chicom. I like it."

Stroh frowned. "Let me know when you get ready to shove off. Probably around daylight sometime, I'd think. Give you more set-up time in Calcutta."

"Remember, Stroh, this is the mission you guaranteed us that you would come along on. I've got a submachine gun with your name on it."

Stroh started to respond, but DeWitt and Murdock turned and walked down the companionway toward the SEALs compartment. They both grinned, the look of astonishment and then fear on Stroh's face had been reward enough. Now, they had to get a fast list of the ammo and other arms they might need.

10

Tijuana, Mexico

Juan Lopez looked at the Tijuana Police Department detective and gave a small inward twitch but nothing that anyone could see. He had heard about Mad Dog Sanchez many times. This was the first time he had met him. It was said that Mad Dog had more confessions than any detective in all of Tijuana. The little border town had grown to more than a million people. Juan Lopez wanted to go right on living there and not in a cemetery.

"Yes, yes, I told you. I go to the El Gallo Colorado sometimes. They have good food and lots of girls. That's no crime."

Juan didn't see the blow coming. It was from behind into his right kidney and he doubled over from the pain. He wanted to vomit but he knew they would make him clean it up. He sagged, then slowly stood.

"Juan, you can make this easy. We know that you have met Chuci Hernandez many times. He also liked The Red Rooster. Now he is dead, you are alive. Curious, no?"

"Why would I want to have anything to do with hurting *Señor* Hernandez?"

"You? Not you. You only follow orders. We know you work closely with El Padre. The big man has not seen fit to help a poor policeman like me with my living expenses. We know that you set up Cuchi with some *gringo* hit man. We want to know who and where we can find him."

Juan felt his face freezing, his skin going pale. This was Mad Dog talking. He too, was acting on orders. How did

Mad Dog know that he had contacted the *gringo*? It didn't matter how.

"So, you dead chicken, you ready to crow?"

Juan looked up. "I don't know what you're—"

This time he saw it coming and tried to duck. Mad Dog had been in the ring for five years. He followed the duck, hit Juan with a straight left jab and then a thundering right-hand fist that caught Juan under the chin and lifted him an inch off the floor. He had been ready for it but that didn't help. The room lights went fuzzy, then flickered and went out.

Juan fell to the floor of the Tijuana police interrogation room. A bucket of water sloshed over him and he cried out and then sat up.

"Stand up, you sniveling weasel," Mad Dog shouted. "I know you have a *gringo* name and a phone number. I want it, and I want it today. I don't have a lot of patience. We might do your fingers next."

Mad Dog took a pair of pliers out of his pocket and worked the handles back and forth. They were well oiled and when Juan looked at them he felt a little bit of himself die. He didn't want to die in this stinking cubicle. Where was El Padre? Who would help him?

A man in a business suit came to the door and talked with Mad Dog for a moment. The detective snorted and scowled. Then he started to turn away. Instead of leaving he did a spinning kick and hit Juan in the belly with his boot. Juan went down again and this time he did vomit. He couldn't help it. He was on his hands and knees when gentle hands lifted him. It was the suit.

"Come, Juan. I just talked to the chief. No reason to hold you. Mad Dog is not pleased, but these cops seldom are unless they are paid enough. Let's get out of here before the chief changes his mind."

On the sidewalk outside the police station, the two men walked away slowly. Juan set the pace. He wheezed and had trouble talking.

The suit with the carefully knotted necktie handed Juan an envelope.

"Juan, a nice vacation for you in Acapulco. El Padre says you have earned it. Two weeks and by then Mad Dog will be angry at someone else. Oh, there's a bonus in there for you besides your tickets and hotel reservation. Sorry I didn't get to see you yesterday."

The tall man in the immaculate suit moved away, stepped into a Jaguar sedan and drove down the street.

Juan looked in the envelope, then began to run away from the police headquarters. He found a taxi and went straight to the airport. He had money and could buy whatever he needed. Juan Lopez was glad to be on his way out of Tijuana and out of the reach of Mad Dog.

Washington, D.C.
The White House

General Winston P. Alexander had known the president for twenty years. Now, as chairman of the Joint Chiefs of Staff, he was a prime adviser to the President on international military matters. They sat in the easy chairs in the Oval Office and sipped at soft drinks.

"True, we have no defense pacts with Nepal or Bangladesh or Mongolia for that matter," the general said. "We do have an agreement with India; however, that could be interpreted as being binding on our assistance if she is attacked."

"If attacked," the president repeated. "So far she hasn't been. I don't think China is that stupid to take on another member of the nuclear bomb community."

"So for right now, the chiefs of staff suggest that we simply sit on the sidelines and see what else happens."

"We know that China is going into Bangladesh. Our intelligence operation is better there. Any developments on getting our embassy people out of there?"

The general nodded, glad to have some good news for a change. "Yes, the rescue mission is under way. The SEAL team was way over in the South China Sea, so it has some travel time. As I understand it, as soon as it gets dark over there, they will be moving."

"I'd guess that India knows that China is going to move

into Bangladesh," the president said. "To do that, the Chinese must violate either India's ground space or airspace. As I have been told, there is a narrow band of Indian territory between Bangladesh and China."

"True. Depends how India reacts. We suggest that she will protest, then maybe put up some air power along that strip to slow down any air resupply to Chinese troops on the ground."

"Will India ask us for any air help?"

The general shook his head. "I'd guess not. She has good air power, some good fighters. If China sends up their latest MiGs to defend the transports, it could be a good fight."

"So, damn it, Win, we just sit on our hands and wait."

"Not quite. We have a carrier group moving closer to the problem area. We have four ships in the Bay of Bengal, destroyers and cruisers, but our air power is eight hundred miles away."

"I've seen the map," the president said. "Not much we can do about that, at least for now. So we pick our noses, and see if we get our people out of that war zone."

Calcutta, India

SEAL Team Seven, Third Platoon arrived in Calcutta tired, grouchy, and hungry. They had been up half the night getting their gear ready, finding the ordinance they wanted from the Navy stores, and getting on the COD Greyhound for the four-hour flight. It turned out to be five.

They arrived at noon at a military airport near Calcutta and were promptly fed and put down on cots for a six-hour snooze. Lieutenant Lonnie Brasco had paved the way for them, smoothed the glitches, and given Murdock a tour of the three CH-46s that had been flown in the night before from an amphibious landing ship that was off shore. Murdock took the one with door-mounted guns and a second one that had what looked like a level-headed older pilot.

"We'll crank up at nineteen hundred," Murdock told the pilots. "It's an hour's flight in there. We don't know if it will be a hot LZ or not. From what I hear, the Chinese haven't invaded yet. They must have got their timetable mixed up. But by tonight they could be all over the place."

Murdock tried to get some sleep but couldn't. He heard an announcement at 1430 that the Chinese had invaded Bangladesh, and thereby violated Indian air space. The announcement said that proper responses would be made.

In their makeshift barracks, the SEALs popped up from their cots at different times. The older hands slept longer than the newer men did. They had chow again at 1700 and then worked over their gear.

"Hear this is gonna be a walk in the park," Howie Anderson said.

"Yeah, a park with a Chicom and his submachine gun behind every bush," Mahanani snapped back.

"Chicom?" Ostercamp asked.

"Yeah, Mr. DeWitt used the term," Mahanani said. "It's from the Korean War, fifty years ago. Stands for Chinese Communists. Chicom. Fits."

Murdock and DeWitt inspected their men ten minutes before load time; then they marched out to the choppers and boarded, half on each one.

"It's the royal survival principal," Jaybird said. "When the king and queen go on a trip, they travel separately, so the whole monarchy won't go down in one fell swoop."

"That makes you the court jester, Jaybird," Jefferson said, and they all laughed.

All fifteen men had their ears on. Vinnie Van Dyke was still on the *Stennis,* getting the chunks of a lead slug out of his chest and lung. Murdock checked with DeWitt on the other chopper once they were in the air. Despite the loud noise of the rotor and motors, they could communicate. It was fully dark when they took off.

"DeWitt. We'll have a hot LZ. We'll go in as planned. You take the front door, and my squad and I will hit the back door. The birds will lift off and circle out of trouble until we call them in with a star shell and radio. They have our frequency."

"That's a roger, Murdock. We're set here. Nothing for the door gunner to do yet. We've been over Bangladesh for twenty minutes and I don't see any sign of fighting or Chinese below."

"Same here. Coming up on a larger town. Hope the pilots go around it. Could be some action there."

Just as he said it Murdock felt some rifle or machine gun rounds hit the chopper. The pilot zigged to the left then lower and to the right and went a mile to the side of the gush of lights below to what had looked like swamps, lakes, and some farming.

"Anybody get hit?" Murdock asked in the mike. Nobody answered, "Net check," Murdock said and listened as his six men checked in. "Good. DeWitt, any casualties?"

"One arm wound, not serious. Mahanani is on it. We're okay unless we have to do some rope climbing."

They saw a sea of light ahead of them, Dhaka.

"Nine million people down there," Fernandez said. "Bigger than Los Angeles. And looks about as spread out. Hope the pilots know how to find the place."

"They do," Murdock said. "We double-checked."

Rifle fire came again, but nothing hit the chopper. The pair of birds swung down a main street that looked like it ran for miles. On the other end was a large park that would be dark now, and on the other side of the park was the U.S. embassy. It was a former prince's palace.

A speaker in the top of the chopper came on. "Target located, we hit the LZ in about two minutes. The light is now red. When it goes green, the crew chief will open both doors and the rear ramp. Suggest you use all three. We're at the LZ parking lot just behind the embassy. Good luck."

The crew chief watched the lights. Murdock had the first door open on one side, and the rear ramp was halfway down when the wheels touched the ground.

"Go, go, go," Murdock bellowed and the SEALs streamed out all three doors.

Murdock charged toward the back of the embassy. He saw a man with a flashlight waving them forward. Jaybird got to him first. "Friendly," Jaybird shouted and ran for the back door of the embassy, which stood open. Ten seconds later all six of Alpha Squad were inside the embassy.

Lights were on. The man who had been outside came in and looked at the SEALs.

"God, am I glad to see you guys. We have a dozen Chinese out front trying to talk their way inside. They came through the security fence with explosive charges."

Murdock waved the man forward. Small-arms fire exploded from the front of the embassy.

DeWitt had seen the Chinese. They were standing around with their weapons down or on the ground. Two men, probably officers, were at the front door where they kept banging on it.

The SEALs went prone and when DeWitt whispered a "now" on the Motorola, all eight of them opened fire on the Chinese. Eight went down in the first barrage. The two at the door turned around, then dove for the ground. When they did they were quickly dispatched. Nobody had wanted to fire into the door and probably through it inside.

"Khai, make sure on the ten," DeWitt said into his mike. Khai jolted up from his prone position with an H&K G11 with caseless rounds and surged forward, kicking bodies as he came to them. One groaned and took a round to the head. One ten feet away sat up and tried to bring his rifle to bear. DeWitt scrubbed him out of the picture with a four-round burst from his Alliant Bull Pup, driving the 5.56mm slugs into the man before he could fire.

Khai fired one more shot, then waved the SEALs forward. DeWitt knocked on the door and bellowed that they were U.S. SEALs. The door opened a crack outward, then swung wide, the SEALs ran inside, and the door closed.

DeWitt found Murdock who talked to the ambassador and his number one man.

"Only trouble we've had so far," Ambassador Theodore Borone said. He was a compact man of five feet eight, with gray hair, glasses, and a twist to his nose over a thin lipped mouth. "I think the wind blew most of the paratroopers off their target. We've been expecting them for two days now.

"Trouble, people," Jaybird said. He had remained behind

at the front window. "Looks like twenty fly boys with boom sticks. They want to come in and play."

The SEALs scattered, four to the front windows. Four rushed upstairs to find front-facing windows and four more went to the rear to check on any troops there.

Murdock pulled the ambassador down behind a wall. "Where are the rest of your people?"

"No basement. Fifteen are in my office. It has no windows and seemed to be the safest place."

"Good, get there and don't open the locked doors unless you know it's a SEAL. Move."

The ambassador was not used to taking orders. He frowned, then nodded. "Yes, yes, right away." He started to stand up but Murdock pulled him down to the floor.

"Crawl, Ambassador. If you stand up they can see you outside and you could be dead in a second."

Murdock reached up and turned off the lights in the room. the rest of the rooms went dark and a moment later rifle rounds drilled through the embassy windows and slammed into woodwork, furniture and glassware.

"All SEALs," Murdock said into his mike. "Take them out. Open fire. Make a safe LZ so we can get the hell out of here."

Ed DeWitt used the Bull Pup and put two explosive 20mm rounds just beyond the front gate into a tree. He saw the explosive power of the round and fired two more. One Chinese soldier didn't like that rain of hot lead. He leaped up and charged from the outside fence toward a foot-thick tree inside. He never made it. Four slugs cut him down and dropped the rifle as he sprawled in the dirt.

Murdock had a report of no troops in back.

"DeWitt, keep up the fire. I'm taking half Alpha Squad through the back and around the side and get the bad guys in a cross-fire. Moving, now."

Murdock took four SEALs and slid around the end of the embassy building and could see the Chinese riflemen shooting at the front of the embassy.

He placed his men and then they all opened fire. Murdock used the Bull Pup and lasered two rounds on a tree near the front for air bursts. Both rounds exploded in the air and rained hot shrapnel down on the Chinese. Two tried to stand and retreat. Both fell to rounds from Murdock's men.

Two minutes later the firing from the front stopped. "Make sure," Murdock told Kenneth Ching. He charged forward, fired one shot, then gave an all clear front.

Murdock put his four men in a perimeter defense around the front of the building and fifty yards away. He told DeWitt to put a screen to the rear. Then Murdock and two other SEALs took a tour of the grounds looking for any hiding Chinese. They found one, who jumped up and tried to run. He had lost his rifle. He didn't make it.

"Grounds look secure," Murdock said on the radio.

"Agree, rear is secure," DeWitt said.

"Fire one red star shell," Murdock said.

"Got it," Lam said and sent the red flare skyward. A moment later it burst and drifted away to the right.

A garbled message came over Murdock's Motorola. He listened to it on the second transmission.

"The birds are coming back to us. Get the embassy people to the front by the door. Divide them into two groups. Go, we don't have much time."

Before DeWitt had the civilians all at the door, Murdock heard the choppers coming. He went outside. "Mother Hen, chicks are ready when you are. Come on down."

"That's a roger. We have you in sight."

He saw them, then, dodging over trees as they hugged the ground. The first chopper landed, and right behind it the second one. Before the dust had cleared, DeWitt had ten civilians running for the open chopper doors. They were onboard when he motioned for the next group.

Murdock had moved the SEALs back into a tight security circle around the choppers.

DeWitt waved for the second group, and Jaybird released them from the front door. They were thirty yards from the second chopper when the whole bird burst into flames as a rocket hit it and exploded the fuel tanks. The civilians scat-

tered backward, and DeWitt corralled them and sent them
to the first chopper.

"Onboard, get on, all of you. Now. Crew Chief, as soon
as all the civilians are on board, get the hell out of here.
We'll find our own way back. Take off. Now."

The door clanged shut and the chopper leaped off the
ground just as four more rocket rounds slammed into the
complex. Two of the small rockets hit the front of the embassy and one beside it. The fourth hit where the chopper
had been before it lifted skyward.

Murdock had seen and heard what happened. He ap-
proved. It was the only way. "Out the back of the place
and into those trees," Murdock shouted into his mike.
"We'll take stock, check for wounds and then try and figure
out what the fuck we're going to do."

11

The fifteen SEALs charged directly through the deserted embassy, out a gate in the rear wall and into a two-acre grove of hardwood trees two hundred yards behind the building.

"Any wounds?" Murdock asked the men who clustered around him in the brush.

"Small chunk of shrapnel in my leg, but it don't bother me none," Howie Anderson said.

Mahanani went over to the big gunner's mate and checked it, pulled up his pants leg and treated it.

"The metal went through, a slice," Mahanani said. "Bandaged it up and Howie is fit for service."

"Good, let's haul ass out of here. We're a little north and west of the bulk of the city. A couple of miles will get us away from any Chinese reaction to the embassy. We'll head generally west, that's where India is. Let's move it, double-time."

Lam was out front a hundred yards as the SEALs did their ground eating trot that would consume a mile in eight minutes. The area was built up but they found a field here and there and a road that seemed to lead nowhere bounded by a few poorly made houses. They saw no one in the area, and there were no Chinese troops that they encountered.

Fifteen minutes from the embassy, Murdock called a halt. "Now, planning session. We have two general choices. We can hike from here back to India to the west, which must be about a hundred miles."

"We could steal a truck," Jaybird said. "Done it before."

"Yeah but I don't see a hell of a lot of roads heading that direction," Jefferson said.

"Hijack a plane?" Ostercamp asked.

"Chicoms will have the airports stitched up tight," Franklin said.

"Ganges," DeWitt said. "I saw it on the map. It's somewhere just to the west of the capital."

"You mean float down the sacred river to the bay?" Will Dobler asked.

"Or find a boat with a motor," DeWitt said. "The Chicoms are going to be worried about taking control of the country. They won't spend a platoon hunting us."

"How far?" Bradford asked.

"If it's a hundred miles to India on the west, it has to be a hundred and twenty to the Bay of Bengal," DeWitt answered. "The mouth of the Ganges is more than a hundred miles wide down there, it shatters into dozens of channels that wander all over the map."

Murdock looked at Jaybird, then Dobler and Mahanani. They all said, "wet."

"If we go wet, and float, at five knots, it would take us twenty-four hours to get to the mouth of the river," Murdock said. "We better try to find some motorized transportation." He looked around in the darkness. "Anderson, you still have that SATCOM?"

"I do, sir."

"Let's see who we can raise. They gave us that ship frequency offshore. The cruiser. Try it."

Anderson set up the antenna, aimed it in the direction of the satellite and had a beep on the radio showing it was aimed correctly.

"Wet One, this is Mother Hen. Do you copy?"

There was no response. He tried twice more. Murdock shook his head. "We have the wrong frequency or they don't have their ears on. We'll try later."

"So let's get moving to the west," Dobler said. "Lam out a hundred. Those Chicoms had cammies on that looked a lot like ours. From a distance we'll even look like Chinks. Might come in handy with the natives."

They hiked again this time in a single file with Alpha
Squad first and Bravo behind. Ed DeWitt brought up the
end of the line as rear guard. They soon found the area
more and more built up until they were in a residential
section of a small town. Now they had to work down
streets, past occasional street lights. Now and then they saw
a car or small truck. They saw no Chinese troops for two
hours.

"We must have come ten miles," Murdock said as they
took a break in one of the few open fields they had seen
lately. Murdock checked his watch. It was 2330.

"Six, maybe seven hours to daylight," Murdock said.
"We need to have a boat and be sailing downstream before
the sun comes up. Let's move it faster."

A half-hour later they came to another section of houses
and streets. They had passed over three bridges, but they
seemed to be swampy areas and not the river. They went
around a building and Lam talked to them on the Motorola.

"We've got some Chicoms dead ahead. Looks like a patrol. Seven or eight. They're coming directly for us down
this street."

"Get out of the way and we'll have a surprise for them,"
Murdock said. He motioned for his men to move to the
side of the street, into doorways and in the openings between buildings.

"We let them come up to fifty feet of us, then we open
fire. We have silenced weapons?"

Six men replied. "Silenced only if that will do it," Murdock said. "Hold your fire until I give you a go on the
Motorola."

All was quiet in the strange little street. Then they heard
some chatter and laughter. Not good patrol behavior. Murdock tightened his grip on his Bull Pup hoping he wouldn't
have to use it.

They saw a lead Chinese soldier come into the street
shortly. He looked around and waved the rest forward.
When all were in sight and less than twenty yards away,
Murdock gave the order to fire.

The six weapons stammered out deadly rounds. None of the eight men in the patrol had time to fire his weapon. All went down to the muffled sound of the SEAL guns.

"Make sure, Franklin."

The SEAL came away from a building and ran forward checking each of the Chinese. The Motorolas spoke.

"All down and out, Skipper," Franklin said.

"We move forward."

A half-hour later they came to a series of small streams and then the banks of the Ganges, the holy river of India. The bank had been terraced and concrete platforms built at the water's edge so pilgrims could come and wash themselves in the sacred water.

"Upstream," Murdock said. "Maybe fewer platforms and a dock or two with a boat."

It was a quarter of a mile farther before they found any boats. Most were flat bottomed and too small to carry even six SEALs. A hundred yards on upstream they found a sturdier dock that angled into the river. Tied up there was a thirty-foot boat that looked large enough to hide the fifteen SEALs. Lam looked it over and came back with a grin.

"Looks like a winner. She has a diesel engine, room for fifteen, and if I read the gauges right, lots of fuel. There's no guard onboard or anyone else, and I didn't see anyone on the pier."

"Let's go steal a boat," Murdock said.

They moved up and watched the boat and the pier for ten minutes. Nothing happened. Lam and two men slipped on board and checked the craft again. Two minutes later, Lam waved from the gangplank and the SEALs hurried onboard.

"Can you start the engine?" DeWitt asked Lam.

"Hey, does a dog have fleas? You betcha. You ready, Skipper?"

Murdock waved and Lam vanished into a small wheelhouse. A moment later the engine coughed, stuttered, then came the rhythmic beat of a diesel engine.

"Cast off," Murdock said, the bowline came off the dock, and they moved out into the Ganges. In the dark, the river looked a mile wide. Lam headed for the middle of the channel and turned downstream. He saw no other boats on the river.

The craft had been used to haul freight down the river, but now was empty. It was just large enough so all of the SEALs could sit or lie out of sight.

"We're making ten knots," Lam said. Murdock nodded. "That means it will take us twelve hours to get into the bay."

"From the wear on the throttle lever, looks like five to maybe seven knots is the normal cruising speed," Lam said. "That five knots with the current of five should keep us at ten knots. I could goose it up a notch, but we might burn up the engine."

"Keep it at the ten knots," Murdock said. "Then we might have some reserve if we need it."

Nobody had mentioned it, but they all knew that China had a Navy. Had they brought over any boats to this area? It was a long way from China. They may have taken over some Bangladesh river patrol boats. Either way they would be just as deadly. Murdock hoped that they didn't see any.

He kept trying to watch the shores. Usually they faded into distance and the haze. For a small country with such a large population, the place seemed relatively uncrowded here in the country. He saw only an occasional light, and no real town along the banks. But it was a long river.

In the bright moonlight he could see where massive flooding had taken place recently. The country was mostly a flat plain and made up of the silt of millions of years from the Ganges. That made it almost at sea level and tremendously at risk for flooding. Every few years devastating floods hit the country. Murdock remembered that ten years ago when the floods hit, there were thousands dead and over twenty-five million homeless.

They plowed down the river. They had been on the river since 0030. That meant they had another five, maybe six hours before daylight. That was when Murdock expected trouble. There would be no way the Chinese would know where to look for them. The trouble might come if a Chi-

nese patrol boat came alongside to inspect the boat or just
to harass the crew.

Lam had the con. Vinnie Van Dyke was their best small
boat sailor, but he was still in the hospital on the carrier.
Most of the SEALs had sacked out on and below the
deck. Murdock hadn't named any lookout. He did the job
himself. Lam would need some relief at the helm. Bradford
would be the next man up.

Murdock went into the little wheelhouse and waved at
Lam. There was a small light over the control panel.

"So far, we're winning," Lam said.

"Lots of miles to go yet, sailor. In another hour I'll get
you a relief pilot. What's the routine, stay in the middle of
the channel and hope we don't hit a sandbar?"

"About the size of it. Saw some small arms fire back
there a ways. None of it came our way."

"If the Chicoms are all over the place, I can't see them,"
Murdock said. He paused staring into the moonscape.
"Maybe they're just in the population centers."

Two hours later somebody nudged Murdock awake
where he had been sleeping in the hold.

"Trouble, sir. Looks like a patrol boat."

Murdock came awake in an instant, recognized Mahanani's voice and jumped to the deck.

"Twin lights and a searchlight coming at us. Range
maybe two thousand yards and closing."

"Wake up the troops and have them lock and load. We
could be in for some action." Murdock wished he's brought
a pair of binoculars. This wasn't supposed to be long-range
work. He stared into the moonlit darkness ahead of them.
Yes, running lights and a searchlight swinging back and
forth over the water. The boat was on the far side of the
river working the far bank. Already Lam had angled the
craft toward the right-hand bank.

Murdock moved up beside him. "Want me to shut down
the power and let the current run us downstream?" Lam
asked.

"Take longer to get by him that way. No sense in giving
him more chances to see us. With his motors running he

won't be able to hear us in this little tub. Wonder what kind of armament he has?"

Murdock had checked the book on Bangladesh before they left the carrier. She had three frigates in the 340-foot class. With any warning at all, those craft should have put to sea until the problem on land was resolved. He couldn't remember the type of patrol craft they had but they would probably have some in the 195-foot class and more of the 120-foot size.

Murdock guessed that the larger ones had taken off for sea, as well, which would leave the smaller ones to be captured and used until the Chinese Navy arrived. That type patrol craft would probably have radar, missiles, and some 25mm twin guns. Way too much firepower for them.

"Let's find some overhanging trees or vines and try to hide behind them against the shore," Murdock said.

Lam eased the craft closer to shore, scraped over a sand bar and moved out again. "That won't work," Lam said. Ahead they could see a small river entering the main flow.

"Give it a try?" Lam asked.

Murdock checked the patrol boat. Still twelve hundred yards off.

"Yeah, nose in easy against the flow and see if it has a bottom."

The small ship angled more sharply to shore, had to turn back against the current to get into the downstream slant of the river entry. Then Lam edged forward a few feet at a time. A small curve in the tributary showed just ahead. Lam checked the riverbank. They were nearly screened from the patrol boat.

"Another twenty yards, Skipper," Lam said.

"Go."

The little boat edged farther up stream until Lam decided it was far enough in, then he used just enough throttle to keep the boat in the same spot against the two-knot current of the small stream.

Murdock saw his men moving into firing positions around the craft. He hoped they didn't have to work against the missiles and the 25mm twin guns, which could chew this little wooden boat into shreds in minutes.

"All quiet on the boat," Murdock whispered into the mike. The SEALs knew the drill. They didn't talk, move or lift weapons. It was as quiet as a tomb, which is where they could be if somebody made too much noise.

Now they could hear the growl of the larger boat's diesels as it strained upstream against the five-knot current.

"Almost opposite us," Lam said. "Can't see them, just a feeling."

They waited.

Fingers were outside trigger guards to prevent any accidental firing.

They waited again.

They all heard it then, the high-pitched whine of the diesel at full throttle as the larger boat on the Ganges revved up its motor and charged more quickly up the muddy flow toward the capital. The men listened to it for sixty seconds.

"Getting fainter," Lam said. "The bastard is heading upstream to see the king."

They waited five minutes until they could barely hear the ship's diesels, then Lam eased the boat backward out of the small stream into the Ganges and they powered downstream at their usual ten knots.

Twenty minutes later Murdock saw lights of what had to be a fair-size city on the far shore. The sound of small arms and machine-gun fire erupted along the shoreline, then all went quiet.

"Wasn't aimed at us," Murdock said into his mike. He could sense the men relax. Bill Bradford took over the ship's controls and steered the craft toward the opposite shore as they passed the lights of the city. When they faded, Bradford took the boat back to the middle of the wide river.

"Has to be a half mile across along here," Bradford said.

"From the maps I saw the river is sometimes two miles wide and at times ten to twelve miles across with hundreds of small islands."

"How do I know where the channel is?" Bradford asked.

"This is the Hindu's holy river," Murdock said. "Maybe a little prayer at this time would help."

"Think I'll pass on that one, skipper. I don't even speak Hindi."

Murdock checked his watch. 0235. Maybe four hours of darkness left. He should have checked sunrise in this part of the country. Why? He was only going to be gone three or four hours to the embassy and back in the chopper.

A star shell burst far down the river.

"What's the range?" Murdock asked.

Most of the SEALs had drifted back to sleep. Bradford growled and then tried. "Three miles?"

"We couldn't even see it at three miles. Two miles at the most, maybe a mile at the least. What I'm more curious about is who shot it off and why? Is it a signal or are the Chinese troops just nervous as hell this first night in a foreign country?"

"Hope they're nervous, skipper."

"Howie, are you sleeping?" Murdock asked the mike.

"Not so you could notice it, skipper. Want to try the SATCOM again?"

"Roger that. We shouldn't be moving too fast for a fix with the antenna. Give it a whirl."

A short time later, Howie came on the net.

"I've got somebody, Skip, just don't know who they are. You want to give it a go?"

"Be right there."

Murdock moved a dozen feet aft and took the mike. "This is Wet One looking for Mother Bird," he sent out.

"Yes, Wet One, not sure what frequency this is. We're a unit of the Indian Army in Calcutta. Who are you?"

"Could you contact Mother Bird on this frequency and do some relay work for us?"

"Yes, indeed. Heard there were some Yanks in town. Just a minute."

The air went dead for two minutes.

"Wet Ones, you are well known here. Your Mother Hen says she's aware of your situation. If you can give them coordinates they will attempt to have a meeting."

"Best we can do on coordinates is the central mouth of the Ganges. We're now in transit at ten knots."

"I say, you have been moving. Will relay."

Two more minutes passed.

"Wet Ones, Mother Hen says a CH-forty-six will find you if you can give them an ETA."

"Problem. We're now about twenty miles south of Dhaka. We'll kick our boat up to fifteen knots and we should be about forty miles from the Bay of Bengal by 0630. Should be daylight by then. We'll keep going best we can after daylight but can't promise we'll get there, depending on Chinese activity. Got that?"

"Right, have it down. Relaying."

It took five minutes this time before they were on the air again.

"Mother Hen says she will send the bird to the mouth, then track north on the best channel and look for you. No trouble for you chaps to get in that bird in flight?"

"Done it a hundred times. Tell the bird we will watch for him and use red flares."

"Will do. Congratulations on your exfiltration so far."

"Many miles to go yet. Thanks."

"Hey, Cap. Come take a look at this," Bradford said from the small wheelhouse.

Murdock told Howie to keep the set turned to receive and adjust the antenna every five minutes, then went to the wheel.

"Far shore, maybe a thousand yards up there. Dark now but won't be for long if they repeat."

Murdock watched. A sudden flash of a string of lights erupted along the far shore followed at once by a series of loud explosions.

"The bang-bang are an added attraction," Bradford said. "What the hell do you think this is all about?"

12

Murdock watched the flares far ahead on the bank glow for a moment more, then snuff out. "Let's move to the other shoreline, we have plenty of river here. Looks like a combat situation. Flares and lots of firepower. But they didn't sound like small arms."

"Shoulder rockets of some kind?" Bradford wondered. "Sure as hell nobody getting any sleep over on that bank."

"If that is some holdout Bangladesh military up there, we can't help them because we don't know which side is which."

Before he finished talking, an engine whine and growl came across the water.

"A boat," Bradford said. "Doesn't sound as big as that last one, maybe a thirty, forty footer."

"Even a small patrol boat will have a pair of machine guns," Murdock said. "Hope he doesn't have a searchlight."

They watched ahead but couldn't tell if the boat was coming toward them or just moving around the fighting area. Now small arms fire did filter though the darkness.

"Machine guns," Murdock said. "Lots of rifle fire and auto rifle. Somebody is throwing out a lot of lead up there."

"Just so it's not aimed at us," Bradford said.

"Sounds like they will be too busy working over each other to worry about us, even if they did spot us, which I'd bet they won't. If that patrol boat has radar, it won't be aimed at us either."

Murdock called on the radio and had Dobler rouse the troops.

"Better be ready in case they do spot us and one side

decides we shouldn't be here," Murdock said.

"Yeah, heard the ruckus. Doesn't sound too large, maybe a platoon against a platoon. No real heavy stuff."

"Neither kind would be good for us. Have the men ready, just in case."

The small boat powered down the river a little faster now. They had boosted their power until Murdock figured they were making their fifteen knots. He wasn't sure what they should do come daylight. Hide everybody except one man at the wheel. Keep at their fifteen knots and hoping that the Chinese didn't have any patrols down this far. From what he remembered on the map the broad spread of the mouth of the Ganges looked like one big floodplain with hundreds of low-lying islands that must be under water half the time. Nothing would be built up in an area like that. So why would the Chinese want to patrol it? He did remember one town on the east side of the area, but he didn't know how large it was. Wait and see.

They eased past the firing on the far shore. A flare popped up now and then to cast a bright light on the bank, and firing increased, then the flares snuffed out and the shooters were blind again. The boat they had heard was quiet as well. Murdock worried that. If they had a radar it would surely pick them up. It just depended if the operator was interested in the far side of the river.

They were slightly past the firing on the far shore, when a searchlight snapped on less than two hundred yards ahead of them and the boat's engine roared as the craft came straight for them.

"Kill that light," Murdock thundered into his mike. The long range guns barked, a Bull Pup gave off the familiar sound of a 20mm round being fired. The searchlight died but a machine gun chattered at them. A half dozen more of the heavy coughing sound of the twenties blistered into the night, and a moment later the MG on the boat went silent. At the same time the engine died.

In the pale moonlight Murdock could see a shadowy shape ahead. His boat was overtaking the other craft. Now they came closer at their fifteen knots and they could see the ship turn slowly.

"Adrift," Bradford said. "Our twenties must have knocked out the crew as well as that damn machine gun."

"Small favors we will take," Murdock said.

They were past the firing on shore now, and Bradford moved the small craft back to the center of the river. He figured it was at least three-quarters of a mile wide here.

Murdock slumped on the small deck outside the wheelhouse.

"Give me a yell if anything shows," he said and told Ostercamp on the radio that he had the watch. That done, Murdock cushioned his head on his arms and slept.

Ostercamp worked around and over bodies to the wheelhouse and grinned at Bradford.

"Sure as hell leveled that patrol boat with the twenties," he said. "Wonder what else we'll find downstream?"

"That's what you're here to watch for," Bradford said and they both kept quiet then and looked downstream.

Murdock awoke at 0530 and checked around. He was tired and sore from sleeping on the wooden planks. He stretched and looked at the wheelhouse. Dobler held the wheel and waved at Murdock.

"Welcome to the world, skipper. No action since that patrol boat got greedy."

"Good." Murdock rubbed the sleep from his eyes. "Be light in a half hour, Chief. Any suggestions?"

"Keep to the middle of the water and pray that we've been making more than fifteen and that we're closer than forty miles to the damn Bay of Bengal."

"What are the odds?"

"Damn slight. Depends what the Chicoms have had time to set up as a defensive unit down here in the mud flats. You ever seen such a wide river? Islands all over the place. Just passed a big island on the right that looked like Minnesota."

"No buildings?"

"Oh, hell no. Looked like it was half marsh and the rest ready to be flooded with the first rain upstream."

As the light came up, they could see more details along the shoreline. It had pinched in now along another big island and the more firm looking land to the left.

"Trouble," Dobler said. "Small boat coming upstream. Range two thousand yards."

Stray bars of light splintered into the darkness from the east. The whole river took on a different tone as the light drove in devouring the darkness.

Ten minutes later they could see the boat plainly. It worked upstream at seven or eight knots.

"Patrol boat for sure," Murdock said. "I'll take the wheel. You get everyone awake and out of sight and locked and loaded for bear. We're going to have a fight with this guy."

Murdock watched the other boat closely as it approached. They were closing at about twenty-five knots. Soon he could see a machine gun mounted on the front. Was it Chinese or still a Bangladesh craft? He saw no flag. Then he spotted a flag on the stern. What was the Chinese flag? Then he had it. A gold star in the upper left hand corner on a pure red field. Yes. He had no idea what the Bangladesh flag looked like. He stared at the fluttering flag. Then he could see it, a red field and star.

They were still five hundred yards off each other.

"Twenties, fire at will," Murdock said. He sighted in on the ship without using the laser and fired. Two more rounds came almost at the same time. Two of the rounds hit the Chicom ship and exploded. The first took out the man just crawling behind the machine gun on the fore deck. The second hit the wheelhouse but most of the damage was on the outside.

In close order six more rounds hit the Chinese craft before the crew had a chance to return fire. The man at the helm vanished, the thirty-foot craft plowed straight ahead for ten seconds, then the engine died. With no one at the wheel, the little craft nudged against the current for the last time, then swung to port and began to drift slowly downstream with the current.

Two rifles fired from the small ship, but neither hit the SEALs' boat. The Chinese patrol boat drifted toward the far shore, and Dobler steered his craft to the opposite side of the half-mile wide river.

By then it was brightly light. The sun was up soon and a warm, humid day approached. Dobler coaxed another knot of speed from the ka-thumping diesel engine and they moved back to the center of the roiling, muddy water.

Ten minutes later Lam called from the center of the boat.

"Chopper coming from due north."

"Too early for the forty-six," Dobler said.

"Doesn't sound like a forty-six," DeWitt said. "Keep those twenties with full magazines." Three of the men switched to full mags and waited.

"Still coming downstream," Lam said. "Engine sound is wrong, so it's not one of ours."

"We let him make a flyover. Everyone flake out like you're sleeping. We might fool him into thinking we're some of his own."

"Not likely," Jaybird said.

Canzoneri spotted it first. "A speck over the far bank at about eleven o'clock looking that way."

"Yeah, working the bank," Murdock said. "Might be part of that attack we came past last night. He's not one of our choppers, for damn sure."

"He might not even see us," Lam said.

"No chance, he's looking for something, somebody," Jaybird said. "I think he just found us."

The chopper had picked up speed and turned directly toward them. "Let him have one flyover free," Murdock said.

By then the bird was only a hundred yards away. Murdock stood with Dobler at the wheel. The chopper came closer. It was a large one for troop transport. two rotors. They could see a machine gun mounted on the door with a man behind it. The helicopter came closer, then did a slow circle around the SEALs in the center of a thirty-yard circle. It moved away, then came back with the door gunner on the right side positioned to fire at them.

"Weapons free, let's knock him down," Murdock said. He lifted the twenty and fired twice from the hip, then came up and sighted in on the bird. The door gunner got off one burst, then an exploding 20mm round churned his face into pulp and knocked him out the far door. He was only a minor splash before the chopper took a dozen hits, turned slightly, then the rotors stopped and began free wheeling just before the fuel tanks exploded in one giant fireball and the chopper dropped like a bucket full of concrete and slammed into the water. The craft resisted the water for a moment, then the remains eased under the muddy flood and were gone.

"Home, James," Jaybird chirped and everyone laughed reliving the tension.

"Sonsobitches, brothers, did you see that asshole explode?" Howie Anderson yelled. "Went up like a possum gutted out by a load of buckshot."

DeWitt chuckled. "Couldn't have said it more colorfully myself."

Where is this damn forty-six we're supposed to meet?" Train Khai asked. "Shouldn't he be showing up sometime soon? How long does it take a forty-six to go forty miles?"

"How long?" Lam asked. "At a hundred and fifty-five miles an hour they move about two point five miles a minute, or about sixteen minutes for forty miles."

"Where the fuck is he?" Fernandez asked. "Hell, it's been light for over twenty minutes."

Lam stood and looked around. "Somebody coming. He stared at the sky again, turned all the way around then looked back north. "Yeah, coming fast and it ain't no chopper. Got to be a jet fighter heading south."

"We won't nail a MiG with our twenties," Murdock said. "And he has twenties of his own."

"Unless he's hunting us on purpose, he won't know we're hostiles," DeWitt said. "Not at his speed. We just play it cool and don't show any guns or objections. Fact is, we could wave at him if he's anywhere under a thousand feet."

They waited and watched. Two minutes later the jet streaked over at eight to ten thousand feet.

"Damn, he couldn't even see us down here," Jefferson said.

"Good, now where's my chopper," Jaybird said.

They worked past another huge island on the left and smaller one on the right. At last the surface of the water seemed to be changing.

"A little salt water creeping in," DeWitt said. "We should be able to smell salt air before long."

"That MiG is coming back," Lam said. "Lower this time, lots lower."

It came from the south right up the channel and when they saw it they were almost too late. It slashed past them at a hundred feet off the water, slapping them with the jet blast of sound as soon as it jolted pas them at seven hundred miles an hour.

"That time he saw us," Murdock said. "Now, the question is, will he make a gentle turn and come back and blast us into toothpicks with his twenties?"

They waited.

Two minutes dragged by. They began to grin and relax.

It came at them from the north. The first they heard were the rattling of the rotary guns pumping out 20mm rounds at their boat. Then it roared over them at less than hundred feet and rocked the boat twenty degrees. None of the 20mm rounds hit the boat.

"Missed us, by God," Chief Dobler screeched. "At that speed one of those rounds hits the deck about every fifty feet. He has to be damn good to do us any harm."

"He might get lucky, do we abandon ship, Cap?" DeWitt asked.

Murdock figured he had two minutes to decide. The next pass the pilot would get more altitude and concentrate his fire when he dove at them. Snap decision, combat pure.

"Over the side, everyone. Leave everything except your weapon. Kill the engine. If he misses we'll swim for the boat. Swim away from the tub on each side. Abandon ship, now."

Murdock grabbed his Bull Pup and jumped the six feet into the Ganges. He did a scissors kick as soon as he hit and kept his head above water, then lowered his face into the water and kicked hard and used one arm to power himself away from the boat. He felt the pull of the current. Good, if the boat lasted they wouldn't have so far to swim to catch it.

Murdock was thirty yards to one side of the boat when the jet came down again. He could hear the plane and he was higher, diving this time to concentrate his rounds. This pass with the 20mm cannon riddled the boat, knocking huge chunks out of the deck on one side. The next pass by the MiG blasted a hundred exploding rounds into the small craft. The wheelhouse vanished and toppled into the water. The deck exploded in a million splinters and the whole left side of the craft caved in as the holes in the bottom let the dank Ganges pour in. A minute later the boat sank.

Murdock looked around. He saw two swimmers.

"Over here," Murdock bellowed. "Assemble over here." He looked for the nearest land. One of the many islands poked out of the water ahead and to the left downstream. The two men near him were Mahanani and Jaybird.

"That next island, Jaybird," Murdock called. The two men headed that way. Murdock yelled again, but could see no other swimmers near him. He surged upward out of the water and yelled at the top of his move. "The island to the left," he called. "Get to the island to the left."

Then he swam for the land, holding the Bull Pup in one hand and swimming hard with the other. The current helped and he washed on shore three minutes later. The other two were there yelling into the morning sunlight. They spotted two more men and helped them up the beach. The land here was barely two feet out of the water.

Murdock thought of his Motorola. It was wet and dead. They weren't made for underwater work. He doubted if any of the men took time to waterproof the little radio set before they dove in. He felt his shoulder and saw that he still had two flares. Some help.

He had four men out of fourteen. Where the hell were the other ten?

13

Where were those guys? Murdock stared into the glare of the early morning sunshine. Another island to the right fifty yards. He squinted. Yes, somebody was over there.

Jaybird came up. "I've got five more men on that next little island to the right," Jaybird said. "Looks like it's about flooded over. We going over there or have them come over here?"

"Here," Murdock said.

Jaybird adjusted his Motorola. "Hey guys on that other island. If you've got your ears on, Skipper says come over here. See me, I'm waving."

Jaybird had no response to his call.

"My radio is dead," Murdock said. "How did you have time to get yours waterproofed?"

"Did that the minute I saw that MiG making his first run. I'll go up as far as I can on this land and yell at the guys. It ain't that far away."

Mahanani came up. "Hey, found two more slippery SEALs. One is talking about a hurt leg, Franklin. Don't know how bad yet. How many men we missing?"

"Still short three. They must be here somewhere. The current isn't that strong, no downpulls."

"Where'n hell are you guys?" Mahanani's ear piece asked.

"Hey, I've got a live one here. Who is this and where are you?"

"Ostercamp you jerk. Three of us found this little reef, sandbar, whatever. We're sitting in six inches of water but it's easier than swimming. Where are you?"

Jaybird came running up from where he'd been up the island.

"Good count on that other island, Cap. I've got five over there. That makes fourteen chicks in the basket. Everyone accounted for."

"Good, where's DeWitt?"

"Must be on the island. They're going to swim over here. Haven't spotted the sand bar guys yet, but they can't be far away. I'll make another run down the island."

Mahanani, Lampedusa and Howie Anderson looked at their platoon leader. "So, what the hell we do now, Skipper?"

"First we get the men together. Where are the three sand-bar sitters?"

"Where are you guys on the sandbar? Can you see a big island maybe three four feet high anywhere? Probably behind you. How far downstream did you go before you got to the reef?"

"Not sure," Ostercamp said. "Big island. Small one in front, oh yeah, now I see it. Behind us, maybe, what three hundred yards."

"Jaybird should be showing up at your end of the island. If you can see him, give him a holler. We've found everybody now."

Murdock moved down the island until he could see where his five men were swimming across the fifty yards from the other one. They came in pairs fighting the five-knot current. The last pair came slower, drifted farther downstream and Murdock saw that one man was helping the other one.

They were going to be swept by the end of the island, but Howie Anderson swam out and pulled them in. The last two were DeWitt and Will Dobler. Dobler was the one getting help. Murdock ran up to them where they both lay on the beach.

DeWitt motioned Murdock to one side. "Will must have taken some shrapnel from one of the twenties. Got him in the upper leg and doesn't look good. We better get a couple of first aid kits off the men. Mahanani is looking at it. Not fatal, but he won't be walking much for a while."

"Glad to see you guys. We've got three fish sitting on a sand bar downstream about three hundred yards. Ostercamp and two others. They have a working radio. I took mine for a swim."

"So what now?" DeWitt asked.

"We're not moving downstream a hell of a lot farther," Murdock said." He looked around, saw Lam, and called the tracker over. "Do a quick survey of the island. Let me know what we have. Any vegetation, where it's the driest, any concealment. Go."

Lam took off on a trot heading for the far side of the island.

"I figure we're still about thirty-five miles from the mouth of the Ganges," DeWitt said. "Hope that chopper pilot doesn't get nervous about charging into enemy territory up the river."

"That's what we pay him for," Murdock said.

He rounded up the men he had and moved then down the island. Two SEALs helped as Dobler hobbled along on one foot. The land was a quarter of a mile long, maybe half that wide. There was no vegetation of any kind on this side, just mud and sand. The dry part was three to four feet above the river level. Toward the center of the island it rose to twenty-five or thirty feet. Murdock moved the men up there.

"Mahanani, contact Jaybird and see if he can spot those three sandbar guys."

Mahanani made the radio call. He waited a minute and looked up. "Jaybird says Ostercamp has Jefferson and Khai with him. All are okay. He says they don't want to do the swim back upstream just yet. Give them another half hour and they will join us."

"Good. Tell Jaybird to stay there and keep in contact with them and ride herd."

Murdock looked at the island. He moved the men to the highest point. It was dry there. They flaked out, tried to get the Ganges silt out of their ears, and dried out a little. Everyone had a weapon except Will Dobler.

Lam caught up with Murdock. "Looks like a little bit of brush and grass over on the far side about halfway down. Might be enough to conceal us if a chopper comes around. That's about it for this bit of Bangladesh soil."

Murdock went with Lam to take a look. By the time they made it back to the top of the island, the three reef sitters were back on dry land and telling how hard it was swimming in the grime of the Ganges against that five-knot current.

"What a bunch of wimps," Howie bellowed. "My grandmother could swim up there and she's ninety-two."

Murdock called the men around and in typical SEAL fashion laid out the problem.

"You know our situation here, let's have some input. What should we do?"

"What the hell can we do to get closer to the bay?" Jaybird asked.

"We can't swim down forty miles with a wounded man," DeWitt said. "No way. Dobler has the leg wound."

"Hell I can still swim," Dobler said.

"Yeah, and we'd have a pack of sharks following down your blood trail," Mahanani said.

"Our Motorolas are good for maybe five miles," Howie said. "Oh, shit. I left the SATCOM on the boat. It's long gone by now."

Murdock scowled. "Next mission I'm gonna staple the fucking SATCOM to your ears. So, the SATCOM is out. Next I want everybody to make a hide hole here in this brush. It isn't much, but better than raw sand. Get a spot fixed so you can go invisible at fifty feet. You know the drill. Let's do it now, and hope that we don't need it. Be thinking on this small situation we're in."

The SEALs moved ten feet apart and scraped out foliage, leaves, and dirt until they could lie down, and cover themselves with the material, leaving only their faces showing. To those they applied new steaks of wet mud to break up the visual image.

They were done in ten minutes.

"Now, any new ideas," Murdock called. Murdock was

next to Dobler and had helped him with his hole.

"The obvious," Jaybird said. "We wait for that forty-six to come and spot us."

"Play stranded and lure a boat over and capture it," Jefferson said.

"Yeah, the place is just teeming with traffic this morning," Howie snapped.

"Send our two best swimmers downstream, maybe with a float log, and watch for the chopper, and guide it back up here." Mahanani said it. He was the best swimmer in the platoon.

"Find some native girls and settle down on our island and grow pineapple and sugarcane?" Canzoneri asked with a grin.

"I'm for that one," Bradford yelped.

"Back to business," Murdock said. "At least my watch works. We send one waterproofed Motorola with the swimmers. It's almost eleven hundred. We should have seen that chopper by now."

"Must be a dozen good-size channels branching off the Ganges," DeWitt said. "The pilot could have picked any one of them and been wrong."

Lam stood and looked to the north. "Chopper coming, moving quickly."

"Let's hit our holes, men. No firing. Weapons undercover as well as usual. Go down, now."

The SEALs vanished into the brushy area where the tallest of the growth was only three feet. They waited. Murdock had his face almost covered, but he could see out a hole to the south. It was a chopper like the last one, two rotors, and could have troops inside. It moved slowly forward, pausing at each small island. He hoped the bird was high enough so the downdraft from the rotors wouldn't blow away their camouflage.

It moved closer. The SEALs remained motionless. Then in a burst it was over their island working one side, then back up the side where the SEALs lay. Murdock saw a door gunner waving his machine gun around. He didn't fire. The chopper hovered over the patch of brush but at more than a hundred feet so the rotor blast wasn't enough to move the sand and leaves.

It hesitated again, then moved on to the end of the island and back down the other side.

"Footprints in the sand," somebody said. "We must have left a batch of them along the shore."

"They didn't see them, or didn't believe them," DeWitt said. "Let's get up, should be safe now."

Before he finished saying it, a jet fighter blasted overhead. It was more than five hundred feet and Murdock knew the pilot couldn't see them, still he ducked down again and waited.

"Just what we need, some damn MiG to find our forty-six and blow it out of the sky with a rocket," Mahanani said.

The SEALs came out of their holes slowly.

Murdock looked downstream, then to the north. "We don't have much choice," he said. "We move two swimmers downstream. Take a radio, check with us at five miles and we'll see if we can receive. We'll keep a Motorola on here while you're gone. Find that damn CH-forty-six for us."

Mahanani peeled out of his webbing and shirt. The sun came down like a warm blanket. The others were sweating. Mahanani looked around, waved at Howie. "Get your gear off, sailor. Let's see if you can swim."

Howie yelped and pulled off his webbing and shirt. "Boots, too?" he asked.

Murdock shook his head. "Better keep them on for protection. They aren't that heavy. Stay near the shore and you might find a log you can use for a float. Five knots drifting with the current is good, don't push it.

"No weapons," Murdock said. "Unless you have hideout revolvers. Take no chances. If you find the forty-six, use one of the flares in your pants knee pockets. Then come get us. If he misses you, and finds us, we come get you. The flare again. Questions?"

"Civilians?" Howie asked.

"Keep clear. Don't think you'll see any people out here unless they have a boat. Still stay clear."

The two pushed into the water and stroked evenly into the current and let it take them downstream. Within five minutes they were out of sight.

"Stay near the brush," Murdock said. "We don't want any surprises. Nothing we can do. Will, how is that leg?"

"Hurts like hell, Skipper. Damned if I know how I got it. Must have been kicking on the surface at just the wrong time and in the fucking wrong place."

"You get some morphine?"

"Not yet. We don't have much. One ampoule in each aid kit. I'll wait until I really need it."

DeWitt came over and sat down in the leaves. "What a mess. How did we get into this one?"

"We must have volunteered. Just glad we didn't have any of the embassy people on that second bird when the Chicoms got the range."

They looked at each other. Both thinking about the same thing. Was this the fucked up mission that was going to wipe out the whole platoon? Murdock drove that idea out of his head. He checked over the men. They were doing fine so far. No food for eighteen hours or more. Water would be the big need, and soon. So far they had toughed it out. Who needed canteens on a four-hour mission?

He deliberately thought about something else. Something pleasant, fun, beautiful. Which brought Ardith Jane Manchester to mind. *Oh, yeah.* She had been one of the really fine bits of life to happen to him so far. Tall and blond and svelte and sexy as all hell. *Oh, yeah.* A smart woman, a lawyer on her senator father's staff in D.C. *Yeah, and maybe moving up to a better spot as some department or cabinet officer's assistant. Or maybe just yank her out of D.C. with a wedding ring and bring her out to Coronado and let her play with some free legal clinic for the Chicanos, blacks, and Asians. She would go for that. Had they talked about it? Dozens of times.* He wondered what she was thinking of right now.

"High and dry, this is Wet Two with a friendly log moving downstream," Jaybird's Motorola came to life. "Figure we're four miles plus. Do you copy?" The sound of the Motorola filled the brushy area.

"Read fives, buddies," Jaybird said. "Keep floating. Bring us back a big fucking, hairy assed chopper."

"Amen to that bro. We're moving again. No more transmissions. Don't see any people, no boats, no planes, but then no hungry sharks either. We're out of here."

"Good swimming, guys."

Five miles down and no chopper. Where the hell was that bird? Murdock tried to get his mind back on Ardith, but somehow it wouldn't turn on. He thought about their situation. Damn bad. He thought about their chances. All depended on that one lone forty-six they hoped was coming. It had been arranged. Yeah, they had set it up, so where was he? Range was right, should be no enemy action on the water or around the multiple mouths of this hundred mile wide delta of the Ganges.

Wrong mouth? Yeah. He wondered how many of the channels the bird had been working up and then back down. How long for a forty-six to fly forty miles? Sixteen minutes as Murdock remembered.

Damn it to hell, where was that chopper?

Lam heard it first, a faint hum that grew from the north and became louder.

"Boat, Skipper," Lam said. "Coming this way fast."

"All of us back in our holes, and keep your weapons locked and loaded so you can lift up and fire when I bellow. This one could get sticky if the boat has troops and they are searching the islands. They might be looking for that chopper crew or the patrol boat crew. Then again, they could be searching for us.

"We stay covered up from right now until all problems are past. If we have to lift and shoot, Alpha Squad take the beached boat and riddle it. Bravo work on the search party. Should be a barrel of laughs. Or it might be a boat traveling downstream and not even wondering about this island."

The boat came closer. Murdock lifted slightly so he could see it. A patrol boat, forty footer, maybe. Would need a small boat to get men ashore. Yeah, that big a craft was damn bad news. Where the hell was that chopper?

14

The black-and-blue patrol boat raced toward them down-stream at what Murdock figured was twenty knots. The closer it came the more he could see. It had a big machine gun mounted on the bow, Probably a .50 caliber. It had a high cabin and a walk around the front deck. He could see men on it, one ready on the MG, two more in the aft area. He couldn't tell if they had rifles or not. The craft had to be forty, maybe forty-five feet. Normally a boat like that could have a crew of four and carry up to ten troops.

Now the boat was fifty yards off their island coming toward the north end. Suddenly the craft throttled down, did a quick turn to the left, then a small circle and used just enough power to hold its position near the point of land of the SEALs hide-away island.

The boat revved up the engine then and did a slow look around as it eased downstream twenty feet from the shore. When it came opposite the highest area, down from where the SEALs hid, the .50 caliber opened up and the gunner slammed a hundred rounds into the built-up section.

Murdock gritted his teeth. For sure when they came up the other side of the island they would do the same thing to the brush patch. He had to decide to take out the craft before that, or lose half, maybe all of his men. When to do it? Should they lift out of their holes, get to the back side of the high ground and take the boat before it got to their brushy hidehole position?

"Looks like trouble," Will Dobler said from his hole. "They use that fifty and we're dead ducks sitting here."

"Damn straight, Chief."

The patrol boat worked farther down the quarter-mile island and at last it was out of sight of the SEALs. Murdock sat up.

"Listen, you guys. We're ducks in a row here. Come out of your holes and we move to the back side of that high ground. As soon as he gets the boat around the bend down there. When we're shielded we move over there and take him out when he comes up on this side of the island. No other way."

"Hold it right here for about five," Dobler said.

They waited for the five minutes, then Murdock stood and the SEALs came to life. "Bradford, give the chief a hand here. He needs a third leg."

"That's what his wife keeps telling him," somebody cracked, and Dobler grinned through the pain in his right leg.

"Jaybird, look over his wound as soon as we're behind that rise," Murdock said. "Might need a new bandage."

They moved quietly, by twos, dashing across the fifty yards to the rise in the land, keeping out of sight of the patrol boat.

Dobler and Bradford came in last. The SEALs spread out five yards apart along the reverse slope of the rise so they could just see over the top. Weapons were ready.

"How are we on ammo for the twenties?" Murdock asked. The word went down the line. The figures came back and it came out to about eight rounds per man. That was for each of the five guns.

"Use the rounds carefully," Murdock said. "Everyone fire what weapon you have. Range shouldn't be a problem."

"We knocking it out or just disabling it so it floats downstream?" Ken Ching asked.

"Knock it out," Murdock said. "She might have ten troops in there. Don't want to share our island with them."

They waited.

Five minutes more and they heard more fire from the fifty downstream. Then the sound moved closer.

"I've got him in my sights," Tran Khai said. He was the last man in the row downstream.

"Hold fire until he gets to the middle of our line," Murdock said. "If he shoots at this rise like he did last time, open fire at once."

Again they waited.

Soon they all could see the boat. It dodged closer to shore, and the fifty fired again away from the SEALs, then it was at the middle of the line.

"Let's do it," Murdock said. He sighted in on the little wheelhouse, and fired.

The 20mm impact-fused round exploded just below the console where the driver stood. It blew the man and his steering gear out of the boat.

In rapid succession five more rounds hit the boat. One caught the machine gunner in the chest and punched him halfway over the side of the ship. The rest of the small arms chattered, drilling holes all over the boat, jolting one man over the side.

"Cease fire," Murdock said. The gunners held fire then and watched. The craft's engine sputtered but kept running. "One more round each on the twenties. All the others, ten seconds firing," Murdock said and the weapons spoke again. This time two 20mm rounds hit at the water line, and blew large holes in the fiberglass hull. The engine cut off. They saw two men dive overboard and be swept downstream with the current.

The boat gave in to the current and drifted away. She took on water fast and listed to that side, then began to sink. One more man swam away from the boat, but by then it was well into the current. The man wouldn't be able to get to their island. Another fifty feet and the small patrol craft slid under the water. They saw two men working downstream, not wanting to tangle with whoever had sunk their boat.

"No troops on board," Murdock said. "Good. They don't know we're here yet."

"Nobody knows were here," Dobler said. He closed his eyes and shuddered.

"Jaybird, get over here with two morphine for Dobler."

Jaybird ran over and dug out the ampoules and gave the senior chief the shots.

"Hey, Chief, that's going to make you feel better. That damn chopper is coming any minute now and we'll get you some real medics."

"Yeah, sure, Jaybird. About the same time elephants fly."

Jaybird looked at Murdock. There wasn't anything either of them could say.

"Back to our hide holes," Murdock said. "We may have some more aircraft over here."

It took them fifteen minutes to get back to their camouflage area with the small brush. Murdock checked his watch. It was 1400. Where the hell was that chopper?

They got into their camouflage spots but didn't cover up. They would have warning enough if they needed to.

Lam stood up. "I hear a chopper. Faint." He scowled than shook his head. "Shit, it faded out. Had one for a while. Not even sure what direction it was."

They waited.

Half of them went to sleep beside their holes. The rest probably thought about food and water, Murdock figured. He stood and scanned the skies to the south. Not a damn thing.

"Got it again, damn right," Lam shouted. "Stronger now and getting stronger, coming from the damn west, not the south."

"Holes, everyone," Murdock bellowed. "We don't know who this could be. Cover up. Wake up the sleepers. Let's move, people."

They slid into holes and covered up with the leaves and dirt. Murdock sat up and watched west.

"Still coming, Lam?"

"Yeah and getting louder. You should be able to hear it."

Then, Murdock could. It was a chopper. But he had no idea if was theirs or ours.

"Yeah, I hear it," Bradley said. Then the others came on with shouts.

"Hold it, men. It could be another Chicom."

"Coming from the west?" Franklin asked.

They waited.

Five minutes later Lam saw a smudge on the flat horizon to the west. "Oh, yeah, he's coming this way. He'll go half a click to the south of us."

A few moments more and Jaybird cheered. "It's a damn forty-six, I've heard that sound before. Got to be a forty-six."

Lam nodded. "Sounds like a forty-six, Cap. We'll know shortly. Yeah, he's swinging north. Damn, looks like he's coming dead at this island."

"Hey castaway little buddies, you looking to the sky for some help?" the sound came from Jaybird's Motorola.

"Oh, yeah are we ever? Mahanani, is that your bones?"

"Sure as sour cream curdles, pardner. How would you like a short lift in some first-class accommodations?"

"Oh, yeah, bring that lovely, beautiful, amazing forty-loving-six right into papa."

Soon it was close enough that they could see the white star and bars on the fuselage and the "U.S. NAVY" print on the side.

Then the chopper sat down on a flat stretch fifty yards upstream from them and the big rotors idled.

"Move it," Murdock bellowed. "Get in that bird. Dobler, on me. Take it all with you. We don't want the Chicom to know we were here."

"What about that twenty-mm brass up on the hill?" Fernandez asked.

Murdock scowled. "Fuck it, leave it there. Let's get in that lovely little chopper."

Murdock and Dobler were the last ones in. Mahanani had the chopper's first aid kit opened and put Dobler on the floor of the bird and checked his leg.

"Thought I told you to stay off this leg and get bedrest and look at pretty nurses with big boobs, Chief. What the hell happened?"

"Shit happened, Doc. It always the fuck does. Got any joy juice? I could use some."

Before the conversation was over the doors slammed and the bird took off in a blast of dry sand.

Murdock talked with the pilot.

"Damn glad we found you, Commander. Those two guys of yours flagged us down on our eighth or ninth trip up one of these wide fucking channels. Must be twenty of them. We spotted your guys' flares and then I thought they would wave their arms off."

"Good men. Where we going?"

"Orders say to take you directly to Calcutta for medical. Then you'll pick up orders there. I saw a COD hanging around the field, maybe it's for you."

"Could be," Murdock said. "You have anything to eat? My boys haven't had a sugar tit to chew on for going on twenty-four."

"Nothing but some emergency MREs."

"Sounds like a banquet. Your crew chief can get them?"

The SEALs gratefully gobbled up the MREs long before they sighted Calcutta. Then the CH-46 came in and landed at the military airfield near the big town. The SEALs were taken to a barracks and told chow would be served in half an hour. Murdock and Dobler headed for the base hospital.

The doctors fussed over Dobler for a half hour. None of them had seen a shrapnel wound like that one before. They cleaned it, stitched it up and bound it firmly.

"Your man should stay off that leg for a week," the doctor said. "I suspect you'll be traveling. If you do, have your medic watch the leg closely. Should heal up with no problems. We just don't want the stitches to break open and it get infected."

They released Dobler, who had a wheelchair ride to an ambulance, which took him and Murdock to the barracks.

The Indian Air Force had some orders for Murdock from the U.S. Navy. The first envelope held a radio message from Don Stroh:

Congratulations on the Bangladesh Embassy rescue. All the nationals from there are safe in Calcutta. Hear you were picked up an hour ago by a chopper in the

Ganges Delta area. A wet place. You'll get orders to
hang out with the Indians there for a day or two. The
brass here and in Washington aren't sure what to have
you do next. Evidently, there is a whole pot-full of
projects needing your special touch. Whatever it is,
it will be interesting. Yes, I'm still going through
channels, Navy channels, that is. So take the day off,
go fishing, play pocket pool, have fun. The next job
probably will be a bit more complicated than this one.
But I'm still going through channels.

Murdock read it, then read it to the rest of the men who
were back from the special chow.

"Sounds like that wimp Stroh is cooking up a good one,"
Jefferson said.

Murdock opened the second envelope. It had a computer
printout Navy logo on the top of the page.

Lieutenant Commander Murdock:
    Well done on the embassy run. Glad you made it
back with only one wounded. You are to remain in
place for up to two days. New orders coming.
    In the Bangladesh invasion, China and Pakistan
overflew parts of India north of Bangladesh. India is
furious. They have threatened to shoot down any
more aircraft from Pakistan or China that try to fly
over the area. India's Air Force has the planes to
match the Chinese MiGs. Be aware of this critical
situation.
    Orders will follow in this form through e-mail
since it's our only military hard copy equipment
available to deal at these distances.

It was signed by Captain Irving Robertson II, captain of
the *Stennis*, CVN 74.

Murdock read the orders to the men.

"What the hell does that mean?" Jefferson asked.

"Means we have all day tomorrow to clean our weapons
and wash our clothes," Ostercamp said.

• • •

The same day the SEALs went into Bangladesh to bring out the embassy people, the Chinese and Pakistani peppered the sky over the corridor of India between Bangladesh and China with more than fifty transport planes with paratroopers. Fighter-bombers took out the main military airport near Dhaka and the civilian airport, blasting them into junk but not damaging the runways.

It took the jumpers just six hours to secure the military airfield, then the planes came in with resupply, food, and essentials to an army in the field. It went just the way the Chinese had planned it. By nightfall of the first day, more than half of Bangladesh was in control of the paratroopers.

The surprise raid on the military air field wiped out two squadrons of MiG-29s of the Bangladesh Air Force and three transports and six Chinese-made P-5s and F-6s. The Bangladesh Air Force had been destroyed except for one squadron of the older MiG-19s. The Chinese didn't know where that squadron was home based.

Just before the attack, the king of Bangladesh and all the royal family had flown in their private jet to Calcutta to be out of danger. Most of the city facilities had been captured by the end of the day. The police were routed, the small military garrison nearby nearly wiped out by the high-powered Chinese and Pakistani assaults. A dozen helicopters flew in the first afternoon, then big transports with armored personnel carriers arrived.

On the second day, Chinese fighters were refueled and armed at the Dhaka military air base and roamed the countryside searching out the Bangladesh-type 54/55 tanks and a few Chinese-made type 59 tanks. Six were blown up the first morning. By noon of the second day, the war in Bangladesh for all practical purposes was over.

The SEALs ate and slept and watched reports of the war on the TV sets. The second day they were there, Murdock received permission from the base to take the men on a conditioning run.

"How far?" the military policeman asked.

"Ten miles."

The corporal swallowed hard. "Well, sir, you can go down the outer boundary of the air base, follow it around. That should cover about eight miles."

"Good," Murdock said. "We'll do it twice."

After they got back, showered, and dressed in fresh cammies the Indian Air Force provided them, a messenger came with an envelope for Murdock.

He opened it, read it, and grinned. "Hey, guys, gather round, we've got news." He read the letter.

Murdock and SEALs, Third Platoon, SEAL Team Seven. Calcutta, India.

Hey, troops, your old buddy Don Stroh giving you some advance warning. Tomorrow morning you'll get official through-channels orders to move back to the good old flattop *Stennis,* which is about where you left her in the Gulf of Thailand. They have it worked out how you'll get there.

Then comes the fun part. Did I say Hong Kong? I certainly did not. I can't say anything until you get the official through-channels orders. So. Have a good night's sleep. Oh, I'm on the carrier, so when you guys get in, the beer's on me.

"Hong Kong? that's part of China now," DeWitt brayed. "The British turned it over three or four years ago. Stroh suggesting that we're going into Hong Kong? He must be nuts."

"Probably, but it does give us something to think about," Murdock said. "At least we won't have to do a conditioning run tomorrow."

"Hong Kong?" DeWitt said. "Must be fifty thousand Chinese troops around that place. This has to be some fucked up Navy mistake. Just got to be."

15

Tijuana, Mexico

Detective Sergeant Mad Dog Sanchez had two men watching Juan Lopez's house. Lopez didn't go back there after the talk he had that afternoon with the police. He didn't go there that night or the next day. Nobody knew where he was.

Mad Dog shrugged and went to the next step. El Gallo Colorado was open at five in the afternoon. It was not the best bistro and cantina in town, but one of the better ones. They had two ex-fighters on the door as bouncers. They kept out people they wanted to and threw out those who caused trouble inside. Both men were heavyweights, six-one and six-three. Mad Dog did not wish to tangle with either one. He had fought welter and now was no more than 165 pounds.

He waved at the two men who knew him. One opened the door without a word. Inside there were about fifteen patrons. Most at the bar. Two danced on the small hardwood floor. Six were actually eating the food from the little kitchen at the side.

He knew the barkeep, who dropped his wipe rag and looked at the far door behind the bar, which had a two-way mirror showing on this side.

"Ayeeee, Detective Sanchez. What would your pleasure be for a drink on the house?"

"Tequila," Sanchez said. Nobody called him Mad Dog within his hearing.

Sanchez tasted the liquor, then put the glass on the bar.

"Pedro, what do you know of Juan Lopez, the creep who hangs around here?"

"Haven't seen him for two days. Someone said he died in a cell at police headquarters." Pedro looked confused and hurried on. He mopped at sweat on his forehead. "At least that was one story going around. You know how stories can grow."

"He was in good health yesterday afternoon when I walked him out of headquarters. You haven't seen him since then?"

"Not the shadow of him, I swear."

"So, where is Adolfo?"

"I don't believe he's here yet?"

Mad Dog grabbed the barkeep's expensive silk shirt, bunched it in his hand and dragged the startled man off his feet and belly up on the bar.

"Don't lie to me, Pedro. I saw you look at Adolfo's door and make some signal. Get back there and tell him I want to see him. Now it will be pleasant. If I have to chase him down, it will be most unpleasant and it will be private."

"Yes, yes. I bring him," Pedro gasped out the words. His air supply was getting halfway cut off by the tight shirt collar. Sanchez let him down to the floor and straightened his shirt.

"Go get Adolfo, now, Pedro."

Pedro wiped his hands on the rag, tossed it on a table behind the bar and scurried down the bar and through the door. Sanchez sipped at his tequila. A good drink should never be hurried. They had some of the best tequila in Baja California. Sanchez carried the drink down to the end of the bar well away from anyone who could hear their talk.

Most of the bar patrons suddenly became interested only in their drinks or food. No one even looked in Sanchez's direction. He smiled thinly.

The man who moments later pushed through the door at the end of the bar and stepped behind it, was about sixty, with graying hair, a white moustache and a white goatee. He wore glasses and squinted through them now at Mad Dog. He wore an expensive sport shirt and slacks. He nodded.

"Ah, yes, Detective Sanchez. Has Pedro been taking care of you? How about a steak diner, my compliments?"

"No, business, old man," Sanchez spoke softly so only the two of them could hear. Pedro had not returned. "I'm looking for a killer who comes to your bar often. Lives here sometimes. I want his name. He's a *gringo*, big guy, could be military. He's been buddy-buddy with Juan Lopez, and now Cuchi Hernandez is dead. I want to talk to this *gringo*."

"What can I do?" Adolfo said. "I have seen him, he's a customer. I have more than a hundred of our fine *Norte Americanos* in my establishment many nights. I can't know details about each one. I know of him, but not a name. He pays his bill, he tips the girls. What is to know?" Adolfo had spoken softly as well.

Adolfo stood away from the bar out of reach of Sanchez.

"You know a lot more than you're telling me. You know him well, Adolfo. I want his name, address, and phone number. I can close you down in two hours, old man. Remember that. Now, once more. Tell me the *gingo*'s name and his phone number. He murdered Chuci and you know it. Now spit out the name or you may not be able to spit anything any more."

Adolfo paled. His forehead showed a sheen of moisture. Twice he coughed and then ran his hand over his face. "Detective Sergeant Sanchez. I understand your wanting to catch a killer. We have too many murders in our town. It is bad for my business. But there just is no way that I can help you."

"No way? I have a way. I'll use Cuchi's favorite game. I'll slice you a few times and see if your memory improves." Mad Dog Sanchez took out a throw knife and flipped it outward holding tight to the handle. A five-inch blade of shiny sharp steel flicked into place and locked. Sanchez pointed the honed steel at Adolfo.

"One last chance old man, or you may wish you had taken up telling nursery rhymes to *niños*." He leaned over the bar and touched the tip of the knife to Adolfo's chest.

Sanchez heard the *cantina*'s door open but ignored it. A

moment later a hand pressed down hard on the side of
Sanchez's neck and he turned. He saw three men larger
then the bouncers at the door who now stood just behind
him. All wore dark blue suits and ties and all had hard faces
showing scar tissue and old wounds. One man's eyelid dan-
gled half closed.

"Is there a problem here, Adolfo?" the taller of the three
said. He took his hand off Sanchez's neck. The detective
turned slowly to stare fully at the three men. All wore the
trademark dark blue suit of an El Padre organization man.
El Padre ran the huge drug wholesale trafficking business
in Tijuana that reportedly channeled 90 percent of all cocaine and marijuana through the west coast of Mexico and
into the United States.

Sanchez shrugged. "A small matter, a difference of opinion."

The tallest of the three with a scar from his right eye in
a curve to his chin spoke again softly so no one else could
hear. "Detective Sanchez. We want you to understand that
there are no hard feelings here. We are businessmen and
we help Adolfo with his protection. If he's in trouble, it's
our job to straighten it out."

Sanchez had heard of these men, or others like them, but
he had never met any of them before. He closed the knife,
slid it in his pocket, and shrugged.

"Simply a small disagreement. He shouldn't have trou-
bled you gentlemen."

None of them smiled or showed any emotion. Sanchez
felt sweat under his arms. His nose itched. He frowned
slightly. "Is there anything more?"

"Yes, we need to end this here, now. We understand that
you are worried about the death of one of our representa-
tives. Yes, he died and no one knows who did it. This man
was a problem of ours, and we resolved the matter. We
would appreciate it if you could simply let the matter rest."

"I have a responsibility as a police detective—"

The taller man held up his hand stopping Sanchez.

"We're sure that you have other cases much more prom-
ising that you should be working on. To encourage you to

do that, we wish to make a contribution to your favorite charity through you." He turned to one of the other men who handed him two thick stacks of peso bills. He held them out to Sanchez.

"This is eighty thousand pesos, roughly ten thousand U.S. dollars. We hope that this act of charity on our part will help you to move on to other cases."

Sanchez felt a surge of delight, then fear. Buying him off? Why? What else had to be behind this? On the other hand, if he refused their money, he was sure that he would be taken into the back room and shot twenty times in the head.

His hands trembled when he reached for the money. "My captain said I had already spent too much time on the Chuci case. He ordered me off it this morning. Yes, yes I think that I can move on to other problems. I'll see that this money goes to a good charity."

Adolfo relaxed.

Sanchez thought his knees would collapse.

The three large men in dark blue suits only smiled, nodded and walked out the front door. Sanchez sipped at his tequila until it was gone, then slid the stacks of bills inside his uniform shirt and made sure they were safely stowed, stopped by his belt. Then he turned and with as much dignity as he could muster, walked out the cantina door and found his car. He was the good charity that the El Padre men had referred to. He had eighty thousand pesos. He would open a separate bank account that even his family would not know about. He drove a mile away but became angrier with each yard he traveled.

How could they do that? Walk in and buy him off in front of a witness? How? He had their money, El Padre's dirty drug money, but they couldn't buy his soul. He'd find out who the *gringo* was, and he knew exactly how. He did a U turn in the middle of the street and swore at the driver who swore at him. He drove back within a half a block of the cantina he had just left and parked. He walked to the back door of El Gallo Colorado and waited. The girls would be coming soon. He saw them arriving from where he stood in the shadows of the next building. They were bright, pretty, and available for two hundred pesos. He waited for the older one he had seen before called Teresa. A minute later, he stopped her and motioned her into the shadows of late afternoon.

"Sergeant Sanchez," he said.

Her face turned upward quickly. "So?"

"I'm hunting a young *gringo* who comes to the cantina often. Sometimes stays several days. Do you remember him?"

"There have been two lately. One in his forties. Bad tipper. The other one doesn't even pay. He's twenty-five or -six. Keeps his hair short but it's blond. Must be six foot three. Yeah, I know him."

"I want his name and phone number."

"Why?"

"He's a hired assassin for the Mexican Mafia or for the drug cartel. Not sure which, but one of them. He recently murdered a man."

"Haven't seen him for a week."

"So, a name?"

"Only one he uses is Howie."

"Phone number?"

"I don't carry that around with me. It's home somewhere."

"Let's go, my car is right down the block."

"I got to go to work."

"The assembly line won't break down if you're a half hour late. Come on. Or I could just arrest you."

She nodded and they went to his car.

Ten minutes later they walked into a modest apartment. It was furnished better than Sanchez's home.

She moved to a small desk and looked through a book, then wrote something on a piece of paper and handed it to him.

"This a San Diego number?"

"Yes."

"No area code. Need one up there."

"You'll have to find that out by calling them."

"Cheeky little whore, aren't you."

She smiled. "You men like some fire, you don't get any at home."

"Since we're here . . ." He reached out and began to unbutton the blue blouse she wore. She caught his hand.

"Three hundred pesos."

He slapped her so hard she staggered two steps to the side.

"No more talk," he said. "Take them off. I have a lot of work to do before the end of the day."

16

Gulf of Thailand
Onboard the *John C. Stennis,* CVN 74
The SEALs arrived back on board the carrier the same way
they had left it, on a COD. They had landed almost twenty-
four hours earlier and now they were getting ready for their
new mission.

They were two men down. Vinnie Van Dyke was still in
the ship's hospital with his chest shot. Dobler was in no
shape to go along. He was in the carrier's medical unit
where they were fighting infection in his leg wound.

"The Ganges might be the holy river of India, but it's
also the main sewer system," one of the Navy doctors said.
He had checked all of the men for any kind of infections
or lung problems, gave them a clean bill of health, and sent
them back to duty.

The twelve SEALs worked over their gear for this special
mission. Murdock and DeWitt had been in a conference
half the morning trying to iron out the logistics. None of
the men had a clue except the two words, *Hong Kong,* that
Don Stroh had told them in his radio message.

"No way it could be Hong Kong," Jaybird chirped. "Hell,
that's right in the middle of about a hundred million Chicoms. They going to sit twiddling their tits while we walk
in and take something or somebody away from them? Hell
no. Even a million rifles is a lot."

"Bet he meant King Kong. He's taking us to that new
movie," Franklin said.

"Oh, no, it got canceled before it was made," Lampedusa
said.

Murdock and DeWitt entered the compartment. There was no call to attention. This was the SEALs and no brass was present.

"So?" Ching called.

"You won't believe this," DeWitt said. "Yes, it is Hong Kong." He waited for the cheers, and yells and catcalls to subside. "I know, I didn't have a clue what we could do in Hong Kong in the middle of all those Chicoms." He shook his head. "I'll have the skipper tell you. He must understand it better than I do."

Murdock snorted. "Not much to understand. Believing it is a different story. The mission is this. There's a Panamanian-registered cruise ship in Hong Kong on a world cruise with almost twelve hundred Americans on board. The Chinese have stopped the ship from sailing, saying that there are spies onboard and they must interview each of the twelve hundred and detain any they consider to be spies. The interviews began yesterday. By the end of the day, they had made it all the way through twenty little old ladies with blue hair and ten older men with prostate trouble.

"Our job is to go in after dark, take out the Chinese security men onboard, get the ship under way, and without clearance or permission to help the crew sail her out of Hong Kong Bay and into the glorious South China Sea."

"That's all there is to it?" Bradford yelped.

"About the size of it. Any suggestions?"

"You give them a plan?" Howie asked.

"No. We were trying to figure out the odds and if it was a risk that the U.S. Navy and the State Department could take."

"Must been a yes," Fernandez said.

"We will have all kinds of support. The carrier is charging toward the area now at thirty knots to get within striking range of the F-eighteens and the Tomcats."

"Sounds like an act of war we're talking about here," Jaybird said. "Tomcats blasting what, Chinese patrol boats?"

"Yes, and maybe a destroyer or two in the harbor," Mur-

dock said. "The State Department says that China has perpe-
trated a mass kidnapping, and any act is acceptable in world
opinion and in diplomatic circles to recover our people."

"We don't have to worry about that part of it. If they
say go, we go. How are we going to rescue a ship of that
size?"

"At night, for sure," Ching said.

"Do we know how many Chinese troops or guards are
onboard?" Mahanani asked.

"No way of knowing right now," DeWitt said. "We
might be able to find out."

"We go in by Pegasus, then underwater to the pier," Canzoneri said. "Then what?"

"How about we go in with our wet suits over civilian
clothes," Paul Jefferson said. "We get onboard with our
weapons and tools, and strip off our wet suits and then we
can blend with the passengers and not be so obvious."

"Good idea, I like that," Murdock said.

"Does the ship need a tug to get away from the pier?"
Howie Anderson asked. "Most of those big rigs do."

"We're clear on that one," DeWitt said. "One of the men
at the meet said this ship can get away from the pier on its
own. More work and slower, but it can be done."

"So, we get onboard, take out the guards and any soldiers
in residence, and get the captain out of his bunk to take the
ship out of port in the middle of the night," Franklin said.

"We still have our EAR weapons," Ostercamp said. "We
should take both of them on the attack."

Murdock looked at Jaybird.

"Yes, sir. We should take them for sure. We used up the
batteries, but they can be charged up and ready to go with
ten shots each in about an hour."

"Good," Murdock said. "Now, how do we get from the
harbor water onboard the liner?"

"Should be ladders all over the place there from water
to dock," Bradford said. "First we take out any guards on
the dock and gangplank. Then we get out of our wets and
go onboard with drag bags holding all of our weapons and
wet gear."

"Once we get onboard?" DeWitt asked.

"Hell, we know ships," Khai said. "We get to the spots the Chicoms would guard: the engine room, the bridge, security, communications room, and engineering. We get them, and we own the ship. Then we clean up on any more guards on the craft."

"Damn, we did you officer guys' work for you again on the planning stages," Jaybird said.

"Glad for the help. The captain says we have been making thirty knots now for two days, over fourteen hundred miles. He says we will be in range for his eighteens and Tomcats by dusk today. He has three units off Hong Kong about forty miles, including a guided missile destroyer that can land a forty-six. As soon as the carrier gets in range for the forty-six to get to the destroyer, we'll be in a go mode."

"When will that be?" Jaybird asked. "The forty-six has a range of about four hundred miles."

"We'll leave that up to the navigators upstairs," Murdock said. "So, let's get ready to travel."

"What about the civilian clothes?" Jefferson asked. "I didn't bring any with me."

DeWitt nodded. "I'll talk to our carrier liaison. I want the sizes of all of you guys. We'll have to borrow civvies from the men onboard. Might take some time. A three by five card for each of you with your pants size, shirt, etc. Do it now."

Murdock went back to the carrier's captain who was playing chess with Stroh in his cabin.

"Stroh, I didn't even know you could play chess."

"He can't," Captain Robertson said. They all laughed.

"Captain, we can do it. I've talked to my planning committee. We've got a weapon that is non-lethal, called the EAR. That stands for 'enhanced acoustic rifle.' It sends out a high-powered blast of air that knocks out the people it hits for four hours. Be ideal. We'll need a Pegasus to get us near the harbor. Then we go underwater to the pier of this ship. What's its name?"

"*Queen of the Seas.*"

"When we get to the dock, we'll take off our wet suits and have civilian clothes on underneath. We take out any guards on the dock and the area with the EAR, then board the ship. We figure to go up the gangplank about oh one hundred."

"What about worst-case scenario?" the captain asked.

"If we can't get to the ship, we retreat, call in the Pegasus on the SATCOM and return to the destroyer. If we get onboard and find ourselves outgunned, shot to pieces, and unable to do the job, we go wet, find our Draegr rebreathers and get back to the Pegasus. That isn't going to happen."

"Very well, Commander. Our navigator tells me we'll be within range for the chopper to reach the destroyer about fourteen hundred. Will that give you time to get onboard set up the Pegasus and get to your swim point on time?"

"Looks good, Captain. If there're any glitches we can delay by twenty-four. As I understand there's no time crisis onboard the ship."

"That's right. But the sooner the better the CNO says."

"Understood sir."

"Good luck, Commander. That will be all."

Murdock stood, came to attention, and walked out of the captain's quarters with Stroh.

"You didn't say much in there, big hairy CIA man."

"Nothing to say, your party." He frowned. "Speaking of hairy, I'm not too sure about this one. Too damn many variables we can't tie down. What if they have a company of troops quartered a block away and they get a panic call from some Chicom on the ship? What if—"

Murdock held up his hand. "Hey, we know all the 'what ifs.' We've talked out a lot of them, we'll go in and do it by our plan, our book. If that doesn't work, we adapt, we innovate, we change, we go a different way. Many ways to skin this big ship cat."

"Yeah. Figured you'd have an answer. I still think it could turn into a whole bucket full of worms."

"If it does, we'll throw the bucket overboard." Murdock turned and looked hard at the CIA man. "Hey Company man, you have any late dope you aren't telling me about?"

"So help me, Murdock. Just what you heard. The captain of the *Queen of the Seas* is a Dutchman who speaks good English. He has a lot of Filipinos in the crew as well as Dutch and Greek. Most of them speak English. Best I can do."

"Tell the president we'll do our best. I better get back with the men."

The SEALs hooted at some of the clothes that came for them. They at last found something to fit everyone that wasn't too outlandish. None of them looked exactly like upper-class tourists, but the only ones they had to fool were the Chicoms.

The timeline held. At 1400 they took off in a 46 chopper heading for the destroyer. It had positioned itself thirty miles off shore from Hong Kong. It would be an hour and a half on the Pegasus at twenty knots average. Murdock didn't think about the timing. He'd do that after they were on the destroyer and had checked out the Pegasus and all of their equipment. They wore their civilian clothes to get used to them. Murdock chuckled as he watched his men in the chopper. What a motley crew they were. They looked like some college tennis team heading for a match.

An hour later, Murdock settled into the quarters they had provided. His crew was fed and then told to get some sleep. They would be up all night and would need the rest.

Murdock and DeWitt talked with the destroyer's captain, a three-striper named Lason.

"We'll have a SATCOM on line with you on channel two," Larson said. "The Pegasus will also be on the channel with a SATCOM. As I understand it, any exfiltration support you need will come from the *Stennis* in the form of F-fourteens and F-eighteens. Now, how do we work out your timing?"

They kicked it around figured an hour and a half in the Pegasus to a point just off Hong Kong Harbor.

"We can get you within two miles of the harbor entrance, but beyond that we could get in big trouble. There's a whole shitpot full of islands around there, and the harbor is on the north side of the island. We're south of that."

"Two or three miles out will be fine. A warmup for our work on shore. Do we have any idea where in the harbor the cruise ship is?"

"No, but those things always have a million lights on them. Should stand out like a WP flare."

They decided they would shove off in the Pegasus at 2200. That would be an hour and a half for the boat ride, a half hour to swim into the port and another half hour to find the ship. Then they could be in position by 0100 to take her down.

For weapons assignment, they decided on taking all of the H&K MP5s they had.

"Should all be close-in work," DeWitt said. "Be sure to have a pistol along and two mags."

Murdock had the only Bull Pup for any long-range action, and Bradford and Mahanani were given the EAR guns. They wound up with ten MP5s, the Bull Pup, two EARS, and one Colt M4A1 with grenade launcher. Their drag bags were light this time. They would carry only weapons and ammo, and a few grenades. Murdock decided to take a few quarter-pound chunks of TNAZ in case some of the Chicoms barricaded themselves.

When the Pegasus slowed to five knots, the SEALs could see the massive lights of Hong Kong across the water.

"Looks like a circus over there," Ching said.

"Over ten million people," Jaybird said. "That's the size of New York City and Chicago thrown together."

The Pegasus had the throttle at five knots as they worked through the West Lamma Channel due north to the East Lamma Channel and on north until they could see the sweep of Victoria as it rounded the north side of the Hong Kong island. It would be a three-mile swim around Victoria and then slightly south into Hong Kong Harbor itself.

They could see Kowloon just across the bay from the harbor and New Kowloon to the north, one giant sea of lights.

The young ensign named to lead the Pegasus crew was not happy. "Hell I'm ten miles inside territorial China already," he wailed. "You guys can do three miles, can't you? Figure that's about how far it is around the city of Victoria there to the harbor."

"No sweat," Murdock said. "When you come back for us, if you have to, we'll get to this point. We hope to be sailing out on the ship with a batch of Navy fighter escorts."

The SEALs had been suited up in their wets and Draegr rebreathers. Murdock gave hand signals and the SEALs went into the water, one by one. Both squads were tied together with buddy lines that stretched between the eight men with Bravo and the six on the Alpha Squad. They went down fifteen feet, checked their compass bearings and headed for the harbor.

After a mile, Murdock surfaced with his men and saw thirteen dark blobs in the water nearby. They swam together compared notes and dove again. Their next surfacing would be at the edge of the harbor to see if it was like the charts they had seen.

They swam through the dark waters in their two teams, counting strokes until they came to what should be two more miles. Murdock came up last, and found DeWitt eying the harbor. The big luxury cruise ship wasn't hard to find. It indeed had five to ten thousand white lights outlining the ship itself, on the lines from the bow and stern to the highest point on the ship, and glowing on every deck.

"Half mile more," Murdock said. They dove again. This time they had tied all fourteen men together. Now was no time to get lost.

They were about to surface when they heard the snarl of a motor through the water. They went deeper and felt the ship plowing the waters overhead as it moved out the channel.

Murdock gave two sharp jerks on the buddy line and surfaced. Soon all the SEALs were spitting water and breathing fresh air. Murdock found DeWitt.

"Big freighter," DeWitt said. They all heard the next sound, the eerie whine of a high-speed engine. They turned toward the harbor and saw a patrol boat with searchlight

and flashing red lights heading directly for them. It was
only a hundred yards away.

"Dive, dive, dive," Murdock said and the SEALs pulled
on their rebreathers and duck dived, then stroked surely
downward to get to twenty feet. Murdock scowled through
his mask. How could anyone know they were there? How
could a Chinese patrol boat be coming after them?

17

The SEALs, still tied together, swam forward underwater. Murdock could hear the craft coming closer. All he could think of were depth charges. What if the boat had them and set one at twenty feet? It would blow all of the SEALs right out of the water and into hell. No, no, patrol boats didn't have depth charges. He'd been seeing too many submarine movies lately. So what was the patrol boat doing?

It came closer and Murdock wanted to hold his breath. Then the engine sounds were louder until they rumbled directly over the SEALs.

A moment later it was gone, speeding away, and the sounds coming softer with each minute. Murdock gave two quick tugs on the buddy line that were repeated down the row and the SEALs went up. Murdock looked around as soon as his face broke the surface. They were off course. They were around the point of Victoria and could see into the harbor. Another quarter of a mile.

He pointed down and they dove and swam forward on Murdock's new course. He used the underwater compass and moved strongly forward. Just inside the harbor, the SEALs surfaced again. Now they could see the luxury liner at the dock. The huge white-painted ship was awash with light from all the strings of bulbs. Murdock surveyed the area.

Jaybird popped up beside him. "That old dock just aft of the cruise ship might be a good spot to set up."

"You and Lam check it out," Murdock said. He gave three jerks on the nylon line and the SEALs untied themselves. They were a hundred yards from the old dock.

"We'll move slowly toward shore," Murdock whispered to the man closest to him and the word was passed to the rest. They submerged and swam toward the shoreline that was built up to the water's edge with warehouses, docks, and a pair of freighters.

Jaybird met them just off the freighters. "Lam is scouting out the area again, but it looks good. Nobody around. Hasn't been used for a while. Some construction going on topside. Plenty of room below it and a dry route to the dock. Puts us about fifty yards from the end of the liner."

"Let's move," Murdock said and the SEALs swam on the surface doing an easy breast stroke with only their faces out of the water.

The water ended twenty feet from the foundations for the pier and the ground was mostly dry. The SEALs found their spots and pulled off their wet suits and Draegrs and put them in their drag bags. They arranged the bags so their weapons were on top. Then they checked out each other. They had on their civilian clothes and while not looking like your ordinary middle-age tourist, they might pass for the part.

Murdock and Lam went to the top of the steps up to the dock, and surveyed the luxury liner. There were three soldiers guarding a closed loading hatch that was dock level a quarter of the way down the long ship. At the gangplank near the center of the ship were eight guards, four on each side. Two more Chinese soldiers stood guard at the top of the gangplank.

"Get an EAR up here," Murdock whispered down the steps. Bradford came up.

"She's fully charged and ready to go," Bradford said. He looked at the targets. "Should get all eight of them at the gangplank first with one shot. Then a second one ten seconds later for the three guys at the hatch."

"Bring up the other EAR," Murdock whispered down the steps. Fernandez came up with it. Murdock moved aside to make room for the other gunner. "Bradford, take the gangplank, then when the two men at the top start down, nail them."

"Fernandez, you have the three men at the loading hatch this side. Let's do it."

The men both nodded. "Sight in and fire on my command. Ready, and fire."

The soft *whooshing* sound of the enhanced rifles hardly made a dent in what they realized was a low level hum of late night traffic on the island.

The eight guards at the gangplank dissolved into masses of sleeping jelly, as they fell where they had been standing. None of them moved after hitting the concrete. Some excited chatter filtered down from the guards at the top of the gangplank. Fernandez's round had blasted the three closer guards and they wobbled a moment, then went down, their rifles clattering on the concrete dock surface.

Bradford watched the guards at the top of the gangplank. They hesitated then both ran down the steps. Bradford led them just a hair and fired. The blast of enhanced air slammed into the two men. Knocked one man off the gangplank to land hard on the concrete twenty feet below. The other one sagged and passed out on the steps themselves.

The SEALs had on their new Motorolas, replacements for the ones they had taken swimming in Bangladesh.

"Jefferson, Bradford, and Ching on me," Murdock said. "We're the first up the gangplank. We'll clear and then the rest of you charge onto the ship in a rush and get to your assigned areas. Let's move."

They ran down the forty yards to the gangplank, carrying their drag bags, their weapons out and ready, locked, and loaded.

"Hell, we don't come close to looking like tourists," Jefferson said. Murdock, Ching, Bradford, and Jefferson stepped over the prostrate soldiers as they approached the gangplank. The ship rode low on the tide and the ramp up to the rail was only twenty steps. Murdock led them. Their line would be that they were new crewmen just assigned. Just as they topped the plank and stepped into the lobby-type two-story entryhall of the ship, a Chinese soldier came out of a doorway and stared at them. He saw their weapons and reached for a pistol. Bradford hit him with an EAR round and the soldier took a step backward, then collapsed like a rag doll on the soft red carpet of the ship.

Before the four could signal the others, three Chinese in civilian dress left another door and headed for the gangplank. They were drunk and walking with just a slight stagger. They laughed at some joke, continued past Murdock and his men without paying any attention to them, and headed down the gangplank.

"Let them go," Murdock whispered into his mike.

A stream of Mandarin sounded directly behind them. They turned to see a Chinese soldier with officer epaulets. He shouted something in Mandarin, then he saw the SEAL's weapons and lifted a submachine gun. Before he could fire, Murdock sent a silenced three-round burst from an MP5 subgun into his chest. He slammed backward against the wall and slowly crumpled, the weapon falling to the carpeted floor. Bradford and Jefferson caught the dead Chinese officer by the arms and dragged him through a door into a dark office and hurried out.

"SEALs, come on up," Murdock said on his Motorola. The four men looked around, saw no more guards, and headed for their objective, the bridge. It would be forward at the top level of the ship. Murdock saw the elevators and led his men that way. The doors on the elevators opened and a couple came out. Their arms were around each other and they had some trouble walking. The girl giggled and stared up at the man. They turned and weaved down a companionway, not even noticing the SEALs who had held their weapons behind their legs. They still carried their drag bags, looking for a good place to hide them.

The elevator took them to the top to the Lido deck. It was open in the center with a swimming pool and deck tennis courts there and a two-story bridge area at the bow of the big ship. The SEALs headed that way. They had just passed the swimming pool and hurried around the tennis courts when a Chinese soldier jumped out from behind a wall and challenged them.

Below on the dock, the other SEALs quickly bound the hands and ankles of the thirteen unconscious Chinese sol-

diers, then raced up the gangplank. All had assignments and
headed into the areas where they could find their targets.

On the Lido deck, Ching shouted something at the Chinese guard who had jumped out and confronted the four
SEALs. It startled the soldier and confused him. In that
fraction of a second, Bradford put him down with an EAR
shot. The man shuddered, then his eyes went wide and
closed as he slumped to the floor, his submachine gun clattering away from him.

Just ahead they saw a door marked "Bridge, Authorized
Personnel Only." Murdock tried the door, it was unlocked.
He and the rest of the SEALs dropped their drag bags in
the corner of the deck and opened the door. Inside was a
corridor with doors opening off it. Straight ahead forty feet
they saw stairs. They took them to the upper level. Another
door blocked their way.

Murdock tested the handle, turned it gently and pulled
the door open an inch. Inside he saw the bridge, a wide
expanse with windows around the entire area. Near the
front was a large console with various video monitors and
a set of controls. A crewman in white uniform stood there
watching everything.

On the far side Murdock saw three Chinese playing some
kind of game at a small table. Another soldier with epaulets
of an officer watched the crewman at the console. Murdock
pointed to Bradford, and held up three fingers pointing to
the left. Bradford moved up beside Murdock, saw the targets and aimed the weapon through the door. Then Murdock shook his head and pulled Bradford back.

"Too confined a space. Everyone inside would be out.
We'll go in and cover them. Use silent rounds if needed.

The four SEALs burst into the room, weapons up, covering the Chinese. The officer's eyes widened, then he
scowled and slowly reached for a pistol at his waist. Murdock shot him in the shoulder and he bellowed in pain but
didn't fall. The three Chinese at the game, stood slowly.
None had a weapon within reach.

"Who the hell are you guys?" the crewman asked.

"Navy SEALs," Murdock said. "Come to get your ass

out of the fire. We'll need your help. Get your captain up here, now. Tell him we're onboard and taking you out of Hong Kong."

The SEALs tied the four Chinese hand and foot with riot cuffs and cinched them tight. They bound up the officer's shoulder wound to stop the bleeding.

The crewman held out his hand.

"Norm Hadilston, from Chicago. I'm the second officer. Glad to see you guys. This is fantastic. I thought we were stuck here for a month or so. How can you break us out of this jail?"

"Not sure, Hadilston. That's why we want to talk to your captain." Murdock's earpiece sounded.

"Cap. Lam. We're at the engine room, but there are some problems here. We haven't attacked yet, but there are six Chinese in there and all are awake and armed. No sign of any crew. We're working on it."

"Roger that, Lam. Take it slow and quiet. Keep them away from the intercom. We don't want any loud speaker jazz."

Hadilston watched the interchange. "I'll call the captain at once. He isn't a sound sleeper. Should be here in five minutes."

"If we get you free of the Chinese onboard, can you move the ship away from the pier and head out the channel without any tugs?"

Hadilston scowled then slowly nodded. "Yes, I've seen it done. Not easy but with a little luck we can do it."

"Good, now we need control. My man said some problem in the engine room."

"The Chinese are fascinated with our engines. They have some engineers down there, I think, besides the soldiers."

Several decks below the bridge, Lieutenant (j.g.) DeWitt stared at the door marked "Communications." No one had entered or left as he and two men watched. There had been no passengers in the companionway.

He and Ostercamp and Mahanani moved up on each side of the door, then DeWitt tried the knob. It turned and he jerked the door open and jumped inside. One sleepy crewman lifted his head out of his hands and stared at them.

"Who the hell are you guys?" he asked.

DeWitt cleared the room with darting glances. There was no one else in the room filled with radio equipment, fax machines, readout screens, and video monitors.

"We're the guys who are going to get your ass out of a sling," Ostercamp said. "Any Chicoms usually stand guard in here?"

"Nope, no Chinks at all. Who are you guys?"

"U.S. Navy SEALs," DeWitt said. "Can you lock the door from the inside and keep everyone out?"

"Sure, but—"

"Good, we've got other jobs to do. You should be getting instructions from your Captain shortly. Just hang in here with us. We hope to be moving this ship before daylight."

All of the SEALs heard the warning in their earpieces.

"Tran at the gangplank. We've got trouble. Two army trucks just pulled up with what looks like fifteen men in each one. I've got the EAR. Should I use it if they start to board?"

"Yes," Murdock said at once. "Put them down now, even if they don't start to board. They'll find the guards down."

At the gangplank, Tran "Train" Khai sighted in on the closest army truck. The fifteen men had gathered around it and he fired.

He watched the Chinese soldiers shiver and stare in astonishment, then they fell down like dominoes, one after the other. Some shouts came from the men at the other truck.

"Eight thousand, nine thousand, ten thousand," Tran counted, then he fired at the second truck. The Chinese there had started to run for the first truck and two of them evidently were outside the effects of the EAR. The rest at the truck went down and out. Tran kept his weapon trained on the two men who stopped and looked back at their own truck. They both ran back and began to look at their unconscious buddies.

"Nine thousand, ten thousand, eleven thousand . . ." Tran fired again nailing the last two men. He touched his mike.

"Last of the thirty men down and out," he said on the Motorola.

On the bridge, Captain Omar Prestwick hurried through the door. He had on his white uniform shirt and pants, but he hadn't taken time to tuck in his shirt. He was also barefooted.

"Damn, real live U.S. Navy SEALs?" He held out his hand. "Prestwick here. Wonderfully glad to see you. Can you really get us out of Hong Kong?"

"Going to try, Captain. I'm Lieutenant Commander Murdock. We have control of the communications room. We're working on the engine room, engineering, and security. What else do we need to control to get the ship under way?"

"Move it, tonight, without tugs?"

"Doubt if we could call up a tug or two without Chinese permission. I understand you can move away from the pier without tugs."

"Yes, but damn hard. Hell, worth a try. If we can control the ship. You have commo. We need engineering and engine. Takes some time to get us ready to move. Not like kick-staring a Harley."

He stared at Murdock and the other men's weapons.

"You have real bullets in those guns, I'd guess. Be careful so you don't shoot up a batch of my passengers."

"We're taking all precautions, Captain."

Murdock held up his hand as his earpiece spoke.

"Skipper, Fernandez at engineering. We're inside. We have half of it. There's another big room two Chicom soldiers ran into and we're not sure how to get them out."

"Hold, we'll send you some help. DeWitt can you move to engineering and assist."

"That's a roger, skipper. We're on our way."

"Captain, my man says two Chinese are in a second room at engineering. Is that the vital one?"

"Yes, we need both rooms to move the ship. They have to get in there without damaging anything. Let me get our chief engineer down there to help them." The captain moved to the phone and dialed.

Two decks below at the security office, Hans Kok, checked the security monitors that covered twenty-four main sections of the passenger areas of the big ship. Earlier he had seen what looked like some young men with weapons, but he figured it must be some kind of program the entertainers were working on. But it was late for that.

Then he spotted another one, this time there was no doubt, it was a man with a submachine gun moving cautiously down a hall. What the hell was going on? He was about to call his supervisor when he saw the time: almost 2:00 A.M. The Chinese soldier guard who had been stationed with him snored softly to one side where he sat in a soft chair. His automatic rifle lay across his chest, the butt on the floor.

Kok checked the other monitors. Twice more he saw young men with weapons moving around the ship. They were in civilian clothes, but acted like soldiers. What should he do? Notify the Chinese? Now that would be dumb. Call the captain? At 2:00 A.M. that would be bold. Just wait and see what happened?

He looked up as the door to the room burst open and three men with weapons surged into the room. He looked at the ugly snouts of the three submachine guns pointed at him and slowly raised his hands. He pointed to the Chinese soldier. Without a sound, one of the men eased up to the Chinese and hit him on the head with the side of his machine gun. Then the man grabbed the rifle as the Chinese slumped unconscious.

"Do you speak English?" Jefferson asked.

On the bridge, Murdock heard a message in his earpiece.

"Cap, we've got real troubles down here in the engine room. We're in the first section, but the next section seems to be the important one. The Chicoms must have seen us coming. They have the door locked down and five or six of them have firing positions inside all aimed at the door. You better get down here and see what the fuck we can do."

18

Captain Prestwick found his shoes and led Murdock and Bradford down to the engine room. They met no Chinese on the walk.

"How many Chinese onboard?" Murdock asked.

"About thirty. Most of them are sleeping in vacant rooms. I don't even know which ones. The purser should know. I'll call him and he will give me the room numbers."

At the engine compartment Murdock was surprised at the size of the place. In the far end was a closed off space where the controls and instruments were situated. Lam materialized from behind some huge pipes.

"Skipper, not sure how to dig these guys out. The door is locked but we could go through it. Trouble is, I don't know what a fire fight with live rounds might do to these tubes and pipes."

"Good thinking," Captain Prestwick said. "I have a key to open the door, but what then?"

"An EAR round," Bradford said.

"What if we get a bounce back here and it puts all of us down as well for four hours?" Murdock asked.

"Yeah, the quarters are a bit close."

"Flash bang?" Lam asked.

"Could do it," Murdock said. "Three of them. I have one."

They found three, the captain took out a master key and three men pulled flash-bang grenade pins and held down the arming handles.

"Open the door only six inches," Murdock said. "We

pitch the flash bangs in to the middle of the area." He nodded at the captain.

"Unlock it and pull it open."

He did. The men threw in the grenades, felt one rifle round hit the metal door, then the captain pushed the door shut and latched it as the strobes went off inside and the six loud explosive sounds came though the walls.

The moment the sounds died, Murdock jerked open the door and the SEALs charged into the room. There were no shots fired. The six Chinese were all on the floor moaning and holding their ears. All had their eyes shut. The SEALs bound them with riot cuffs and found the two crewmen in a locked side room. They came out, and the captain told them that they might get under way in a few hours. The men began to check controls and instruments.

"Commander, you said there were some problems at engineering?" Captain Prestwick asked.

"Yes, can you take us there?"

Five minutes later they came to the engineering section where Fernandez watched a door.

"In there, Skipper. Two of them, they saw me and holed up. That room important?"

"If we want to run the ship," Murdock said. "Captain, any ideas? A back door, flood the thing with teargas?"

"No back door, no tear gas. It's a small room. One of those flash bangs should do it."

Fernandez had one. The captain unlocked the door, Fernandez threw in the non-lethal grenade and two minutes later engineering was back in friendly hands.

The captain smiled. "I think I own my ship again. No, those other Chinese with their submachine guns could still kill some of my passengers. Let's wake up the purser and find out which rooms the Chinese are using.

"The thirty men you mentioned, did that include the guards out front?"

The captain shook his head. "No, thirty onboard. You've accounted for some already, four on the bridge, six in engineering, maybe three or four more. That should leave twelve or fourteen sleeping. We need to surprise them before they can get to their guns."

The purser was not pleased to be rousted out of bed at 0245, but when he saw the SEALs he became absolutely chipper and ecstatic.

"Damn right I know where they are, the fourteen rooms they demanded. All in the crew quarters. I put them in the four to a room area. I call it our dormitory rooms. They have four of them side by side. I'll show you exactly where they are."

Murdock called in reserves on the Motorola. He had eight men marching down the corridors to the crew deck. The purser opened the first door and four SEALs charged in, binding hands and feet on two Chinese before they knew what happened. One soldier put up a fight but was promptly knocked out with a slash of an MP5. They went to the end of the four rooms and opened that one.

In the last of the four rooms there were only three men, and one was awake and got off a shot with a pistol. The round missed and Howie Anderson charged him and broke his arm taking the weapon away from him.

"Little shit, I should break your neck," Howie brayed. He was the closest to the fired round.

Captain Prestwick couldn't keep a delighted smile off his face. It was 0323 when the last Chinese was bound. All were walked to the Promenade deck and their ankles retied. They would be put off the ship as soon as it was ready to pull away. The ship's engines fired up, and the crew alerted, bailing out of warm beds ready for action.

The captain said it would take at least an hour to get the ship ready to move. There were no other large ships docked near the *Queen of the Seas*. The SEALs counted twenty-eight Chinese ready to be kicked off the ship.

"The other two were the ones at the gangplank," Lam said. "That makes the thirty we need. No stowaways."

By 0430, Captain Prestwick said they were ready. The SEALs cut the plastic cuffs on the Chinese men's feet and led them down the gangplank. Once on the dock their feet were bound with another riot cuff and they were added to the tethered Chinese on the dock.

Murdock was the last SEAL up the gangplank before it was released by the ship. It would be stowed on the dock later.

Murdock hurried to the bridge. He wanted to see the captain maneuver the big ship out into the channel. At the same time, he called on Howie Anderson to bring up the SATCOM. Time to alert the fly boys that they might be needed. It wouldn't take them long to get to Hong Kong, and if they were in the area it would be even better.

"*Queen* here, CAG," Murdock said on the SATCOM. "We've cast off our lines and are starting to maneuver into the bay. So far no Chinese other than those unconscious or tied up, know what's going on. There could be an alarm sounded at any time. Quicker here the better."

"We've had cover on you for about an hour," the CAG on the aircraft carrier *Stennis* said. "You can talk to them on channel two on your dial. I'll turn you over to them."

Murdock made contact on the first transmission.

"Skyhigh, this is the *Queen*, glad you're nearby. We're pushing away from the dock now. No alarm yet. Will let you know what's happening."

"Good, *Queen*. We're flying CAP about ten miles off shore. Can be in your area in three or four minutes. Good luck."

Murdock watched the huge ship edge away from the pier. She used some kind of side thrusters that blew water to the side of the ship to ease her into or away from a dock. At last they were twenty feet away, but not anywhere near far enough to start a turn. The engines purred and they moved like a snail with an outhouse on its back.

Murdock scowled. Damn, what about those destroyers he heard were based in Hong Kong? They could do thirty to thirty-two knots. The *Queen* could make twenty if she were at top speed. No contest if one of the Chinese destroyers was sent on a chase. He had no idea where the nearest Chinese military air base might be. The Tomcats could take care of the fighters, and the F18s could handle patrol boats, but would they sink a destroyer?

They were forty yards away from the pier when the nose of the big ship began to come around so she could head out of the harbor, and to the northwest at the same time. A siren wailed from the pier and Murdock could see the flashing lights of a police vehicle.

"Somebody knows that we're gone," the captain said.

Soon they were turned and picked up speed as they headed northwest out of the port. Far back, Murdock could see lights coming toward them, could be a patrol boat. He went to the Motorola.

"Gunners on the EAR, how many shots do you have left on this charge?"

Bradford came on first. "I'd say six."

Train answered next. "Near as I can tell I have seven left."

"Good, both of you get on the Pomenade deck. One on each side as far forward as practical. We may have some company soon. I see one, now three sets of lights heading our way. We'll wait until they get in range and listen to them order us back to the dock. When they are close enough and before they open fire, we hit them with one round of EAR. That should put them dead in the water."

"That's a roger," Bradford said. "Weapons free?"

"No, on my command."

"Roger," Train said.

Captain Prestwick moved over by Murdock. "This is quite a team you have here. You really get things done."

"Our job, Captain. I just hope we don't have any major problems, like a Chinese destroyer or a frigate. Both could do serious damage to your bridge, which is where they would shoot with machine guns and rockets."

The captain paled and Murdock hurried on.

"We have jet fighters for support if we need them. They will track any warship and fend it off well out of range. At least we hope they will. We can handle the smaller patrol and harbor boats.

"Patrol boat coming up fast on our stern," one of the crew on the bridge said.

"Right. Steady as she goes. We need to get away from here as fast as we can."

"What's that, Captain, twenty knots?"

"We're going twenty-two right now. We'll see."

"Coming up fast, Skipper," Bradford said. "She looks to be about a forty footer."

"Let her come by you both. EAR guns hold your position near the bow on the Pomenade. That's where your shots will be from. The patrol craft will try hailing us first, I'm sure."

"If not?" Train asked.

"If any shots are fired by the craft, you have weapons free to fire one round."

"Confirmed," Bradford and Train said almost at the same time.

"Patrol craft at three hundred yards astern, Captain," the First Officer said.

"Noted."

Murdock left the bridge, ran down the steps to the Promenade deck and hurried forward. He was on Train's side. He spotted the SEAL about forty yards ahead of him. He could also see the first patrol boat jolting through the quiet waters at top speed and closing the gap between the boats.

Train turned as Murdock came up. "My side," Train said. "He can't be fifty yards off."

Train held the EAR weapon tightly against his thigh to make it hard to see as the patrol craft caught the luxury liner and moved ahead toward the bow. It slowed opposite the high bridge and a loudspeaker sounded.

"*Queen of the Seas*, you are commanded to throttle back and take on boarders. I say again, throttle back to all stop and prepare to take on boarders."

The big ship kept moving, turning away slightly from the patrol boat. The small craft matched the turn and gave the warning again. When there was no response to the command, a man hurried on the fore deck of the craft and sat at what looked like a machine gun.

"Fire, Train," Murdock said. It took him a moment to refine his sight on the broad side of the ship and fired. The *whoosh* came and then almost at once the man on the machine gun fell off the seat and lay on the deck. The boat kept moving but Murdock figured there was no one conscious on board. Lam was still on the bridge.

"Lam, ask the captain to make a sharper turn, I think the patrol boat is on auto pilot. The personnel on board are taking a nap."

Murdock saw the big boat swing more to the left. This time the patrol boat did not follow, it kept moving straight ahead and would, Murdock decided, until it ran out of diesel or was boarded by friendly forces.

He turned to look for the other patrol boats he'd seen before as lights. He found only one, and it was five minutes away.

"Anderson, find me on the forward Promenade deck with the SATCOM." Two minutes later Murdock took the handset.

"Skyhigh, this is *Queen*, talk to me."

"*Queen*, holding ten out. Any problems?"

"We had one patrol boat that we took care of. Another set of lights coming but about the same size. How long does it take to get a Chinese destroyer up to power and moving after us?"

"I'd say three hours. Could have personnel problems. In two hours you'll be well into international waters."

"What about those channels and all the islands? Doesn't that mean the international part is twenty beyond them?"

"Not sure, *Queen*. I'll ask the professor."

There was a lot of empty air. The boat behind them was gaining rapidly. It must be doing forty knots. Still two minutes away.

"*Queen*, nobody awake is sure. You're hitting the West Lamma Channel, I'd bet. That puts you nine miles from the tip of the north end of Victoria and you're past the last Chinese Island. That's a half hour for you guys at twenty-two knots."

"Sounds better. We have one small problem in that patrol boat. She's almost here. Hold."

Murdock still carried the Bull Pup. He worked aft to a good firing position and waited. He knew the Chinese patrol craft would be in radio contact with each other. When the lead boat went dead on the air, the back one wouldn't take any chances. Its commander would open fire as soon as he was within range. Murdock checked the laser sighting on the boat and figured it was about a mile and a half away. In another half mile the patrol boat's .50 caliber would be in range, and Murdock would bet the ranch that he would fire.

Time seemed to crawl by. Murdock checked the patrol rig twice a minute. That didn't make it come any sooner. Now Murdock was following the boat with the scope and the laser. He could see someone onboard, on a .50-caliber machine gun. The man charged in a round. Do it now.

Murdock lasered on the boat and fired. The jolt to his shoulder as the 20mm round went off and spun out of the barrel was as usual; but it had been a while, and it surprised Murdock. He got on target with his scope again and saw the round explode in the small boat's antenna. He worked the bolt and fired again, this time the round exploded on target slightly forward, smashing out the glass in the small bridge area and probably killing the driver.

The boat made a slow turn to the left and then went dead.

"Nice shooting, Skipper," Train said. "That motherfucker was about ready to rake us with some fifties, wasn't he?"

"He was."

"Now what other problems can we try and stay away from?"

"Skipper," Lam called.

"Go, Lam."

"The captain wants you up here pronto. To the bridge."

"I'm moving."

Three minutes later, Murdock walked into the bridge and looked at Captain Prestwick who put down the phone and scowled. He shook his head and then saw Murdock.

"Our commo people have been monitoring Chinese radio

in the port. The boys over there are mad as hell. They know they have lost two patrol boats and they are working on getting a frigate under way. The frigate was due to sail at six this morning which is just a little more than two hours from now. So she was getting steam up and going through pre-sailing procedures. They just compressed those and the frigate will be ready to sail in thirty minutes.

"We've turned around the tip of Victoria, and are on a heading almost due south, but we have about ten miles to sail to get out of the islands down there. So technically we'll still be in Chinese water. In a half hour we should make it to the islands, but not out the twenty miles of territorial water that China claims. You better call in your big guys with the wings on them for some help."

19

Murdock picked up the SATCOM handset and hit the send button.

"Skyhigh give us a call. This is *Queen*."

"Read you, *Queen. Que pasada?*"

"Small problem. A frigate in Hong Kong was getting ready to sail on an exercise at oh six hundred. They will now shove off in twenty-three minutes. We'll just about be at the edge of the Chinese islands down there by the time they catch us. Any ideas?"

"We'll discourage them before they get to you. Some flyovers, maybe a rocket or two across their bow. Give them the idea we don't want them following you."

"Sounds good to me. You have guns free?"

"Will check with CAG but we should be free."

"Weapons we have can't stop a frigate. Good luck, Skyhigh."

"Same-o, same-o in the wet."

Captain Prestwick looked at Murdock. "That's pretty heavy action you're talking about."

"Only kind the Chinese understand. A slap in the face doesn't help much. A roundhouse right to the jaw is more effective. A CIA guy I know says our State Department has authorized extreme measures to rescue your ship. They say the Chinese have committed an extreme act of barbarism in kidnapping four thousand people. They say the international community will accept any action to get you back, including what otherwise might be considered an act of war. See how important this ship and you people are?"

Captain Prestwick smiled. "Well now, it's good to know

that we were missed. When we get free, we'll have some other problems to deal with. For example we're three days behind our schedule. We might not have dockage at our next stop, and our supplies might run a little low."

"Damn," Murdock said. "The rich guys will have only one entrée instead of their choice of three?"

The captain laughed. "Yeah, I guess that's about the size of it. But will we get complaints!"

"Tell them they have been a part of history, and work up something in your print shop to commemorate the occasion. Then sign it for all twelve hundred and you should have a winner."

The captain brightened. "Well now, that does sound like a good idea."

The phone rang and a crewman pointed to the captain. He took it and listened for a minute. "Yes, understood." He hung up.

"One more small problem. Our overhead radar reports that a flight of three aircraft is approaching us from the east at mach one speed. They suspect they are Chinese fighter aircraft."

Murdock took the SATCOM handset again.

"Skyhigh, we have any Tomcats up there? We just picked up three bogies coming in from the east. Probably MiGs. You have any data?"

"We have them. Three Cats will meet them for some friendly conversation. The Cats don't have weapons free unless fired upon. We have your ship in sight, will buzz you in about five to let you know we're in the area, then check on that Chinese dinner delivery frigate."

"That's a roger, Skyhigh. Good luck."

Murdock had the Motorola on while he talked to the pilots. Now he had some reaction.

"Hey, Skipper, would the EAR work on a MiG?" Jaybird asked.

"Might, if he came in close enough. Say you had a head-on shot when he was on a strafing run. Might knock him out, which would in effect shoot down the sucker."

"What's the range of the EAR?" Bradford asked. "Know we've used them out six hundred yards."

"Don't remember anything farther," Murdock said. "Something we should test when we get a chance. Set up targets and watch for a blast effect. Or maybe just put Bradford out a thousand yards and see if we can get to him."

"I'll pass on that one, skipper."

Murdock went down from the bridge to the Lido deck to watch for the jets. He wondered if there would be a long-range missile duel, or if they would come up, and do flybys, and wave at each other.

The pair of F18s thundered by at two hundred feet over the *Queen of the Sea*, one on each side. The cracking, roaring, blasting sound of the jet engines must have awakened half the ship's people. Then the Hornets lifted up, and kept flying toward Hong Kong where the Chinese Navy frigate should soon be getting under way.

Anderson brought the SATCOM to the Lido deck where he set it up and they followed the aircraft talk on channel two.

"Tom One, I have three bogies at twenty thousand feet out about forty miles and closing."

"Roger that, One. No radar yet. If they lock on, we've got a war on our hands."

"If they lock and fire, we do the same. Roger that, Tom Two."

Captain Prestwick came down and stood with them. "The Chinese Navy radio, unscrambled, just reported that the frigate *Dandong five forty-three* has just cast off and is on the way. We are twelve minutes to the bottom of the islands. It should take the frigate thirty minutes to move the thirteen miles to the bottom of the islands at twenty-six knots. We may just slip out past the Chinese islands, but still be well within the twenty miles of territorial waters that China claims."

"*Queen* calling from Skyhigh. Your ears on?"

"Yeah good buddy, you must have been on the road with your CB. What's cooking?"

"CAG says we can't overfly Hong Kong, so we're sliding back into your area and around the islands. How long before the frigate gets to your position?"

"Skyhigh, the captain estimates we'll be six or eight miles past the islands into territorial waters when the frigate catches us."

"Oh, yeah. We can claim anything past three miles is international waters. He won't be there for another twenty-eight minutes. We're low on juice, going to take a drink from a tanker and be back. Watch the store for us."

"Roger that, Skyhigh."

The three men stood there, watching the sky, then looking at the island they were passing. Chinese territory. A few minutes later they all looked at their watches.

"We still have twenty-two minutes before he catches us," Anderson said.

The speaker on the SATCOM came on.

"*Queen,* can you read the Tomcats?"

"Loud and clear, Toms."

"We're edging back out of Chinese air, and taking the bogies with us generally west of your position. Teasing them away from you. We'll keep in the territorial zone if possible. So far they are coming to us. No radar, no lock-ons, no firings."

"Good, Tom One. We don't want them raking the *Queen* with twenty-millimeter fire."

"Roger that. We'll keep in contact."

The men stood there watching the blue water boiling past the big ship. Were they moving fast enough? Murdock wished that he knew. They worked slowly past a big island on the left that must be five miles long. He could see lights from at least one town, so it was inhabited. That was the last one, the one they had to get out beyond three miles to claim international water.

Murdock watched to the rear to see if he could see the Chinese Naval frigate coming up. Not so far. It would have lights, or maybe not. He wasn't sure. He did know that they would beat the frigate to international waters but not by much. Once there, the F18s would have their say. Now all he could do was stand and watch.

"*Queen,* come in," the SATCOM speaker said.

"Yes, *Queen* here."

"Tom One. The MiGs are going with us. Estimate that we're about two hundred miles from your position. MiGs are hanging back, must be trying to figure out what we're doing. We penetrated their air space by ten miles, now we're back in the wet and going generally northwest. They keep about five miles behind us. So far no radar targeting, which is what we like. Take care."

"Thanks, Tom One. Be careful up there."

Captain Prestwick had been staring to the rear and he nodded. "Yes, I can see the frigate. She's showing lights and charging along. Maybe a mile behind us. What time is it?"

"Four twenty-five," Murdock said. "It gets light here about what oh five thirty? Another hour of darkness."

"Frigate should overtake us in another half hour. See the island over there? That's Pok Liu Chau. I've seen her on the charts often enough. Five miles long and the end of Chinese territory around here. Three miles beyond that and we're in better shape."

"*Queen*, this is Skyhigh."

"Skyhigh, the frigate is closing," Murdock said. "We'll just about be in the three-mile area when she matches us."

"If she fires any weapons at or near you, we have weapons free," the pilot said.

"Any plans before then?"

"Yeah, going to do our circus act. Two and I will do a fly-by at mast-top level one on each side of the ship, coming from her bow. Shake her up a little. Let her know for sure that we're up here."

"When is the show? We figure she's about half a mile behind us."

"Any minute now, we're making our turn and lining up. You'll hear us after we pass you."

"That damn frigate is gaining on us. I'm waiting for her to fire a shot across our bow and order us to stop."

"Would you?"

"Not a chance. Another few minutes and we'll be past

the island and then three lousy miles and we'll be in generally considered to be international water. She won't have
the guts to fire into us, even with a machine gun."

"We hope," Murdock said.

The two jets screamed past the big ship a quarter of a
mile away not over fifty feet off the water and roared into
the distance showing fiery jet exhausts behind them.

"I'm always amazed at the raw power those jets have,"
Captain Prestwick said. "I wonder if this will slow down
the frigate at all? I better get back to the bridge." He turned
and left.

"Couldn't we use the EAR on the frigate?" Howie Anderson asked.

"She won't get close enough for that," Murdock said.
"They know about the patrol boats, that they were disabled.
They won't know how we did it, but they'll stand off just
to make sure. She might try to cut in front of us and make
the liner turn, hoping to turn her all the way round and
back into Chinese waters."

"We just cleared that big island," Howie said.

"*Queen,* I guess you heard us go by."

"Skyhigh, you were low on that one. Any reaction from
the frigate?"

"Not that we could see. She's about a thousand yards
behind you and gaining."

"Anything else you can do, Skyhigh?"

"Only thing we're authorized to do is fire some twenty
millimeter over her bow. Discouragement."

"We're well within range of her guns, but I don't think
she'll fire on us. Will she fire on you?"

"I don't think so, unless we hit her with some of our
warning shots. We'll make damn sure not to hit the frigate.
We're moving on her now before she gets too close."

Murdock and Howie ran to the other side of the ship
where they had a better view of the dark shadow of the
frigate boiling up behind them. Now she was about five
hundred yards back.

The F18s came in one at a time, strafing with 20mm
rounds across the bow of the destroyer thirty yards out. The

big ship hesitated, then went back to full throttle.

Murdock and Howie Anderson ran up to the bridge and got in contact with the planes again.

"*Queen*, she isn't going to give way. I can't shoot her until she shows some aggressive act."

"Understand, Skyhigh."

"She's coming closer," Captain Prestwik said. "She's trying to cut us off."

Murdock touched the Motorola mike. "EAR guns, get on the port side, both of you now."

Murdock watched the 350-foot-long Chinese frigate bristling with guns, rockets, and antennas charging toward them. The Chinese man-of-war was less than fifty yards behind them and Murdock felt his stomach twist.

"She's not trying to cut us off, Captain, she's going to ram us. EARs are you ready?"

Murdock listened to the earpiece.

"Go, go," both SEALs said.

"When she gets to twenty-five yards and is still aimed at us amidships, blast the bridge and control area with three shots each. On my command."

Murdock watched the Chinese frigate move closer, it turned away a moment, then came back heading directly for the side of the big luxury liner.

"Fire," Murdock said into the Motorola mike.

"Captain, hard right rudder to get away from her."

The captain hesitated, then gave the command and slowly the big ship began to turn away from the frigate.

The first two rounds hit the frigate's bridge, but Murdock couldn't tell if they penetrated through the row of windows. He watched the second two rounds hit and sensed a change in the big frigate. It slowed, then slowed more until it was simply coasting ahead on its momentum.

The shooters sensed it too and aimed their third shots at men near deck guns. The men went down and didn't get up. The big luxury liner turned like a four hundred foot long log. Slowly, ever so slowly. The frigate came closer, closed the gap but it was only coasting along on the speed it had built up.

"Nobody at the controls," Murdock said. "Our enhanced audio rifle knocked out everyone on the bridge. She's dead in the water until new personnel realize something is wrong and rush to the bridge. By that time we'll be well out to sea."

They watched as the *Queen* veered away from the frigate that slowed and then stopped. It was a half mile behind them in minutes and the Captain shook Murdock's hand.

"She was going to ram us, damage us so we would have to return to the closest port, Hong Kong. It would be reported as an accidental collision in the South China Sea. Those damn Chinese are always plotting, aren't they?"

"They were this time."

"*Queen*, what the hell happened down there?" Skyhigh asked on the SATCOM. "Looked like that frigate was going to slam into the *Queen* amidships, then she slowed and stopped."

"Our secret," Murdock said. "We zapped them with our new secret weapon. We knocked out everyone on the bridge. They'll wake up in four hours with the granddaddy of all headaches."

"Can we fit one on my eighteen?"

"Sorry, these are for grunts only. Thanks for slowing her down."

"We'll cap you until you're outside their twenty-mile zone, then we better head for the home field."

"Roger that, Skyhigh, and thank the Tomcats for us, too."

20

Coronado, California

Master Chief Petty Officer Gordon MacKenzie, switched the phone to the other hand. He wiped perspiration off his palm and then mopped his forehead with a tissue from a box on his desk.

"Oh yes, Mrs. Fernandez, I am worried about what this might do to Nancy Dobler. That's why I want you to be the one to tell her. Will Dobler has been wounded in action and survived and is still in the platoon. I want to be sure that she understands that the wound is not critical, he's in no danger of dying, and that he should be treated there in the hospital onboard the aircraft carrier and then he'll be sent home to Balboa here in about two weeks."

Maria Fernandez had cringed when the master chief called her, sure that her husband had been wounded. She had relaxed a little when she realized that it was Will Dobler. Then she was even more worried—about Nancy.

"Master Chief, I'm glad you called me first. I'll go over and see her today, set up a movie date for us and Milly DeWitt. We're her support group. We'll handle it. Tell her before we go out and get any crying jag over with, then have dinner and a movie. . . . Yes, I'll call Milly at work and see if she can meet us at Nancy's place." She hesitated, wondering if the master chief should be the one to tell Nancy with her two friends there. She changed her mind and closed the talk on a high note about having the master chief over for a real southern crawfish dinner.

Maria put down the phone and frowned. Nancy had been a little better lately after her last problem. She had cut way back on her drinking and refused to have any drugs in the house. For now, that is. Maria made reservations for three at eight o'clock at the Seafood Grotto. Nancy did love good seafood. Two hours at Nancy's should be enough to get the crying all done. She smiled. She was sure before it was over, all three of them would be crying. At least a little.

Milly offered only a quiet, "Oh, no," when Maria told her the news. She said good idea about the dinner and movie. She'd be at Nancy's by six.

Maria had been to several Navy-sponsored forums and talks about how to handle the stress on a family of wounds and MIA and KIA. They had been aimed at wives and even children of Navy personnel. Maria had gone out of a sense of duty, because her husband was in one of the most dangerous jobs in the Navy. Now she wished that she had paid better attention and learned more. She remembered some of it. Should they have a priest or minister there? No, that would be for a KIA notification. That would scare Nancy into an immediate blowout.

Maria called Nancy that afternoon and suggested the night out. It had been over a week since they had done anything like this. Nancy had been delighted.

"I even know what film I want to see. It's that new one with Andrea Hightower in it. She is going to be a big star for years. Did you see her in *Wicked Can't Hide*? Andrea was just fantastic. Now this new one is *Where Virgins Dare Not Walk*. It has good reviews. Dinner first, right, then the movie. We can get it at the Ken Theatre at nine forty-five. We can eat and run."

That night at six-thirty, after Maria stumbled through the carefully thought-out way she had worked out to tell Nancy about Will, Nancy blinked once and nodded.

"Well, thank God he isn't critical. I don't know how I'd finish raising these kids without him." Nancy didn't cry. Not a tear not a wail and no hysterics or storming around the house.

When Nancy didn't cry, Milly was startled, and then deeply concerned. "This is the kind of injury that the military used to call a million-dollar wound," Milly said. "It wouldn't kill you, wouldn't mess up the rest of your life, but it was serious enough to get you sent home."

"Master Chief MacKenzie didn't want to tell me himself, did he? I'll tease him about that. That rough, tough old coot is a big jelly roll inside." She paused and took a deep breath. "Well, we have that out of the way, why don't we go to dinner early? I've left food in the oven for the kids. They'll do fine here until we get back."

They all splurged with lobster and steak and each one paid her own check as usual. The meal was served well; the background music was delightful; and the lobster was local, fresh caught, and cost a small fortune. Milly watched Nancy for any sign of cracking, any small fissure that might grow and build into a huge cave-in somewhere in the near future. She saw nothing. If anything, Nancy was better than usual. Now she was making plans for what they would do when Will came home.

"How long do you think he'll be in Balboa?" Nancy asked.

"When Miguel was wounded more than a year ago, he was in the hospital for three weeks, but he had a nasty chest wound that they had trouble with. This wounded leg sounds far less serious. He could be out in a week at the most."

"Good," Nancy said. "When he gets home we're going to go see every one of the San Diego county parks. There are something like twenty of them. We'll go picnic or hike or swim and whatever the park is about. I've always wanted to do that. This is the perfect time."

"We got up to see the Flower Fields at Carlsbad this year," Milly said. "We try every summer, but this time we made it. The blooms are gone now, mostly renunculas. Fifty-five acres of them, so many brilliant colors sweeping up this half mile of hill. Amazing, truly amazing."

They chattered away over coffee and then decided on dessert. The dinner lasted so long they missed the movie they were going to see. Milly was pleased. The whole situation looked to be under control. Nancy was acting hurt and a little bewildered, but seemed genuinely pleased that Will would be coming home soon, maybe within the week.

Yes, they had been lucky this time. This was exactly the kind of shock or trauma that might set Nancy off again.

They left in their individual cars, so nobody would have to backtrack. Nancy's three-year-old Chevy was in immaculate condition. Will kept it that way. She was his newborn and he babied her.

"Take care, you guys," Nancy said. "We'll see you next week for our regular dinner. It's at my place this time. Bye."

The three women got in their cars. Nancy drove off. Maria waited a minute until Nancy's car was out of sight, then she went over to Milly's car.

"What do you think?" Milly asked.

"Not sure, but she sounded good. No wild screaming or ranting and raving. This time she had just cause to get upset, but she didn't. Seemed to me like she took it well."

"I hope so. I had the same impression. Maybe we got lucky this time." They looked at each other.

"Hey, I'll call you if I hear anything else about the platoon."

"Yes," Milly said. "We've got to stay in touch." They both drove out of the restaurant parking lot.

Down the street a half mile, Nancy slowed and pulled to the curb. It was a residential only a few blocks from her home. She put her head on the steering wheel. The tears came in a rush, then the pain and anger stormed out of her, and she screamed in fury and beat the steering wheel with her hands. Wetness streamed down her checks. She couldn't just sit there. Nancy jumped out of the car and ran down the block fast. She sprinted and didn't even feel the strain. She sprinted back to the car and began to wheeze and cough and then slammed her fist against the hood. It didn't dent but her hand hurt so much she thought she might have broken it.

"God damn it, why me?" Nancy bellowed into the night sky. "Why am I always the fucking punching bag?" The second scream was almost as loud as the first one and brought a flash of room lights on the second floor of a house across the street.

Now the exhaustion hit her from the two long blocks of sprinting. She sagged against the car, then opened the door and slumped into the driver's side.

"Harry's Place," she said softly. Nobody knew her from Marilyn Monroe at Harry's place.

At first she stayed in a booth near the back, drinking quietly and quickly. On her sixth bourbon on the rocks, the waitress asked her if she was sure that she wanted it.

"You're alone, honey. You have somebody to come take you home? I can't let you out of here if you're driving."

Nancy looked up at her and brushed new tears away from her cheeks streaking the already smudged mascara. She stared back at the waitress and tipped up the bourbon and didn't lower it until the glass was empty.

"I'll go call you a cab. The manager is worried about you."

As soon as the waitress left. Nancy pushed out of the seat, almost topped over, fell against the table and gained her balance. She looked at the front door, then headed for the side door. The manager ran in front of her.

"Lady, I can't let you go driving in your condition. Now just relax. I called a cab and I'm paying for it. Give me your keys and you can come get your car tomorrow afternoon. We open at two."

Nancy stopped, reached into her purse but what came out was her fist that she used to take a swing at the manager. He jumped back then stepped ahead inside and caught both her arms.

"Get your hands off me you slob," Nancy snarled.

"Lady, I'd love to, but I could lose my license, understand? Nothing personal, it's just business."

She looked away, and when he looked in that direction she brought up her knee and rammed it into his crotch as hard as she could.

The manager bellowed in pain and swayed backward, dropping his hands from her arms and slumping to his knees. He held his crotch and keened in pain, then fell over on the floor, his hands protecting his genitals from any more damage.

Nancy looked at him a minute, snorted, and went out the side door to her car. She saw a taxi flash into the parking lot and turn toward the front door.

She hurried then, almost fell, bounced off a fender but kept her feet. She found her car, slid in, and locked the doors, then started the Chevy. She backed out of the slot slowly, with elaborate care, and cautiously turned toward the street.

Nancy prided herself that she had never had to ask someone to drive her home or get a cab after a few drinks. Always made it home. Always.

She shook her head and stared at the street. *Which way? Oh, yeah, to the left.* She hit the gas and spurted into the street and barely missed a car coming at her in the right-hand lane. She blew her horn at the guy and laughed, then blinked to get a better view of the street. *So damn dark out there. Lights were on, yeah, mine? Yeah.* She thought the street was narrow and before she could correct, she side-swiped a car parked at the curb.

She scowled and drove on, just a little crinkle fender, no big deal. Had to get home. She heard some horns honking at her but ignored them. Somebody behind her? She speeded up. *Fifty miles an hour on a Coronado street? Oh, hell yes. Get home faster that way.*

The light had just turned red, and she was thirty feet from it. No way she could stop. Hell, nobody coming this time of night. She hit the accelerator to slip through fast before a cop saw her and then she caught just a flash of yellow to her right.

Nancy wasn't sure what happened next. She felt the impact as her front bumper slammed into the driver's door of a yellow convertible. She jolted forward. Her head hit the steering wheel, and then the wheel smashed into her breasts. After that everything whirled and spun and she saw the convertible tip over and her Chevy ride up onto the wheels and undercarriage of the other car. A moment later she passed out.

South China Sea
John C. Stennis, CVN 74

Lieutenant Commander Blake Murdock and Father O'Connor went to see Senior Chief Boatswain's Mate Willard Dobler in the hospital section of the huge carrier.

Dobler looked up, saw Murdock and grinned, then frowned when he saw the crosses on the other officer's collar.

"I know I've missed mass for a few years, Father, but you didn't have to come all the way out here—" He stopped. Neither of them was going to laugh. His grin turned to a frown tinged with the redness of fear. "What is it? My family?"

The priest looked at Murdock who had asked to lead the team.

"Yes, Will. Nancy was in a car crash. She got banged up a little bit but only spent one night in the hospital."

"Thank God. Were the kids with her?"

"No, she was alone. Your Chevy is pretty well totaled."

"So, we can replace the car. Is Nancy really okay? She must not be, why else would you both be here? What's the problem?"

"She ran a red light, Will. Broadsided a couple of kids in a convertible. One of them died. She was drunk, Will. The manager of the bar she left said he tried to stop her. She fought with him, kneed him in the groin, and rushed out of the bar. Five minutes later the kid was dead."

Will ducked his head and covered his face with his hands. "She went off again. Did she know about my getting wounded? That must have set her off. Damn, she must be in jail."

"She is, Will. It only happened two days ago. Yesterday they had the arraignment. She's being charged with second-degree murder.

Will had been sitting up. Now his face sagged, his eyes watered and then closed and he lay back on the bed.

"Will," Murdock said.

"Get the hell out of here, both of you. Go. Just go. God

damn it I thought she could hold it together a few more months. God damn it to hell. It's my fault. I should have known it was coming. Happened often enough before. God damn it to hell, what the fuck am I going to do now?"

Murdock waved the priest out of the small room and sat in the chair beside the bed.

"Listen up, Chief, and I'll tell you exactly what you're going to do. I've arranged for you to fly out this afternoon on the COD to T'aipei. From there you catch an ambulance aircraft with a couple of stops and then you hit San Diego and Balboa in fifteen to twenty hours, something like that.

"When you get to San Diego, a lawyer I know who is a top man in criminal law in town and owes me a bunch of favors will take your case pro bono. Not a red cent. He usually gets twenty-five thousand down and three hundred an hour. He will tell you what he's going to do. First he'll get the bail knocked down from a million dollars to something like fifty thousand, since you're Navy and Nancy is not a flight risk. Then he'll get Nancy home and get you out of Balboa and she'll settle down. Is every little thing clear?"

Will looked up. "Yes, sir, Commander, yes sir. Sorry I lost it there."

"Next, the priest is coming back in here so you can apologize to him for your bad language and atrocious manners. Then we'll see about getting you in motion."

Coronado, California

Four days later, Senior Chief Dobler came out of the Balboa Naval Hospital in San Diego in a wheelchair and hobbled on crutches into Maria Fernandez's Chevrolet.

"Good to see you, Will. Hear you're healing like a whirlwind. That lawyer of yours is a dandy. I was in court yesterday. He pulled out all the strings and got the bail battered down to thirty thousand. We'll drive by a bail bondsman. You said you could write him a check for three thousand, which is the ten percent. Then Nancy should be out and waiting for us to pick her up by noon tomorrow."

Dobler eased into the cushion and tried to keep tears out

of his eyes. "Everyone's been so damn good to us. I certainly do appreciate it, and I know Nancy does."

Maria looked over and smiled. "Hey, Chief, you're family. We're not gonna let our family down. Your kids have been at my place but they insisted they would be fine at home now that you're going to be there. Helen says she's fifteen now and can be chief cook until her mom gets home and Charlie will be bottle washer."

Two hours later, the bail was posted and the process started at the Las Colinas Women's Detention Center in nearby Lakeside. Maria drove over the Coronado Bay bridge from San Diego and up to the Dobler house. Both kids waited on the front lawn for him and rushed out and grabbed him. He used the crutches to get to the house, then spread out in his favorite recliner chair and the two kids hugged him again.

Maria went back to the car and drove home. Dobler had assured her that Miguel was fine, hadn't been injured or wounded and was a good man to have on your side.

Will didn't remember what Helen had fixed for dinner that night but he complimented her on it and she glowed. Then he settled down in his recliner, channel surfed the TV for a while, then took a nap. He was home. Nancy would be there tomorrow, and they would work through whatever problems faced them. Together, they would do it together. The lawyer had talked briefly with him that evening and said that if they didn't want to go to trial there would almost certainly be some kind of a plea bargain they could make. The charges would get knocked down to manslaughter two but the chances of Nancy having to do at least two years in prison would be hard to get around. Dobler understood. A young man, twenty-two, had died and his girlfriend would be in a wheelchair for six months to repair the damage to her legs. He understood. He didn't like it, but he knew there was no way around it. They would simply have to adapt.

At noon the next day, Maria and Dobler picked up Nancy at the discharge point of the Detention Center in Lakeside, seven miles north and east of San Diego. Nancy had her head down as she walked to the car. Maria put her in the back seat with Will, but she sat on the side as far from him as she could get.

She wouldn't talk. Will moved over toward her, then pulled her over to him and put her head on his shoulder. Slowly she relaxed and before they were at the bay bridge, Nancy Dobler began to cry softly, wetting his shoulder and bringing dampness to Will's eyes as well.

By the time they pulled up in front of the Dobler home, Nancy had her head on Will's chest and her crying had stopped. His arms were around here. Neither of them had spoken yet. Maria eased out of the car so the two could be alone. She walked up to the house and talked with the kids who had been waiting.

Will tried. "Baby, I'm so sorry." The words came out softly yet smothered with so much emotion that he could hardly understand them himself. Nancy turned and looked up him.

"Sweetheart . . . I didn't mean . . . I didn't try to hurt that boy." She broke down again and he held her while she sobbed.

It was a half hour later before Nancy opened the door and helped Will out of the car and onto his crutches. His right leg was still heavily bandaged, and he wore shorts to give the wrappings room. He eased onto the crutches and they walked slowly up the sidewalk and into the door.

Maria had been talking to the kids, and now Helen and Charlie waited inside, and let their mother come to them. She did, hugged each one and kissed them. Being home made her feel better. Yes. Holding the kids was what she needed. Nancy thanked Maria, hugged her and then walked her to the door.

When she came back Nancy felt like her old self. She looked around and then at the kids. "Okay, you guys, who have you hired to clean up this place? It's practically spotless."

"Dad pulled an inspection," Charlie said. "Gave us all morning to get the place ready."

Nancy laughed. It was the first time in almost a week.

"Yep, that sounds like our Will. Navy right down to the old gonads." That made them all laugh.

Helen had been making dinner. She continued. There would be broiled herb chicken, mashed potatoes and gravy, frozen peas, a fruit salad, and ice cream sundaes for desert. Nancy watched her with amazement.

"Whoever taught you to cook, young lady?"

Nancy turned, a sparkle in her eye. "A wise old Hindu monk who came only when I was alone in the kitchen." Then she smiled. "I've been watching you for years, Mom. You're a great cook."

Nancy felt the tears coming again and thanked her daughter and left the room to find a box of tissues. It was so good to be home if even for a short time.

The phone rang and Nancy grabbed it out of habit. She always got the phone because sometimes raucous shipmates from years before would call up and usually Will didn't want to go meet them for a drinking bout.

"Yes, good afternoon."

"Mrs. Dobler. I'm Harry Justin, your lawyer. We met briefly at your arraignment. We need to do a lot of backgrounding. Could I come over tonight for a couple of hours?"

"Mr. Justin I appreciate what you have done for me and are doing. But I just now made it home. I'd really like to have tonight with the family. Would that be all right?"

"Yes, but I'll call tomorrow. There is a lot I need to know about the stress of being a SEAL wife on top of the normal Navy problems. Yes, let's do it tomorrow. I'll call you about noon and set up something."

That night after dinner, they turned off the TV and played dominoes the way they used to when the kids were learning to add and subtract.

"Been a long time, Mom," Helen said.

"You can talk, you're a hundred points ahead," Will cracked.

Later that night, Nancy tenderly made love to Will, being careful of his wounded leg.

"Yes it was good for me," Nancy said, poking Will in

the shoulder as they lay side by side relaxing. "Tonight was a wonderful time. Something to remember."

"Baby, I think it's time we talk about my getting out of the platoon. I want to stay in the SEALs, but I won't be on field duty. We talked about it once before. I'll be in a support group somewhere, maybe supply or the boats. Lots of spots where I can save my rate. Then I get in the rest of my twenty years and we'll talk about me finding some other type of employment."

"But you love the SEALs, sweetheart. You've told me a dozen times that if you had to leave the platoon, you'd just as soon quit the Navy. I don't want you to have to make that decision. Not on account of me. Look, Will. I understand this DUI I've got and the murder charge or manslaughter two, or whatever it comes down to. I know that means I'm going to have to do some time. That fancy lawyer is good, but he can't get me a walk. We both know that. So, no more talk about quitting the platoon. Your wound won't keep you out. You're only thirty-seven. You've got another two good years with the kids out there swimming around. Now keep quiet. Has Big Boy down there had a long enough rest? I'm still just as horny as hell and there's only one way to stop that itch."

"Damn, sexy woman, it's only been a half hour." He laughed. "Hell, yes, Big Boy is coming up again and raring to go."

The next morning, Will drove over to the SEALs base. It was only a little over two miles and he proved to Nancy that he could drive. He braked with his left foot.

Nancy went back inside the house and sat a moment looking around the place. Then she did a clean-up, putting everything in place. She laid out the menu for dinner that night, and made sure that all of the food was in the refrigerator or on the shelf. The kids were in school and would be home about three thirty.

Then she went into the bedroom, picked up a leather bag from the night stand, and took it into the bathroom. She cleaned the room until it sparkled, then sat down in the tub, and pulled the shower curtain so it hung inside the tub.

Nancy took the .45 caliber automatic pistol from the leather pouch and racked the slide back the way Will had taught her years ago. Yes, a round moved into the chamber. She flipped off the safety and put the muzzle up to the side of her head just above her ear.

Nancy said a short prayer, then pulled the trigger.

21

South China Sea
John C. Stennis, **CVN 74**

The SEALs had struggled through two whole days off. They hardly knew what to do with themselves. Ed DeWitt found a new chess opponent in the ward room and they had a best-three-out-of-five series going.

Murdock tried to follow the war. Bangladesh and Nepal were entirely subjugated. Nobody could figure out why. Then word came that ten divisions of Chinese infantry with armor support had moved into Pakistan with the country's blessings and were concentrating on the Iranian border. Speculation was all over the place about China's intentions. Murdock couldn't figure it out. If they wanted territory, why not go for Afghanistan or India? No, India would retaliate with a nuclear weapon and end it in a rush. So Why Iran? True, those Arabs have some oil. Murdock looked it up. Iran has a little over ninety billion barrels of oil reserves. But they also had 1.4 million men under arms.

India was still hot over the resupply of Chinese forces in Bangladesh. The Chinese planes had to fly over a small strip of India to get to Bangladesh. The shortest route was sixty miles across India between China and Bangladesh. Twice India had threatened to shoot down any more transports. Then a day ago they did, downing three large transport planes that had no fighter escort.

Today, China announced that MiG fighters would now escort their unarmed supply transports across the line into Bangladesh. India had asked for U.S. assistance, calling on the mutual defense treaty with the United States. They asked for an AWACS plane to monitor the area for Chinese flights, and for fighter aircraft to help counter the MiG escorts. Washington was taking the request under advisement. India said they must have the help within four days or it would not be of any value.

Murdock put down a confidential bulletin he had from Don Stroh and shook his head. "What the hell are we doing in this mess anyway, Stroh? Do we really have a mutual defense treaty with India?"

"Of a sort. It's a broad multinational thing that covers many areas, and it could be interpreted as being for military aid when attacked. That's what State is churning around about. No worry about that for a while. What the Washington boys are really wondering about is China and Pakistan. Word leaking out is that China is not looking at Pakistan as a partner in this crazy war. We're not sure why, but relations between the former allies seem to be weakening and could collapse."

"That with three hundred thousand Chinese troops now inside Pakistan where they were invited guests?" Murdock asked. "That's like inviting a fox into your chicken coop."

"Could well be. In the meantime, State and New Delhi are whipping up a new wrinkle. They want to launch what looks like an attack on Nepal and see how the Chinese react. Will they fight to hold the country or was that just a warm up for the rest of the war? We could find out fairly soon."

"A fake attack, timed charges, loudspeakers, tapes of machine, and mortar fire, the whole thing," Murdock said. At least we won't have to worry about that one."

"Didn't I tell you?" Stroh asked. "Something is coming through channels right now, but then I can't talk about it."

Murdock sat up straighter in the ward room where he and Stroh were working on coffee. "Of course you can't talk to me about it, but if you were simply thinking out loud . . ." The men looked at each other and laughed.

"Yeah, I think out loud a lot. That's what gets me in trouble with the brass around here. Remember I was thinking about that fake attack on Nepal and the Chinese. I didn't tell you but there could be the SEALs' name tag on that one. If it comes through. Hell, a walk in the park. Anyway, you guys are getting bored just sitting here eating three times a day, sleeping ten hours. Hey, your men must be going nuts."

"Yeah, that's straight. Me too. Nepal. Why don't they just base us in Calcutta for a while? We'll be a lot closer to the action."

"You could be a lot closer tomorrow." Stroh held up both hands. "Hey, you didn't hear it from me. I'm just having a cup of java here with some wild-assed SEAL. I know nothing."

"Yeah, you and Sergeant Schultz from the old Bob Crane TV series about the Stalag Seventeen WW two prison camp." They both chuckled.

"Well, guess I better get busy and see if my guys are up on their shots and everything."

"I don't know what the hell you're talking about, Sailor. Me, I got to go see a movie."

Murdock finished his coffee and headed for the SEAL compartment. He had some getting ready to do.

He stopped by at the hospital. Every day he visited Vinnie Van Dyke. He was improving. The red tag was off his chart. In another week he should be well enough to be flown back to Balboa Hospital.

"Vinnie, you didn't miss a thing in Hong Kong. We didn't even get shore leave."

"You guys took down a whole damn luxury liner?"

"Just the bad guys onboard, about thirty of them as I recall. They weren't special troops. China has some good ones. These were just soldiers, and didn't know what they were doing."

"Hey, docs say I might get out of here and back to Balboa in another week, isn't that great!"

"Yeah, in Balboa those three girls you have on strings can come see you. Just be sure they come on different days."

"Hey, Cap, not three. Just two and one of them I'm trying to dump. Yeah, I'm looking forward to going home."

Murdock left and checked over his remaining men. The sixteen-man platoon was down to fourteen. Jaybird had been filling in for Dobler doing the senior chief's chores. He hated to lose men, even for a few missions.

If they did do a show for China along the border, it wouldn't be much. They would need a pair of trucks and would have to go in after dark and set up the whole thing to launch a night attack on the next day at dusk. That would leave Mr. Chinaman twelve hours of darkness to worry about an attack.

At 1400 the messenger came. Murdock and planning team wanted in the admiral's cabin. Murdock, DeWitt, and Jaybird went to the meeting.

Captain Robertson and two more Captains faced the three SEALs. Don Stroh came in late and took a seat.

"SEALs, you've heard about the idea of sending in a team to create the illusion of a massive attack on the Nepal border at one of the roads that leads into the mountains."

"Yes, sir," Murdock said.

"Good, what's your reading on the idea?"

"Can be highly effective if done right and at the right time of the day. We did a good one during Desert Storm in the Gulf. Pulled several divisions out of the primary target to defend a beach that was never invaded."

"I know about that one," one of the other captains said. "Will it work here?"

Murdock considered it a moment. "Yes, sir, but it will take a mile of frontage and a platoon of forty Marines to help us plant the explosives and run the generators and loud speaker systems. It's a hell of a big job."

"How much explosives?"

"Fifty pounds every one hundred feet. That's five hundred times fifty. That's twenty-five thousand pounds. Twelve and a half tons."

"What if we cut the amount in half at each spot, set them off in a pattern, not all at once, so it would seem more like the real thing?" Jaybird asked.

The captain looked at Murdock.

"Sounds interesting, sir. We haven't had time to do any planning on this."

"Let's do it now. The floor is open."

Murdock looked at the captain, he was serious. He turned to DeWitt. "Ed, will we need anything that can't be detonated with a radio signal?"

"No, there should be forty-eight point timers on board. Two sets would give us ninety-six. We string the charges in sequences of five to each frequency."

"What about rockets without warheads, to slam over the border and into Nepal but no bang on the other end?" Jaybird asked.

"Yeah, I like it," one of the captains said.

"Machine gun fire on tape played over loud speakers," Murdock said. "We can throw in dozens of explosions, too. We time the whole thing for a half hour."

"Space out the heavy explosions?" Captain Robertson asked.

"That would help us play out the half hour," Murdock said. "Give them time to listen and make some reports to China GHQ in Katmandu."

"We don't have that kind of explosives onboard," the third Captain said. "We can't use our usual ordnance, too much risk of bomb fragments."

"Dig up what black powder you have, C-four and C-five," Murdock said. "Wish we had a battle wagon around. The sacks of powder on those big guns would be about right." He frowned.

"So, we gather up all the safe explosives you have here, get shipments from the other ships in your fleet, and then ask India to supply us with the difference, three or four tons of dynamite."

Ed DeWitt sat there shaking his head. "Captain, this is too big, too long, too many chances for foulups. We can do the same thing with a quarter-mile-long front. Get the point across. Cut our powder needs to three tons and still have all the generators and loud speakers we need to ram the point across the border."

"How many speakers?" Jaybird asked.

"Four and four generators," DeWitt said. "Do the job. We set the charges, work them in sequence through the half hour. We'll have a hundred charges, set every one hundred ten feet apart."

Captain Robertson looked at Murdock. "You go along with the shorter field?"

"Yes. Fits better. We'll still need twenty Marines to help us lug and tote. We'll need trucks to haul the men and explosives up to the front."

"What about Indian approval?" Jaybird asked.

"This was their idea," the carrier skipper said. "They said they will cooperate with us in any way they can. They have a spot picked out, two hundred and seventy miles from Calcutta on one of few roads that crosses the border."

"Timing," Murdock said.

"We'll ask Calcutta to furnish the three tons of powder and let them drive it north. Give them two days. By then we'll have the SEALs and twenty Marines on hand in Calcutta. You'll fly up in choppers we'll bring to Calcutta from our ships offshore."

"We set up one night, then set them off as soon as it's dark the next night," Murdock said.

"Generators and speakers?" DeWitt asked.

"We can furnish those from the carrier. Send them in the COD with the SEALs," one of the Captains said.

Stroh listened to the plan, made some notes.

"This was Indian Intelligence's idea. I'll coordinate it with them. They said they could furnish us with most of what we need if we ramrod it. Timing?"

"As soon as you can set it up," Captain Robertson said. "We'll have the SEALs and Marines from one of the ships down there in Calcutta by noon tomorrow."

"Mr. Stroh," Jaybird said. "Don't forget we'll need radio detonators, a radio signal board for one hundred, and all the other material for the radio detonation."

"Yeah, Jaybird. Coming up." He nodded at the captain and hurried out of the room.

"Captain, we'll be ready to get on the COD on two-hour

notice," Murdock said. "You said sometime about day-light?"

"Right, Commander. You've made the run before. This time I think we'll leave you in Calcutta for a while. Cheaper than flying you back and forth."

A half hour later in their SEAL compartment, DeWitt had just finished briefing the rest of the men about the job coming up.

"So that's it, a no-sweat, no-return-fire kind of operation. We should be scaring any border guards pissless up there on the front line. As soon as the show is over, we pick up our toys and go back to Calcutta."

"We don't do any small arms work ourselves?" Howie Anderson asked. "Damn be a good time to knock over some Chinkomen."

"They might not even have border guards up at that point," Murdock said. "India picked out the target."

A messenger came into the room and looked around, went up to the nearest SEAL and asked him a question. Canzoneri pointed the messenger to Murdock.

The sailor handed Murdock an envelope, and hurried away.

Murdock frowned, opened the sealed business-size envelope and took out the paper. It was a radio message. He read it quickly. His face sagged and his eyes closed for a moment. No reason to tell the men just before a mission. At once he changed his mind. There also was no reason not to tell them.

"Hey, gather around." He waited for the men to come up in a group around him.

"Just received a radio message from Master Chief Petty Officer Gordon MacKenzie. It reads: 'Regret to inform you that Nancy Dobler killed herself in her home Tuesday night. She had just been released on bail from police custody after her DUI auto wreck where a young man was killed. She was charged with second degree murder. Will Dobler is devastated. More to follow.' "

22

Coronado, California

Detective Sergeant Mad Dog Sanchez sat in his rented car across the street and down three cars from the apartment where the *gringo* killer lived. A secretary in the lieutenant's office who spoke perfect English had made the contact for him on an extremely secretive basis. Her brother could be pulled in on drug charges at any time. Sanchez was sure that she would not tell anyone she made the call.

The San Diego Police had been most helpful with the telephone number and the address it produced. They also had confirmed the name of the man who lived there, Howard Anderson.

Now it was simply a matter of waiting. Twice now he had come to San Diego through the international port of entry. It was easy. Twice he had waited all day and all night but no one appeared at the apartment. He could not make inquiries at the adjacent areas. Someone would remember. It could take him half a dozen trips on his days off, but he would find this *gringo* killer.

Now he ate the tacos he had bought from a stand downtown. Coronado was a small place across a long bridge from San Diego. He ate the second taco and thought it through again. The prostitute at the *cantina* had given him the phone number. He had the right name now and the address. All he could do was wait. But he must remain invisible. No one must remember him. He rented a different car for each trip and parked in a different spot. Sooner or later he would find the man. Detective Sergeant Sanchez settled down for a long wait. He was good at this. He would win in the long run.

Six blocks away on another Coronado street, Will Dobler sat with his arms around his two children. Helen had not recovered from the shock of finding her mother. That afternoon she had run from the house to a neighbor's place screaming all the way. The woman there had checked, then called the police. There was no need for an ambulance, she knew.

Helen whimpered and burrowed against her father, trying to gain from him some confidence, some reassurance. She looked up at him and asked the question she had asked him dozens of times.

"Why, Daddy. Why did Mom do that?"

He shook his head and hugged her tightly. "I'm not sure, honey. I just don't know. I wish I did." She whimpered again, and shivered, then relaxed against him.

Charlie was in better shape. He put up with the group hug but he wasn't all that thrilled with it. He had cried when he found out about his mother, but had recovered well in two days.

Will hadn't figured out how he felt yet. He'd been too busy making arrangements and taking care of the kids. Maria Fernandez and Milly had been tremendously solid friends helping him. The kids insisted on staying in the house. Helen refused to use the downstairs bathroom where she had found her mother. Late at night when the kids had finally gone to sleep, Will paced the living room. Sometimes he went out and walked with his crutches around the block as well as he could. Several times he had cursed the Navy, and the SEALs. It was their fault. The whole damned Navy had caused this. He should have seen it coming. He knew Nancy was on a teetering edge. But she'd been there before. His leg wound had been the clincher, he decided. It had been just enough to blow her over the edge. Maria said she thought that Nancy had taken the news that Will had been wounded extremely well. She hadn't even cried. But then after they left each other she must have splintered

into a thousand pieces and gone back to her one friend who
never let her down, alcohol. Will doubled up his fists and
punched the air.

"It's the god-damned Navy's fault. The fucking Navy has
done this to my family. Gonna ask for a hardship discharge
and get as far away from Navy people as I can. Move out
of Coronado for damn sure." He said the words out loud
not caring if anyone heard. He snorted. He'd decided to
move a dozen times in the last two days. He was so confused and angry and overwhelmed that he didn't know what
the hell he was thinking. Give it some time, his friends told
him. Yeah, some friends. Cremation. He and Nancy had
decided on that a long time ago. Death was the end. Yes,
they both believed that. No heaven, no loved ones waiting
for you "on the other side." You had life and when it was
over, it was over. No afterlife. What a ridiculous idea per-
petrated by religion for it's own ends. Now he was a fucking philosophy major, for Chris' sake. He was really going
off the deep end.

Will wondered how the Platoon was doing. Would it
have a new mission? What the hell could the men do
against China, anyway? Too damn big, too many men, too
many people.

He looked at the TV set and turned it on. Maybe there
was a good war movie on. Yeah, *Bataan* or *Battle of the
Bulge* or even a good John Wayne flick. He began surfing
the channels with the beeper. Tomorrow he had to take
Helen in to see that shrink. A Navy guy who had called
him and volunteered. Damn nice of him. Helen was taking
this the hardest.

Damn car wreck. If she hadn't killed that kid, she would
have been okay. Beat up and angry, and doing some jail
time, but alive. Yeah, alive and getting better. Sometimes
he figured they had the damn suicide thing whipped; then
she would remember her dad and how he had abused her
when she was just ten, and the whole fucking thing flooded
back and she would be out of it for a week or more. How
could a father do that to a kid, to his own kid? He'd never
know. God, he missed Nancy already. What was it going

to be like in a week, then a month, then a year? Damn. He decided to walk around the block again. Wear off some of the tension, maybe get tired enough to sleep three or four hours. At least he hoped so.

Calcutta, India

It took three days to put together all the elements of the "invasion" package. They had to have a TV studio in Calcutta make up the reel-to-reel tape for of the machine gun fire, combat explosions, and aircraft roaring past. That held them up a day.

The explosives were another problem. India at last rounded up enough 20 percent dynamite and some black powder from field guns to do the job. The trucks took another day to transport everything to the small village of Jogbani close to the border with Nepal.

The SEALs and Marines landed from choppers an hour after the trucks arrived in the village. It was dusk, and Murdock began assigning tasks and moving people and explosives. It took four hours to get the explosives set out in the quarter-mile arc aimed at Nepal. Then Jaybird went to each cache and put in the radio-controlled detonator. He had only a forty-eight-frequency board, so he put two detonators with similar frequencies in nearby stacks of explosives. They were simply placed on the ground in the open to give the loudest and most dramatic effect. By 2200 they were ready.

Howard Anderson took care of the sound equipment. He set up the speakers, aimed them, checked over the electric generators, and fired them up to be sure the gasoline engines would start. It was all wrapped up by 2400 and Murdock sent the men into a field to sack out. He had tight security around the whole complex, and Jaybird would sleep with his detonator broadcaster.

A half hour after they stood down, a jeep rolled into the area and an Indian Army General stepped out and asked to see whoever was in charge. Murdock was called, and he came with Don Stroh who was along for the ride.

"Commander, I'm General Gaya Chhapra. I have been

ordered by my commander-in-chief that the diversion you
plan here should go ahead at once and not wait until tomorrow night. It's been too long now. Can you get the
operation started within a half hour?"

Murdock frowned. "Yes, General. I'm not sure who has
command of this operation from a start/stop standpoint.
However, I don't see any reason not to do it now. Please
stand by and watch, then you can report back."

Murdock found Jaybird who roused the rest of the
SEALs who had operational jobs, and he dug out his firing
board. The gas engines sputtered into life and came up to
speed. Jaybird told Murdock on the Motorola that he was
ready.

"Start the loud speakers," Murdock said on the net and
the four speakers began blasting out machine gun fire
and all kinds of attack sounds including big guns, tanks,
and aircraft.

"Fire at will, Jaybird," Murdock ordered.

The first two explosions rocked the countryside. All
those who could move lifted up and ran to the rear to be
away from the rest of the real-life explosions. Jaybird
worked his firing board like a symphony orchestra, some
on the right, then the left and some in the middle. He spread
them out but his last charge went off at a little before the
twenty-minute mark. Murdock let the loud speakers roll for
ten minutes more, then shut them down.

The silence was deafening.

"Wow, is it quiet out here in the country," Ostercamp
said. The others agreed with him.

"Let's get this place cleaned up and get out of here,"
Murdock said. There wasn't much to clean up: A few
wooden explosive cases, the PA systems and generators to
recover and put on the truck.

Lam ran up to Murdock. "We've got company coming
from across the border," Lam said. "A jeep and a truck.
About a quarter of a mile off."

"SEALs on me with your weapons and live rounds.
We're moving out to find some line crossers."

The Marines had their weapons but no ammunition. Murdock's thirteen men assembled quickly and they took off at a trot toward the Nepal border. They had their usual mix of weapons, with one EAR and only one Bull Pup.

They jogged for three hundred yards and went to ground. Murdock crawled up to Lam who had signaled the lay-down.

"Right over there, skipper," Lam said, pointing with his MP5 submachine gun. Murdock took a look. In the wavering moonlight he saw what had to be a dozen men dropping off a six-by type truck with canvas top.

"Move up both squads in a line of skirmishers. I'm thirty yards ahead of you. We have fifteen to twenty visitors. Keep it quiet."

Murdock watched the Chinese infantrymen ahead of him fifty yards as they gathered together while someone talked to them. Murdock was tempted to have the two of them fire while the Chinese were bunched up, but he waited.

The Chinese had just started to spread out when Jaybird hit his Motorola.

"We're ready, Skip, we see the targets."

"Open fire," Murdock said. Fourteen guns blazed in the night sky. Half of the enemy troops went down with the first few rounds from each weapon, then the firing tapered off as targets became scarcer.

Murdock had the one Bull Pup. He put two 20mm rounds into the six-by truck and saw it catch fire. The jeep ahead pulled away, but Murdock tracked it and sent one round into the engine, jolting it to a stop.

"Cease fire," Murdock said into the mike and the guns went silent.

"Don't hear a fucking thing out there," Lam said. "Must be a few of them still on their feet."

"We take any return fire?" Murdock asked on the net.

"Didn't see any muzzle flashes," Fernandez said. "They were too worried about getting out of there."

"Anybody wounded?" Murdock asked.

There were no responses. "Okay, let's haul ass out of here. No formation, just filter back to where we left the trucks."

Five minutes later they loaded in the trucks, yelled at the Marines to get onboard and the whole "invasion" force moved out for the short drive back into the village. The trucks stopped and Murdock spoke with the Indian liaison officer who had been talking to the locals who were concerned that the Nepal war had spilled over into their village.

"I have most of the locals calmed down," the Indian Army captain said in a severe almost-English accent. "We don't have any accommodations for your men, but you can bivouac in a small field just outside of town. We'll get the choppers here for you in the morning for your return flight." The officer paused. "I'd say you chaps did quite well tonight. Must have scared hell out of those Chinese forces nearby and will give the command generals something to worry about."

The Marines bitched about the arrangement until one of their top sergeants chewed out the lot of them, then they settled down.

DeWitt put out two guards for their section of the field and the SEALs nodded off.

Murdock looked up, surprised by the Indian jeep that pulled up and Don Stroh stepped out into the moonlight.

"Thought you were talking with the folks in Calcutta," Murdock said.

"Well, I was, then we had a few signals come through, one right from the CNO himself. While you boys been pissing into the wind down here, there's been a real wild one going on up at the Indian corridor into Bangladesh. India shot down three more Chicom transports. MiGs have shot down four Indian fighters. The U.S. has sent a squadron of Tomcats to the military field near Calcutta, and they have flown thirty-four sorties, watching for MiGs. This morning one of the Tomcats was shot down over the edge of China. We have a pinpoint location of the two men who jumped and neither one is hurt. They're hiding.

"In twenty minutes two choppers will be here to lift you guys into China where you will provide protection and escort service via the choppers to get our men out of there."

Stroh stopped talking and squatted in front of Murdock.

"Are you with me on this? There's no time to go through Navy channels. Right here we're almost three hundred miles closer to those two fly boys than they are in Calcutta. The plane went down in a dagger of Chinese territory that stabs down toward Bangladesh between the Indian area of Sikkim and the small nation of Bhutan. You'll fly from here to Shiliguri, a good-size town in the corridor and about eighty miles from where the plane went down."

"Weapons and ammo," Murdock said. "Are they bringing our other weapons from Calcutta? We have three more Bull Pups there and our resupply of ammo."

"Believe it or not, the brass thought of that, and they have loaded everything you left there except your diving gear onto the choppers. Should have plenty of ammo. This is a run in and snatch operation and fly out as fast as possible. It will be a night operation if possible but could stretch into tomorrow morning. Your guys ready?"

"Let them sleep until the chopper gets here. How far to this supply point?"

"Sixty miles. They will refuel the choppers at Shiliguri, and you'll have time to get your weapons cleaned and ready. Heard you burned up some ammo tonight?"

"A few rounds. Some curious Chinese wanted a closer look. We didn't let them look."

"Oh, just in case you wonder: There will be three forty-six choppers in the flight, one for backup if needed. All will have door-mounted machine guns and gunners to man them."

"Damn, the Navy is finally understanding some of the problems here. Will it last?"

"Until something goes wrong. In case you missed out on the rest of the war, there is now fighting in Pakistan between the locals and the Chinese they invited in. I think this whole charade was a put-on so China could take over Pakistan without a major war. Much easier to fight inside a country than to invade it."

"Why would China want Pakistan?"

"State and our boys finally figured out what may be the answer to that one. Pakistan has two hundred and eight million barrels of oil reserves. That's nine times as much as China has. China is going to be needing more and more oil in the years to come. Why not steal it free from Pakistan?"

"This is starting to make sense."

They both heard the engines and rotors of the big choppers at the same time. Murdock used the Motorola. "Okay, SEALs on your feet. Your siesta is over. We have some work to do. Let's move up and get ready to do some travel time. Move it, SEALs."

23

Shiliguri, India

Murdock watched the town come into view from the open door of the chopper as they came toward a small landing strip. It wasn't a large airport, just a single concrete runway and blacktop taxi strips to four medium-size hangars. He saw two Indian-marked helicopters at the first building and that was the one they landed near.

"We'll be here just long enough to get restocked on ammo, and have a quick meal. Not sure what we'll be eating but pretend that you like it. Get back here fast after eating to check out weapons, and supplies. We'll take off in an hour."

The Indian liaison found Murdock a minute later.

"Lieutenant Singhe," the man said. He was shorter than Murdock, stocky and looked like a lifter. "Commander, we'll have your men through our mess in half an hour. We have a room where you can stash any of your gear you don't want with you. You have enough ammunition to start your own war."

"About what we're going to do, Lieutenant. I'm sure the Chicoms will have people out looking for our flyers as well."

"True, but your AWACS planes say their search planes are fifty miles off the mark."

"Hope they stay that way. What's this country like that we're going into?"

"Himalayas in a word. Mountains, On that side probably twelve to thirteen thousand feet, foothills to the big guys. Not a lot of vegetation up in there. It's a hard, cruel, cold place most of the time. Summer brings a little rain and some wildflowers. Most of that area is above the timber-line."

"Sounds inviting. Any Chinese infantry in the area?"

"None that we know of. There are no real settlements up in those areas. Bleak, worthless country."

"Where is the closest air base?"

"Don't know, Commander. I'll try to find out."

"Don't put up any of your fighters while we're on the mission. Maybe that way no MiGs will be in the area to shoot us full of holes."

"I don't control that, but I'll put in your request."

"Thanks, now I want to get some food and then check on my men and the chopper."

Forty minutes later the fourteen SEALs were waiting for the last flight checks on the two choppers. One squad would be in each bird in case of enemy fire. Stroh was on hand yelling at the crew and waving off Indian personnel. He loved it. Murdock watched and grinned.

The 46s took off on schedule. The SEALs had five Bull Pups with forty rounds per man and double ammo for the rest of the guns. They had extra long guns this time and fewer submachine guns.

The two birds kept in visual and radio contact with each other; in the eerie moonlight, they had their noncombat warning lights on. Thirty minutes out from the landing strip, the crew chief talked to Murdock over the roar of the engines and the rotor noise.

"We're seven minutes from Chinese territory. Our men are supposed to be another twenty-five miles into China. That will take us ten more minutes. We'll use our global locator to zero in on their coordinates."

"Let's hope they haven't had to move."

Murdock looked out the open door past the gunner but could see little. They had climbed continuously from their fifteen hundred foot landing strip to get over the closest of the mountains, which the crew chief had told him would be over thirteen thousand feet.

Jaybird grunted nearby. "Service ceiling on this bird is

fourteen thousand. Hope we have enough oomph."

Ahead, the mountains slanted upward again and the two
46s vibrated as the engines strained in the thin air.

Ten minutes later the crew chief was back.

"We're over the last pass and into China near our target.
Working out final approaches now. Our maps show those
coordinates to be in a valley."

Murdock went back to his men and told them what he
knew.

"How did these guys send out coordinates?" Lam asked.

"Maybe they radioed before they bailed out," Ching said.
"They could have had time to get it nearly right."

"Fly boys jump with any kind of flares in their flight
suit?" Bradford asked.

"Some do, some don't," Murdock shouted so they could
hear.

They all felt the ship head downhill.

"We've pitched down," Bradford said. "Must have some
idea where these guys are."

The crew chief came into the cabin. "Flare sighted, we're
going down. This valley shows at more than twelve thousand feet."

"Let's get ready to get out of here," Murdock said. "The
pilot might not be able to land. He told me if it was too
rough looking in his landing lights, he'd get us down to at
least three feet and hold."

"I can do three feet," Howie Anderson said.

The crew chief came in and the green light snapped on.
He waved at them and pointed to the two side doors for
exit. Three men on each side.

Murdock felt the bird touch the ground. The crew chief
waved them out the doors. Murdock went first. He couldn't
see a thing when he jumped down the three feet from the
bottom of the hatch door to the ground. A swirl of rotor
dust clogged everything. He used the Motorola. "Hold in
place until the birds take off." He could see the other chopper fifty feet to the left. A moment later his chopper lifted
and vanished into the dark sky. Two red flares would be

the signal for the choppers to return to the ground for pickup.

Murdock willed the dust to settle. "DeWitt, on me about fifty feet down the slope."

"Roger that, I have your position."

Murdock's five men came around him.

"I don't see no fucking flare," Anderson said.

"We hold here for a minute. If the airmen can move, they should be on their way to us."

They waited, watching for a flare, a gunshot, anything. The only thing they heard was DeWitt and his seven men moving to their location.

"Anyone see a flare?" Murdock asked.

He had no response.

"Time?" Murdock asked.

"Its just after oh four thirty," Jaybird said. "An hour or so to daylight.

"Any concealment around here?" Murdock asked. He had seen some low brush but not much of it.

Lam had made a circle of their position. He came back shaking his head. "This is rock heaven. A few sparse shoots of grass and some bushes, but not much to hide in."

"We're stuck here until we find out where our men are," Murdock said.

A second later a shot jolted into the night.

"Where?" Murdock asked. Six hands pointed in different directions.

"So we know they're here," Murdock said. "They heard us come in. They must not be able to move. Why we don't know. No options here, gentlemen. We wait for daylight and try for a visual sighting—before the Chicoms do."

"Find a bush and wrap yourself around it," DeWitt said. "Not enough dirt here for hide holes. We'll sit and hope." He looked around in the darkness. "Ostercamp and Jefferson on guard till daylight. The rest of you, sack out."

DeWitt sat down next to Murdock cradling his Bull Pup. "So which direction are they?"

"Guess?"

"Educated professional estimation."

"Down the valley to the left. Has to be downhill. They wouldn't be up the slope." Murdock thought about it a moment. "Lam," he said into his lip mike.

Lam slid in next to Murdock without the officer hearing him.

"How about a little hike downhill?" Lam asked.

Murdock grinned. "You voted for downslope as well?"

" 'Deed I did. I'm ready when you're ready, Cap."

They moved out silently on the rocky ground. The slope was gentle but consistent. They had gone fifty feet when Lam held up his hand and Murdock ran into him.

Something ahead," Lam whispered. "You have your NVGs?"

Murdock hadn't wanted to use them until he had to. They distorted normal night vision when you took them off. He slid them out of the pouch and put them over his eyes scanning ahead. The darkness turned into soft green haze like a green dusk. He could see rocks and bushes and not much else.

"Chicom?" Lam whispered.

"Could be, but why would they wait for daylight? They could charge in and take the guys out."

"Souvenirs, and show time for propaganda," Lam said. "The Chicoms are good at it."

Murdock nodded. They moved forward again, Murdock in front now with the glasses. He figured they had gone down the slope twenty yards to the bottom of the small valley. The footing was easier and the growth bigger. He saw a tree ahead over twenty feet tall. They could hide in there from a cursory air check.

Murdock stopped and went to one knee. Lam floated in beside him.

"Somebody's up there," he said. He handed Lam the NVGs. The scout studied the area, then both sides of the twenty-yard-wide ravine. He handed the glasses back.

"Yeah, I make it two bodies. Could be our guys. They have some camo over them but not enough. No way it's Chicom. Maybe thirty yards up there."

"Let's work closer," Murdock said. They eased their way

forward. It could be a trap, Murdock knew, but he put it out of his mind and stepped down the ravine a cautious half yard at a time.

Twenty feet away. Murdock checked the area again with his night vision goggles. "I see a U.S. flag shoulder patch on one guy," Murdock whispered. He handed the goggles to Lam. The scout nodded.

"Hey fly boys, you the Tomcats we're hunting?" Murdock asked.

There was silence. Lam saw the bodies were moving, maybe getting in a defensive position.

"Tomcats, we're Navy SEALs come with some support. Is that you?"

"Could be, how do we know you're on our side," the voice came scratchy, hard to understand. "Hey, who replaced Johnny Carson on the *Tonight* show?"

"Jay Leno, Tomcats. You wounded?"

"The commander is hurt bad." I'm busted a little but can move. Heard you come in back a while with two choppers. We had some Chinese jets looking for us. They found our Cat, but it has to be twenty miles from here."

"Don't shoot, we're coming in. Two of us." Murdock went to his lip mike. "We've got them, DeWitt. Bring the men down and let's find an LZ. One man hurt bad."

"That's a Roger. How far?

"Maybe three hundred yards. Can't miss us in the bottom of the ravine here."

Murdock and Lam moved in. They found the two airmen in a slight depression behind a small tree that would give them concealment from the air. One man came to his knees and held out his left hand.

"Lieutenant Birnbaum. Damn glad to see you guys. Where are the choppers?"

"Be coming as soon as we find an LZ down here," Murdock said. "Broken arm?"

"Yeah and some other stuff. The commander is out of it again. He slips in and out. He got hit with a twenty before we kicked out. We never saw the MiG who must have run out of missiles."

"DeWitt, we need that LZ in a rush," Murdock said to his lip mike. "Shoot one flare, and charge down here. Get those choppers back. We should have had the SATCOM with us."

"Coming, one red flare up."

Murdock saw it blossom and hoped that the chopper pilots could see it. He prayed they weren't a ridge line over.

"Can the commander stand?"

"We walked in here from where we landed. I mostly carried him. Need a litter if you have one in the chopper. Otherwise we carry him."

"Any Chinese troops around the area?"

"Think so. We heard two choppers come and then go, but not sure how far away they were. After that we heard some small arms fire. Could be infantry looking for us."

"So we use the flares and get out of here before the Chicoms find us," Lam said. He had found two tree branches he broke to the right length. "Let me splint that arm for you, Lieutenant," Lam said.

"We don't want it messed up any more than it is." Lam laid a piece of the branch under the officer's arm and one on top. Murdock held them in place while Lam tied them securely on one end with a kerchief he took out of his pocket. He used the roller bandage from his pocket and wrapped it ten times to secure the other end.

The commander pilot groaned and woke up. "Where the hell are we?" he asked.

"Still in China, Commander. I'm Murdock with SEALs. We're going to get you out of here."

"Cap, I've got an LZ for us," DeWitt said. "About fifty yards from where I see you under that tree. I've got the men in a perimeter defense. Going to be light in about twenty. We've fired three more red flares. Where the hell are those choppers?"

"Should be watching for the flares," Murdock said on the Motorola. "Keep one man on the LZ with two red flares ready to mark it on the ground when the choppers come."

"Roger that."

They waited.

The backseat man sat beside his pilot. He looked at Murdock. "Where the hell is that chopper?"

"Two of them, who are supposed to be here by now. We've fired two more flares. They may have pulled back waiting for daylight to be sure we have found you."

"Them and the Chink infantry," the Commander said. "Yeah, I'm back. Gut hurts like fire. Guess I got gut shot. Damn but that hurts."

"Getting you out of here, Jock, no sweat," Lieutenant Birnbaum said. "Just hang in there, buddy."

"You guys have any kind of a radio?"

"Not with us. Wish we did."

Murdock went over to DeWitt who stood looking uphill at the LZ he had picked.

"Anything closer?" Murdock asked. "The commander is gut shot, so we'll have to carry him."

"I'll work it down this way. It's getting too damn light for our flares to do much good. Where are the damn choppers?"

Twenty minutes later they still waited. Streamers of light had daggered into the darkness eating it up, spreading like a cancer, devouring every bit of blackness it could find.

Lam came on the Motorola. "Cap, I'm out about five hundred in front of our perimeter downhill. Heard there could be some Chicom infantry in the area. I'm concealed and watching another mile of territory downgrade. Damn but these mountains are big ones. Don't have anything like this in Tennessee."

"Any movement down there?"

"Not so far. A little wind blowing which will make it harder, but I'll keep them pealed."

"Roger that, who gave you the five hundred?"

"I did, Cap. Figured you were busy and you'd just say okay, anyway. I've got my Pup with me, so I can engage at a thousand if you want me to, if anybody shows up."

"Hold fire and we'll see how we're doing. No choppers yet."

"Be full light in ten."

"Don't remind me."

Murdock looked up. The other men did as well.

"Chopper," somebody said. Then the sound faded.

"He's over one or two ridges," Murdock said. "Damn, how could he get lost? He's got the fucking coordinates."

Lieutenant Birnbaum shook his head. "Just isn't our day. I should have seen that damn MiG come up from the side. He didn't fire any missiles so I wasn't concerned by his blip. Figured I had worse trouble from the two MiGs firing missiles at us."

"Trouble, Cap," Lam said on the Motorola. "I've got at least twenty Chicom troops moving my way. They are on a search and destroy, kicking every shrub, digging into every nook and cranny. I figure they are about half a mile out. What the hell do you want me to do?"

24

Murdock listened to Lam's report of the Chinese troops.

"Only twenty. Any more coming out of the bushes down there?"

"That looks like all of them, Cap."

"We should keep them away from this area. Use your Bull Pup on them and I'll send down three more Pups to help. The damn chopper has to be coming in soon. Open fire when ready."

Murdock looked around. "I want three more Pups down five hundred to help Lam. Three of you, move now."

Four SEALs lifted up and ran forward. At the same time they heard the report of a 20mm round going off ahead of them. The fourth man at the rear, slowed and stopped. The other three charged down the slope.

"Yeah, love this gun," Lam said in the net. "First two rounds put them on the ground. Don't know how many will get up. I lasered them on the first man and it worked perfectly with an air burst. Oh, yeah, like fish in a barrel. I'm still way out of their range. They must be about seven hundred yards down there."

"Three more Pups coming. No chopper yet."

As he said it, Murdock heard the sounds of choppers coming toward them. Yes.

"Choppers inbound," Murdock shouted.

"Flares now on the LZ," DeWitt barked into the Motorola.

"Lieutenant, let's get the commander up and moving. Bradford, Ching, give us a hand here."

Both U.S. Navy 46 choppers came down the slope and settled into the landing zone.

"Choppers on the ground," Murdock said into his lip mike. "Lam and three buddies, bug out of there and get back up here for a ride. Move now."

The three men carried the unconscious pilot out of the depression and thirty yards up the slope to the 46 chopper. The rear hatch had been lowered and they carried the pilot inside. The lieutenant stayed with him. Chin and Bradford came out and ran back to the area to pick up their weapons.

The first mortar round came in with no warning. It exploded fifty yards up the slope from the choppers. The 46 closest to the SEALs with the pilots on board, lifted off at once before anyone could even yell at the pilot. Murdock screamed at him but he was gone. The second chopper stayed on the ground.

"Load up, all SEALs load up on the last chopper. Move it guys. Somebody has a damn mortar within range."

Two more mortar rounds landed and the SEALs dove into the rocks and dirt. One exploded with a furious blast twenty yards from the chopper. The SEALs were still in the dirt when the second bird revved up and began to take off. A mortar round landed ten feet from the nose of the big chopper and sliced jagged shrapnel through the cockpit, killing the pilot instantly and knocking out the engines. The bird settled to the ground and a fire erupted in the engine compartment.

"Take cover," Murdock bellowed into the lip mike. "Scatter, I want twenty yards between men." He looked downslope and saw the four SEALs moving toward him.

"You Pup men coming up the hill. No rush. We just lost our ride out of here. Lam, how are the Chinese?"

"Three or four of them ran back to where they were, hidden behind a hill or some bush. Fifteen of them must be out of action, dead or badly hurt. No shit, no chopper?"

"Not unless you want to roast marshmallows. The pilot and his backseat man got away in the first chopper."

"So we take a hike?" Lam asked.

"Unless we can sprout wings damn quick."

"I'll stay down here two hundred and see if the Chicoms come back. We gonna move during daylight?"

"Better, unless we want to eat off the abundance of the land."

Murdock went back to the tree and sat down. DeWitt came up a minute later. The two men looked at the still-blazing chopper. None of the three-man crew had escaped. They were killed by the mortar round or the fire.

"Nothing we can do for those three crewmen. Can't even get their dog tags. That burning chopper is going to be a beacon for the Chicoms to come find us. We better get moving."

"They did it to us again."

"We should be getting used to it," Murdock said. "We've got one MRE per man, no local sustenance, and twenty-five miles to hike uphill. We better haul ass. Anybody get hurt from those mortar rounds?"

"No, but the mortar means there are more Chicoms somewhere on the reverse slope of one of these ridges," DeWitt said.

"Call in Lam. As soon as he gets here, we choggie."

"Choggie?" DeWitt asked.

"Hangover from the Korean War where they used choggie bearers to pack food and ammo. 'Choggie' came to mean to move, to hike, to run if you could."

"Thanks for the military history lesson."

The SEALs came in from their spread-out spots they took for the mortar barrage and gathered around the tree. The three Bull Pup shooters came back, and Lam made it a couple of minutes later.

"I've got fourteen heads," Jaybird said.

"Hiking time. Up this slope and then another one and maybe then downhill and to the border. Maybe. We better get moving. Anybody hurt or wounded?" Murdock looked around. Nobody sounded off.

"Okay, let's go, ten yards between men. Lam in front by about a hundred. We're outa here."

The first two miles went quickly. Murdock worried about the mortar but no more rounds were fired at them. The

Chinese could be moving up a squad with a medium mortar and digging it in ahead of them to set up a greeting. Could.

There had been no response from the Chicoms who had been moving up the ravine that Lam took out. Murdock decided they had been on a flushing patrol, not one moving against a known enemy. So were there any more of the probing units of twenty or more men searching these valleys and ravines? He hoped not.

Suddenly Murdock felt a chill race down his spine. This was it. He was living on the edge as almost no one could these days. He was afoot and twenty-five miles inside of red, Chicom, fucking China and had taken enemy fire. It didn't get any hairier than this. Now all they had to do was get out of this death trap.

Two more miles up the hill and Murdock called a halt. He kept the men spread out. The rise came sharper and sometimes they had to use their hands to help get up a slant. Lots of it was slab rock from some giant lava flow a million years ago.

Murdock checked his watch: 0736. Time enough for that bird to get back to India and report in. The pilot had to see the other chopper hit and burning. Murdock could imagine the report of a hot fire fight that pilot and crew would give to justify their leaving without a full load.

"Think they'll send in a chopper to lift us out?" DeWitt asked.

Murdock shook his head. "Not a chance. Think what a wild tale that crew is going to spin about how much fire they took. They might even have a hole or two from shrapnel. Oh, hell no, they won't risk losing another bird in here just for fourteen fucked-up SEALs."

"Yeah, I agree. We need any more scouts out?"

"Lam can do it to the front. No way we can maintain scouts on each flank. Damn walls are getting steeper."

DeWitt checked ahead. "This ravine is petering out on us. In another two miles we'll have to go up the side of the ridge line and hope it gets us to the top of this one and then someway to get down the reverse to the next ridge. How many you guess we'll do?"

Murdock put away his compass. They had been heading almost due south. He figured they were inside the long point of China that daggered south between India's Sikkim area and the small nation of Bhutan.

"It might be simpler to head west and get back across the border to India. If any of our ridges or valleys aim that direction. This whole neck of China can't be more than fifteen miles wide at the broadest, and it comes almost to a point the farther south we go."

"It might come down to which route China gives us," DeWitt said. "Right now I'd bet that they will attack us before we get to the top of this long ravine."

They moved again. Murdock put Lam out two hundred and increased the space between his men to twenty yards. He kept watching the ridge to their left. He didn't know why, unless it was because he had a feeling the mortar rounds came from that side. He went to the Motorola.

"Lam, anyone. See anything to the ridge on the left? I have a bad feeling about it."

"That's where the mortar rounds came from," Lam said. "I checked one ground hit. It's not obvious like an artillery round, but I figured the spray of rock was more to the right than the left. So the round came angling in from the left."

Twenty minutes later the ravine ended in a sheet of rock wall of ninety degrees. Lam had scouted left and right and he pointed to the right. That's when the first mortar round came in. The Chicoms hadn't set in their base plate yet so they couldn't get any accuracy until it was solidly in the ground. The first round was off downhill and onto the side of the ravine wall to the right.

The SEALs had bunched up at the wall. Now Murdock bellowed at them. "Spread out. Two men with Pups go up that left wall and see if you can find that gun. I want it out of there."

Just as Bradford and Ostercamp started up the left slope, rifle fire erupted from the top. The two dove for protective boulders and scurried behind them. The scattering SEALs also found large rock boulders they could hide behind.

The mortars fired twice more, once short, the other one long.

"Have us bracketed," Murdock said. "Stay down. Bull Pups, I want two rounds each along the top of that ridge left. Laser the top of the ridge and hope for an airburst that will sweep the backside clean. Fire when ready."

Murdock lifted his Pup and lasered the light on the top of the left ridge three hundred yards upslope. He fired. He saw three air bursts before his hit with another air burst. The firing from the top slowed, but didn't stop. Four more rounds went off just above the ridge top and the firing from there stopped suddenly.

"Bradford and Ostercamp, on up to the top and hunt that—"

A mortar round went off just off where the SEALs hid behind rocks.

When the round went off, Ostercamp and Bradford hit the ground, but when the shrapnel stopped singing, they jumped up and ran up the slope. Soon they were grabbing rocks with their hands to help them get up. Behind them they heard four more mortar rounds go off. They charged faster, panting for breath, legs stinging from the buildup of toxins. Another twenty feet.

A Chinese soldier lifted up ahead and swung his rifle around. Bradford drilled him with three rounds from the 5.56mm barrel and he slammed backward out of sight.

Two more mortar rounds hit below as Bradford and Ostercamp bellied up to the ridge line and looked over. Forty yards down the slope a gun squad of four men worked the mortar. The SEALs saw two infantrymen on the top of the ridge looking over. Ostercamp pointed at the infantrymen and then at himself. He hosed down the two men with six 5.56mm-rounds each, while Bradford slammed three 20-mm rounds into the mortar crew.

The gun toppled over, blown off its bipod. Two of the men on the gun went down with multiple and fatal shrapnel wounds. The third man carried a round toward the assistant gunner. He dropped it and tried to run, but Ostercamp's three rounds of 5.56mm slugs cut his stomach open and he died in seconds. The fourth man vanished behind some rocks.

The two SEALs studied the ravine. It was a twin for the one they had just come up. Far down Ostercamp pointed to a blob. It had to be a mile away. "What is it?"

Bradford put his Pup scope on it. "A damned Jeep. No wonder they got ahead of us. Range?"

Ostercamp had his Bull Pup up as well and sighted in. "More than a mile. Range on these pups is only twelve hundred. Let's laser it and try a couple of rounds. Shooting downhill we get more distance. Might scare them." They laser sighed on the jeep, and fired. The two rounds air burst forty yards short of the target, but enough shrapnel slammed that way that the jeep-type rig dug its wheels as it raced down the slope and out of range.

"Give the bastard something to think about," Bradford said. He saw something and fired a quick shot from the 20mm at a rock twenty yards from the ruined mortar. A man screamed, lifted up and tried to fire a rifle, then crumpled and didn't move.

"We're clear up here," Bradford said in his Motorola.

"Come on down," Murdock said. "We're going up the other side. Thanks for silencing that mortar. We picked up a couple of scratches in the exchange. Nothing to worry about. We're moving."

"Cap, we scared away a vehicle of some kind, jeep-like. It went blasting out of range down the ravine. We won't have to worry about that mortar or those infantrymen."

"Roger that."

It took the SEALs ten minutes to work up the sharp incline of the right-hand side of their ravine. Once on the crest, they saw that it angled into a far higher ridge in front of them that was slanting more to the west. Murdock checked his compass.

"Yes, let's get down that slope and into the valley down there, more of a ravine, maybe thirty feet wide at the bottom, but it will be easier working to the west."

They hiked.

Twice in the next hour they heard aircraft. Once it was

a pair of what they figured were MiGs slanting across the
sky up high and well to the north of them.

The second aircraft was a chopper. It worked away from
them, then came back. Murdock decided it was following
the ravines, hunting for them. This time it was closer.

"Let's find something to hide under or around. Rocks,
shrubs, anything and get dirt and rocks over you. Can't tell
how close this bastard will come."

They covered up as well as they could. There wasn't
enough dirt and growth here to do a perfect job. Anyone
with good glasses from five hundred feet could pick them
out. Murdock lay in his small depression next to a boulder
and behind a small shrub and hoped.

Then it was too late. The chopper swung over the ridge
and aimed right for them. It turned away from them, and
flew up the canyon to the source two miles away.

"Hold tight, he'll be back" Murdock said in the Motorola. "Be ready for him. If he finds us and fires, we take
him out with the twenties. Be ready to fire."

They waited.

Five minutes later the chopper came back. It slowed fifty
yards from them, then came forward again, slow, then hovered. It was about two hundred feet and the rotor wash blew
away some of the sand on the ground.

Then the Chinese bird inched forward until it was over
the first SEAL. In a quick move the chopper pilot turned
the bird in a small circle around the SEALs and the door
gunner got off a murderous burst with a 30-caliber, door-
mounted machine gun aimed directly at the SEALs.

25

With the first muzzle blast from the machine gun, four SEALs fired with their twenties. The machine gun rounds splattered into the rocks around the SEALs. Three of the four twenties hit the bird and exploded on impact. The gunner slumped over his 30 caliber before he could fire again. One 20mm round detonated inside the cockpit, shattering the instruments, killing the pilot and sending the craft into a whirling and gyrating dance as it dove power on into the ground and exploded fifty feet from the SEALs.

"Any casualties?" DeWitt asked on the Motorola.

"Only the Chicoms in the fucking chopper," Jaybird chirped. "That was a big bird, a lot like our forty-sixes. Must be used for transporting troops. So I wonder where they are?"

"Yeah, Lieutenant, I'm not exactly a casualty, but I've got me a little scratch," Guns Franklin said, his voice missing its usual twang.

"On it," Mahanani said. He lifted from the ground and looked around for Franklin. He was at the edge of the group. The medic ran to him and knelt in front of Franklin. He couldn't see any blood.

"Where, buddy?"

"Arm, a ricochet I'd guess. Fucker hurts like my arm was blown off."

Mahanani saw some blood then, halfway up Franklin's left forearm. He peeled back the cammy shirt gently.

"Yeah, just a scratch, Guns. About three inches long and to the bone. Gonna need some stitches in there. I'll use some butterfly bandages to pull it together."

Mahanani dumped antiseptic on the wound, then pulled it together and bound the whole thing with a roller bandage.

"There you go, Guns. You want a morphine?"

"Hell, no, just a damn scratch."

"Fit for duty, Commander, and ready to roll," Franklin said to his lip mike.

"Yeah, we better move," Murdock said. "If there's any more Chicom air in the area, this burning chopper is another damn signal flare to them where we are. Let's choggie."

They hiked.

Lam kept them on a generally western course, heading into the closest friendly territory, the Sikkim area of India. Murdock wondered if there would be any border guards. India and China had never been on good terms. Now with the overflights and the shoot downs, tensions could be running high. Even so, he figured that border guards up in this remote most northern part of India were unlikely.

They moved out for an hour down the small valley, then had to go up and over another ridge when the valley turned south. They were on the side slope with no vegetation at all when they heard a jet plane.

"Down and don't move," Murdock barked into the Motorola. "We don't know where he is or if he's coming this way. We play it safe."

They waited for five minutes.

The jet sound faded and was gone.

The SEALs moved again to the west.

Murdock couldn't help but think about the pilot on the first 46 that bugged out on them. It was mortar fire, not pinpoint target shooting. Chances were that the bird would not have been hit at all, even with a fire-for-effect, six-round salvo from the Chicom mortar men. A mortar is an area weapon, not a direct targeting one.

When they got out of here, Murdock was going to make every effort to contact that pilot in person and take him apart verbally and physically if possible. The bastard had run out on them. Yellow-bellied out, and Murdock would have some satisfaction.

"You never leave your men behind in combat."

It was a principle that every officer had to commit to. This fucking pilot chickened out and flew away when the first mortar round hit. Murdock let his anger rage as he walked along. He was going to write up a scathing letter of objection, critical and asking for a reprimand, a letter in the officer's permanent personnel file, and a court-martial if possible.

Murdock came out of his reverie with sound in his earpiece.

"Looks like some trouble up ahead," Lam said.

"What?" Murdock asked.

"Not sure, come on up, skipper and take a look."

Murdock called a halt and put the men down, then moved up to where Lam lay at the top of the ridge looking down the reverse slope.

"A blocking force?" Lam asked.

Murdock looked down in the small valley. Six hundred yards ahead he saw six wall tents, cooking fires, a dozen men moving around the tents, and a squad of eight lined up in front of the area for an inspection or getting ready to go out on patrol.

"Infantry, for damn sure," Murdock said.

"Bet they have patrols out blocking every possible route through this area," Lam said. "There could be fifty to seventy-five troops in that camp."

"So we don't tangle with them," Murdock said. "Even with the twenties, because we don't know where all of their men are. Let's not make the ones not in camp mad. We work around and through them, and hope we get a break."

Murdock looked around. "Best bet is we go down this ridge to the valley, up the other side and over that ridge. Gives us about a mile away from the camp. Then we work west and watch for any ambush patrols just sitting there waiting for somebody to walk into their traps. We also look for roving patrols and individual sentries. With that many men they can flood this area."

Before either of them could move they heard a jet pass-

ing over them and thundering away to the west, then it
turned north.

"Never hear those suckers until they go by you when
they're that close," Lam said. "Think he saw us?"

"No. He was looking at the camp down there. Checking
on it. Probably in radio contact with them for any help they
might need. We better get moving."

It took the SEALs almost an hour to get away from the
Chinese camp and into the next ravine-like small valley and
back on their way to the west.

Murdock wondered how long the Chicoms had been in
that blocking position. If they had just arrived by chopper,
they might not have a lot of patrols out yet. His platoon
might get lucky and slip through.

Lam edged up to the lip of another ridge and looked
over. They had to go down the other side and across a
larger valley with the hint of a stream in the bottom. In the
center of the valley beside the now-dry streambed, stood a
tree. In the shade of the tree sat six Chinese soldiers, evidently taking a break and eating from their rice rolls that
usually were slung over their shoulders.

"Skipper, our luck ran out. We've got a six-man patrol
up here on our route."

Murdock hurried up to the spot and looked over.

"Looks like they will be there for a while. Can you see
any radios?"

"Nope. Check it with your Pup scope."

Murdock put the scope on the six and shook his head.
"No radio, but a few twenty rounds could be heard in here
for five miles."

"Skipper, don't look like we can go round this one without backtracking four or five miles. I've been watching this
ridge to our right. That's the way we'd have to go. It's a
sheer cliff two hundred feet high. Not a rat's ass chance
we can get up it. We go through these guys or we backtrack
a mile out of sight and try to go past them on the left.
Which I don't recommend."

"Done," Murdock said. "DeWitt, take a look at this,"
Murdock said in his Motorola.

The tall, slender (j.g.) came up to the spot and swore when he saw the patrol. "They settled down there to keep house for a month or so?"

"Looks like it. No chance to go around them on the right. We could go back a mile and try to get past them on the left."

"More Chicoms over there, it's a bet," DeWitt said. "Hell, we have to go through them and then run like hell west before the rest of those Chicoms come boiling in here to see who's shooting."

"Agreed. We move up the ridge to the closest spot to the patrol, then do it."

It took them fifteen minutes to move along the side of the ridge to the spot Lam had picked for the attack. They spread out five yards apart and set up. The Chinese patrol had finished eating and the men were sitting around waiting. The targets were less than two hundred yards away.

"Fire on my command. Ten seconds should do it. All weapons. Ready . . . fire."

The fourteen weapons cracked, chattered and blasted. The machine gun belted out six-round bursts. The twenties exploded on contact riddling the standing and sitting Chinese infantry. Two crawled behind rocks and returned fire, but they didn't seem sure where the rounds came from. Murdock saw one of the men hiding behind a rock and lasered a round and fired. It exploded ten feet over the rock shredding the back side of the hiding spot with deadly shrapnel.

Twelve seconds into the firing, Murdock called a cease-fire.

Only one Chinese soldier still stood. He raised his rifle, then fell flat on his face.

"Let's move, people," Murdock said. "Down the slope through that little valley and up the other side before our Chicom friends get some support. Go, go, go."

Murdock trotted down the easy slope with the others, double-timed across the small valley edging around the dead Chinese. One of them lifted a pistol and took six SEAL rounds in his chest.

Murdock used the mike as he jogged along. "Okay, logic time. This last hit means the Chicoms will figure out in about twenty seconds where we're headed. Not sure how much farther we have to go, but even if it's two miles, it gives them plenty of time and space to set up a surprise for us. How?"

"Send in a pair of choppers with troops to cover four or five of the valleys we may use," Lam said.

"Could, what else?

"Same choppers could bring in a small tank?" Jaybird asked. "They have birds big enough to lift that much?"

"Unknown. Other ideas."

"A pair of chopper gunships, like our Cobra. The kind built for strafing and rocketing ground targets. They would know to stay out of range of our twenties."

"Yeah," Murdock said. "Three ideas that could happen. So now we work on ways to counter all three of them. So work on them, and in the meantime we blast our way over this fucking ridge and get out of eyesight of the bodies back there. That's in case they have any sub-five-minute mile runners on their Chicom teams."

They soon topped the ridge and worked at a slower pace down the far side. Again it was slab rock, some decomposed granite and a little more sparse growth of grass and a bush here and there.

"Lam, how far have we come since we turned west," DeWitt asked on the mike.

"Six, maybe eight miles," Lam said.

"So, if we only had ten to twelve to go, we could be within two to four miles of the border."

"Hell of a long choggie when a hundred bastards are shooting at you," Howie Anderson said.

They worked down a two-mile-long razor-thin valley that had a dry streambed in the bottom. More growth showed now, with a scattering of brush along the streambed.

Thirty minutes after topping the ridge line, they were though the valley and moving up another ridge. Lam edged to the top and stared over it. Then he stood and waved them forward. They were halfway down the slope before they saw the two camouflaged Chinese armored personnel carriers. Both moved out and machine guns on the hatches pivoted toward the SEALs.

"Scatter," Murdock bellowed and the SEALs darted different directions until they were twenty yards apart. They hit the ground, and at once the heavy machine gun fire came their way.

"What the hell, Skipper," Jaybird barked. "Our twenties won't touch those babies."

"About the size of our V-three hundred Commando APCs," Anderson said. "Which means they could have ten troops inside each one."

"Bull Pups, dig out your armor-piercing rounds and load five in the mag. Then let's see what we can do. Sound off when you're loaded and ready."

Forty seconds later the five men with Bull Pups were ready.

The enemy machine guns chattered again. They were heavy, fifties, Murdock decided. Big enough to tear a man's arm off at the shoulder.

"Fire two rounds of twenty each," Murdock said. He sighted in without the laser and fired. Worked the sight and fired again. Murdock watched the target through his six-power scope. He saw two of the rounds hit and explode with no penetration. One jolted through a viewport and must have exploded inside. The vehicle veered off course and came to a stop.

"One lucky hit," Murdock said on the mike. "What do we do with the other one?"

"I'm hit," a SEAL shrilled in his lip mike.

"Who?" Murdock asked.

"Canzoneri. Caught a splatter of one of their rounds off a rock. Not too bad. I won't be running any marathons for a while."

"Mahanani, can you get to Canzoneri?"

"Roger that, Skipper."

The armored personnel came closer. "She's at six hundred yards," Ed DeWitt said. "Bull Pups, work the treads.

If she turns left or right, get on the side of the treads. If not, hit them head on."

The twenties spoke again and again, but the APC plowed ahead over the hard ground and flat rock.

"Who has the EAR?" Murdock asked.

"On my back," Ostercamp said.

"Charge it and get ready to try for any kind of a port that thing has. Fire when you're ready. Aim at the nose of it where there could be concealed ports. We might get a lucky bounce."

"Cap, we've got ten grunts out of that first APC. They're moving up," Jaybird said.

"Seven hundred yards. Bradford and I will go at them with our Pups, rest of your stay on the baby tank."

Murdock sighted in, lasered and fired. Bradford fired about the same time. Murdock sighted in again as the rounds hit. Four of the Chinese went down. He fired again and so did Bradford. This time three more men slammed into the ground and didn't move. The last three men ran behind the dead personnel carrier.

Murdock heard the familiar *whoosh* of the EAR. They had used it effectively at four hundred yards. He wasn't sure if it would reach out five hundred. The EAR blast sent up a gout of dirt and dust well in front of the tank. Short.

"Wait on the EAR until the APC gets to four hundred yards, then fire five times."

"Roger that, Skipper."

Murdock had been sighting in on the APC. It suddenly hit some glazed rock and one tread slipped slewing it almost sideways. Four Pups barked and rounds slammed into the tread rollers and exploded. One had been an AP round, which bored through some linkage and then exploded. The APC came back on line for the SEALs but the left track wasn't working right. It kept turning the carrier off course to the left.

At four hundred yards range, Ostercamp fired the next EAR round, waited ten seconds for the charge to build and when the red light flicked on, he fired again. Both rounds hit the APC. At first there was no obvious effect. Then gradually the rig began to slow. Ostercamp punched another EAR round at it, and then a fourth. This time the armored personnel carrier came to a stop. Only two men came out the back. They began to run to the rear, but stumbled and waved their arms to get their balance, then fell into the rocks and dirt of the high country of China, and started a six-hour nap.

Murdock waited. No more men came out of the stalled rig. He looked at his Bull Pup. He had only six rounds left. "Ammo count on the Pups," he said.

When the men checked in, they averaged five rounds per man.

"Hold fire on the twenties unless we absolutely need them," Murdock said. "Use the five fifty-six instead."

"Lam, what do you see up there?"

Lam had taken out his eight-by-thirty fieldglasses and stared down the valley. "Not good, Skipper. I wondered why those two men ran to the rear. There are at least three camouflaged tents back there a mile and half. Big enough to hold twenty men each. They could still have forty men ready to fight. Must be some kind of a check point. Not sure but there could be a chopper on the ground almost behind one of the tents. They know we're here. Men running all over the place. I see no vehicles."

There was some dead air on the Motorolas.

"Medic, how is Canzoneri?"

"Gouge out of his right leg. Took out a chunk of flesh and bled like a stuck hog. I've got it bundled up, but he's gonna need a crutch to walk and we'll distribute his equipment and weapon. Not ready for duty."

"Noted, Mahanani."

"I'll be a shit-faced mama whore," Lam exploded. "They just formed up in squads and now are marching this way in diamond formations. A whole fucking bunch more than just forty. I'd say over a hundred. Commander Murdock, what the hell are we supposed to do now?"

26

"What do we do?" Murdock echoed. "First we pull back over the ridge and set up on the reverse slope. When they get in range of the twenties, we hit them with ten of our remaining twenty-five rounds. We take assigned sectors to do the most damage. If that doesn't stop them, we run like hell into the valley behind us. There's enough real dirt down there so we vanish."

"Vanish like in hide holes?" Jefferson asked.

"Exactly. Now, let's get over that ridge line."

The waiting was the hardest. They had moved back to the ridge and went over it, then set up with weapons primed and ready, thrusting over the ridge, and aimed eleven hundred yards down the slope. The Chinese would be still in the valley when they came in range. Murdock hoped that they didn't split up into flanking units.

"Fifteen hundred yards," Lam said. "Remember, shooting downhill you'll get a distortion. Will that make any difference on the lasered sights?"

"We'll find out," DeWitt said.

The troops below seemed to be moving slowly. They acted like they were on an ambush patrol checking every bush and gully. Another five minutes before Lam sounded off.

"I make it eleven hundred yards, Commander. A hundred yards inside our Bull Pup range."

Murdock assigned all five guns to the target with each one a different sector. "I'll fire one round for range and we'll check it," Murdock said. He lasered in on the point of the men in his sector and fired. They saw the flash a second before the sound of the twenty exploding slammed past them like a thundering herd of buffalo.

"Yeah, on target," Lam said putting down his field-glasses.

"Two rounds each on your sectors," Murdock said and sighted in again. All but one of the ten rounds were on target. The Chinese hit the ground after Murdock's first shot. They made a better target that way for an air burst. Two men ran to the rear. One whole diamond formation was neutralized with dead and wounded.

Two other formations regrouped, and with what must have been strong leadership, began walking forward.

"Let's move it," Murdock said. "Down to the dry river-bed. Twenty yards apart. Should be enough loose sand down there to make the holes easy. Go, go, go."

They jogged down the slope.

"Twenty minutes," DeWitt said on the net. "Should take the Chicoms twenty to get up that slope the way they're moving. So we need some fast action of the digging."

The SEALs came to the streambed and spaced out along it facing the ridge they had just left. Then they dug with their hands and their K-bar knives, moving enough sand to lay down in the hole and then pull the sand over them as total camouflage. Only their faces would show and the muzzles of their weapons pointing at the ridge line.

All the men worked hard. Canzoneri had given his weapon and combat vest to buddies and Mahanani helped him make the trip down to the dry streambed.

"Hurts like hell, Maha. Maybe one of those capsules when you get time."

Both were digging in the sand with their combat knives. Mahanani gave Canzoneri a shot of morphine, then made sure he was covered and ready before he finished his own hole.

"Short time," Murdock called. The last man slid into his hole and pulled the last bit of sand over his arms and chest.

They were good. Murdock looked ahead and could see only one lump of sand that looked unnatural. It should work.

Again they waited.

Murdock has positioned himself so he could see the ridge line they had just left. That's where the first Chicoms should appear.

Another five minutes crawled by before Murdock saw the first Chicom head lift tentatively over the ridge line and then vanish. Two more took a look, then another, probably an officer, edged up and used fieldglasses.

"Our company has arrived," Murdock whispered into his lip mike.

The Chinese became bolder. One man sat on the ridge-top. Another stood and pointed his rifle down into the small valley. The enemy troops were less than two hundred yards from the SEALs. If they marched across the streambed they would probably step on one of the SEALs. If they kicked one man out of the camouflage it would be a close-in deadly fight, and the SEALs would not have a chance. Would they come down?

As he watched, Murdock saw three men slide over the edge and move forward. Good move, send out a patrol. The three men moved with nervous hesitation. They looked across the valley and at the far ridge line. It was a thousand yards away, but they had been hurt before at that range. If the patrol kept coming, Murdock knew two of them would miss the SEALs. One man would be inside the group. He couldn't see exactly where. Then they were so close, Murdock ducked his face into his hand and slid his cammy colored floppy hat over his head.

He heard nothing for three minutes. Murdock knew it was three minutes because he counted: one alligator, two alligators, three alligators . . . when he reached a hundred and eighty, he cautiously lifted his face off his hand and peered out. He could see a few heads over the closest ridge line. Where was the three-man patrol? He moved his head slightly and slowly so he could see downstream. There they were. The men had crossed the dry bed and were halfway up the far ridge. They all had been below the SEALs or the one who went through the patrol hadn't stepped on anyone.

A voice bellowed at the patrol from the near ridge, an order of some sort. The patrol turned and began jogging back. If they kept their course they would miss where the SEALs were hidden.

They all waited.

Murdock used the lip mike. "Hold fast everyone. The patrol is heading back to the ridge. Their route will miss our location."

"What happens if they decide to leave a lookout up on that ridge, Skipper?" Jaybird asked.

"Then we all go to sleep until it gets dark," DeWitt answered.

Later Murdock used the mike again. "Anybody see the patrol?"

"I've got them," Lam said. "Almost to the top of the near ridge they came down."

"Just hold on, guys. We played Indian this way for four hours at a time in training, remember?" Two minutes later, Murdock wondered about the wounded man. "Canzoneri, how are you doing?" Murdock asked.

There was no immediate reply.

"Cap, I think he went to sleep," Mahanani said. "He had an ampoule and he was getting sleepy when I helped him with his hole. He should be okay. Just so he doesn't sleep-walk."

They waited again.

"The patrol just went over the ridgeline, Skipper," Lam said. "I haven't seen any heads up there for ten minutes. You want me to ease up there and see if they all left?"

"And what if they haven't left?" DeWitt chimed in.

"Then I'm a dead Mandarin duck in goose sauce," Lam said. "Yeah. Guess not a good idea."

"Can anybody can see his watch?" Murdock asked.

"Yeah," Ching said. "I'm a little claustrophobic so I always get my watch where I can see it. Almost seventeen hundred."

"Roger, seventeen hundred," Murdock said. "Should be dark in another two hours. Everyone take a nap. No wet dreams you guys, you'll shake all the sand off your bodies."

Murdock moved slightly, then again. He felt some of the
carefully placed sand, dirt and rocks spill off him. Couldn't
be helped. He had to get better look at the ridgeline. Now,
he had it all. Where he had seen heads and an occasional
rifle before, now there was nothing. Were they playing possum on him, waiting out his next move? Or did they give
up and figure that the SEALs had bugged out over the next
ridge and were running like crazy? Could be either one.

He waited.

Now he had moved so he could see his watch. Time
dragged. He thought of something pleasant. Like Ardith
Manchester the only woman in his life for the past three or
four years. Yes, beautiful, tall, Ardith with the long blond
hair, a svelte sexy body, and a sharp lawyer's mind. Still
in D.C. working with her father the senator from Oregon.
Murdock was still trying to persuade her to leave D.C. and
move to San Diego. Move in with him. Maybe, some time
soon.

He shifted minutely and felt the sand and dirt shift. Not
good. Murdock checked his watch. Past eighteen hundred.
Could be dark in a half-hour.

Murdock looked at the ridge again. Hell, he should move
up there and check it. He got the men into this trap. He
should be the one to get them out of it. He moved one leg,
then stopped. Give it a few more minutes.

His earpiece sounded off. "Don't go, Murdock," DeWitt
said. "I know what you're thinking. It isn't time yet. Wait
for dusk at least."

"Hadn't crossed my mind."

"Don't let it. After dark we can get back on our westward
trek and be home free in India before morning."

"I'm taking bets on that," Murdock said.

They waited.

Ten minutes later, Murdock looked at his watch. It was
nearly dusk. Time to move out. He freed one arm when his
Motorola responded.

"Cap, good news," Lam said. "The fucking fucked up
Chicoms have bugged out from the ridge. Not a sight nor
sound of them up here. No wonder, I got ten feet away

from you guys, and I couldn't locate any of you. I'd say it's time to rock and roll."

"Lam, didn't I order you not to go up there," DeWitt barked on the radio.

"Yes, sir, Lieutenant sir. You told me not to go up there at that time. You didn't tell me not to come up here later on. It's done, so sue me."

"Enough," Murdock said. "Let's rise and shine, you guys. Count heads to be sure we don't leave somebody sleeping. Up and at 'em."

Murdock got to his feet and watched the river bottom erupt with bodies every twenty feet. It was weird, surprising even though he knew there were twelve other men down there. They all came up spitting and coughing. Within two minutes they had cleared their weapons, cleaned any problem areas, locked and loaded and were ready to travel.

"Lam, out front by fifty, keep us in sight if possible. We'll head due west across this valley and up the other side where the Chicoms think we already went. Anybody want to put a ten spot on our getting into India by midnight?"

"No way, Skipper."

"Not a chance."

"Not with our luck so far."

"At least you guys put your mouths where your money isn't. Let's roll." A moment later Murdock remember the wounded man.

"Canzoneri, what's your status?"

"Up and moving, Skipper. Looking for a sturdy stick I can use as a cane. Leg don't hurt much. I can walk, just don't know how far or how fast."

"Mahanani and Canzoneri up front. You set the pace. We've got ten hours of blessed darkness to get to India."

They walked ahead, through the valley and up the slope to the ridge. Murdock figured they were making about three miles an hour. Not bad considering Canzoneri's wound.

They went down the far side into another ravine-like valley and over two more ridges before Lam called a halt.

"Can't be sure, Skip, but sounds damn like a war is going

on up ahead. Can't be more than two or three miles off.
I've got machine guns, rifles, and what sounds like artillery
rounds all blasting away. Come on up and take a listen."

Ten minutes later the platoon was convinced.

"We got a fucking war on out there," Jaybird said.

"Could be the Chicoms and the Indians going at it on a
border clash," DeWitt said. "They have been having trouble
along half their frontier for the past twenty years."

"Great, so we pick the one spot where it's flared up on
the night we want to cross," Murdock said. "We keep moving straight ahead until we see how broad the front is. Then
we go around the closest end in a student body left."

"A sweep," Anderson said. "Yeah we used to use that
one when I played some college football."

"Cost us some time but what else can we do?" DeWitt
asked.

"We're going to have to slow down again," Mahanani
said. "Canzoneri is down. He can't walk on that leg anymore. We're going to have to carry him from here to the
border."

27

They kept moving straight ahead as Murdock had ordered. Each man who weighed as much or more than Canzoneri's 190 pounds was detailed to carrying him. The man packing Canzoneri farmed out his webbing and vest and weapon to others. The assignment was for a quarter of a mile. Then the next man took over.

It worked remarkably well. There were six men in the platoon who outweighed the injured man. Murdock took the first carry and kept his position as second in the line of march with Lam out in front and the rest stretched out behind at five-yard intervals.

They went down the next ridge and across another valley.

"Why can't we follow more of these snarks downstream a ways?" Ching asked.

He knew the answer before he finished the frustrated question. Obviously, the downstream direction was not the one they wanted to take.

Murdock turned the carrying job over to Howie Anderson after almost a half mile. He was winded but not done in. After that he would make sure they stuck to the quarter-mile distance.

They moved a little slower. The up and down ridge lines slowed them more and Lam estimated they were doing well to get three miles an hour.

Slightly after 2000, Lam called a halt. "Better take a look up here, gents," he said on the net. Everyone worked forward to another ridge line. This one had a scattering of taller brush than they had seen lately. Now the sound of gunfire and bursting shells could be heard plainly. In the distance almost due west they could see some flashes as the larger shells exploded.

"An artillery exchange?" Murdock suggested.

"Maybe, but what are those machine guns doing?" Ed DeWitt asked. "Artillery would be four to six miles between the shooters."

"Supporting an infantry attack," Lam said.

They watched the flashes. Most of them were coming from the right-hand side of the battle area.

"How far away are they?" Jaybird asked.

Lam frowned. He knew it was coming. "I'd say not over two miles for the strongest artillery hits."

"Let's swing on a forty-five to the left," Murdock said. Lam headed out on that bearing and Paul Jefferson lifted Canzoneri on his back and claimed the second spot in the line of march. So far they had been through the six men and were ready to start over.

"Jeff, I'm sorry man that I fucked up and got in the way of that round."

"Shut up, Canzoneri. Not your fault. My job to get you down the line another quarter. So let's ride happy back there."

They had slowed again. After another mile, Murdock called a halt. He and Lam went up a ridge that looked higher than the others hoping they could see the battle area. They could.

"Holy shit, look at that," Lam said.

In front of them a broad valley opened that looked to be ten miles long and half that wide. In the middle of it they could see tracers and hear small arms, and machine guns firing. The big guns pounded farther back. There was a war on down there, infantrymen, and on a flat fighting surface.

"My guess the international border runs right through the middle of the valley, half in China, half in India," Murdock said. "A damn good spot to hold a battle."

Lam studied the area in the sometimes moonlight. A cloud scudded away from the moon and he stared through his binoculars. "If we can get down another mile, we can hit the very edge of the valley and creep along it into India. We should be two, maybe three miles from the fighting."

"But you can bet that both sides will have patrols and lookouts in the areas," Murdock said.

"So, we watch them. Take them out with the EAR. Is there any battery left on it?

Murdock shook his head. He'd checked.

. Murdock took over the carry work as they climbed down the side of a steeper ridge and headed for the flat lands of the valley. Franklin's arm wound broke open and they stopped to let Mahanani rebandage it. Then they moved again. DeWitt brought up the rear.

A half hour later, Lam and Murdock looked out past a pair of good-size trees at the valley. They were fifty feet off the floor itself and could see where the fighting raged. The artillery still probed. The ground fighting was about a mile across the valley from them.

"This side should be best," Murdock said. "We work along the side, just off the valley itself. A lot more trees and brush here we can hide in if we have to. You stay out front two hundred and keep in constant contact with your Motorola. Let me know what you see, what you hear, what the brush is like, everything. Be a chatterbox."

"You got it, Skipper."

When the troops came up, Mahanani carried Canzoneri like he was no more than a second pack. The big Hawaiian's 240 pounds did the job easily.

Murdock and the rest of the SEALs heard Lam.

"Working along the side of the valley," Lam said. "Almost across from the fighting. Looks like the two sides are dug in about two hundred yards apart. Deadly no-man's-land in the middle. Bush is thick here. Moving closer to the valley. Hold it, a patrol."

The ear pieces went silent for thirty seconds.

"Okay, troops, that was close. Finally made out that it was a Chicom bunch, eight of them working along the edge of the valley, watching for line crossers, my guess. So keep twenty yards up in the brush and move slowly. No rush now. Maybe the next patrol I spot will be the Indians.

"Yeah, okay. The brush thins. I'm actually directly across from the fighting now. An occasional round comes this way, but not often. Fighting seems to be slacking off. No more MGs that I can hear. A little bit of rifle fire. Even the big stuff has gone silent. Now the patrols will be out in force. Wait a few, visitors."

Again the radio speakers went silent. It was two minutes this time before Lam came back on.

"Oh, yeah. That was closer. This bunch of six Chicoms poked into the brush. I had to go flat and not move. One guy would have stepped on me, but his sergeant called him back two steps before I'd be greasepaint. They're gone now. Watch for this bunch. I'm going to hold up and make contact with you. Have a feeling I'm too far ahead of you. Skipper?"

"Good idea, Lam. Not sure how far ahead you are. We saw the one Chinese patrol but not the second. Hold there."

Five minutes later Murdock saw the second Chinese patrol. They had left the edge of the valley and moved out fifty yards working silently forward.

Murdock looked around a few yards later and Lam stood beside him.

"How do you do that?"

"I'm half Apache, didn't I tell you," Lam said grinning. "I'll stay in better touch. I'd say another half mile and we could be in Indian territory. I don't expect a welcome gate, but there could be a marker fence of some kind." He vanished into the brush ahead without making a sound.

Murdock knew that his platoon had slowed. The horses were getting tired. Canzoneri was a load. Murdock had done duty three times so far and it was starting to tell. His legs felt a little rubbery, and he hadn't felt that often in his SEAL career.

Past a thick growth of brush, Murdock found Lam leaning against a tree.

"We've got an outpost ahead. Sand-bagged bunker with two machine guns sticking out of it. One is a fifty, the other a thirty, I'd guess or comparable. I've heard at least four men in the bunker. Not sure what is behind it or how we get to it. There are firing lanes cut into the brush back fifty yards. That's fifty yards we need to cross to get to the bunker. Let me borrow your NVGs."

Lam took the night vision goggles and vanished for a pair of minutes. When he came back he nodded. "Oh, damn, they have NVGs too. One of them lifted up to check something in the goggles, and I nailed him, spotted him. Which means it will take me a few minutes longer. I'm going to circle around and come up behind them. I'm counting on their not having any mine fields in this area. If so, I'm so much canned mush. If I can get around them and come up and talk to them, I'll keep my lip mike open, and tell you when to come across."

"Any other way?" Murdock asked.

"Not unless you want to blast them out of there with the twenties, or knock them out with the EAR. Don't think they would appreciate either one."

"You're sure these are Indians and not Chicoms?"

"Dead sure, Cap. I heard one of them chattering away in English. It's the second language in India."

"Go."

"Get all of our people down in good cover positions in case I mess up and that fifty starts whacking away. Make damn sure everyone is protected. Those fifties would cut right through here even out of the firing lanes."

"Roger that, now move."

It took Murdock five minutes to get everyone down and behind a tree or log or rock for good protection. Then they waited to hear from Lam.

Lam worked into the brush at a right angle turn away from the bunker. He moved without a sound, without breaking a stick. When he was fifty yards away from the valley, he did a due west turn and moved a hundred yards through the thinning brush and a few trees. Then did another right angle turn toward the valley. This should put him a hundred yards behind the bunker. He could watch for backup and any camped out troops in support. Twenty feet from the edge of the woods, he found a rough road that ran toward the bunker. He kept near it yet still in the brush.

Just behind the bunker were six small two-man tents laid out in a neat company row. Yes. Good. He moved closer and now could hear the men in the bunker talking. Some spoke what he figured was Hindi. Others spoke English. Definitely Indian and not Chinese. He moved closer, watched a shift change. He was six feet from the back entrance to the bunker when an officer came out. He said something to the men inside in English then turned to head for the small tents.

When he turned, Lam stood directly in front of him with both hands up, his weapon slung around his neck.

"I'm a friend, an American, we need your help. We intend you no harm. Hey, we're on your side."

The man's face went taut, his eyes bulged and his mouth dropped open. Then he gave a yell.

"Americans? You're the U.S. Navy SEALs we've been told to watch for. It's been all over the military radio on this end of India for the past two days."

"We're SEALs. Lost our transport inside China and have been looking for you. Can our people come on in? They're out in front of your firing lanes about fifty yards."

"Yes, yes. You have a radio. Just a minute." The officer went into the bunker. "Hold your fire. Friendlies coming in. Hold your fire."

He came out. "Tell your people to come in. How many?"

"Fourteen of us and one is wounded. Do you have any medical people here?"

"Just an outpost. You must have seen the fighting. We have a field hospital up there five miles. I'll get a jeep down here to take your man to the medics. We have two choppers that can transport you. Take you down to Purnia, then on to Calcutta. Let me phone my Commander. He'll be overjoyed to know you're safe."

Calcutta, India
Less than twenty-four hours later, the SEALs landed in Calcutta. Medics at the field hospital had treated Canzoneri's

leg. It had become infected, and they did what they could and sent him along with the rest of the SEALs.

In Calcutta he went to the best civilian hospital in town under Don Stroh's direction and the SEALs settled down in their semipermanent quarters on the military airfield nearby. Franklin's arm was cleaned out, stitched up and bandaged and he was returned to duty.

Murdock tried to find the chopper pilot of the 46 who had chickened out on them in China. Don Stroh lent his efforts and at last they tracked him down and got his name, rank, and serial number. Murdock wrote a scathing after-action report especially for the air operations officer who had the pilot under his command.

Murdock asked that the man be court-martialed for cowardice under fire and desertion of troops in a combat situation. He gave a second by second account of the incident and the resulting abandonment of fourteen U.S. Navy SEALs in the wilds of hostile China. When he was through he had two pages of single-spaced accusations. He made six copies and sent one to the pilot's commanding officer, one to the CNO, one to the temporary field where the choppers flew from in northern India. He gave the rest to Don Stroh to see what good he could do with them. Then he took a long, hot shower and hit his rack for fourteen hours. He couldn't remember being so tired or worn out in his life.

The next morning, Ed DeWitt woke him up.

"Hey, fourteen hours in the sack should be enough. Stroh said not to bother you, but I figured you'd want to know. We have twenty-four hours to get out of here. I mean get out of the Far East or wherever the hell this is. Hey, Murdock, do you understand? We're done here. We're used up. Don Stroh said to pull us out now. We're going home on commercial air, first class. We're getting class A uniforms and traveling cash. We should be home in two days."

Murdock had come out of his long sleep slowly, but the news about going home did the trick. "Home, yes. Good. What about Canzoneri?"

"He's on the manifest. He's fit to travel. We're all getting out of here and Stroh is going along to smooth out any problems."

"Stroh as our traveling companion. Now that will be a treat. What about the big war?"

"Simmering down. Now there is only sporadic fighting in Pakistan. The Chicoms bit off a bigger mouthful than they could chew. Looks like during this whole mess China was after the huge oil reserve that Pakistan has. That was their purpose all along. Now it looks like China will pull out of Pakistan and they will get the contract to build a huge pipeline from Pakistan into China to a refinery complex. So looks like China got what it wanted after all."

"Yeah, but they'll have to pay for the oil. The other way they could simply steal it. Good old Chicoms are at it again." Murdock rubbed his face trying to get fully awake. "Was it a bad dream or do I remember you saying something about Don Stroh is flying home with us?"

"That's the word."

"Wow, wow, wow. Isn't that going to be a bucket of fun."

28

Coronado, California
SEAL Team Seven Base
Lieutenant Commander Blake Murdock eased into the chair at his small office in Third Platoon headquarters and relaxed. Good to be home again. It had been a start-and-stop trip via commercial air from Calcutta, India, and he was glad it was over. They arrived at Lindbergh Field in San Diego late last night. They found their luggage in the form of cardboard boxes containing their weapons without ammo and combat vests and personal gear. After they checked in at the equipment room there on the base, Murdock had given everyone a five-day liberty.

His boss, Commander Masciareli, top ass kicker of SEAL Team Seven's 230 men, would chew him out for a week. Hell with him, the men needed some time off. They deserved it. Master Chief MacKenzie had met them and cut the orders at 0100 for them. Murdock had been up at five this morning for a two-mile run along Coronado's beach. He had slept himself out on the five or six planes they had been on coming home. Now he stared at the stack of paperwork he had to do, which Master Chief MacKenzie had dropped on his desk last night.

Canzoneri had been taken directly to Balboa Naval Hospital in San Diego's Balboa Park. The emergency-room crew had examined his leg, did some quick surgery to repair one area and then bandaged it up and admitted him. The estimate was that he would be there a week before being returned to light duty.

Franklin's left arm was checked, two stitches replaced

ones that had popped loose, and he was bandaged and released to duty.

By 0930 Murdock had only started on his paperwork
when he looked up and saw Senior Chief Will Dobler
standing in the doorway. He wasn't sure how long the chief
had been there.

"Senior Chief, come in." Murdock stood and held out his
hand. They shook and Murdock pointed to the chair beside
his desk.

"Senior Chief, I can't tell you how sorry I am about what
happened. I didn't think the problem was that severe or I
would have grounded you in a second."

"Not your fault, Commander. It was all mine, and I have
to live with that. I've had some time, but it's going to take
some more. I have to decide what I'm gong to do. I have
to make a living. Navy is the only thing I know. I'm too
damn old to be playing your kid games anymore. I've filed
with Master Chief a request for transfer to one of the non-
field jobs in the Team. I'm grounding myself, Commander.
I hope you understand."

Murdock nodded. He had hoped that this wouldn't happen, but he was almost certain it would. Dobler was having
trouble keeping up some days on their training runs and
swims. At thirty-seven, he was by far the oldest man in the
Platoon.

"I know how it is getting older in this game. I figure I
have two, maybe three more years before I cash out. You'll
be missed in Third Platoon, you know that."

"MacKenzie has a short list of three men he's recommending to move in here. All three are in the same job in
other platoons. Seems like everybody wants to get shot at."

"Yes, I'll have to get on that today. You know any of
the three?"

"One of them, and he wouldn't be my top pick."

Neither man spoke for a moment, each reliving some
action they had been in during past days.

"Has MacKenzie found a berth for you yet?"

"He's working on it. He says there's a cross-referencing
spot open at the CIA in Washington, D.C. for a SEAL.

Man who was there for two years just retired. Don't know if I would like rubbing shoulders with those spooks."

"Be a good berth for you, Dobler. Your combat, and your platoon action experience would be an eye opener for them. You've been there and done that. You'd be a top man for the spot. Has Masciareli done anything about it?"

"Don't think so."

"His word would help out a lot in D.C. I'll bug him about it today."

"Kids would have to change schools again."

"True, but it would move you out of that house and the memories. Might be just the thing."

Neither spoke again for a minute or two.

"You still have twenty days or so on your leave. You going to get away somewhere?"

"No sir. I'm spending all the time I can with my kids. We do something every day after homework. A show, a ride, go surfing, or swimming. I even went fishing with them at some lake."

"Good. I'm going to call the top dog and urge him to recommend you for that referencing spot at CIA. Get out of here so you won't hear the nice things I'm going to say about you."

Senior Chief Dobler grinned for the first time. "Aye, aye, sir. I'm moving my butt. I'll bug MacKenzie again. His coffee is better than yours, anyway."

Murdock smiled when the chief left. There had been just a trace of the spark from the man that he knew. Maybe Dobler was starting to come out of his depression that must have wracked him after Nancy's death. He reached for the phone to talk to his boss about Dobler.

The phone rang before he could pick it up.

"Third," he said.

"And a good morning to you, Commander. You slipped over the Quarterdeck without my checking the polish on your shoes this morning."

"Sorry, Master Chief, wasn't thinking what I was doing. Just talked to Dobler. You in the process for our recommending him for that CIA cross-check spot?"

"That I am lad, sir. I talked to the commander. He's with me on it. We're putting together a package. I e-mailed Stroh not to let them fill the slot before they get our material on Dobe."

"Good. Now about his replacement here."

"You want to interview the three candidates this morning?"

"Are they ready?"

"They've been on standby since 0800."

"Send them over an hour apart starting at 1000. You have any preference?"

"Me sir? I'm just a lowly master chief not fit to be making such officer-type decisions."

"Yeah, right. And your mother washed your pants in her chowder. Who do you like best?"

"He'll be the second man over. The first one is to sharpen your interview techniques. The best man is number two. But I didn't say a word. Sir."

"I hear you. Did DeWitt get his tail moving?"

"He went on a five day. Something about the high country around Denver."

"Good, as far from water as he can get. Take care, Chief." Murdock hung up and went back to the stack of paper on his desk. There must be a better way, but he hadn't found it yet.

Detective Sergeant Sanchez pushed down in the front seat of the rented Chevy where he sat twenty yards down from Howard Anderson's apartment. The man was in town. He had caught just a glimpse of him last night when he came to his place and then left almost at once before Sanchez could get to the door. Then Anderson had slammed through the sparse nighttime traffic at such a pace that Sanchez lost him before they made it to the bridge into San Diego. He was furious that the damned *gringo* could outdrive him when the man didn't even know he was being followed. Sanchez went back to the apartment to wait through the night, but Anderson didn't come back. Another two hours, and he was going back to Tijuana. This had been the closest he had come to the big American. Another two hours. Sanchez swore softly. He would get this *gringo* pig, it was an obsession now. He had to get him.

Tijuana, Mexico

It was well after two o'clock in the morning when Howie Anderson banged on the back door of the El Gallo Colorado cantina. He kept banging with his fist and then with a chunk of wood he found nearby until someone opened the door.

One of the girls in a half-open robe, looked at him.

"Hey *gringo*, we closed."

"You're always open. Get the hell out of the way. Where's Teresa?"

"She's busy."

"Same room?"

"Yes, busy. All-nighter."

"I'll throw the bum out. Got business, funny business." He laughed. Then Howie hurried up to the second floor. Teresa always had the same room, number one. He tried the door. Locked. He pushed against it just a little with a shoulder slam and it popped open.

The light was on, but low. He surged into the room, saw Teresa with the long black hair on the bed, naked with a nude man beside her. Howie grabbed the sleeping man's arm and pulled him off the bed. He swore in Spanish and jumped up ready to fight. But when he looked up at Howie's six feet three inches and 240 pounds, he backed off. He put on his pants as Howie glowered at him.

Teresa woke up and recognized Howie. She told the man in Spanish he better leave. He yelled in Spanish and hurried out the door. Teresa sat up and stared at Howie. He liked the way her bare tits bounced and rolled.

"What are you doing here?"

"Celebrating. I'm still alive. I want me some good hot pussy and I know where to get it."

"Not tonight. You heard of Mad Dog Sanchez, Tijuana police?"

"No, who's he?"

"Toughest, most vicious cop in town. He was here looking for you. Something about a dead dopehead."

Howie who had killed a six pack of beer driving to TJ
sobered up in a rush. "Some cop is looking for me, by
name?"

"Yes. I told him I didn't know you."

"Why's he looking for me?"

"Some big-time dope supplier got himself shot twice in
the head with a small-caliber weapon. He thinks you did
it. This Mad Dog Sanchez is the worst of the cops around
here. He gets more confessions than anybody. Also, more
of his suspects die during questioning than anyone else's."

"Why didn't you tell me he was asking about me?"

"I called you twice, no answer both time."

"Been out of the country."

"You better get back across the border. He catch you
down here you're turkey meat. Know what I mean?"

"Yes, Teresa. I know. Hell, while I'm here . . ." He unzipped his fly. Teresa caught his hand.

"No. It isn't safe for you here, not even for five minutes.
You better go right now."

"Hell, I been through a lot lately—" He stopped, zipped
up his fly and swore. "Fuck it, I'll go north and then head
for Arizona. He'll never find me in Arizona." Howie stood
there a moment, his alcohol-fuzzed brain spinning. "Wait a
God-damned minute. Why am I gonna run just because
some pussy tells me to? Hell, why should I be afraid of
some little greaser cop? I ain't afraid of no cop." He
laughed, unzipped his fly again and dropped his pants, then
his shorts. He pushed Teresa back on the bed and dropped
on top of her.

"Hell, I ain't wasting a drive all the way down here just
to get pushed out the door by some damned greaser detective."

"Howie. I'm serious. Hanging around here could get you
killed."

"Look at me, pretty woman. I'm shaking in my boots.
I'm so scared I can't get it up. Like shit. Look at this dandy.
He's ready to get to work."

"Hell, I warned you. Sanchez has checked me three times now, looking for you."

"So let him come."

An hour later, Howie had drifted off to sleep when the door with it's lock broken eased open. Sanchez grinned. The other girls had agreed, this was Anderson, the *gringo* Teresa knew, who Juan Lopez knew. The American lay on his back, hands over his head. He was a big one. Sanchez took a lead-filled sap from his pocket. He hit Anderson's genitals first. The blow brought a wail of pain from the *gringo* who sat up. The second blow slammed hard on the big American's head and he flopped down unconscious half off the bed.

Teresa heard the cry and jumped out of bed on the other side and scurried out the door. Sanchez didn't need her anymore. He always knew where to find her. He was more interested in Anderson.

Sanchez knew how to use the sap. He had swung it dozens of times and knew how hard to hit a man's head to knock him out and how hard to kill him. Anderson would wake up soon. The cop used plastic riot cuffs to bind Anderson's wrists and ankles where he lay on the bed. He found a glass half full of whisky on the night stand. He threw the liquid into Anderson's face.

The big SEAL came awake screeching in pain and frustration.

"What the hell. My hands? Who kicked me in the balls. What's going on here?" Anderson shook his head to clear it, then slowly focused on Sanchez standing beside the bed, his Glock pistol out and aimed at Anderson's head.

"Howard Anderson?"

"Hell no, I'm Regis Philbin. What the hell are the tie strips for?"

"To keep you in control, Anderson. You're a wanted killer. I have to be careful."

"You a cop?"

"Right, and I have you for murdering Raymundo Cuchi Hernandez in cold blood in his apartment."

"Proof, you bastard, it takes proof to arrest somebody."

"Not in Mexico, *gringo* bastard. You're going inside for a long, long time."

Howie had been in some tight spots but nothing like this. Maybe the little detective did have some proof. He couldn't take the chance with a Mexican jail. This cop had been in a rush and had cinched up his hands in front of Howie. Bad move. Howie sat there slack jawed, head down, evidently broken and despondent.

"Look at me, *gringo*. Look at me as I shoot you as we struggled in this whore house."

Howie didn't move. Sanchez pushed in closer, the Glock now off at an angle he was so close. His head was inches from Howie's face. Howie exploded his two-handed fist upward jolting into the cop's windpipe then on up into his chin blasting him backward. Sanchez was unconscious before he hit the floor.

Howie rolled to the floor, groaned at the pain in his testicles, and found his pants. He pulled out a three-inch knife, and cut his hands and feet lose from the plastic. Then he grabbed the Glock pistol still in the cop's hand before he checked the small man's throat for a pulse. He had one, faint, but it was there. Howie dressed quickly.

Teresa looked in the door. "Praise Mother Mary and all the saints, you're safe." She looked at Sanchez. "Is he dead?"

"No, and I better get out of here. You didn't see me. I was never here. Make any of the girls who saw me understand this. I'll carry Sanchez into the alley and dump him where somebody will find him. He won't be able to prove he was inside, or that he saw me, let alone arrested me. Go now and talk to the girls. What time is it?"

"Almost four o'clock."

"Good, it's still dark." Howie hoisted the small Tijuana cop over his shoulder and carried him down the steps and into the alley. Halfway down he dumped him, made sure he was breathing and had a pulse.

"Robbery," he whispered. "Yeah he was mugged and robbed." Howie took the Glock, the cop's billfold and wrist watch, but left his police ID badge. It would be put down as a robbery.

A mile from the border checkpoint, Howie threw the cop's pistol out the window and his billfold after taking out two U.S. hundred dollar bills and two thousand in pesos.

Now he really was going to go to Flagstaff, Arizona. He'd stop by his apartment for some clothes and some more cash and his ATM card, then he would be moving. There was only a slim chance that this cop knew where he lived. He wasn't listed in the phone book. The SEALs would never give out his home address, even if this Mad Dog Sanchez did learn that he was a SEAL. Hell no, the cop couldn't be that good. Howie figured he'd take his five days liberty in Flag and then get back to work with the SEALs.

29

Coronado, California
Third Platoon Headquarters

Murdock picked up the phone on his desk on the third ring. He had been reading over background reports and service files on the three senior chiefs as possible replacements for Will Dobler.

"Third Platoon, Murdock."

"Oh yes, it's good to hear a calm, friendly voice."

"Lampedusa. Sounds like trouble."

"Just a little bit, sir. It's Jaybird. He did his thing last night and is now incarcerated in the Vista jail."

"Oh, boy. What is it?"

"We were driving in that little Toyota of his north into Carlsbad when this guy in a new Caddy cut us off and laughed, gave us the finger, and laughed some more. When Jaybird got his rig under control he took off after the bastard. Needless to say, the little Toyota topped out at about ninety-five and the Caddy just walked away from us. Finally got Jaybird cooled down a little and slowed down, and we hit a bar in Carlsbad. The Jaybird got sloshed in an hour.

"He kept yelling at this Cadillac guy, and the barman almost called the cops once, but I talked him out of it. He threw us out half hour later and Jaybird was still spitting mean mad. You know the routine then. He kept swearing at the Cadillac driver and peeling off his clothes and throwing them down. I was the rag picker. In five minutes he was jaybird naked walking in and out of stores there in Carlsbad at 1400. Broad daylight. Ten minutes later three

260

Carsbad police cars arrived. They convinced Jaybird to go with them. I gave them his clothes and that was it. No resisting arrest, no punches.

"At the jail in Vista they told me it was a misdemeanor and after he sobered up he could post three hundred dollars bail and be released. He has a court date, but if he doesn't show the bail becomes the fine and it's off the books."

"How many times is this for him?" Murdock asked.

"Just two with me. You said he'd done it before then."

"Ask him how he got his nickname sometime. I can check his file, but I'd say this is at least five times. Different towns, different states even. Get him wrung out and released. Where you guys headed?"

"Not the faintest. Decided to drive out two days, then drive back two days."

"Have fun. Damn quiet around here."

"You working on a new senior chief?"

"Yeah. Hate to lose Dobler. But he's made up his mind. You take care of Jaybird. We need both you guys."

Murdock hung up and went back to the file folders. All were good men. He didn't have the slightest idea which one he would pick. The interviews would determine that. His first one was for 1000. He had a half hour more.

Tijuana, Mexico

It was almost daylight before a wandering street person saw a man in the alley. Good shoes. Yes, the man had good shoes, about the right size. If he didn't know how to keep his shoes, he didn't deserve them. The bum ran up quickly, looked around and saw no one protecting the man. He noticed that the guy's pockets had been turned inside out. Robbed. Yeah. Wrong neighborhood. He had the guy's right shoe unlaced when the man groaned and moved.

The street knight jumped back, then saw the police shield on its leather folder laying beside the body.

A cop?

The bum frowned and took another step backward when the body groaned again and with great effort sat up. He said something but the words came out garbled. The man's face flushed darkly, his glance darted around, his mouth dribbled saliva as stark fury raced through him. At last he motioned to the man, stood with pain and leaned on the bum as he staggered toward his car. Gingerly he felt in his pocket. Yes, he still had his keys. Could he drive? Yes. He had to get to a hospital. His throat felt on fire, he couldn't talk. That damn *gringo* had surprised him. He wondered if he would ever speak again. He had to. Now he had a personal reason for wanting to find the *gringo*. There would be no expense to the state to prosecute this Howard Anderson. It would be a matter of attempting to escape and a tragic accidental shooting.

The street bum helped Sanchez into the car, then stepped back and ran as fast as he could away from the car. Sanchez hardly noticed. He had to concentrate to get the car started. Small actions like turning they key that usually were totally automatic now had to be thought out carefully.

It took him twenty minutes to drive five miles to the closest hospital. He parked in the emergency entrance where ambulances usually came and layed on his horn until a cop and three doctors and a nurse rushed out to help him.

Coronado, California

Will Dobler sat at the dinner table in the Fernandez house and nodded. This was what friends were for. He was lucky. Maria and Miguel had invited him and the kids over for supper. It had been a fine meal and he was feeling more like his old self. The kids had gone to play a computer game, and the adults worked on second cups of coffee.

"We're really going to miss you down at BUD/S, Senior Chief," Miguel said.

"Hey, you won't have me to yell at you anymore. You'll miss that with pleasure. Truth is, I'm getting too old to play these kid games. I'm right near to thirty-eight. Do you know that I'm the oldest man in the whole Team Seven in the field platoons? Oldest one. I am until Master Chief MacKenzie gets me slotted in somewhere. Hey, ain't like I was shipping out. I'll be over for coffee now and then."

Fernandez nodded. "Hey, you know what I'll really miss.

You were one of only four men in the platoon I could beat
on the OC. My times were getting better, but that damn
obstacle course is a true torture chamber.

"Oh yes, the OC. I won't have to worry about that anymore." He paused. "Know we came out pretty clean on this
mission. Vinnie was the only one with a bad wound. That
chest shot is still giving them trouble over at Balboa. Not
sure if he'll get back to the platoon or not. My leg slice
isn't so bad. I could come back. But not sure about Canzoneri. Damn shrapnel tore a chunk right out of his leg.
Gonna be a long time in rehab before he can even walk
good again. He could make it back if he works hard
enough."

"How's your leg coming along?"

"Good. I still use a crutch sometimes, but the medics say
in six months the only thing I'll remember about it is the
three-inch scar on my leg. I'll settle for that."

"Any regrets about being a SEAL, Senior Chief?" Maria
asked.

"Sure, the big one." He wiped at his eyes. "Hell, I can't
bring her back. Damn it, I should have known, have
watched her a lot closer. My fault, and that's a damn big
regret. When I can get past that, I have loved this SEAL
life. Our platoon is on the cutting edge of world politics
and national crises everywhere. Think what we've been a
party to in just the past two years. It's awesome. Yes, that
aspect I'll miss. But getting shot at, I won't miss."

"You've been on some good missions, Dobe."

"Aye, and some really fouled up ones, like walking out
of Chicom China with them shooting at us."

"We made it back. We completed our mission. Those are
the two important elements."

"I like that part about you getting back," Maria said.
"That's the most important part to me. You bet we worry.
Milly and I are still going to meet every week. We've just
about decided on Sunday afternoon. We can do girl talk,
and yell at the Navy, and say a little prayer for your safe
return."

Will Dobler wiped at his eyes again, then took out a

handkerchief and wiped the moisture away, turned, and blew his nose.

"You girls were wonderful for Nancy. She used to say what a blessing it was to have the two of you for friends. She said you talked about all sorts of things, including her drinking." His eyes misted again. "Oh, damn." Will stood and walked to the front windows and blew his nose again and wiped his eyes. He came back and sipped at his coffee, using it as a prop to avoid saying anything.

"We understand a little of what it's been like, Will," Maria said. "We lost our firstborn when he was just a year old. It was the greatest shock of our lives, before or since. I cried for a week. I came close to doing something terrible. A good friend helped Miguel and I through it."

They talked for another hour, then the coffee went cold and Maria reminded them it was a school night. Will gathered up Helen and Charlie and went out to the car.

"Sunday dinner here," Maria said. "We always have chicken with gravy and stuffing and the whole thing. Be pleased if you and Helen and Charlie can come."

Helen looked at her father. "Daddy, can we come, please. Linda has some of the best computer games."

"They're easy, that's why Helen likes them," Charlie said. Helen swatted at him but missed.

"Sure, we'll be here. Don't let us wear out our welcome."

"No danger of that Senior Chief. Hope you get a good slot in the Team."

"I will, or I won't take it. Nineteen years of seniority still means something in this man's Navy."

They waved, and Dobler drove the car away and toward his house.

Murdock picked up the phone in his office. "Third Platoon, Murdock."

"About your second interview. He should be over in about five minutes, will that be all right with you, Commander?"

"Ardith, when did you . . . No, I won't ask. You and your contacts. I've been back for almost twenty-four. Where have you been and what took you so long?"

"That's what I like, a warm welcome for a traveler," Ardith Manchester said a catch in her voice and a beautiful smile coming over the line. "I've missed you, too. Now about lunch. I'll pick you up, no I don't have my car. I'll see you on the Quarterdeck about one o'clock. The Master Chief says you should be done with interview number three by then. We could have a fancy lunch where they serve those little bitty things that are attractively arranged and taste like wallpaper, or we could go to Jack-in-the-Box, or that little Italian place here in Coronado where they have that combination lunch/wine tasting."

"I think I just bought a wine-tasting lunch. What's new around the Beltline?"

"The usual. Lobbying, vote trading, pork barreling, and backbiting. All the regular D.C. stuff. That's why I like to come west."

"I like you to come west. How about Ensenada, Mexico, for a couple of days. I can wrangle some liberty."

"Sounds good, rush that interview, will you?"

"Can do. Oh, you'll know me by the white carnation between my teeth. I'll probably be the only one with a flower."

He rushed the interview. This senior chief wasn't the man he wanted. He had already made up his mind on number two, the one Master Chief MacKenzie liked. He changed into civvies and hurried up to the Quarterdeck.

It was four days since Detective Sergeant Sanchez had been found dazed and injured in the alley behind the El Gallo Colorado. They kept him in the hospital for two days until his voice cleared up. His trachea has been bruised and his voice box shaken up but not damaged. At once he had applied for two weeks' medical leave and had come north to watch for the *gringo* sonofabitch who had assaulted him. He carried two weapons, had a third hidden under the seat of the rented car, and his Tijuana Police credentials.

For two days he waited at the Anderson apartment, but the big man didn't come. This was the third day and he had hopes. About noon a car stopped in front with two men in it. One was Anderson. Sanchez had to order himself to wait, it had to be when Anderson was alone. Not yet.

An hour later, Anderson came out of his apartment, got in a car in the parking lot and drove. Sanchez followed the man a short distance out on the Strand heading toward Imperial Beach. Anderson turned off right into an un-marked parking area in front of several one-story buildings. Sanchez was so surprised that he kept on driving past. There was no gate, no guard. He had to drive down several miles to turn around and when he did it was in the Silver Strand State Beach. He turned around and drove back. This time he turned left into the same parking lot Anderson had. Only then did he see the sign, "NAVSPECWARGRUP." He memorized the strange words or combination of words, turned around and drove out. No one paid any attention to him.

There was no area around that parking lot where he could wait in his car. He drove back to the Anderson apartment and parked. He wrote the strange assortment of letters on a pad and studied it. They made no sense whatsoever. He took the pad and walked down the street. Sanchez stopped the first man he met.

"Sir, could you help me? I have this long word, and I don't know what it means."

The middle-aged man in a suit and with a pin on his lapel looked at the pad and chuckled. "You're not Navy are you, son? That's not a word, that's an acronym, sort of. Stands for 'Navy Special Warfare Group.' So it's really four words. That's just out on the Strand. Where the Navy SEALs do their training. SEAL stands for Sea, Air, Land. The Navy SEALs. The toughest, meanest, roughest bunch of killers the world has ever seen. They can be nasty. I used to be Navy. Retired Commander. That answer your question?"

"Yes, Commander, thank you," Sanchez said and walked away. SEALs. He had heard of that elite bunch of special warfare men. So was this Anderson a SEAL or just visiting someone there?

He could sneak up to Anderson's apartment before he came home, slip the lock, and check inside. But that would be risky. Anderson might be home any minute. Still, it might be helpful. He wanted the man down and dead before the sun came up. No, he would break into the place. Too risky. So how?

Challenge him? Yes. Put up a challenge, *mano a mano*. One on one. Him against the SEAL. Knives. He'd heard the SEALs like to use knives. Good. Only the SEAL would not know that it would not be a fair fight. The man was a killer, a hired assassin. He didn't deserve to be treated fairly.

Sanchez took his notebook, and with a ball-point pen printed out the challenge.

"Anderson. I'm Sanchez. We met in Tijuana last week. I demand satisfaction. You and me, one on one, at a neutral site. Weapons of your choice. We fight until one man can't get up. You shamed me. I must fight you and win. Tonight at midnight out on the Silver Strand State Beach. Beside the first restroom. I'll be there. Will you be there or will you chicken out?" He signed it Sanchez.

The detective sergeant folded the note once and fastened it to Anderson's front door with two strips of tape from a roll in his pocket. Then he left as any salesman might, got in his car, and drove down the street several blocks to a shady spot, and took a nap in the front set. He might need it before the night was over.

In the early evening he ate a good dinner in a Mexican restaurant, then walked four miles before he went to his car. On a quiet residential street, he parked. He dropped down on the grassy parkway, and did a hundred pushups. Then he sharpened a fighting knife that he carried. The fine stone let him put a razor-like edge on the six-inch blade. Nothing else to do but wait. At eleven o'clock he drove to the state beach and checked it out. No other cars there. He put his car at the far end of the parking and walked back to the first restroom building. He would wait in the moon shadows at the far side of the structure. There anyone driv-

ing in couldn't see him. Yes, the headlights would give
away the oncoming car.

It was 11:05. Detective Sergeant Sanchez relaxed against
the building. Several cars zipped along the highway heading toward Imperial Beach or the other way into Coronado.
None of them slowed or stopped. It could be a long wait.

Howie Anderson saw the note on his door the moment he
went up the steps to his second-floor apartment. He didn't
find a lot of notes taped there. He ripped it off and read it.

"How in hell—" Howie stopped, looked around the complex parking lot, then unlocked his door and stepped inside,
closing the heavy door quickly.

There was no way the little Mex detective could find him
there in Coronado. But he had. He had even offered him a
challenge a fight, just the two of them. More like a bush-
whacking as soon as he poked his nose into that parking
lot. Yeah, a fair fight, it would be fair all right. Fairly
deadly. The little bastard had been totally humiliated when
he had his ass kicked in TJ. He could settle the score only
by killing the man who did it to him.

Howie guessed that the detective would have some kind
of an automatic weapon. He would need the same. He
grinned and went into his bedroom, removed a false bottom
in a big chest and lifted out a nearly new H&K MP5. It
was the one that they had "lost" one day on a training
mission. He had seen Khai drop it when hundreds of wasps
had attacked them. Their nest had been accidentally kicked
over and destroyed when the SEALs were running across
some sparse territory in their private shooting grounds up
in the mountains beyond Pine Valley. Two days later Anderson went back alone and found the submachine gun. The
loss was written off as a platoon training accident and nobody had to stand a statement of charges.

He hefted the little weapon and picked up two loaded,
thirty-round magazines. If sixty rounds wouldn't do it, he
didn't know what would. With the shoulder stock pushed
in, he could hide the weapon under a floppy shirt on a cord
around his neck. Surprise, surprise.

He strapped on a .38 ankle hideout and kept a .45 on his hip. Yeah, that should do it. He'd make mincemeat out of the little Mexican cop in twenty seconds. Would he let the cop fire first? Not a chance. Shoot first, kill first, an old SEAL tradition.

Midnight was the call-out time. His watch showed 2200, two hours yet. He'd go early, get there about eleven, drive out partway, the last two miles with no lights and park on the shoulder. He knew a place. Then walk in circling around to come at the restrooms from the back. Yeah.

It worked out just that way. He came into the state beach on the bay side and went to ground studying the area. One car in the far end of the parking spaces, a quarter mile away. No threat. He couldn't see anyone behind the restrooms, but that wall was in deep moon shadows.

In those shadows, Sanchez thought he heard something behind him. He turned and scanned the darkness there illuminated somewhat by the bright moon. Now his Army training came full circle. He had been with the Mexican Army Rangers, line crossers, the elite of the Army's attack and covert forces. He could smell an enemy soldier at fifty yards.

Now he came fully alert. There was someone or something out there. A coyote, a rabbit, or a man, maybe Anderson. He slid around the corner of the restroom still in the shadows, lay on his stomach and peered out from ground level at the area he suspected. Nothing, not yet, just that vague hypersense that alerted him.

Howie Anderson was not the quietest man in the platoon, but he had learned to move over ground with a minimum of sound. Now he used that technique, walking crouched over to cast a smaller shadow, testing each footstep to be sure it would not break a stick or kick a rock. Soon he was fifty yards from the restroom. He could see nothing in back of the restroom in the shadows.

He wished now that he had a pair of night vision goggles. He'd have cut the little Mexican cop into pieces by now. He had to be there. He said he would, and he'd come early. But where, damn it, where was he?

Howie moved again, slower now, easing his feet into the sandy black top of the parking lot. The bastard was here close, somewhere. But where? Had he moved around the edge of the building? Had he somehow figured that being a SEAL, his target would come in the unexpected way?

Sanchez rubbed his eyes and stared into the darkness again. Had he seen a moon shadow down there thirty yards moving slowly toward him? Or had it been a cloud? No, not a cloud. He lifted the M16 assault rifle fitted with a laser aiming light and brought it around to where he figured the shadow had been. A damn SEAL would come in the back way. He'd park out of hearing and walk in, then attack soundlessly. He probably had a submachine gun.

Yes! The shadow moved. It came another step toward his position, then went prone watching forward. Sanchez clicked on the laser sighting light. It would project a red dot on the target wherever the barrel was pointed. Get the dot on target and the bullet would follow with incredible accuracy. The rifle had been charged with a round while he was still in the car and the safety put on. Now he snicked off the safety and swung the barrel around at the target.

Howie Anderson thought he heard something, a safety on a weapon sliding to the off position? He wasn't sure. He rested a minute. His heart was hammering in his chest. He hadn't had such a high since he'd taken out that drug supplier in TJ. He moved a foot forward, then saw something on his hand.

Christ! A laser dot. He dove to the left away from it just as the M16 opened fire on full automatic.

Howie felt the first bullet hit him in the arm. It was a long trail of fire up his arm into his shoulder. Then another slug ripped into his upper chest and a third and he stopped rolling. He had slued sideways so his body was open to the rounds. Three more thundered into his unprotected chest. Howie felt them hit, he tried to scream, but nothing came out. The pain boiled through him then, searing, scorching like a blowtorch on his bare skin. The agony zoomed a million times, churning, tearing at him, smashing his whole nervous system into a mass of wreckage. He felt more rounds hitting his legs and then working back up to his chest. The faint moonlight faded, and a moment later Howie Anderson gave a shrill scream that ended when two rounds drilled through his head, slamming him backward into the sandy blacktop paving and straight into hell.

Sanchez stopped firing. He ran to the crumpled man who lay on the parking lot dressed in his desert cammies. A submachine gun lay at his side. Sanchez was tempted to take it. No let the weapon stay there. It would be a puzzle for the police and the Navy to solve.

Detective Sergeant Sanchez lifted his M16 rifle and trotted toward the rented car in the far end of the lot. He drove into Coronado on the Strand, then through the quiet streets and over the Coronado Bay bridge into San Diego. He was halfway to the border on U.S. 5 when he took out a cell phone. He dialed 911 and spoke quickly and clearly.

"There has been a shooting on the Silver Strand State Beach just down from Coronado. It's serious. Someone has been shot several times."

"Yes, I understand," the operator said. "Who is this and where are you?"

"On the Silver Strand State Beach, a man is seriously wounded. Send an ambulance at once."

"Yes. I have that, a unit is on the way. Are you close by? Stay on the phone, please so I can get some more . . ."

Detective Sergeant Mad Dog Sanchez of the Tijuana city police broke the phone connection, and nodded. Sometimes the law wasn't enough. Killers had to be dealt with in the only way they understood.

Ensenada, Mexico

It was two days before they located Lieutenant Commander Blake Murdock. That happened only because he called in when Ardith was napping to see what was going on.

"Commander, some bad news," Master Chief MacKenzie said. "One of your boys has been killed, shot eighteen times, the coroner tells us. It's Howard Anderson. He was on the state beach out on the Strand. The strange part is he was in his cammies and had three weapons with him including that MP-five we lost six months ago on a training exercise. Coronado homicide got a warrant to search his apartment. They found four automatic weapons, two more that we show as missing from Third Platoon inventory, as well as boxes of ammo and grenades and even two Claymore mines. Something wasn't right about that boy."

"Anything I can do?"

"Police have it in hand. They say they had a nine-one-one call about midnight, but the man caller wouldn't identify himself or remain on the phone. The operator said she was sure it was a Spanish accent that she heard in the voice. That's all they have. Oh, the rounds that riddled Anderson were NATO five fifty-sixes; the police think they were fired from an M-sixteen."

"Any good rifling on the rounds?"

"Plenty, Commander."

"Have every weapon in our Platoon armory that uses the five fifty-six for the M-sixteen uses test fired and the rifling checked against that of the death slugs."

"Will do, Commander."

"Any of our men across the Quarterdeck that day?"

"No sir, not a one."

"I'll be back in twenty-four."

"Commander, sir. Nothing we can do. Finish your mini-vacation. Relax. There will be enough to do when you report back in three or four days."

Murdock shook his head and took a deep breath. "Yeah, Master Chief, I think you're right." He looked over at Ardith who had just come awake, long blond hair trailing down over her shoulders and half hiding her bare breasts. She smiled at him and he almost dropped the phone.

"Anything important?" Ardith asked.

Murdock grinned and shook his head. She sat up on the hotel bed and her hair fell away from her chest.

"Nothing important," he said. He lifted the phone. "Master Chief, I'll see you on the Quarterdeck in three or four days."

SEAL TALK

MILITARY GLOSSARY

Aalvin: Small U.S. two-man submarine.

Admin: Short for administration.

Aegis: Advanced Naval air defense radar system.

AH-1W Super Cobra: Has M179 undernose turret with 20mm Gatling gun.

AK-47: 7.63-round Russian Kalashnikov automatic rifle. Most widely used assault rifle in the world.

AK-74: New, improved version of the Kalashnikov. Fires the 5.45mm round. Has 30-round magazine. Rate of fire: 600 rounds per minute. Many slight variations made for many different nations.

AN/PRC-117D: Radio, also called SATCOM. Works with Milstar satellite in 22,300-mile equatorial orbit for instant worldwide radio, voice, or video communications. Size: 15 inches high, 3 inches wide, 3 inches deep. Weighs 15 pounds. Microphone and voice output. Has encrypter, capable of burst transmissions of less than a second.

AN/PUS-7: Night-Vision Goggles. Weighs 1.5 pounds.

ANVIS-6: Night-Vision Goggles on air crewmen's helmets.

APC: Armored Personnel Carrier.

ASROC: Nuclear-tipped antisubmarine rocket torpedoes launched by Navy ships.

Assault Vest: Combat vest with full loadouts of ammo, gear.

ASW: Anti-Submarine Warfare.

Attack Board: Molded plastic with two handgrips with bubble compass on it. Also depth gauge and Cyalume chemical lights with twist knob to regulate amount of light. Used for underwater guidance on long swim.

Aurora: Air Force recon plane. Can circle at 90,000 feet. Can't be seen or heard from ground. Used for thermal imaging.

AWACS: Airborne Warning And Control System. Radar units in high-flying aircraft to scan for planes at any altitude out 200 miles. Controls air-to-air engagements with enemy forces. Planes have a mass of communication and electronic equipment.

Balaclavas: Headgear worn by some SEALs.

Bent Spear: Less serious nuclear violation of safety.

BKA, Bundeskriminant: Germany's federal investigation unit.

Black Talon: Lethal hollow-point ammunition made by Winchester. Outlawed some places.

Blivet: A collapsible fuel container. SEALs sometimes use it.

BLU-43B: Antipersonnel mine used by SEALs.

BLU-96: A fuel-air explosive bomb. It disperses a fuel oil into the air, then explodes the cloud. Many times more powerful than conventional bombs because it doesn't carry its own chemical oxidizers.

BMP-1: Soviet armored fighting vehicle (AFV), low, boxy, crew of 3 and 8 combat troops. Has tracks and a 73mm cannon. Also an AT-3 Sagger antitank missile and coaxial machine gun.

Body Armor: Far too heavy for SEAL use in the water.

Bogey: Pilots' word for an unidentified aircraft.

Boghammar Boat: Long, narrow, low dagger boat; high-speed patrol craft. Swedish make. Iran had 40 of them in 1993.

Boomer: A nuclear-powered missile submarine.

Bought It: A man has been killed. Also "bought the farm."

Bow Cat: The bow catapult on a carrier to launch jets.

Broken Arrow: Any accident with nuclear weapons, or

any incident of nuclear material lost, shot down, crashed, stolen, hijacked.

Browning 9mm High Power: A Belgium 9mm pistol, 13 rounds in magazine. First made 1935.

Buddy Line: 6 feet long, ties 2 SEALs together in the water for control and help if needed.

BUD/S: Coronado, California, nickname for SEAL training facility for six months' course.

Bull Pup. Still in testing; new soldier's rifle. SEALs have a dozen of them for regular use. Army gets them in 2005. Has a 5.56 kinetic round, 30-shot clip. Also 20mm high-explosive round and 5-shot magazine. Twenties can be fused for proximity airbursts with use of video camera, laser range finder, and laser targeting. Fuses by number of turns the round needs to reach laser spot. Max range: 1200 yards. Twenty round can also detonate on contact, and has delay fuse. Weapon weighs 14 pounds. SEALs love it. Can in effect "shoot around corners" with the airburst feature.

BUPERS: BUreau of PERSonnel.

C-2A Greyhound: 2-engine turboprop cargo plane that lands on carriers. Also called COD, Carrier Onboard Delivery. Two pilots and engineer. Rear fuselage loading ramp. Cruise speed 300 mph, range 1,000 miles. Will hold 39 combat troops. Lands on CVN carriers at sea.

C-4: Plastic explosive. A claylike explosive that can be molded and shaped. It will burn. Fairly stable.

C-6 Plastique: Plastic explosive. Developed from C-4 and C-5. Is often used in bombs with radio detonator or digital timer.

C-9 Nightingale: Douglas DC-9 fitted as a medical-evacuation transport plane.

C-130 Hercules: Air Force transporter for long haul. 4 engines.

C-141 Starlifter: Airlift transport for cargo, paratroops, evac for long distances. Top speed 566 mph. Range with payload 2,935 miles. Ceiling 41,600 feet.

Caltrops: Small four-pointed spikes used to flatten tires. Used in the Crusades to disable horses.

Camel Back: Used with drinking tube for 70 ounces of water attached to vest.

Cammies: Working camouflaged wear for SEALs. Two different patterns and colors. Jungle and desert.

Cannon Fodder: Old term for soldiers in line of fire destined to die in the grand scheme of warfare.

Capped: Killed, shot, or otherwise snuffed.

CAR-15: The Colt M-4A1. Sliding-stock carbine with grenade launcher under barrel. Knight sound-suppressor. Can have AN/PAQ-4 laser aiming light under the carrying handle. .223 round. 20- or 30-round magazine. Rate of fire: 700 to 1,000 rounds per minute.

Cascade Radiation: U-235 triggers secondary radiation in other dense materials.

Cast Off: Leave a dock, port, land. Get lost. Navy: long, then short signal of horn, whistle, or light.

Castle Keep: The main tower in any castle.

Caving Ladder: Roll-up ladder that can be let down to climb.

CH-46E: Sea Knight chopper. Twin rotors, transport. Can carry 25 combat troops. Has a crew of 3. Cruise speed 154 mph. Range 420 miles.

CH-53D Sea Stallion: Big Chopper. Not used much anymore.

Chaff: A small cloud of thin pieces of metal, such as tinsel, that can be picked up by enemy radar and that can attract a radar-guided missile away from the plane to hit the chaff.

Charlie-Mike: Code words for continue the mission.

Chief to Chief: Bad conduct by EM handled by chiefs so no record shows or is passed up the chain of command.

Chocolate Mountains: Land training center for SEALs near these mountains in the California desert.

Christians In Action: SEAL talk for not-always-friendly CIA.

CIA: Central Intelligence Agency.

CIC: Combat Information Center. The place on a ship where communications and control areas are situated to open and control combat fire.

CINC: Commander IN Chief.

CINCLANT: Navy Commander IN Chief, atLANTtic.

CINCPAC: Commander-IN-Chief, PACific.

Class of 1978: Not a single man finished BUD/S training in this class. All-time record.

Claymore: An antipersonnel mine carried by SEALs on many of their missions.

Cluster Bombs: A canister bomb that explodes and spreads small bomblets over a great area. Used against parked aircraft, massed troops, and unarmored vehicles.

CNO: Chief of Naval Operations.

CO-2 Poisoning: During deep dives. Abort dive at once and surface.

COD: Carrier Onboard Delivery plane.

Cold Pack Rations: Food carried by SEALs to use if needed.

Combat Harness: American Body Armor nylon-mesh special-operations vest. 6 2-magazine pouches for drum-fed belts, other pouches for other weapons, waterproof pouch for Motorola.

CONUS: The Continental United States.

Corfams: Dress shoes for SEALs.

Covert Action Staff: A CIA group that handles all covert action by the SEALs.

CQB: Close Quarters Battle house. Training facility near Nyland in the desert training area. Also called the Kill House.

CQB: Close Quarters Battle. A fight that's up close, hand-to-hand, whites-of-his-eyes, blood all over you.

CRRC Bundle: Roll it off plane, sub, boat. The assault boat for 8 SEALs. Also the IBS, Inflatable Boat Small.

Cutting Charge: Lead-sheathed explosive. Triangular strip of high-velocity explosive sheathed in metal. Point of the triangle focuses a shaped-charge effect. Cuts a pencil-line-wide hole to slice a steel girder in half.

CVN: A U.S. aircraft carrier with nuclear power. Largest that we have in fleet.

CYA: Cover Your Ass, protect yourself from friendlies or officers above you and JAG people.

Damfino: Damned if I know. SEAL talk.

DDS: Dry Dock Shelter. A clamshell unit on subs to deliver SEALs and SDVs to a mission.

DEFCON: DEFense CONdition. How serious is the threat?

Delta Forces: Army special forces, much like SEALs.

Desert Cammies: Three-color, desert tan and pale green with streaks of pink. For use on land.

DIA: Defense Intelligence Agency.

Dilos Class Patrol Boat: Greek, 29 feet long, 75 tons displacement.

Dirty Shirt Mess: Officers can eat there in flying suits on board a carrier.

DNS: Doppler Navigation System.

Draegr LAR V: Rebreather that SEALs use. No bubbles.

DREC: Digitally Reconnoiterable Electronic Component. Top-secret computer chip from NSA that lets it decipher any U.S. military electronic code.

E-2C Hawkeye: Navy, carrier-based, Airborne Early Warning craft for long-range early warning and threat-assessment and fighter-direction. Has a 24-foot saucer-like rotodome over the wing. Crew 5, max speed 326 knots, ceiling 30,800 feet, radius 175 nautical miles with 4 hours on station.

E-3A Skywarrior: Old electronic intelligence craft. Replaced by the newer ES-3A.

E-4B NEACP: Called Kneecap. National Emergency Airborne Command Post. A greatly modified Boeing 747 used as a communications base for the President of the United States and other high-ranking officials in an emergency and in wartime.

E & E: SEAL talk for escape and evasion.

EA-6B Prowler: Navy plane with electronic countermeasures. Crew of 4, max speed 566 knots, ceiling 41,200 feet, range with max load 955 nautical miles.

EAR: Enhanced Acoustic Rifle. Fires not bullets, but a high-impact blast of sound that puts the target down and unconscious for up to six hours. Leaves him with almost no aftereffects. Used as a non-lethal weapon. The sound blast will bounce around inside a building, vehicle, or ship and knock out anyone who is within range. Ten shots before the weapon must be electrically charged. Range: about 200 yards.

Easy: The only easy day was yesterday. SEAL talk.

ELINT: ELectronic INTelligence. Often from satellite in orbit, picture-taker, or other electronic communications.

EOD: Navy experts in nuclear material and radioactivity who do Explosive Ordnance Disposal.

Equatorial Satellite Pointing Guide: To aim antenna for radio to pick up satellite signals.

ES-3A: Electronic Intelligence (ELINT) intercept craft. The platform for the battle group Passive Horizon Extension System. Stays up for long patrol periods, has comprehensive set of sensors, lands and takes off from a carrier. Has 63 antennas.

ETA: Estimated Time of Arrival.

Executive Order 12333: By President Reagan authorizing Special Warfare units such as the SEALs.

Exfil: Exfiltrate, to get out of an area.

F/A-18 Hornet: Carrier-based interceptor that can change from air-to-air to air-to-ground attack mode while in flight.

Fitrep: Fitness Report.

Flashbang Grenade: Non-lethal grenade that gives off a series of piercing explosive sounds and a series of brilliant strobe-type lights to disable an enemy.

Flotation Bag: To hold equipment, ammo, gear on a wet operation.

Fort Fumble: SEALs' name for the Pentagon.

Forty-mm Rifle Grenade: The M576 multipurpose round, contains 20 large lead balls. SEALs use on Colt M-4A1.

Four-Striper: A Navy captain.

Fox Three: In air warfare, a code phrase showing that a Navy F-14 has launched a Phoenix air-to-air missile.

FUBAR: SEAL talk. Fucked Up Beyond All Repair.

Full Helmet Masks: For high-altitude jumps. Oxygen in mask.

G-3: German-made assault rifle.

Gloves: SEALs wear sage-green, fire-resistant Nomex flight gloves.

GMT: Greenwich Mean Time. Where it's all measured from.

GPS: Global Positioning System. A program with satellites around Earth to pinpoint precisely aircraft, ships, vehicles, and ground troops. Position information is to a plus or minus ten feet. Also can give speed of a plane or ship to one quarter of a mile per hour.

GPSL: A radio antenna with floating wire that pops to the surface. Antenna picks up positioning from the closest 4 global positioning satellites and gives an exact position within 10 feet.

Green Tape: Green sticky ordnance tape that has a hundred uses for a SEAL.

GSG-9: Flashbang grenade developed by Germans. A cardboard tube filled with 5 separate charges timed to burst in rapid succession. Blinding and giving concussion to enemy, leaving targets stunned, easy to kill or capture. Usually non-lethal.

GSG9: Grenzschutzgruppe Nine. Germany's best special warfare unit, counterterrorist group.

Gulfstream II (VCII): Large executive jet used by services for transport of small groups quickly. Crew of 3 and 18 passengers. Cruises at 581 mph. Maximum range 4,275 miles.

H & K 21A1: Machine gun with 7.62 NATO round. Replaces the older, more fragile M-60 E3. Fires 900 rounds per minute. Range 1,100 meters. All types of NATO rounds, ball, incendiary, tracer.

H & K G-11: Automatic rifle, new type. 4.7mm caseless ammunition. 50-round magazine. The bullet is in a sleeve of solid propellant with a special thin plastic coating around it. Fires 600 rounds per minute. Single-shot, three-round burst, or fully automatic.

H & K MP-5SD: 9mm submachine gun with integral silenced barrel, single-shot, three-shot, or fully automatic. Rate 800 rds/min.

H & K P9S: Heckler & Koch's 9mm Parabellum double-action semiauto pistol with 9-round magazine.

H & K PSG1: 7.62 NATO round. High-precision, bolt-action, sniping rifle. 5- to 20-round magazine. Roller lock delayed blowback breech system. Fully adjustable stock. 6×42 telescopic sights. Sound suppressor.

HAHO: High Altitude jump, High Opening. From 30,000 feet, open chute for glide up to 15 miles to ground. Up to 75 minutes in glide. To enter enemy territory or enemy position unheard.

Half-Track: Military vehicle with tracked rear drive and wheels in front, usually armed and armored.

HALO: High Altitude jump, Low Opening. From 30,000 feet. Free fall in 2 minutes to 2,000 feet and open chute. Little forward movement. Get to ground quickly, silently.

Hamburgers: Often called sliders on a Navy carrier.

Handie-Talkie: Small, handheld personal radio. Short range.

HELO: SEAL talk for helicopter.

Herky Bird: C-130 Hercules transport. Most-flown military transport in the world. For cargo or passengers, paratroops, aerial refueling, search and rescue, communications, and as a gunship. Has flown from a Navy carrier deck without use of catapult. Four turboprop engines, max speed 325 knots, range at max payload 2,356 miles.

Hezbollah: Lebanese Shiite Moslem militia. Party of God.

HMMWU: The Humvee, U.S. light utility truck, replaced the honored Jeep. Multipurpose wheeled vehicle, 4×4, automatic transmission, power steering. Engine: Detroit Diesel 150-hp diesel V-8 air-cooled. Top speed 65 mph. Range 300 miles.

Hotels: SEAL talk for hostages.

Humint: Human Intelligence. Acquired on the ground; a person as opposed to satellite or photo recon.

Hydra-Shock: Lethal hollow-point ammunition made by Federal Cartridge Company. Outlawed in some areas.

Hypothermia: Danger to SEALs. A drop in body temperature that can be fatal.

IBS: Inflatable Boat Small. 12 × 6 feet. Carries 8 men and 1,000 pounds of weapons and gear. Hard to sink. Quiet motor. Used for silent beach, bay, lake landings.

IR Beacon: Infrared beacon. For silent nighttime signaling.

IR Goggles: "Sees" heat instead of light.

Islamic Jihad: Arab holy war.

Isothermal layer: A colder layer of ocean water that deflects sonar rays. Submarines can hide below it, but then are also blind to what's going on above them since their sonar will not penetrate the layer.

IV Pack: Intravenous fluid that you can drink if out of water.

JAG: Judge Advocate General. The Navy's legal investigating arm that is independent of any Navy command.

JNA: Yugoslav National Army.

JP-4: Normal military jet fuel.

JSOC: Joint Special Operations Command.

JSOCCOMCENT: Joint Special Operations Command Center in the Pentagon.

KA-BAR: SEALs' combat, fighting knife.

KATN: Kick Ass and Take Names. SEAL talk, get the mission in gear.

KH-11: Spy satellite, takes pictures of ground, IR photos, etc.

KIA: Killed In Action.

KISS: Keep It Simple, Stupid. SEAL talk for streamlined operations.

Klick: A kilometer of distance. Often used as a mile. From Vietnam era, but still widely used in military.

Krytrons: Complicated, intricate timers used in making nuclear explosive detonators.

KV-57: Encoder for messages, scrambles.

LT: Short for lieutenant in SEAL talk.

Laser Pistol: The SIW pinpoint of ruby light emitted on any pistol for aiming. Usually a silenced weapon.

Left Behind: In 30 years SEALs have seldom left behind a dead comrade, never a wounded one. Never been taken prisoner.

Let's Get the Hell out of Dodge: SEAL talk for leaving a place, bugging out, hauling ass.

Liaison: Close-connection, cooperating person from one unit or service to another. Military liaison.

Light Sticks: Chemical units that make light after twisting to release chemicals that phosphoresce.

Loot & Shoot: SEAL talk for getting into action on a mission.

LZ: Landing Zone.

M1-8: Russian Chopper.

M1A1 M-14: Match rifle upgraded for SEAL snipers.

M-3 Submachine gun: WWII grease gun, .45-caliber. Cheap. Introduced in 1942.

M-16: Automatic U.S. rifle. 5.56 round. Magazine 20 or 30, rate of fire 700 to 950 rds/min. Can attach M203 40mm grenade launcher under barrel.

M-18 Claymore: Antipersonnel mine. A slab of C-4 with 200 small ball bearings. Set off electrically or by trip wire. Can be positioned and aimed. Sprays out a cloud of balls. Kill zone 50 meters.

M60 Machine Gun: Can use 100-round ammo box snapped onto the gun's receiver. Not used much now by SEALs.

M-60E3: Lightweight handheld machine gun. Not used now by the SEALs.

M61A1: The usual 20mm cannon used on many American fighter planes.

M61(j): Machine Pistol. Yugoslav make.

M662: A red flare for signaling.

M-86: Pursuit Deterrent Munitions. Various types of mines, grenades, trip-wire explosives, and other devices in antipersonnel use.

M-203: A 40mm grenade launcher fitted under an M-16 or the M-4A1 Commando. Can fire a variety of grenade types up to 200 yards.

MagSafe: Lethal ammunition that fragments in human body and does not exit. Favored by some police units to cut down on second kill from regular ammunition exiting a body.

Make a Peek: A quick look, usually out of the water, to check your position or tactical situation.

Mark 23 Mod O: Special operations offensive handgun system. Double-action, 12-round magazine. Ambidextrous safety and mag-release catches. Knight screw-on suppressor. Snap-on laser for sighting. .45-caliber. Weighs 4 pounds loaded. 9.5 inches long; with silencer, 16.5 inches long.

Mark II Knife: Navy-issue combat knife.

Mark VIII SDV: Swimmer Delivery Vehicle. A bus, SEAL talk. 21 feet long, beam and draft 4 feet, 6 knots for 6 hours.

Master-at-Arms: Military police commander on board a ship.

MAVRIC Lance: A nuclear alert for stolen nukes or radioactive goods.

MC-130 Combat Talon: A specially equipped Hercules for covert missions in enemy or unfriendly territory.

McMillan M87R: Bolt-action sniper rifle. .50-caliber. 53 inches long. Bipod, fixed 5- or 10-round magazine. Bulbous muzzle brake on end of barrel. Deadly up to a mile. All types .50-caliber ammo.

MGS: Modified Grooming Standards. So SEALs don't all look like military, to enable them to do undercover work in mufti.

MH-53J: Chopper, updated CH053 from Nam days. 200 mph, called the Pave Low III.

MH-60K Black Hawk: Navy chopper. Forward infrared system for low-level night flight. Radar for terra follow/ avoidance. Crew of 3, takes 12 troops. Top speed 225 mph. Ceiling 4,000 feet. Range radius 230 miles. Arms: 2 12.7mm machine guns.

MIDEASTFOR: Middle East Force.

MiG: Russian-built fighter, many versions, used in many nations around the world.

Mike Boat: Liberty boat off a large ship.

Mike-Mike: Short for mm, millimeter, as in 9 mike-mike.

Milstar: Communications satellite for pickup and bouncing from SATCOM and other radio transmitters. Used by SEALs.

Minigun: In choppers. Can fire 2,000 rounds per minute. Gatling gun-type.

Mitrajez M80: Machine gun from Yugoslavia.

MI-15: British domestic intelligence agency.

MI-16: British foreign intelligence and espionage.

Mocha: Food energy bar SEALs carry in vest pockets.

Mossberg: Pump-action, pistol-grip, 5-round magazine. SEALs use it for close-in work.

Motorola Radio: Personal radio, short range, lip mike, earpiece, belt pack.

MRE: Meals Ready to Eat. Field rations used by most of U.S. Armed Forces and the SEALs as well. Long-lasting.

MSPF: Maritime Special Purpose Force.

Mugger: MUGR, Miniature Underwater Global locator device. Sends up antenna for pickup on positioning satellites. Works under water or above. Gives location within 10 feet.

Mujahideen: A soldier of Allah in Muslim nations.

NAVAIR: NAVy AIR command.

NAVSPECWARGRUP-ONE: Naval Special Warfare Group One based on Calmoloi Cal. SEALs are in this command.

NAVSPECWARGRUP-TWO: Naval Special Warfare Group Two based at Norfolk.

NCIS: Naval Criminal Investigative Service. A civilian operation not reporting to any Navy authority to make it more responsible and responsive. Replaces the old NIS, Naval Investigation Service, that did report to the closest admiral.

NEST: Nuclear Energy Search Team. Non-military unit that reports at once to any spill, problem, or Broken Arrow to determine the extent of the radiation problem.

NEWBIE: A new man, officer, or commander of an established military unit.

NKSF: North Korean Special Forces.

NLA: Iranian National Liberation Army. About 4,500 men

in South Iraq, helped by Iraq for possible use against Iran.

Nomex: The type of material used for flight suits and hoods.

NPIC: National Photographic Interpretation Center in D.C.

NRO: National Reconnaissance Office. To run and coordinate satellite development and operations for the intelligence community.

NSA: National Security Agency.

NSC: National Security Council. Meets in Situation Room, support facility in the Executive Office Building in D.C. Main security group in the nation.

NSVHURAWN: Iranian Marines.

NUCFLASH: An alert for any nuclear problem.

NVG One Eye: Litton single-eyepiece Night-Vision Goggles. Prevents NVG blindness in both eyes if a flare goes off. Scope shows green-tinted field at night.

NVGs: Night-Vision Goggles. One eye or two. Give good night vision in the dark with a greenish view.

OAS: Obstacle Avoidance Sonar. Used on many low-flying attack aircraft.

OIC: Officer In Charge.

Oil Tanker: One is: 885 feet long, 140 feet beam, 121,000 tons, 13 cargo tanks that hold 35.8 million gallons of fuel, oil, or gas. 24 in the crew. This is a regular-sized tanker. Not a supertanker.

OOD: Officer Of the Deck.

Orion P-3: Navy's long-range patrol and antisub aircraft. Some adapted to ELINT roles. Crew of 10. Max speed loaded 473 mph. Ceiling 28,300 feet. Arms: internal weapons bay and 10 external weapons stations for a mix of torpedoes, mines, rockets, and bombs.

Passive Sonar: Listening for engine noise of a ship or sub. It doesn't give away the hunter's presence as an active sonar would.

Pave Low III: A Navy chopper.

PBR: Patrol Boat River. U.S. has many shapes, sizes, and with various types of armament.

PC-170: Patrol Coastal-Class 170-foot SEAL delivery vehicle. Powered by 4 3,350 hp diesel engines, beam of 25 feet and draft of 7.8 feet. Top speed 35 knots, range 2,000 nautical miles. Fixed swimmer platform on stern. Crew of 4 officers and 24 EM, carries 8 SEALs.

Plank Owners: Original men in the start-up of a new military unit.

Polycarbonate material: Bullet-proof glass.

PRF: People's Revolutionary Front. Fictional group in *NUCFLASH,* a SEAL Team Seven book.

Prowl & Growl: SEAL talk for moving into a combat mission.

Quitting Bell: In BUD/S training. Ring it and you quit the SEAL unit. Helmets of men who quit the class are lined up below the bell in Coronado. (Recently they have stopped ringing the bell. Dropouts simply place their helmet below the bell and go.)

RAF: Red Army Faction. A once-powerful German terrorist group, not so active now.

Remington 200: Sniper Rifle. Not used by SEALs now.

Remington 700: Sniper rifle with Starlight Scope. Can extend night vision to 400 meters.

RIB: Rigid Inflatable Boat. 3 sizes, one 10 meters, 40 knots.

Ring Knocker: An Annapolis graduate with the ring.

RIO: Radar Intercept Officer. The officer who sits in the backseat of an F-14 Tomcat off a carrier. The job: find enemy targets in the air and on the sea.

Roger That: A yes, an affirmative, a go answer to a command or statement.

RPG: Rocket Propelled Grenade. Quick and easy, shoulder-fired. Favorite weapon of terrorists, insurgents.

SAS: British Special Air Service. Commandos. Special warfare men. Best that Britain has. Works with SEALs.

SATCOM: Satellite-based communications system for instant contact with anyone anywhere in the world. SEALs rely on it.

SAW: Squad's Automatic Weapon. Usually a machine gun or automatic rifle.

SBS: Special Boat Squadron. On-site Navy unit that transports SEALs to many of their missions. Located across the street from the SEALs' Coronado, California, headquarters.

SD3: Sound-suppression system on the H & K MP5 weapon.

SDV: Swimmer Delivery Vehicle. SEALs use a variety of them.

Seahawk SH-60: Navy chopper for ASW and SAR. Top speed 180 knots, ceiling 13,800 feet, range 503 miles, arms: 2 Mark 46 torpedoes.

SEAL Headgear: Boonie hat, wool balaclava, green scarf, watch cap, bandanna roll.

Second in Command: Also 2IC for short in SEAL talk.

SERE: Survival, Evasion, Resistance, and Escape training.

Shipped for Six: Enlisted for six more years in the Navy.

Shit City: Coronado SEALs' name for Norfolk.

Show Colors: In combat put U.S. flag or other identification on back for easy identification by friendly air or ground units.

Sierra Charlie: SEAL talk for everything on schedule.

Simunition: Canadian product for training that uses paint balls instead of lead for bullets.

Sixteen-Man Platoon: Basic SEAL combat force. Up from 14 men a few years ago.

Sked: SEAL talk for schedule.

Sonobuoy: Small underwater device that detects sounds and transmits them by radio to plane or ship.

Space Blanket: Green foil blanket to keep troops warm. Vacuum-packed and folded to a cigarette-sized package.

Sprayers and Prayers: Not the SEAL way. These men spray bullets all over the place hoping for hits. SEALs do more aimed firing for sure kills.

SS-19: Russian ICBM missile.

STABO: Use harness and lines under chopper to get down to the ground.

STAR: Surface To Air Recovery operation.

Starflash Round: Shotgun round that shoots out sparkling fireballs that ricochet wildly around a room, confusing and terrifying the occupants. Non-lethal.

Stasi: Old-time East German secret police.

Stick: British terminology: 2 4-man SAS teams. 8 men.

Stokes: A kind of Navy stretcher. Open coffin shaped of wire mesh and white canvas for emergency patient transport.

STOL: Short TakeOff and Landing. Aircraft with high-lift wings and vectored-thrust engines to produced extremely short takeoffs and landings.

Sub Gun: Submachine gun, often the suppressed H & K MP5.

Suits: Civilians, usually government officials wearing suits.

Sweat: The more SEALs sweat in peacetime, the less they bleed in war.

Sykes-Fairbairn: A commando fighting knife.

Syrette: Small syringe for field administration often filled with morphine. Can be self-administered.

Tango: SEAL talk for a terrorist.

TDY: Temporary duty assigned outside of normal job designation.

Terr: Another term for terrorist. Shorthand SEAL talk.

Tetrahedral reflectors: Show up on multi-mode radar like tiny suns.

Thermal Imager: Device to detect warmth, as a human body, at night or through light cover.

Thermal Tape: ID for night-vision-goggle user to see. Used on friendlies.

TNAZ: Trinittroaze Tidine. Explosive to replace C-4. 15% stronger than C-4 and 20% lighter.

TO&E: Table showing Organization and Equipment of a military unit.

Top SEAL Tribute: "You sweet motherfucker, don't you never die!"

Trailing Array: A group of antennas for sonar pickup trailed out of a submarine.

Train: For contact in smoke, no light, fog, etc. Men directly behind each other. Right hand on weapon, left hand on shoulder of man ahead. Squeeze shoulder to signal.

Trident: SEALs' emblem. An eagle with talons clutching a Revolutionary War pistol, and Neptune's trident superimposed on the Navy's traditional anchor.

TRW: A camera's digital record that is sent by SATCOM.

TT33: Tokarev, a Russian pistol.

UAZ: A Soviet 1-ton truck.

UBA Mark XV: Underwater life support with computer to regulate the rebreather's gas mixture.

UGS: Unmanned Ground Sensors. Can be used to explode booby traps and claymore mines.

UNODIR: Unless otherwise directed. The unit will start the operation unless they are told not to.

VBSS: Orders to "visit, board, search, and seize."

Wadi: A gully or ravine, usually in a desert.

White Shirt: Man responsible for safety on carrier deck as he leads around civilians and personnel unfamiliar with the flight deck.

WIA: Wounded In Action.

Zodiac: Also called an IBS, Inflatable Boat Small. 15 × 6 feet, weighs 265 pounds. The "rubber duck" can carry 8 fully equipped SEALs. Can do 18 knots with a range of 65 nautical miles.

Zulu: Means Greenwich Mean Time, GMT. Used in all formal military communications.